THE TACKSMAN'S DAUGHTER

Donna Scott

Copyright © 2022 by Donna Scott. All rights reserved.

ISBN: 978-1-7349248-4-8

All rights reserved. No part of this book may be reproduced in any form or by any means without the prior written consent of the author of that part, except for including brief quotations in a review. With the exception of some well-known historical figures and events, the names, characters, and incidents depicted in this book are products of the author's imagination or are used in a fictitious situation. In all other respects, any resemblances to actual events, locations, organizations, incidents, or persons—living or dead—are coincidental and beyond the intent of the author.

Sigh, wind in the pine;
River, weep as you flow;
Terrible things were done
Long, long ago.

In daylight golden and mild
After the night of Glencoe
They found the hand of a child
Lying in the snow.

Lopped by the sword to the ground
Or torn by wolf or fox,
That was the snowdrop they found
Among the granite rocks.

Oh, life is fierce and wild
And the heart of the earth is stone
And the hand of a murdered child
Will not bear thinking on.

Sigh, wind in the pine,
Cover it with snow;
But terrible things were done
Long, long ago.

--poem entitled **Glencoe** by Douglas Alexander Stewart

Part One

THE TACKSMAN'S DAUGHTER

Chapter 1

February 2, 1692
Alt Na Munde, Glencoe, Scotland

It was not the frigid air easing through the crack next to the window that covered Caitriona's arms in gooseflesh, but the parade of foot soldiers that appeared at the snowy edge of the loch that February afternoon. Most noticeable were the Redcoats, their scarlet wool stark against the loch's pewter water and the thick copse of naked oaks behind them. But there were others too—clansmen—their tartans indistinguishable in the blue-grey morning light. Caitriona hugged herself as she watched the men struggle to lean into the wind that slowed their progress.

Above them, a murmuration of starlings dipped and circled. The soldiers seemed undisturbed by their presence, but her nape tightened at their flying dance. She stared at the birds, their swooping and swirling mesmerizing and beautiful. They were usually gone by winter, and she wondered if the flock had stayed in Glencoe to warn her of these men now in approach. Starlings signaled change—good or bad, that was yet to be seen.

"What has ye so taken, Cait?" her mother asked.

Caitriona didn't turn to face her. She pulled her *sgian dubh* from its sheath, then twirled it between her fingers, hoping the repetition of movement would soothe her mind as it had in the past. "Have Sionn and Finnean been creating mischief again?"

Her mother joined her at the window, her hair lightly streaked with silver above her ears. "Stealing cows? Even yer cousins would agree 'tis too cold for that."

"Then what do ye make of the men entering the glen?" Cait asked, her fingers and blade closing over the scar on her left palm, a painful reminder of the last time soldiers had arrived in their quiet village.

"Some are Englishmen." Her mother continued to stare at the landscape, her gaze moving higher to the starlings now flying past the loch. "This isnae about a few missing kine."

With each passing moment, more soldiers inched their way into Glencoe from the west. As they edged closer, their muskets and black pikes poked through the blanket of mist hovering over the loch and its shore. Cait's shoulders stiffened. This had nothing to do with stolen cattle.

Ma's brow crinkled. "Fetch yer da."

Cait scrambled down the stairs and almost fell into the gaping hole on the landing, the laird's lug hatch wide open. She grabbed the rope railing and peered down the wooden rungs into MacIain's secret chamber. Torchlight bounced off the rough stone walls below.

"Who's that up there? Spying, are ye?" MacIain asked, his words touched with a bit of humour. His voice was low and deep as if it arose from a vast cavern.

Cait smiled. "No spying. I'm simply searching for my da. Is he too deep in his cups to climb that ladder?"

MacIain's mane of white hair crept into view. "What makes ye think he's down here with me?"

"He's wherever the whisky is, and I'm guessing you've a dram or two in yer hands this very moment."

MacIain's head popped out of the hatch first, his great white whiskers concealing much of his flushed face. Slowly, his huge form emerged from his secret room like a beast from the loch. Then Da appeared, a bottle peeking out from inside the tartan draped over his shoulder. He climbed out of the hole, then lowered the hatch carefully.

"'Tis one of my beauties!" Da held up the bottle. "I hope you've come for something important. MacIain and I have a pint between us and two hours of daylight left to finish it."

"*You* will be the one to tell me if 'tis important or no. There's a group of men coming into the glen. Some are English soldiers. Some clansmen."

MacIain took a quick swig from the bottle. "A group? How many, lass?"

THE TACKSMAN'S DAUGHTER

Cait shrugged. "A hundred. Maybe more. The line hadn't ended when I last looked."

Da turned to the chief. "Do ye think it has something to do with yer Oath of Allegiance to the king?"

MacIain seemed to consider Da's question. "I dinnae see how. I swore the oath before Campbell himself. I've a letter from Hill to prove it."

He was telling the truth. Cait had heard the story from the ghillies who had traveled with MacIain to attend to his needs. According to them, MacIain had given his oath—albeit five days late—in January. But that was understandable. MacIain hadn't heard about the king's demand until the day before it was due, so with no time left, he'd chosen to travel north to Inverlochy instead of south to Inveraray, thinking he could get there faster and swear his oath at the fort. Once he'd arrived, Colonel Hill had said he wasn't authorized to take it, so he wrote MacIain a letter of protection that he was to present to Campbell of Ardkinglas in Inveraray. After plodding through a blizzard he'd said was sent by the devil himself, MacIain explained the delay and presented Hill's letter assuring Ardkinglas that MacIain had only the best intentions to swear his loyalty to King William and Queen Mary. One of the ghillies known to be a bit of a nashgab, had whispered to Cait that Ardkinglas refused to listen at first, but then MacIain wept, begging for forgiveness, and Ardkinglas took his oath the next day. Cait knew the story to be true—all except for the weeping. She couldn't imagine MacIain, the chief of the MacDonalds of Glencoe, shedding a tear in front of a Campbell.

Da asked, "Then why do ye think there are English soldiers in Glencoe?"

MacIain swatted the air with indifference, then took another drink. "They're likely headed to the garrison at Inverlochy. Or Fort William. Whichever ye wish to call it. Either way, I have a feeling we'll soon find out."

She had never heard the chief refer to the garrison by its new name. *Fort William.* Could he truly, in his heart, be loyal to King William?

MacIain turned to her. "Dinnae look so glum, lass. Nothing is going to happen to the MacDonalds while I'm chief."

She allowed her shoulders to loosen with his reassurance, but her fear of Englishmen maintained its grip.

Her stomach growled, reminding her that she'd missed the mid-day repast, her mind too occupied with the soldiers in approach. She meandered down to the kitchens to see if Lilas, the cook, had any porridge to spare.

Her mouth watered as the smell of warm bannocks reached her nose. Lilas stood at a long table kneading dough, her brow furrowed in concentration. Caitriona leaned into the warmth of the hearth, her outstretched hands capturing some of its heat. Beside her sat two round loaves still on bannock stones. "May I take a wee bit of bannock, Lilas?"

"Heavens no, lass. Can ye no see they're broken apart?" Lilas swiped her cheek with the back of her wrist, leaving a streak of flour behind. "Ye dinnae want to eat those. They're rife with ill fortune."

A single broken bannock meant that a stranger would pay a visit. More than one was a bad omen indeed. "There are soldiers in the glen. But MacIain says we needn't fash over it."

Lilas stopped kneading, then yanked Cait over to the end of the table, where a large woven basket sat. The cook jabbed her finger at it twice. "Look at that! We have nothing to fash over?"

Inside the basket were at least a dozen bannocks broken into crumbly bits. Cait's stomach tautened.

With a crinkled brow, Lilas pounded the lump of dough, and a fine cloud of flour floated into the air. "'Tis a sure sign of misfortune, it is. Never saw a clearer one."

Cait left the kitchens, no longer having much of an appetite. Her mother stood in MacIain's great hall with a gaggle of women, their murmurs and chirping echoing off the thick stone walls. Cait signaled to her with the wiggle of a finger, and Ma left the others briskly.

"Did ye find yer father?"

"Aye, but he and MacIain paid no heed to my warning."

"Well, I suppose they would know best." Cait's mother sighed, her hand picking nervously at the blue sapphire that hung from her necklace. The walnut-sized stone had been handed down through generations of MacDonalds and was believed to be the largest sapphire in all of Scotland. Ma never took it off. "Perhaps 'tis nothing."

Cait peeked behind her mother at the gaggle of women too busy chatting to notice her agitation. "I was in the kitchens, though, and Lilas showed me a basket filled with broken bannocks."

Ma grabbed her arm and squeezed. Cait's heart raced. The message was clear to her too. "'Tis why I came to find ye. Da may think nothing of the soldiers, but we know better."

"What are you two whispering about over here?" Davina MacNab—the niece of the Earl of Breadalbane, the Chieftain of Glenorchy—leaned into them, her son seated drowsily on her hip. He reached up and tugged on a messy blonde curl that had escaped her haphazardly pinned-up hair. "Have ye finally decided on a husband for Cait, Mistress Cameron?"

THE TACKSMAN'S DAUGHTER

Ma stood straight, her smile unable to hide her concern. "A husband? What would Cait need with a husband?"

Cait bristled. It was the wrong thing to say to Davina, whose life was ruined because she had no husband. The man who had filled her head with sweet tales of their future together, then bedded her, had left before she could tell him she was with child. Davina had told Cait that her world since then had been filled with only heartache and woe, caring for her son alone. The scorn of her parents and her powerful uncle rained down on her daily in every cross look and sharp word.

Davina shrugged one shoulder. "She's of marrying age. Eighteen, aren't ye, Cait?"

Cait nodded, but she had no interest in marriage. Certainly not to any of the eligible men in Glencoe who smiled at her as if she would be their last meal.

"Ye should marry her off before some lad comes around and puts her in a pickle like me."

Ma's brow raised in shock. "Cait would never succumb to a honeyed tongue full of empty promises. Mind yerself, Davina."

Davina sank. "I never meant disrespect—"

"Aye, but ye did." Ma's attention snapped towards the entry to the hall. "There's MacIain. I'll tell him about the bannocks."

"And the starlings!" Cait shouted after her.

Ma left them, turning back once, her eyes narrowed at Davina.

"Ye know 'twasn't like that, don't ye, Cait?" Davina shifted her son to her other hip. "We were in love. We were to be wed."

Cait brushed her fingers through little Sandaidh's dark downy hair as he clung to his mother's breast. His eyelids dipped slowly with each stroke. "Of course ye were."

Davina had never told Cait who the father was. The only thing she'd ever confessed to her regarding his identity was that he was a soldier who'd traveled to Glenorchy from Glasgow. Even her uncle, Breadalbane, who'd threatened her with a public flogging, didn't know who'd got Davina with child. Cait had heard gossip, of course, that she was seen with a dark-haired man, but no one knew who he was for certain, for it had all happened so fast. After a few months, the evidence of how Davina had spent her time alone with him started to show.

Sandaidh snuggled deeper onto his mother's chest. Cait wasn't sure if she should mention the soldiers entering the glen. It would likely send Davina running out into the snow in a frenzy. "Yer bairn is fast asleep. Why don't ye set him down so we can have a wee blether. The last time I saw ye was at harvest. Surely there's plenty to tell since then."

Davina handed the laddie to a servant girl, then joined Cait on a bench by the hearth. "Very little happens in Glenorchy."

Cait laughed. "'Tisnae much different here. A cow disappears and it sends everyone up in arms. If it weren't for the steady trouble with the Campbells, I think I'd die of boredom."

Ma returned with MacIain and Da, interrupting their gossip. Da's face was now flushed with drink, his eyes a little watery but still filled with humour. "Away with yer foolish wives' tales. Yer upsetting yerselves for naught."

This was no foolish wives' tale. Cait grabbed his hand and squeezed. "When was the last time ye saw starlings in Glencoe in the middle of winter? And what of the broken bannocks? 'Twas a whole basket. I saw them myself!"

Davina stepped closer, her head tilted to the side. "What did ye see, Cait?"

Da ran his hand down his face. "There are soldiers in the glen, and Cait thinks—"

Davina perked up. "Soldiers!"

Da flipped his hand in dismissal. "Aye, but there's nothing to fret over. MacIain sent John and a few men down to the loch to meet them."

The knot in Cait's neck loosened. John, MacIain's son, would know if they were friend or foe. Either way, she hoped they had no plans to settle in Glencoe.

Chapter 2

The snow found its way inside Edward's collar and shirtsleeves. He pulled at his broad-brimmed hat, praying for some protection from the wind. His feet were wet and numb from having accidentally stepped in a shallow stream he'd thought was frozen over. He and the others had been marching for weeks now, since December, to meet the Earl of Argyll's regiment in Inveraray. Sir John Dalrymple, the Master of Stair, had sent the orders, conveniently forgetting—or not caring—that it was the middle of winter and almost impossible to travel through the snow-covered passes. If Edward and his men didn't perish from trying to navigate the dangerous Highland terrain, they'd die from the cold.

Now with the regiments joined, Argyll's men marched ahead, most of them Scottish and faring slightly better cocooned in green plaids with their blue wool bonnets protecting their ears from the wind's frosty teeth. Edward tugged his hat lower, hoping to ease the icy burn on his forehead.

Alexander, his brother, marched farther up front, his shoulders hunched liked all the others, the wind forcing his head down, his chin to his chest. Even with the north and south sides of the glen framed by tall ridges, there was no respite from the freezing gusts.

The only sounds were the howling wind and the crunch of their boots as they made their way through the snow. After a while, Edward found it difficult to tell if the noises were real or if his mind had simply allowed their interminable rhythm to play in his head.

"Edward!" Alexander called to him with an urgent wave. It was an unnecessary gesture, for Edward could spot his brother in any crowd. It was like looking in a mirror. They were both a half a head taller than most men, their shoulders straight and broad, their hair long and dark. The only remarkable difference lay in their eyes—Alexander's the colour of weak tea and Edward's blue. Like his mother's.

The regiment stopped. Edward edged by some soldiers to join his brother. "What is it?"

Alexander nudged his chin towards the brae. "It looks like Highlanders near Argyll's troops. Could mean trouble."

Edward scanned the sloping hillside down to the edge of the loch. There were men there, maybe twenty or so, but they didn't appear to be armed. "They don't seem as if they mean harm. I see no weapons."

Alexander laughed without humour. "They are Highlanders. Each one of them has five blades hidden in his plaid."

Edward blew into his hands, then rubbed them together. "A bit of an exaggeration, don't you think?"

"They are armed. Trust me. Come."

They trudged through the snow to Argyll's men and reached them just as Captain Campbell yelled, "Order your muskets! Order your pikes! Rest on your arms, men!"

One large Scot descended the hill first, the others trailing behind. Edward guessed he was in his early thirties and seemed to have the respect of his men. He was likely not the clan chief, but he displayed the confidence of a man in charge.

Alexander moved slightly, resting his hand on the hilt of his sword. He was always so distrustful, too quick to attack.

"Stay your hand, brother," Edward urged under his breath.

The Scot's eyes narrowed, his breath streaming out in front of him in great white gusts. He pressed his faded blue bonnet to his head as he hopped over a small burn, his expression wary. He speared an unfriendly glance at Captain Campbell whose reddish-blond hair heavily threaded with grey blew wildly in the wind. "What business do ye have here, Glenlyon?"

Campbell inched in front of Alexander, then shifted uneasily. His voice was nervous and a little too loud. "We only need shelter until the storm breaks, John. The fort is full, and we cannae go any farther with the snow as deep as it is."

Edward watched as John took his time studying Campbell's face. They knew each other, but it didn't appear to be a friendly acquaintance.

Leftenant Lindsay stepped out from the regiment, then reached into his coat and pulled out a folded piece of parchment, offering it to John. "I have papers signed by Colonel Hill requesting that the clan chief provide our two companies quarters while in Glencoe."

THE TACKSMAN'S DAUGHTER

John made no move to accept the missive. Edward waited while he scanned the expanse of the regiments, his rough-looking men behind him on the hill unmoving. Edward tried to read their gazes as they danced from one soldier to another, but they gave away nothing.

Finally, John took the sealed parchment and read it. A gust of wind caused it to flutter wildly in his hands. Edward pressed his hat tightly to his head, his cheeks burning from the icy blast.

After a minute or so, John folded up the missive, then handed it back to Lindsay. "John MacDonald, son of MacIain." They eyed one another, their expressions stoic.

John turned to Campbell, one eyebrow raised. "Kin or no, if you've come to make trouble, you can turn around now and head back home."

They were kin? A MacDonald and a Campbell? The bad blood between the two clans was no secret. They differed on everything—religion, politics, loyalties. Edward had heard from the Scots in his troop that they stole each other's cattle and raided their lands regularly. So, for the captain to enter MacDonald lands and ask for hospitality was no simple request—it was a risk.

Campbell nodded, both hands raised in surrender. "We're only here for lodging and a wee bit of food until the weather lifts."

Edward sensed the thick wall of distrust between them, Campbell's hand extended to John, waiting.

After a moment, John took it, his arm moving slowly as if weighted with reluctance.

John signaled to one of his clansmen on the hill. "Tell my father we're on our way. And be quick about it, aye?"

Edward leaned towards Alexander. "He's sending them up there to give the chief enough time to prepare. They don't trust us."

Alexander smirked. "Us or Campbell?"

"Perhaps both." Edward had only just met Campbell, but something about the man didn't sit well with him. He seemed desperate, and desperate men do desperate things.

They resumed their march up through the glen. Campbell walked beside John, Alexander and Edward only a pace behind and close enough for Edward to eavesdrop.

"Yer headed north?" John asked.

Campbell adjusted his bonnet. "Aye. We were sent to punish Glengarry for not taking the Oath of Allegiance."

John looked at him sideways. "Ye need two hundred men to do that?"

Dozens of thatch-roofed cottages sprinkled the small village, smoke from their chimneys flying erratically in the wind. Not a soul was outside. Not a goat. Not a hen.

Like a squatting giant amongst dwarfs, a large stone manor sat on the brae overlooking the croft-houses below. Several feet of snow rested on the rooftop, some settling in the jagged nooks in the stone walls. It wasn't a castle exactly, but it was clearly a home befitting a man of great importance.

Edward tucked his hands into his armpits, but even they were cold. "I imagine that is the chief's home," he said, thinking out loud.

"My father's. Aye." John pulled his tartan tighter around his shoulders, then turned to Lindsay. "Tell yer men to wait here." He pointed at Edward and Alexander. "You two and Glenlyon will come with me."

Glenlyon patted John on the shoulder. "Of course, of course!"

A cluster of MacDonald Highlanders stood at the manor's entrance by a snowdrift, their arms crossed in front of them, gazes piercing, as if to remind Edward and the others that they were merely a step away from slitting their throats, if need be. John quickly mumbled something private to his clansmen, then turned to Edward. "You three will leave yer weapons here."

They disarmed, then followed John inside. The smell of baking bread and roasting venison hung thick in the air. It had been more than a week since Edward had eaten meat, the last time when he'd shot a red grouse in Inveraray outside of their encampment. He'd roasted it over the fire, its flesh tender and earthy, but hardly aromatic.

Edward's stomach growled, and John hmphed. "Dinnae start smacking yer gob just yet. Ye need to get past MacIain first."

Edward didn't mind waiting for MacIain. He was finally starting to thaw, his fingers and toes now bending without pain and the snowflakes on his coat melting into the scarlet wool. He inhaled deeply, the mixed aromas wafting in from the kitchens giving him something to look forward to.

In a burst of commotion, several large Scots entered the hall, led by a large white-haired man with a full beard and moustache that hid most of his face. There was no doubt that this man was the clan chief, his shoulders squared and blue eyes piercing.

John stopped him in his approach and whispered something in his ear, his sight set on Captain Campbell. MacIain rested one hand on his son's shoulder. "Tell the cottars and tacksmen that we have guests. These men are the king's soldiers and should be treated as such."

MacIain turned to Edward. "Some of ye will billet here, and the others will have to find lodging with the cottars. We're a small village, so you'll have to make do."

THE TACKSMAN'S DAUGHTER

Edward nodded once at the huge beast of a man. "Much obliged. Your generosity is appreciated, sir."

"Alasdair MacIain, Chief of the MacDonalds of Glencoe, but you will call me MacIain like all the others." He stared at Edward and Alexander through narrowed eyes, his thumbs hooked in the belt that held his sporran. "Brothers? *Lethaonan?*"

Alexander's face screwed up with confusion. *"Lethaonan?"*

A man even taller than the chief with unruly golden hair, stepped from behind MacIain and spoke with a strong brogue. "Twins. He means *twins.*"

Edward and his brother had been asked the same question many times. He rubbed his forehead. "Not twins. We share the same—"

"My father is the Earl of Wetherby." Alexander bowed slightly. "Please allow me to introduce myself. I am Leftenant Alexander Gage, Baron Mansfield. And this is my half-brother Edward. His mother is . . . not the countess."

Edward wanted to add *yet I was the child born out of love*, but he didn't. Instead, he took a deep breath and smiled tightly. "We are four months apart."

MacIain grunted. "Aye, well, ye share the same blood, and that makes ye brothers."

That was about all they shared.

MacIain's thick hand nudged Edward ahead. "Taran will show ye to the kitchens so ye can fill yer wames." He searched the faces around him, his full mane of snowy hair swinging back and forth as he scanned the hall. "Taran! Where are ye, laddie?" His voice boomed off the walls.

A small lad tapping a long wooden stick on the ground just in front of his feet clickety-clacked into the room. He stared straight ahead with crisp, clear grey eyes unfocused and fixed. His free hand reached out to MacIain, fingertips gently touching his heavily draped belted plaid. "Aye, MacIain."

MacIain bent down and tousled Taran's hair. "Take these men to the kitchens, and tell Lilas to give them something hot and a wee bit of drink too."

"Follow me." He waved them ahead with his little hand. Edward found it strange that the chief would choose a blind child to lead the way, but this little boy's shoulders were straight and confident. His cane rhythmically swept the floor before him as he walked, his fine blond curls bouncing with each of his steps.

"Are you kin to MacIain too?" Edward asked. "A grandson, perhaps?"

"Nay. I'm the *bard's* grandson. We're nae MacDonalds. We came from the Isle of Harris, sent by our master, the MacKenzie Earl of Seaforth, to deliver a message to a man in Inveraray. We had to stop here on our way back because of the weather."

Edward shot Alexander a look of surprise. It was a long distance to travel, especially in the winter.

"And how long have you been in Glencoe?"

"A month. Maybe more, maybe less." They reached a narrow stairwell, and Taran stopped, the tip of his cane dipping onto the first step.

Edward and Alexander trailed behind him through a short hallway and into the kitchens. Edward inhaled the tangy, peppery smell of well-seasoned roasted venison. His mouth watered.

An older woman crouching before a low hearth, her hands wringing her apron, muttered something. She finished it off with a "Please, God." Alexander coughed, and the woman startled upright. "Oh heavens! I didn't see ye there."

She took in their scarlet coats and the weapons on their hips, then pulled Taran to her side. "What is it that ye want, gentlemen? I am in no need of any trouble."

Edward stepped closer, and she shoved Taran behind her. "We mean no harm, mistress. The chief sent us down here to get something to eat."

"And drink," Alexander added.

"MacIain sent ye?" she asked.

"He did."

She reached into a basket at the end of a table and lifted out two flat round loaves of bread, chunks missing from the edges. "Ye can start with these. They're still warm."

She motioned for them to sit on the bench, then set down wooden plates and a pot of jam. Taran situated himself across from Edward and Alexander, his arm out in front of him, searching for the bread.

The woman gasped. "Taran! Dinnae touch those!" She hastily whispered something in his ear, and the lad jerked back his hand and quickly set it in his lap.

Edward was surprised at her cruelty. There were plenty of loaves left, enough to feed ten hungry men. "You can have some of mine, Taran." He broke off a piece and held it out, nudging his arm so he could find it. But Taran wouldn't take it.

The woman rushed to Taran's side, her hand firmly resting on his shoulder. "The laddie will have something else. These bannocks are for *you*. Only for you."

Chapter 3

Davina gritted her teeth with each painful stroke of the hairbrush, the bristles pulling her strands out one by one. How could she have let her hair go so long without a decent brushing?

"Hold still," Cait begged, her fingers separating Davina's hair into sections. "Yer as jumpy as a cat with its tail too close to the fire."

"Can ye see who is out there?" Davina asked. She couldn't see out the window from where she was sitting, but she was sure Cait could. She knew the soldiers had arrived but had no idea how many or from which regiment they'd come. "I wish I had a nicer gown. Brown wool will never catch a man's eye."

Cait pulled the brush through with a sharp tug, indicating a fairly good-sized knot, and Davina winced. "A smile will grab a man's attention more than a gown."

That was easy for Cait to say. She had a perfect oval face and lips as red as a September berry on a Rowan tree. A smile from her would cause a whole platoon to come running. But it wasn't the same for Davina. At least not since her sweet little Sandaidh had come along. "Sometimes I smile so much, I think the men believe me to be daft."

Cait laughed, the last of the evening light catching in her pale green eyes. "Yer a lovely lass, Davina. Any man would be lucky to have ye."

Davina truly only cared about the desires of one man, but without a word from him since they last parted, she wondered if he'd even remember her. She twisted in her seat, stretching to catch a glimpse of tartan or red coat out the window. "Tell me, Cait, how many do ye think there are?"

"Too many. Hundreds, I imagine."

Davina sat taller. "Hundreds?"

"More or less." Cait leaned closer to the diamond-paned window, lifting Davina slightly out of her chair by her hair. "I hope they move on quickly."

Davina's heart raced. Could he be here? Come to claim her as his bride? She nudged Cait aside and hurried to the window. She pressed her face to the cold glass, but it was too wavy and pitted for her to see anything short of movement. She collapsed back into the chair, picturing Sawney's father's face the first time he pulled her close, the heat of his large hands burning through her gown at the small of her back. Cait resumed her brushing and Davina relaxed into the memory, the rhythmic stroke of the brush slowing her fluttering heart.

The door burst open, and Davina startled. Cait's younger sister, Gillian, blew into the room, rosy-cheeked and out of breath. She was a miniature replica of Cait—hair as black and shiny as the feathers on a raven's wing and a thin, straight nose that turned up only slightly at the very tip. "MacIain wishes for us to stay upstairs until the soldiers are settled in for the evening."

Cait's hands froze, the bristles of the brush still against Davina's scalp. "They're staying?"

Gillian nodded. "We mustn't leave."

That would ruin Davina's plans for making her way through the ranks. "I'm sure he meant only you and Cait. Not me."

"He said all lasses. Married ones too," Gillian insisted.

Little Gilli was only seven, still too young to understand that having a child wasn't the same thing as being married, and Davina wasn't about to explain the not-so-subtle difference to her.

Cait slowly resumed brushing. "Then it will be dark before we can return home."

Gilli sat at the foot of the bed, her feet unable to reach the floor. "MacIain said we will all stay at Alt Na Munde until the soldiers leave. He thought it would be safer for us here since Da offered our cottage to a bunch of them."

Davina liked that idea. The sisters could share her bed and help keep her warm at night, if only for a day or so until the snow stopped and the soldiers could travel safely. As if to remind her that the weather had no intention of letting up, an angry gust shook the rooftop. "You'll stay in here with me and wee Sawney. Like three sisters in a bed. I couldn't wish for better."

Cait kissed the top of her head, then bent to whisper in her ear. "Ye dinnae fool me, Davina. You'd trade us for a big hairy soldier in a trice."

THE TACKSMAN'S DAUGHTER

The next morning, Davina awoke to deep voices vibrating from below. She wrapped herself in a shawl and inched open the window. It was peaceful, quiet outside, the full moon still visible in the early morning grey light. Gently, she latched it closed and tiptoed out of her room, careful not to wake Sawney, Cait, and Gilli. She padded down the long passage in the direction of the noise spiraling up the dark staircase. It wasn't until she reached the bottom that she spotted several dark-haired soldiers in scarlet coats standing in the great hall. Englishmen. Armed strangers. She never thought MacIain would allow that in his home. Then she noticed that they were empty-hipped, their scabbards not belted around their middles.

Perhaps one of them was Sawney's da. She desperately wanted to take a few more steps into the room to get a better look.

"Davina MacNab!" She spun to face Mistress Cameron on the steps above her, hands on hips, lips tightened into a straight line. "What are ye doing down here in naught but yer shift? Get back in yer chambers this instant, or you'll be sure to suffer the same fate as ye did the last time soldiers were nearby."

Davina scampered past her up to her room, her cheeks aflame. It was too early in the morning to be chastised. Could she go one day without someone reminding her of her costly indiscretion?

"There ye are, lass." Cait lifted Sawney out of his cradle and rubbed her cheek on his wild hair. She swayed side to side, patting the bairn's back with light taps. "For a second I thought you'd run off with one of the soldiers and left us to mind wee Sawney here."

Cait wore a smile when she'd said it, but nonetheless, Davina didn't care for her comment. She would never do such a thing. Sawney was a blessing, even if he signaled her ruin to everyone else. She reached out for him and kissed the warm rosiness of his cheeks. "Help me dress, Cait."

"But aren't we to stay put until—"

"Lilas must need our help. How are the kitchen maids to feed all these men?"

Davina sensed Cait's apprehension. Something had happened years earlier that soured her opinion of soldiers, but whatever it was, Cait hadn't shared the details. It had left her with a mean scar across her palm and a permanent scowl when they were near. But with the chance that Sawney's father could very well be under the same roof, Davina wasn't going to let Cait's fears interfere with a possible reunion.

They dressed quickly, left Sawney to play with Gilli, and scurried down the stairs directly into the kitchens. Lilas and three other kitchen maids bustled back and forth between the hearths and the larder, carrying baskets and platters, true determination on their stern faces. Lilas occasionally reprimanded one of them or ordered them to 'make haste' or 'move aside'. Davina stood pressed against the wall with Cait, afraid to interrupt the chaos. When Lilas finally caught sight of the two of them, she asked, "Are ye here to help or get in the way?"

"I was hoping to get something to eat," Cait said sarcastically. "But Davina's looking to—"

"Do ye need someone to serve, Lilas?" Davina asked, shooting Cait an angry glance.

Lilas hesitated, then used her apron to wipe her brow. "Here." She handed Davina a jug of ale and Cait a stack of wooden bowls. "Take these and come right back. No lingering. Now go on."

Davina drew in a deep breath and headed into the hall, Cait right behind her. The room was cold and dim with only a few pine torches lit, their light flickering off the walls and the great beams on the ceiling that stretched from one end of the hall to the other. English soldiers sat separately from the Scots, their starkly different uniforms marking a clear line between the troops. It was not as if she could ask any of them if they knew of Sawney's father, for she was ashamed to admit she didn't know his surname. She'd never confessed that to her parents or uncle or anyone, not even Cait, and the humiliation of that truth lay heavy on her heart.

Davina's hands began to tremble. What if he was here? Could she confront him in front of all these men? Her mouth started to water, a wave of nausea washing over her. She wasn't sure she could do it.

Davina scanned the scruffy faces of the fifty or so soldiers that had already arrived for breakfast, the jug wiggling in her shaky hands. None of them was Sawney's father.

She busied herself pouring ale for the men, when a heavily bearded Scot with not a single hair upon his pink, splotchy head beckoned her. "Come here, lass. A bonnie kitchen wench, ye are."

Davina approached, careful to stay close enough to pour his drink but far enough away to avoid a roaming hand. "Drouthy, are ye?"

A few more men trickled into the hall. She swallowed the saliva pooling in her mouth, a sudden chill traveling up the back of her neck.

"Don't ye have anything stronger than that to start the day? A wee dram of whisky, perhaps?" the Scot asked with a wink.

She wiped her cold, sweaty brow with her sleeve. "If I did, I'd have drunk it already."

"What's that, lass?"

She hadn't realized she'd said it aloud. "I'm sure we have some back in the kitchens, but I doubt the cook . . ."

THE TACKSMAN'S DAUGHTER

Out of the corner of her eye, she spotted movement at the far end of the hall. Two English soldiers entered, partly hidden by the shadows cast by a large wooden partition near the entrance. Davina ignored the shouts and lewd remarks from the men trying to get her attention and concentrated on the faint sounds of the newcomers' voices. They stood together with familiarity yet formally, one nodding intermittently as the other spoke. Suddenly, they moved out of the shadows and farther into the hall, the elder and shorter of the two with a hawk-like nose and a curled white periwig, and the other dark and straight-backed.

And then she saw it. That way in which the younger soldier brushed his hand down the front of his coat, first fiddling with the top two buttons, then sweeping his hand to his waist. She'd seen it before. Many times.

Her pulse raced, whooshing steadily in her ears. Her fingers grew weak and her grip on the jug loosened, sending it clanging on the floor, its contents seeping across the stones. Blood rushed to her cheeks, and heat flooded her chest. It was him.

Cait rushed over to her, her brow crinkled with worry. "Are you unwell?" She scooped up the jug, waiting for Davina to respond. But Davina couldn't seem to make her lips form the words. Cait pressed her hand to Davina's forehead. "Come back into the kitchens, and I'll fetch ye something to drink."

Davina didn't want to leave, not now that her lover had returned to her. The father of her bairn. She pressed Cait's hand between her own. "He's here."

"Who?"

"My . . . Sawney's father."

Cait's mouth fell open. "Here? In the hall?"

Davina nodded, a hard burning lump the size of an acorn in her throat.

Cait slowly turned her head, a look of worry on her face. But she wouldn't know who he was. Nobody knew, except for Davina.

He was walking in her direction, the elderly wigged soldier at his side speaking with large hand gestures, in his grip a handkerchief waving erratically with each word. Davina didn't know whether to escape back into the kitchens or face what she'd been dreaming of doing for more than a year and a half now. She couldn't simply inform him of the son he had playing upstairs. And she certainly didn't want to do it in front of the older man who carried on incessantly about something he obviously found extremely important. He was coming closer, and if she didn't make up her mind soon, her fate would be decided for her.

Cait remained pinned to her side, one hand gripping her own tightly. "Would ye like me to stay with ye?"

Davina pressed a hand to her stomach, trying to keep it from flopping around like a fish out of water. "I dinnae think I can . . . I'm not sure I know what to say."

Cait leaned in close. "Ye mayn't have to say anything. He'll take one look at yer bonnie face and tell ye how much he missed ye."

"Do ye really think so?"

Cait cupped her cheek. Was that pity in her eyes? "Aye. I do."

Davina inhaled, her insides quaking, her heart pounding furiously. She tried to move, but her feet stayed rooted to the ground.

Cait gave her a gentle push, and Davina took a step. "Go on."

Davina swallowed hard, her lip quivering with hope or fear, she didn't know which.

Before he could sit on the long bench along with other English soldiers, she touched the back of his sleeve slightly. He turned his head and smiled but said nothing.

She cleared her throat to use a few seconds to calm her heart and steady her voice. "It's been a long time."

He tilted his head slightly, confusion in his half-smile. "Forgive me, madam. Have we met?"

"Davina?" It was Cait's voice. "Give her some room!"

Davina opened her eyes. She was lying in Cait's lap, a blur of faces above her, all male. Red patches of light and spinning objects swirled before her. She squeezed her eyes shut again and shook her head.

"Can ye hear me, lass?" Cait touched a bottle to Davina's lips, the fire of its contents stinging her nose. She took a quick drink and sputtered a cough, its burn racing down her throat.

"What happened?" she asked.

"Ye fainted. Almost hit yer head on the stones had this man not caught ye in time." Cait nodded to her right, and Davina turned to see a fuzzy sea of red and gold. After a few seconds, his face became clearer, his hair, his collar. And then it all came back to her in a hot rush of humiliation. He didn't remember her. She thought she might retch.

Cait resituated the damp cloth that Davina realized she wore on her forehead. "Tell me now if I need to fetch the chirurgeon."

"I'm fine." *Embarrassed, ashamed, torn into pieces.* "Help me up, will ye, Cait?"

"Here." The soldier—her soldier—gently reached under her arm. "I'll do it."

THE TACKSMAN'S DAUGHTER

She didn't want him to touch her. It was far too painful, but she had no choice in the matter. He lifted her, his chest pressing into her back for leverage. She closed her eyes, remembering all those times he had held her like that, his arms wrapped around her, his lips on her neck. As much as she didn't want to face him, she had to. At least to thank him.

She turned, his hands still on her arms. "Thank ye for yer kindness. I—"

She questioned her memory as she stared at him closely. Was his jaw always that squared? His hair so wavy? Then she noticed. Her heart suddenly steadied. It wasn't him. This man's eyes were blue.

Chapter 4

That night, Cait sat with Gillian at the *ceilidh*, listening to the old bard from the Isle of Harris tell a tale about a young wife who lost her husband at sea. According to the legend, shortly after his death, a large beast with antlers that stretched as wide as a ship's sail would appear in the wild moors, scaring the sheep with its sad braying. The widow, knowing it to be her husband, had heard its calls late one night and went out searching for it, never to return.

Gilli squeezed Cait's hand and shuffled closer on the bench. "Would you follow a beast into the night?"

"Nay. I wouldn't, lassie. And neither should you." Cait patted her knee, hoping to comfort her little sister. "Men are nae worth the trouble."

Gilli nodded, quick to believe the words. She had to learn sometime—even now at the age of seven—that she needn't bother with men. It was a lesson worth knowing. Da had taught Cait how to sell and barter goods and work with numbers. That was one of the benefits of not having brothers. Her father treated her like a son. And immediately after the soldiers had left the glen a few years back, Da had taught Cait how to defend herself, promising that as long as she kept a blade with her at all times and learned how to use it, she would never fear another man. Or need one. It was only a matter of time before he took Gilli aside and taught her to fight with a knife too.

Cait observed the Englishmen and some of the Lowlanders as they listened to the bard, scratching their beards and shooting questioning glances at one another with every word of Gaelic. Everyone else sat still, heeding the haunting story, their agape mouths and gasps the evidence of their understanding.

THE TACKSMAN'S DAUGHTER

Gilli wriggled in her seat, plainly uncomfortable with the bard's description of the dark night and the faerie spirits that roamed free on the moorlands. "What do ye think happened to the woman? Did the beast take her?"

Cait had to answer this carefully or Gilli would keep her up all night, croodling and clinging to her like ivy to an oak tree. "The beast took her to a village where the grass stayed green all year round, there was plenty of meat to eat, and the wild berries grew as big as yer hand."

Gilli licked her lips with a sharp smacking noise. "Did she ever have to eat Finnan haddie again?"

Cait knew how much Gilli hated the fish, having watched her surreptitiously feed it to the village cat that wandered into their home on occasion. She leaned in and nuzzled her close. "Never."

Gilli's feet swung happily, the tips of her slippers barely scraping the floor.

More than a hundred soldiers lined the walls with their scarlet coats and unfamiliar tartans. Why had MacIain invited the soldiers to join them that night in the great hall? Englishmen!

Cait ran her thumb over the scar on her palm, her nerves on end, then shivered as if a cold breeze had tickled the back of her neck. It had been almost five years since she had seen a soldier, but it felt as if it were yesterday. She didn't want to allow that memory to ruin her night, so she released a long breath, expelling every horrible thought that fought to stay lodged in her mind.

The bard finished, and Big Henderson of the Chanters emerged, his normally wild blond hair tamed back with a leather thong. Standing an inch or two taller than MacIain, he began playing his pipes, the high-pitched music filling the hall and lightening the mood. He was a common sight here in Carnoch, this part of Glencoe, and since the arrival of the soldiers yesterday, he was never more than a step away from MacIain's side.

Before Cait knew it, she was tapping her foot and keeping time to the trilly beat.

Gilli stood and brushed down her skirts. "I'm going to look for Taran."

Cait spotted the bard against the wall, but Taran wasn't beside him. "With his grandda nearby, he must be here in the hall. Dinnae go beyond it without someone ye know escorting ye. Not a soldier, mind ye."

Cait stood to watch Gilli push her way through the crowd. She breathed a sigh of relief when Gilli found Taran, then turned her attention back to Big Henderson, whose rosy cheeks puffed out with each deep breath, his bushy brows lifting every time he reached a high note.

"Enjoying the music?"

It was the soldier Davina had mistaken for her own. Cait couldn't blame her for wanting to find her son's father, but at the same time, part of her wanted to scold Davina for placing so much hope in a man. And an Englishman nonetheless.

"'Tis lovely," she said, eyes fixed on Big Henderson.

He motioned to the empty seat on the bench beside her. "May I join you?"

Although he'd been kind to Davina when she collapsed, he still wore the scarlet coat of an English soldier. "There must be other seats."

"None that I have found."

She glanced at MacIain who stood against the wall, his arms crossed firmly in front of him. He was watching them intently. She raised her brow in question, and he offered a brief nod. Although he'd given his approval, she wasn't happy with it.

She shrouded her discomfort with a half-shrug, then scooted a little to her left, giving him just enough space to sit. He wouldn't dare behave improperly with the clan chief not ten paces away.

"When we were introduced earlier, your name sounded familiar, but I couldn't quite place it." He tapped his finger to his temple and winked. "But now I know who you are."

She didn't care for that wink or the implication of what he was saying, his closed grin likely hiding some vulgar thought. Her father had told her that every man imagines a woman naked within the first ten seconds of an introduction. She crossed her arms over her breasts. "Ye know me?"

"Your reputation extends all the way to Fort William."

Heat crept up her chest and into her neck. She didn't like the sound of that. Fame and infamy were the same—never amounting to anything good and impossible to hide from. Could the story of what happened years ago have traveled back to the garrison? Had the soldiers lied about the events? "My reputation, sir? Clearly, ye have me mistaken for another lass."

"I don't believe so. Caitriona Cameron, is it?"

"Beg pardon, but I forgot yer name." As soon as he told it to her, she was going straight to MacIain to see that he was given a proper lesson on how to speak to a lass on MacDonald lands.

"Edward. Sergeant Edward Gage."

"Well, Sergeant Gage, if you've come here thinking to slander my good name or seek some sort of pleasure—"

"Not at all. You misunderstand me." He pressed his hand over his heart, his brow furrowed, the shadow of a smile fighting to stay hidden. "I meant your reputation with a *sword*."

Cait's shoulders loosened.

She didn't mind her skill with a blade being the subject of conversation, but clearly the tales of her expertise were skewed. She couldn't imagine besting an opponent with her father's claymore. A few parries with that heavy sword would be exhausting.

"If I have a reputation at all, it lies with the way I throw my *sgian dubh*."

She forgot that he was English and probably had no knowledge of the Gaelic, so she corrected herself. "Black knife." She wasn't about to show him. It was hidden under her skirts. "A small blade, but it can kill a man all the same."

The sergeant smiled, his blue eyes catching the firelight of the hearth nearby. He had shaved since the morning incident, only a fine dark stubble now shading his jaw.

She continued, "Especially if it catches him in just the right spot. The base of the skull, the throat, the fleshy part just below the chest, the back of the knee . . ." If he'd been thinking of behaving disrespectfully, she was certain her clear understanding of how to kill a man would change his mind.

"I don't doubt you, miss," he stated, brow raised.

The man to his right, portly and red-faced, slid a pewter flask out of his plaid and handed it to him. Sergeant Gage turned it up to his lips and took what appeared to be a hearty swig. He wiped his mouth with the back of his hand, winked, then offered it to Cait. Was he being impertinent?

As much as she would've liked a sip or two, she held up her hand in refusal. "A black knife is much quicker than a pistol. Nothing to reload."

"True. I—"

"I'm quite good with a dirk too. 'Tis simply harder to conceal."

"That it is." He took one more pull from the flask. She'd never seen an Englishman savor the taste of whisky before. The last time the English were in Glencoe, they'd complained that it tasted like horse piss.

He returned it to its owner, who was showing signs that this was not his first flask of the evening. "I never expected I'd have a discussion about weapons with a fair lass such as yourself."

"Better to learn of my skill through discussion than at the tip of my blade." That should keep him from winking at her again. "So why are ye here, Sergeant Gage? Ye cannae arrive on MacDonald lands with Robert Campbell of Glenlyon at yer side and no have a lot of folks talking."

"Why all the concern? I heard him mention he is kin to the MacDonalds."

She should've known Glenlyon would play the kinsman card. "'Tis true. His niece married MacIain's younger son, Alasdair Og. But calling us kinsmen is a bit of a stretch, ye see. Ye cannae erase hundreds of years of stramashes with a single marriage vow. So, if I appear concerned, 'tis for good reason."

Gage shrugged. "My regiment joined his in Inveraray. I barely know the man."

That might be true, but why join forces with *him?* And then choose MacDonald lands as the place for both regiments to rest their weary feet? "I suppose yer here for some purpose. And dinnae tell me 'tis to punish Glengarry."

"Then what am I to tell you?" he asked, his brows raised in question.

"The truth."

"But that is the truth. We were on our way to Glengarry but stopped in Glencoe because of the weather. We cannot get through the pass during the storms or at least until the snow melts. Surely you know that."

"Why should I trust ye?" He was an English soldier, after all.

"What other reason would there be?"

She searched his eyes for a sign of deceit, a twitch, a quick look away. But his gaze remained steady. If he was telling the truth, then why did her skin prickle every time the soldiers were near? The sooner they left, the better. *"Gheibhear a-mach an ceann sreath."* She realized the Gaelic probably skimmed over him like it did with all the other Englishmen in the room. "I said—"

"All will be revealed in good time'." He offered her a brief nod, then turned to the red-faced man beside him and pointed to his flask. "May I?" The man, now heavy-lidded and swaying in his seat, handed him his whisky.

She froze, unsure of what she just heard. It took a moment before she could speak. "Ye have the Gaelic?" she asked, impressed and curious at the same time.

"You seem surprised."

"I—I just assumed—"

"That an Englishman couldn't possibly master the language? 'Tis my mother's tongue. She's Scottish." He took a pull from the flask, then swiped his thumb and forefinger down the corners of his mouth.

"Is she, then?" she asked, her shoulders loosening a bit. "I'll remember to take heed with what I say when yer near." She'd never met an Englishman like him before. She snatched the whisky from his grip and drank a good mouthful. The taste of dried figs with a hint of leather coated her tongue and throat. "Where is she from?"

"She's a MacKinnon. Of Skye."

A Highlander. She should've known by the way he handled his drink. "We have some MacKinnons here in Glencoe."

"Do you?"

"There's a spirit of kinship between the MacDonalds and the MacKinnons. They've come to the aid of the MacDonalds of Skye when there's been trouble with the MacLeods." She wiggled the flask, happy that it was still half full, then held it up in a salute. "When ye bear yer blade for a MacDonald, the knowledge of it will be burned in our hearts forever." She swallowed another mouthful, pleased with the burn it carried with it, then offered it back to the sergeant.

"I thought you were a Cameron." Sergeant Gage took a drink. He moved to hand the flask to its owner, but the man was fast asleep, his chin on his chest, his gut stretching the buttons on his waistcoat with each intake of breath.

"Aye, but my mother is a MacDonald and cousin to MacIain." Normally, she wouldn't waste her time explaining her heritage to an Englishman, but this one was part Scot. And he had an interesting smile, crooked but honest. For a soldier. "My father was on his way to Inveraray from Lochaber and had to pass through Glencoe. He spotted my mother with some women, churning butter and making cheese. He said she looked lovely singing with the others, her cheeks pink from the sun. She smiled at him, and that's when he knew she'd become his wife."

"All with a smile?" he asked.

Cait had wondered the same thing the first time she'd heard the story. But her mother was a beauty, her smile beguiling, so she didn't doubt it. "I suppose for some, 'tis that easy."

"And for you? Would you fall so easily?"

Foolish man. "Never."

The next morning, Cait's mouth was as dry as an old bone. It was the second pint that did her in. She remembered the sergeant returning to his seat with another flask and how her tongue had flowed loosely about her family and life in Glencoe. He had shared his story too, although she couldn't remember much of it.

Still in her gown, now crumpled with sleep, she headed down the long passage to the stairwell, one hand clinging to the rope and the other grazing the curved wall as she carefully treaded each wedge-shaped step. She paused at the laird's lug, certain she heard voices below. She waited, listening, trying to make out a word or phrase, but the sounds were muffled, indecipherable. Was MacIain down there? Was he spying on someone in the alcove next to the great hall? If he was, she wouldn't blame him. A room full of soldiers—and English soldiers at that—rarely promised anything fortuitous, but in this instance, it might just reveal a secret or two.

She followed the smells from the kitchen, sweet and heady, her mouth starting to water. "A tassie of heather ale, Lilas?"

The cook took one long look at her and frowned. "Were ye partaking in the wine last night, lass?"

Cait shook her head, which felt like it would topple off her shoulders if she wasn't careful. "The whisky."

"Well, then. It looks like ye learned yer lesson." Lilas set a jug and a cup on the table in front of her with some soft cheese. "Here ye go. The crowdie should settle yer wame a bit too."

"Much obliged." Cait inhaled the spicy honey scent to clear her senses, then downed her drink and quickly poured another. Out of the corner of her eye, she spotted an English soldier standing at the entrance to the hall, his scarlet coat too bright in the dull morning light. He looked like Edward Gage—dark hair, early to mid-twenties—but his laugh didn't match what she remembered. She shook her head slightly, confident she was feeling the effects of last night's whisky.

Her face was buried in her cup when he spoke, his words formal, crisp. "I do not believe I have yet had the pleasure of your acquaintance, madam."

She stared at him over the rim of her cup, then over at Lilas. *She* looked the same—short and round, faery-white hair hanging higgledy-piggledy out of her kertch, her apron smeared with earth-coloured handprints. *Edward*, however, did not. Could there be two of them? He stood hat in hand, straight and tall, waiting for her to respond, but his extreme likeness to Edward prevented any logical thought from forming in her mind and finding its way out of her mouth.

"Madam?"

She set down her ale and exhaled. "Forgive me. Ye share an uncanny resemblance to someone I know."

His smile faded. "I suppose you have met my brother."

"Yer brother?" That couldn't be right. Through the course of the evening, Edward had told her he was raised alone, an only child.

"My half-brother, Edward. I am Alexander." He bowed slightly. "Leftenant Alexander Gage at your service."

"I've never seen half-brothers favour one another as much as the two of you."

He petted the white foam of lace at his throat. "Actually, we both favour my father."

She noticed he didn't say *our* father. This man was pure English, not a drop of Scottish blood in him. But just to be sure, she said, *I'll wager my arse that yer imagining me naked right now* in Gaelic.

He leaned closer, his head tilted to the side, lips pursed, showing no sign of understanding a word she'd said anywhere in his blank countenance.

She couldn't help but smile. "So ye dinnae have the Gaelic."

"I am afraid I do not," he admitted.

THE TACKSMAN'S DAUGHTER

That was plenty good. But she didn't doubt that her father was right, and at that moment, those brown eyes of his were looking right through her clothes.

Chapter 5

Even though it was better than sleeping outside in the unbearable cold, lying with five other men in a room the size of a breadbasket was not to Alexander's liking. It had to be the worst room in the manor. Didn't the laird realize that this was beneath him? He had made it perfectly clear upon their introduction that he was a noble and not some commoner who should be given a tattered wool blanket and a pallet stinking of mouldy straw and cow dung.

All night his men had snored and farted, adding to the sour stench that accompanied their unwashed bodies. It was like sleeping in a poorly kept barn. He wouldn't have even allowed his most incompetent hunting dog to rest there.

To make matters worse, he had to start the morning with the knowledge that Edward had somehow managed to meet the fairest of all the Glencoe wenches before him and insert his greedy claws into her. It was the way she'd looked at him with judging eyes while they were in the kitchens, as if he were somehow inferior to that lowly brother of his, that made his chest burn.

He couldn't wait to leave this place and all its savagery. Dalrymple was right. These people needed to be tamed, brought to their knees in submission to His Majesty, King William, and taught the king's English, for God's sake.

Relieved to be anywhere other than his dismal sleeping quarters, he stood at the window in the laird's drawing room, staring out at the bare larches dotting the hillside behind the estate, their fallen needles buried under three or four feet of snow. There was something about the sky that promised better weather, though. By noon, the fog had lifted, and the sun struggled through slightly parted clouds high above. Alexander leaned his forehead on the cold windowpane, hopeful that the small break in weather would mean they could resume their march and get on with teaching Glengarry a good lesson on loyalty and fealty. That was his favourite part of being a soldier—drawing the haughtiness out of some desperate scoundrel with his blade stretched across his neck.

Of course, Alexander was only a soldier because his father had turned traitor to King William three years earlier and become part of the Jacobite rising. If he hadn't done that, Father wouldn't be in the Tower eating scraps left over from the guards, and Alexander wouldn't have been forced into the military to prove his worthiness to the king. For the moment, the king hadn't used attainder against Father for his treason, but the threat of it lay imminent. If William chose to attaint the earl, Alexander would lose his titles and lands. All of his inheritance. He would become a commoner. The mere thought of it sent him into a horrible sweat.

"There you are." Edward stood at the threshold to the room, his coat off and the top three buttons of his waistcoat undone.

Alexander hated when he appeared so slovenly. He was a soldier, an officer. But then again, he was also a bastard.

"Would you care to join us in a game of baggammon, brother?" Edward asked.

Alexander rubbed his forehead, still cold from the glass pane. "Another game of baggammon? Sounds thrilling."

Edward crossed his arms, feet spread apart. Alexander hated to admit it, but he recognized himself in that stance. Except when *he* stood that way, it was more of a challenge, not a question.

There was only one thing that could entice him to join the others. Alexander asked, "Have they wine? Not that vile whisky, I hope."

It was yet early in the afternoon, and Robert Campbell was already making a fool of himself, half-drunk, loud, and wagering as if he had all the riches in the world. Alexander loathed men like him. They puffed out their chests and expected everyone to applaud when they sneezed.

"What will it be, Leftenant?" Campbell asked, leaning forward in his chair, ready for Alexander to make his next move. He scratched the side of his beet-coloured nose with a stubby finger.

Alexander studied the board, joggling the doubling cube in his palm. With a lucky roll, he would win Campbell's entire lot, leaving the poor sot singing for his soup. He felt the smirk warm upon his face. "I vie."

The soldiers around them shifted uncomfortably, plainly aware that Campbell was about to be defeated. Again.

Alexander released the cube, and in seconds, a recognition of defeat appeared in the Scot's watery eyes. The old man drew a long pull from his flask, then shouted in a husky voice, "Another game! Another game!"

One of the soldiers wrapped his arm around his shoulder. "Nay, Glenlyon. Ye need something in yer wame first. Come to the kitchens with me."

Campbell peered up at him, his face fallen like a child's, then allowed the soldier to lead him away. He was a captain in Argyll's regiment, yet he was drenched in weakness. Alexander leaned back in his chair, disgusted by Argyll's choice in men.

John, MacIain's son, shook his head. "Ye better hold onto yer sterling, Leftenant, for as soon as the old bawheid is sober, he'll come begging for it back."

Alexander wasn't worried. He hadn't seen Glenlyon sober since they'd arrived. He scooped the coins into his palm, then slipped them into his pouch. "He seems to spend an awful lot of time here. Where is he lodging?"

Lindsay strode forward, wiping his nose with a stained handkerchief, his white periwig tilted to the right. "MacIain offered him a bed, but he chose to stay at the end of the glen with MacDonald of Inverrigan."

Alexander thought the fool would've taken quarters with the chieftain of Glencoe, not Angus MacDonald, a mere tacksman. "How does he manage to travel here every day with the snow as deep as it is?"

John answered this time, sarcasm in every word. "I suppose the promise of the burn of whisky in his throat and a seat by the hearth playing cards or gammon are enough to make him trudge a mile through the snow. He's likely cleared a path by now."

Spirits and gaming. Alexander would gladly trade both for the third vice—women. He had spent three days in the village already and not a single lass—save for the black-haired one seated in the kitchens earlier—was worthy of sharing his bed. If their stay stretched out much longer, he would have to lower his standards and take a plain wench from the washhouse or kitchens.

He excused himself to join Edward, who was seated at another table, playing cards fanned in his hand and a small pile of sterling stacked neatly in front of him. The three Scots also at the table, all with hair unkempt and unbound, eyed him warily as if he were a wild boar in approach. Edward must've picked up on it too, for he said in a tone far too jolly for the occasion, "Brother, have you come to rescue me from the gaming prowess of these fine gentlemen?"

Alexander rolled his eyes. *Fine gentlemen, indeed.* "May I have a word?"

Edward gathered his winnings, and they moved into the hall.

THE TACKSMAN'S DAUGHTER

"The weather is showing improvement." Alexander pulled at his collar, now suddenly pressing too hard against his throat. "I cannot wait to leave this place and these barbarians."

"Improvement?" Edward shook his head. "Even if the weather lifts, the pass will still be neck-deep with snow. It will be a week before it melts enough for us to get through."

Alexander's stomach turned. He had to finish his business here so he could get back to England and fight to keep his right of inheritance. Hopefully this time, after he carried out his orders, the king would recognize his loyalty and put to rest the idea of issuing attainder. "The sooner we are out of here, the sooner we can return to England."

"What is the rush? We have shelter and food, and these people have been nothing but hospitable towards us."

"Hospitable?" Alexander glared at him. "I sleep on a straw pallet that reeks of piss and eat hard bread that lies in my stomach at night like lead shot."

Edward laughed. "You seem to be content in the evenings, draining flagons of wine by the hearth."

"Forgive me for finding something to make this stay bearable." Edward was always so self-righteous. So ready to point out the few moments of comfort Alexander managed to scrape up in all the miserable places they camped. "And what are *you* doing to pass the time, brother? Burying your cock in some Scottish whore?"

"Really, Alexander." Edward rubbed his brow. "I'm not like that."

"Anymore, perhaps."

Edward glared at him. "It always comes down to that for you, does it not?"

"I suppose it does." Alexander didn't care what Edward thought of him. He was tired of his condescending ways. He tugged on his lace cuff. "I met someone this morning who knows you."

Edward's brow crinkled. "Who?"

"A lass. I find it amusing that you would not have mentioned me to her, considering the closeness of your acquaintance."

One corner of Edward's mouth turned up. "You're normally opposed to my drawing attention to our . . . relationship."

"I am not in favour of advertising my father's indiscretions, if that is what you are implying." It only served to remind him about the annuity his father had sent Edward's whore-of-a-mother to maintain her as his mistress. At least that had stopped when he was taken to the Tower. Alexander's mother had made sure of it before Father had even been thrown on the back of the wagon and hauled away. "I simply wanted an introduction. But I took care of it."

Edward crossed his arms in front of his chest and sighed. "I'm not sure to whom you are referring."

"The raven-haired beauty with the green eyes. A bit bloodshot this morning, though. Perhaps from too much . . . frolicking."

Edward's lip twitched. "You should stay away from her."

He was so predictable. "You would like that, of course." Alexander leaned close. "Will you speak ill of me to frighten her off?"

Edward poked Alexander in the chest. "*Your* misfortune with the lasses is a result of your shortcomings. It has nothing to do with me."

Alexander swatted his hand away. "Was that true with Lady Berenice? Hmm?"

Edward planted his hands on his hips. "Is that really what this is about? Her?"

Alexander's chest filled with heat. "Do not speak of her as if she were nothing."

Berenice had been everything. His heart. His future. His hope for keeping his title as Baron Mansfield. She had been the solution to all his problems—a solution cut short by Edward. "You ruined my chances at—"

"Am I interrupting something?" They both turned to face the Scottish wench from the kitchens standing at the threshold, her sardonic smile seemingly aimed only at Alexander. Her timing was impeccable.

Alexander offered, "We were just talking about you. Were we not, Edward?"

She drew back, clearly displeased by that announcement.

A look of panic suddenly appeared on Edward's pathetic face. "Cait, I—"

"Calling her by her Christian name, are we?" He pointed back and forth between the two of them, hoping to bring them to shame. "Are you two that *familiar?*"

"Alexander!" Edward grabbed his coat sleeve and yanked him hard.

Cait folded her arms, eyes narrowed, her perfect little mouth tightened. "MacIain sent me to invite ye to the *ceilidh* tonight in the hall, but perhaps he should've thought better of it."

Edward edged closer, his hands extended in supplication. "Please ignore my brother. His anger at me caused him to use a poor choice of words." He twisted back and shot him a sharp glance. "He meant no harm. We were in the midst of a petty quarrel."

"About me," she stated, her jaw tight.

"Not at all," said Edward.

Nothing could be further from the truth. Of course this was about her. Especially her. And all the others that Edward had stolen from under him.

THE TACKSMAN'S DAUGHTER

Alexander gritted his teeth and forced a quick smile. He offered a small nod. "Please forgive me."

She stared at him sideways, as if to decide whether or not she should grant him a pardon. As if she were superior to him. A flicker of exhilaration burned in Alexander's gut. *Oh, how I could bring you down.*

She licked her bottom lip in study. "The piper will be there, and MacIain told the bard to perform in Scots English this time. It will be the bard of Clan Donald, not Matheson, tonight." Her gaze stayed fixed on him, never blinking.

"We would be honoured to be there, of course." Edward bowed.

She left the room, her skirts swirling angrily after her.

Edward was about to say something, but Alexander cut him off. "Tell the men we will start drills tomorrow morning whether or not the weather is fair. Have them ready at dawn."

"At dawn? I imagine everyone will want to attend the festivities tonight. Not a single soldier will be—"

"You were given an order, Sergeant." Alexander sniffed, then cleared his throat with derision.

"Very well." Edward started for the door, then turned back around. "Brother?"

Alexander waited for him to continue, his patience wearing thin.

A crooked smile crept onto Edward's face. "Speak to her like that again, and I have a good feeling she'll demonstrate how talented she is with a knife."

Chapter 6

More than two hundred men and women packed the great hall to listen to the bard. Edward lingered by the hearth, searching through the crowd, hoping to find Cait. He wanted to apologize once more for his brother, but more importantly, he wanted to warn her about him. He probably didn't need to, though. The look of contempt in her eyes when Alexander had insinuated they had been intimate had told him she would likely stay clear of him anyway.

"I know you," a little voice said. Edward stared down at the child tugging on the hem of his coat, her angelic face tilted in wonder. "Ye were with my sister last night."

Edward crouched to her height. Her eyes were big and round and the pale green of a dragonfly's wings. Just like Cait's. "You must be Gillian."

She nodded, her bottom lip caught between her teeth.

"Do you know where your sister is now?" he asked.

She twisted back and forth to the bard's song, rising and falling in a happy rhythm. "She's with Glenlyon."

What would she want with Campbell? Edward was fairly sure she didn't care much for the man. "Glenlyon? Are you certain?"

"Aye. She said she wanted to give him the gift of a pint or two, so she went to look for him by the gaming tables."

Gifting Campbell with whisky? That didn't seem right, unless it was to pour it over his head.

Edward followed Gillian's gaze as she searched through the hordes of revelers. Suddenly, she spun to face Taran in approach, her smile stretching cheek to cheek in an instant. She reached out and snatched his free hand, his other hand busy with his blackthorn cane. "Over here, Taran. 'Tis warm by the hearth."

Taran's mouth twisted to the side in displeasure. "I know where the hearth is. I feel the heat."

Little Taran apparently didn't like being led around by others. Edward patted him on the shoulder. "Of course you do, lad. You probably know your way around this entire estate."

"I know my way around all of Glencoe," he said, his shoulders pulled back, eyes staring blankly.

Gillian jammed her fists on her hips. "How would ye know that? You've spent most of yer time here stuck inside with me."

The poor lad's face fell, his shoulders now slumped. "Only since the weather turned."

His expression tugged at Edward's heart. "Taran is an expert guide, Gillian. I don't doubt that he can cross these fields and ford through streams better than most of the men in this room."

Taran stood a little straighter. "'Tis true. I can."

Gillian threaded her arm through Taran's and smiled sweetly. "When the sun comes out and the snow has melted, I'm going to take ye to the faery pool where *maybe* we can catch a wee one in our hands."

Taran lit up, his dimples starkly pronounced at the corners of his mouth.

The two disappeared quickly, leaving Edward free to search for Cait. He was sure she was up to something. He thought he'd done a good job the other night of convincing her of the truth—that their stay in Glencoe was incidental and not something sinister—but perhaps she still didn't believe Campbell was capable of behaving honourably. Otherwise, why would she want to be near the old man?

He zigzagged his way through the crowd to the gaming room, where Cait stood at Campbell's side. At the threshold, Edward studied the scene for a couple of minutes before he decided to approach. Leftenants Farquhar and Kennedy shot him a doubting look as Campbell placed his next bet. Another questionable stake. The man would never learn.

It was indisputable as to what Cait was trying to do. She leaned into the captain after each roll of the cube, encouraging him to partake in more than his share of whisky, going so far as to hold the pint in front of him if he reached for it too slowly. Edward had to fight back a laugh, careful not to delight at the old man's expense.

"Cait. I mean . . . Mistress Cameron," he corrected himself.

Cait spun to face him, Campbell's pint in her hand. She speared Edward a look that told him he was clearly interrupting something, her eyes narrowed and mouth tight. He considered leaving her to her own devices but changed his mind when the soldier to her right stretched his neck to admire her décolletage.

"Your sister told me I would find you here," he said as he approached.

Her eyes darted between him and Campbell, who seemed completely oblivious of the intrusion. "Did she, then?"

He strolled closer to the Englishman ogling her breasts and laid a heavy hand on his shoulder, casually blocking his view. The soldier attempted a fairly insistent jab to Edward's ribs, which he ignored. "I was wondering if I could have a word with you, mistress."

She smiled down at Campbell, who suddenly noticed Edward standing at the table. Cait handed the old cove the pint, which he took gladly. "I'm a wee bit busy now, Sergeant," she replied through gritted teeth.

"I see that, but this should only take a few moments."

She made no move to leave the table, her gaze fixed on the upturned pint pressed to Campbell's lips.

Edward leaned in to whisper. "Surrounding yourself with a host of drunken men will likely guarantee an unfortunate outcome."

She let out an exasperated huff, then pulled him to the corner of the room by the sleeve of his coat. "I know what I'm doing."

"Do you?"

A few of the men watched them from the table, the others far more interested in the game at hand, including Campbell.

She reached into her skirts and pulled out another flask, wiggling it as she spoke. "A man under the influence of drink, if he speaks at all, usually speaks truth."

His shoulders relaxed. She was only searching for information, not planning some sort of attack once the man was good and soused. "And you think getting Campbell pissed will get him to tell you the truth about what?"

She hesitated, chewing on her bottom lip as if deciding whether or not to divulge her purpose. "I want to know why he's here. Why all of ye are here."

"You still believe that we mean the MacDonalds harm?"

"I take very few men at their word, Sergeant. Certainly nae an Englishman. And never a Campbell."

"You may call me Edward. No one is listening, Cait."

"Dinnae call me Cait." She swept a curl away from her face roughly. "I shouldn't have made the offer of such informality last night. I blame the whisky."

He had to laugh. She was definitely a different girl from the one she was last night. By the end of the evening, that girl had turned playful, on the verge of flirtatious, even. There was no doubt that the spirits had loosened her normally rigid ways. "I think you meant it when you said I could call you by your given name."

She stared down at the flask in her hand. "That was the whisky talking. Not me."

"But a minute ago, you claimed that spirits get men—or women—to speak the truth."

She shook her head in defeat, a smile in her obstinate lips. "Very well. Ye may call me Cait when we are alone."

She started to walk away, but he caught her arm. "There's something else."

She tilted her head to the side, forcing a small crease between her brows.

"I want to apologize for my brother's rude comment earlier."

"Ye already did."

His palms grew clammy, so he wiped them on the sides of his breeches. "And I want to warn you about him."

"Warn me?"

He reached for the flask still in her grip. "May I?"

He took a good swallow, then handed it back. This was going to be difficult. Alexander had questioned him about frightening her off only a few hours earlier. "I worry that my brother is . . . what I mean to say is . . . please take care around him. When he wants something, he takes it."

Her left hand curled into a fist, and her look transformed from curious to determined. "I appreciate yer concern, but ye have no need to worry over me. I can take care of myself."

"Keep it in mind, though."

She nodded, almost imperceptibly, her gaze directly on his. "I think I understand. Yer brothers, but in name only."

He and Alexander had never been close. Alexander had resented Edward's existence from the day he was old enough to understand he had a half-brother, one who stole his father's attentions and affections from him and the rest of his family. Of course, Edward didn't know that until he was a lad of seventeen and met Alexander for the first time.

It was the winter of 1685, and King Charles II had just died. The king's brother, James, took the crown, and Charles's illegitimate son, the Duke of Monmouth, raised an army against him. Edward and his mother privately hoped the duke would take the throne since he was also Protestant. They feared James, a Catholic, would throw the country into turmoil once again if he were victorious.

It was the need to deliver the news that the duke's army had been defeated at Somerset that had driven Father to visit unexpectedly, Alexander in tow.

Edward had sensed Alexander's hostility towards him within the first five minutes of their introduction. But his desire to form a bond had pushed him to accept Alexander's offer to join him down at the pond, where Alexander had held Edward's head under the murky green water until he saw spots dancing before his eyes. He'd said he only did it as a warning, but Edward knew that the threat would've turned deadly had he not fought for his life.

Edward started to speak, but Cait stopped him. "Ye needn't say anything. I see the truth in yer eyes. 'Tis a shame, though."

He shrugged one shoulder. "We manage."

Cait shook her head. "I'm sure ye do. That's nae what I meant."

Through the window, a shaft of sunlight limned her black hair with tiny prisms of colour.

"I . . ." she started, then bowed her head, staring at the floor. "I believe yer brother is well acquainted with the lass ye met yesterday in the hall at breakfast. I think she mistook ye for him."

"I see." That made sense. Her friend had looked at him as if she'd seen a ghost, one from her past, and one she'd known well. "And now you must warn her about him."

"'Tisnae that simple."

He could tell she was fighting the urge to divulge something, but he wouldn't press it. Her eyes were too sad, too full of disappointment. He gave a quick nod and motioned to the other side of the room. "I suppose you should return to your ruse."

They turned back to the others and found Campbell lying face down at the table, his reddish-gold tresses blanketing his face as if to hide his shame.

Cait sighed in defeat. "'Tis too late. The gowk is nae good to me now."

Chapter 7

Davina sat in the cold, bundled under a wool blanket with Sawney, watching the soldiers complete their drills before breakfast. They marched in formation at the foot of Alt Na Munde, their muskets poised on their shoulders and their swords dangling at their sides. To her left, a small cluster of men crowded around Cait as she flung her *sgian dubh* at a straw-filled sack. Each time she hit it, they smacked one another on the arm, surprised. What they didn't know was that Cait could hit that sack dead-center another fifty feet away. Davina had seen her do it many times before.

Davina tilted her face up to the weak morning sun, welcoming its warmth onto her skin. She didn't care that it might freckle her. No man would ever notice her again with a bairn on her lap and ignominy surrounding her name. Not with marriage in mind, anyway.

A huzzah erupted, and Davina watched as Cait curtsied, then broke through the crowd, twirling her blade through her fingers. Her cheeks were flushed with cold, yet she smiled brightly.

Davina patted the space beside her on the bench, inviting her to sit. "I'm surprised yer out here with the soldiers."

Last night, as soldiers and clansmen flowed into the great hall to find seats for the festivities, Cait's father, MacIain's senior tacksman, had mentioned there were over three hundred troops now billeted in Glencoe. It hadn't mattered to Davina since the one soldier she was looking for wasn't one of them, but Cait had cringed at the number.

"I thought it might be a good idea to let them see me with my blade." Cait shielded her eyes with her hand, peering out at the Redcoats and Scots practicing maneuvers. "I dinnae suppose yer still searching for Sawney's father."

It sounded like a statement, but it was a question, and the answer was simple. Her son needed his father. A family. And so did she. Davina shivered. "Do ye think I'd be sitting here if I wasn't?"

Cait reached around her, nestling close, her head on Davina's shoulder. "What'll ye say if ye see him?"

That was a question Davina had asked herself many times. Ever since she had made a fool of herself with that other soldier at breakfast, she couldn't imagine she'd ever have the nerve to approach him—if he actually appeared. But if he did, would their reunion be sweet, filled with soft glances and warm smiles? Would he enfold her in his arms and sprinkle kisses on her head and cheeks, so happy to have her again? Would his eyes brighten with love when he recognized his likeness in Sawney?

Cait's voice pulled her away from her thoughts. "From the smile on yer face, I think yer answer would be something that would make me blush."

Davina prodded her with her elbow, heat creeping into her cheeks. All her memories had been encapsulated in the short span of a month that they were together, but they lived inside of her as if she'd spent a lifetime creating them. "Ye dinnae know what it was like, Cait. He loved me. Hard and deep as if every moment we were joined was our last."

"Yer right. I dinnae know what it was like." Cait set her blade aside and tucked the edge of the blanket tighter around Sawney. She seemed sad, preoccupied, worry settled in her downturned brow. "But what if . . . he isnae the man ye remember?"

"Why wouldn't he be?"

Cait opened her mouth to answer just as MacIain called out to them, Big Henderson and MacIain's sons—John and Alasdair Og—followed a few paces behind him. "Keeping an eye on the soldiers, are ye?" he boomed, his thumb and forefinger grooming his moustache.

Davina struggled to stand, Sawney cradled in one arm, her free hand fumbling with the blanket draped around the two of them. MacIain motioned for her to stay seated.

His white hair blew wildly in the wind, lifting and falling with each blustery gust. He wore leather trews, something her father told her the chief would never do regardless of the cold. It was a sign of his fierceness, her father had said. She remembered a story he'd once told her about a January storm during which MacIain, wearing naught but his plaid and a dirk, wrestled a wild boar that had been terrorizing the village. After four hours of hunting and then fighting the beast, he'd returned to his wife covered in blood from his throat to his shins. She'd thought he was hurt, attacked, but the only complaint he had was that his bollocks were frozen to the point they might snap off. Perhaps he'd started to wear trews after that day.

His green coat flapped around his thighs with a quick gust of wind as he stood staring out at the drilling soldiers. He turned to John but spoke loud enough for Davina to hear. "The snow needs to melt a wee bit faster. If the men bide here much longer, the food will be depleted before winter's out."

Cait hmphed. "Well, *I* willnae keep them from gathering their things and heading on their way."

Davina busied herself with Sawney, pretending she hadn't heard Cait speak so boldly to the chief. Davina wanted the men to stay. At least they brought excitement to an otherwise dreary February. What did it matter that some of them were Campbells? She was too, in a way. After all, her father's sister had married Breadalbane, a Campbell.

"Forgive me, MacIain, but ye cannae blame them for staying," Cait added. "They have a warm place to sleep and enough food and drink to satisfy their wames. You've even welcomed some of them to sleep under yer very roof."

Davina's stomach tightened. Although MacIain often treated Cait like his own daughter, Davina had never heard her speak like that to him.

He stared down at Cait. "Yer suspicious of them, lass?"

Cait stood, her neck stretched high as if to challenge him. "Warfare relies on deception. Ye must make yer enemy believe ye unlikely or unable to attack, then ye strike fast."

MacIain smiled, amused. "I suppose yer da taught ye that."

"He did," she answered.

"Well, he's right. But I dinnae think these men mean us harm. They've had plenty of chances to pull their weapons in the last few days, but they haven't." MacIain's hand reached for the hilt of his claymore as if to reassure himself it remained at his side. "I appreciate yer concern, but there's no need to fash. You lasses should enjoy the extra celebrations and entertainment while they last."

Cait seemed deflated by MacIain's words, but Davina wasn't. She enjoyed the pipers and the *Gillie Callum* the sword dancers performed to the music, their graceful hops and steps keeping playfully to the beat. "I dinnae mind the men."

MacIain lifted one eyebrow. "Keep yer distance, lass. Breadalbane willnae appreciate ye finding trouble in Glencoe while yer under my care. I gave him my word I'd keep ye safe."

There it was again. Did *everyone* think she was merely a common whore and not a girl who'd simply fallen in love? "My uncle knows my heart belongs to Sawney's father and no one else."

"'Tisnae yer heart I'm concerned about."

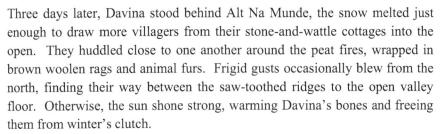

Three days later, Davina stood behind Alt Na Munde, the snow melted just enough to draw more villagers from their stone-and-wattle cottages into the open. They huddled close to one another around the peat fires, wrapped in brown woolen rags and animal furs. Frigid gusts occasionally blew from the north, finding their way between the saw-toothed ridges to the open valley floor. Otherwise, the sun shone strong, warming Davina's bones and freeing them from winter's clutch.

A few MacDonald men played *camanachd* in the open plot between Alt Na Munde and the brewhouse, some men having cleared the snow from a space large enough for a proper game. Davina recognized John and Alasdair Og racing back and forth, long wooden sticks in their hands. Some of Glenlyon's men struggled for the ball, their Campbell plaids wet from falling in the remaining piles of snow.

Nearby, Cait swiped the snow with her boot, clearing a space to get a good footing, as she'd explained to Davina many times. Cait tried to teach her how to throw a blade, but she didn't have much interest in it. If she was fortunate enough to have the free time to do something without Sawney pulling on her gown, she preferred helping in the kitchens.

Cait narrowed her eyes, staring at the sack across the field, then hurled her knife. It hit just to the left of the center of the target. The men clapped, and the soldier Davina had mistaken for Sawney's father smiled, his blue eyes bright and focused on Cait.

"That was the last one," Cait announced.

The blue-eyed soldier stepped out of the circle of men to retrieve her blade.

Every man sighed with disappointment when she left the group and joined Davina. "I heard Wallace MacDonald spent all morning with the chirurgeon, having his leg mended."

"Broken?" Davina asked.

Cait nodded. "The lower part bent to the side like the caman that likely snapped it."

Davina cringed. Each game always ended with more than a few men suffering horrible injuries—huge lumps mottled with black and blue marks, open cuts from the slice of the stick, and broken noses or split lips turning a perfectly braw face into something scarred and misshapen. She'd never understand why they continually chose to endure such torture.

THE TACKSMAN'S DAUGHTER

The soldier returned, and with a bow, handed Cait her *sgian dubh*. "I've been looking for you everywhere."

Cait examined the point of her knife, then twirled it between her fingers before sliding it into its sheath. "Ye seem to have found me."

He laughed. It sounded nothing like Sawney's father's laugh, which, although infrequent, was softer. Somehow, that soothed Davina.

"Word of your knife-throwing travels fast." His smile faded a bit but lingered in the corners of his mouth. "But I can't help thinking that you're purposely avoiding me."

Cait shot a nervous glance at Davina, then stared out at the men playing *camanachd*. "I've been helping in the kitchens."

The soldier cocked his head to one side. "I've looked in the kitchens. I've been down there so often your cook and I have had no choice but to get acquainted. Did you know she has eleven children and almost thirty grandchildren?"

"Of course. I know all but two of them." Cait touched her hair with the lightness of a bee flitting around blossoms. Davina had never really seen Cait fuss about her hair before and wondered if this man standing with them was truly as annoying as Cait made him sound.

As if he could tell she was thinking about him, he turned to her. "Please allow me to introduce myself." He gave a quick bow. "Sergeant Edward Gage at your service, mistress."

Davina stammered, "Aye. We've met. I was the—"

"The fair lass who swooned in my arms."

That was not exactly what she was going to say, but she liked his less-clumsy version of the story better. "'Tis a pleasure, Sergeant." She extended her hand. "Davina MacNab."

The sergeant kissed her knuckle, his lips warm on her cold skin.

Cait looked at her sideways, her eyes narrowed, then suddenly grabbed Davina's arm and tugged. "We were just headed inside. Good day, Sergeant."

"You're not staying to watch the game of shinty?" he asked, his voice playful.

Cait stopped abruptly after a few steps, then turned back to him. "Do ye plan to play, then?"

"I might." He rubbed his palms together while he scanned the field, his cheeks rosy from the cold.

At that moment, two men collided, sending heavy grunts and the sharp crack of their camans into the cold air. Davina winced.

Amusement flickered in Cait's expression. "It might be too rough for an Englishman."

Davina opened her mouth to warn him about the injuries that would surely come his way, but Cait squeezed her forearm, stopping her.

He smiled, then blew into his hands, his eyes full of humour. "I thank you for your concern over my well-being, Cait, but I think I can manage it."

Cait? How well did she know this soldier? Had she been spending time with him outside of the festivities? Davina had spotted them together on a few occasions but hadn't thought anything of it. Cait had made it perfectly clear that men were of no concern to her. But evidently, this was not the case. The frigid Cait had met a handsome soldier—who fancied her—and kept this secret to herself.

Sergeant Gage pressed his hand to his chest. "Would either of you lovely lasses offer me some kind words before I enter into battle?"

Davina couldn't think of anything to say, still surprised by this new revelation.

Cait, on the other hand, looked like she had plenty to say.

"If ye still have yer head when 'tis over, I'll eat my boots."

Davina searched the kitchen cupboards for a fig or some black pudding for Sawney but couldn't find any. The only food visible was a few blocks of hard cheese and some half-eaten bannocks. MacIain was right. The soldiers' presence meant the food wouldn't last until spring.

She sat on a bench with Sawney by the kitchen hearth to thaw, wondering when the men would leave. She supposed it didn't matter anymore since Sawney's father wasn't amongst them. She was about to tell Cait she'd given up on finding him when Taran entered the room and Cait pulled him into the corner by a tower of stacked baskets.

"What did ye discover?" Cait asked.

He reached out tentatively and touched her skirt, his other hand firmly gripping his cane. "Well, the one who sounds like he has drammach stuck in his thrapple is costive. Been complaining of a belly-griping all afternoon. Says he hasn't shat in five days."

Davina stifled a laugh. Taran was only a child, but he often spoke like a man four times his age.

Cait's chin dropped. "That's what ye have to tell me? Shall I make some dandelion tea, then?" she asked sweetly yet biting. She turned to Davina and pointed at the door. "Go get the chamber pot. This could get slitterie."

Davina ruffled Taran's hair. "Stop teasing the lad, Cait. He did what ye told him to do, and that's all he heard."

"Ye didn't stand there long enough, laddie." She shook her head and sighed. "And Glenlyon? Did ye give the gomeral the pint I gave ye?"

THE TACKSMAN'S DAUGHTER

"Aye. Sounded like he drank it too, but it didn't have enough of the devil in it to loosen his gob."

Why didn't Cait believe the soldiers were harmless? *Stubborn lass.* Davina hugged Taran to her side. "Ye did fine, laddie."

A smile finally broke out on his face. "May I go now? If the snow isnae too deep, Gillian and I are going to walk to the faery pond to catch faeries. Rinalda is coming too."

Davina hoped her sweet Sawney would be just like him, full of sunshine and dreams. "The washerwoman?"

"Aye." He nodded once, his loose curls bouncing slightly.

"Go on, then. But watch after my sister, Taran," Cait said. "Tell her she must stay on the path."

"Och, aye. She can be a handful." He was swallowed by the shadows as he walked down the narrow hallway, his cane tapping the floor in front of him.

They sat at one of the long tables, and Davina poured the two of them a cup of ale. Sawney sat quietly beside her, his legs swinging freely to a slow steady rhythm. "Ye should be ashamed of yerself for having that wee lad do yer bidding. Yer chasing a ghost through the fog, Cait. Yer never going to find what yer looking for."

Cait set down her mug, her voice low and serious. "I've had tingling in my ears for days now. Should I ignore that?"

That feeling had only happened to Davina once. It was the night before a fox had dug its way under the fence into the henyard and devoured all six of her hens. Davina shook her head to free herself of the gruesome memory. "I'm simply saying that ye seem to be the only one who believes the soldiers to be a threat. Even MacIain fears nothing. He gave them back their weapons."

"Then MacIain is a fool."

"Cait!" Davina glanced behind them to make sure no one had heard. Cait had gone too far. She lowered her voice so that only Cait could hear. "Ye cannae speak foul of the Chief of Glencoe. People are starting to talk. Ye sound like you've been touched by the devil, and now yer preying on the wee ones. You've snared poor Taran into yer web of mistrust. Truly, Cait. That laddie looks to ye like a sister, and yer scaring the innocence out of him."

She placed one hand on Sawney's shoulder, his head now resting in her lap. "And yer treating others unfairly too. 'Tis a miracle that fine soldier still wishes to speak with ye after ye lash him with yer sharp tongue and wish ill upon him."

Cait stared at her defiantly, but then her eyes changed from tight and piercing to glazed and sad. Davina watched as Cait seemed to surrender to something stirring within her, her fingers loosening around her mug and her shoulders slackening.

Davina reached for her hand. "This suspicion has snared ye like a rabbit in a trap. Let go of it, lass. Yer belief that the soldiers mean to do harm has only made ye lose sleep and bite the hands that wish to soothe ye." Davina waited while Cait considered her words.

"I'll do as ye say, if only to keep ye from thinking I've gone mad." Cait drew in a deep breath, then let it out slowly. "I only pray yer right."

Chapter 8

"Have another drink, lass!" Cait's father's words echoed off the walls near the entrance of the great hall. It was late in the evening, yet people still milled about, one of Big Henderson's livelier tunes playing from within.

Cait had listened to Davina's advice a couple of days earlier and freed herself from the grip of distrust. But that didn't mean she would shed a tear when the soldiers finally left the glen. Nay. She would be the first in line to bid them a hearty farewell. But she didn't want to think about them. It was her birthday, and she was going to make the most of it.

"Yer going to make her sick, Malcolm," Ma said, pushing Da's hand away as he tried to give Cait his flask. "'Tis more than a tot of whisky."

"A daughter of mine can handle her drink!" he said, his face lit up with pride, the crinkles around his eyes sharp and spread like a jackdaw's claws.

The men around them laughed. One of the cottars lifted his drink in response. "I believe you've taught her well. I've seen her throw back her share of the spirits once or twice."

Ma's eyes widened disapprovingly at the man's comment. Cait patted her hand, completely unbothered by his assessment of her drinking experience. "I'm nae ashamed that I can match every one of ye louts drink for drink, but I willnae prove it on my birthday. I'd like to remember it, if ye dinnae mind."

"Birthday?" Edward stepped into the crowd, his face beaming, the torchlight settling on his wide shoulders. "Did I hear correctly? 'Tis your birthday?"

Cait bristled. Her parents stood silent, their faces frozen in shock. They were likely wondering why an English soldier would dare interrupt their circle of celebration. It was an expected response, given that their distaste for Englishmen had only worsened since the last time they'd marched into Glencoe. And they hadn't spent many evenings at Alt Na Munde to witness Cait's growing acquaintance with Edward over the last week. Instead, they had recently elected to remain in their cottage with the billeted soldiers in order to guard their home. That was perfectly fine with Cait. She didn't need them hovering over her. She could take care of herself.

"Nineteenth," she said.

Edward shook his head, merriment in his eyes. He reached inside his coat and pulled out a flask. "Here's to the lass of nineteen! *Deagh shlàinte air do cho-latha-breith!*"

Da's mouth fell open, and his hand flew to his chest. "Ye have the Gaelic?"

Edward wiped his mouth with his knuckle. "Enough to wish a fair lass good health on her birthday."

Cait held her breath, waiting for Da to say something. This could go either way—Da could take offense that an Englishman would speak the language of his kinsmen, or he would be impressed that he could. The men around them shifted nervously, their eyes darting back and forth between them. Finally, Da raised his flask, a slow smile spreading across his face. *"Slàinte!"*

Cait exhaled. Cheers went up, and Da hugged her around the shoulder. After a few minutes of words being exchanged, including a brief explanation of Edward's mother being a MacKinnon, the crowd ambled inside the hall, and she and Edward were left standing alone in an alcove near the stairs.

He stared at her, his smile crooked and dimpled. "You seem happy tonight."

"I am." It was true. It felt good to let go of her fears.

The light from the halfmoon shone through the slit window in the stairwell, washing it in a blue haze. There was something calming about it, soothing.

"You have a lovely smile, Cait. I'm glad I have stayed long enough to see it." Edward's voice was soft, barely above a whisper.

"I suppose I haven't smiled much since ye arrived."

"No," he said sadly. "But I'd like to think it had more to do with hundreds of the king's soldiers being here and less to do with me."

Studying him—the sharp line of his cheekbone and jaw limned in blue light, his eyes sincere, honest—she felt foolish for having doubted him and the others. She reached to brush a white thread from his sleeve.

"Am I interrupting something?" Alexander clamped a hand on Edward's shoulder, a smirk lurking in the corner of his mouth.

Cait's hand dropped immediately. There was something about Edward's brother that made her bristle every time he drew near. It was difficult to reconcile too—one brother being benevolent and warm and the other hard and prickly.

"If you would kindly give us a moment, Alexander," Edward said, his voice controlled.

"Something is surely going on here." His gaze swept from Cait's face to her toes, then settled on her breasts. "Are you not willing to share, brother? Is that not what we do? Share our women?"

He grazed his knuckles across Cait's cheek, and she flinched. A chill ran through her neck and shoulders, her scarred hand closing into a tight fist. Her memory flashed back to when she was standing in the brewhouse four years earlier and that bearded English soldier ran his dirty fingers over her hair. Quickly, she fumbled for her blade through the hidden slit in her skirts.

Before she could use it, Edward slid in front of her, blocking her view of Alexander. "Don't touch her."

"Come now, brother. We can both enjoy your little Scottish whore. There is no need to—"

Edward punched him, the crack of his fist hitting bone echoing throughout the alcove. Alexander's head jerked aside, and Cait jumped back to avoid him crashing into her. He collided with the wall instead, then swiped the blood trailing from the corner of his mouth. He sneered. "Never show where your weakness lies, Edward." His tongue peeked out and dabbed at the split in his lip. "She must mean an awful lot to you for you to assault a superior officer. I could have you court martialed for that."

"You could, but you won't." A sharp glint of moonlight sparked in Edward's eyes. "Would it help your cause if the king knew one of his officers—particularly *you*—was engaging in misconduct not only unbefitting of a soldier, but of a gentleman too? You have more to lose than do I."

Alexander glared at Edward. "Say what you mean, brother."

The muscles in Edward's jaw twitched. "I think you know what I mean."

Cait stared at Alexander, his face partially cloaked by the shadows. Whatever Edward had meant by his statement, it had clearly struck a chord. She stared at the blade still in her hand.

"Cait?" Davina stood in the entrance to the alcove, her gaze traveling from Cait to Edward and then Alexander, partially cloaked in darkness and leaning against the back wall, his thumb swiping at the blood beneath his lip.

Cait slid her *sgian dubh* back into her stocking. A sudden coldness struck her core. She had nearly stabbed him—Sawney's father. The man Davina loved. And one of His Majesty's soldiers.

Davina leaned closer to get a better look at him, and Cait's heart stopped.

Davina took two steps in, the realization that she was staring at Sawney's father lightening her face. "Alex?"

Cait waited to see how he would respond, her stomach in knots, praying he wouldn't hurt Davina. He stepped out of the shadows and into the moonlight, blankness stretched across his features. Cait tried to control her breathing, now jagged with fear for her friend.

Davina reached to caress his cheek, and a sliver of light sliced across her arm. "Are ye hurt?"

He looked puzzled for a moment. His brow twitched with uncertainty, then he smiled and clasped her palm to his cheek. "A minor cut. Your beauty has already cured me."

Cait exhaled, but Edward didn't. He was still standing as rigid as a marble column, his eyes narrowed on his brother, watching, waiting.

Davina pressed into Alexander, her head resting on his chest. "I was beginning to think I'd never see ye again."

Alexander peered over her head at Edward, his voice flat. "I was beginning to think the same."

Davina pulled away slightly and wiped a tear from her eye, her bottom lip quivering. "Could we go somewhere to talk? To reacquaint ourselves?"

"Of course." He turned to Cait, holding out his arm for Davina to take. "If you will excuse us."

Cait stepped aside to let them pass, her stomach unsettled by the encounter. She hoped she was wrong, but he didn't act like someone who had suddenly stumbled upon his long-lost love. How could this be the man Davina gave up her family, her reputation for?

Davina turned to leave with him, and Cait grabbed her wrist, stopping her. Davina gazed at her with that hopeful look Cait had seen so many times before. She wanted to warn her, to save her, but she knew Davina wouldn't listen, her heart and mind already fixed to the idea of a man who bore little moral resemblance to Alexander. Since he'd been at Alt Na Munde, Cait had seen nothing of his gentle nature, his sincerity, his dignity. He was not the person Davina had painted him to be.

She couldn't find the right words to say, so she gave Davina's wrist a gentle squeeze and let her go.

Edward also watched them leave, the corners of his mouth turned down. He released a deep breath. "I assume she knows him . . . well?"

"Aye." If he only knew how well.

"As do I," he said, rubbing his palm over the knuckles of his right hand. "And I can tell you this—he has no recollection of who she is."

THE TACKSMAN'S DAUGHTER

Cait sat through the evening's song and storytelling, but she didn't hear a single note from the piper or a word from the bard. Her mind was too tangled with possible scenarios between Davina and Alexander. Cait prayed she was wrong about him but knew she wasn't. Edward gently tapped her knee half a dozen times to remind her that her leg was bouncing up and down to an impossibly fast beat, but it never calmed her. She couldn't help but feel agitated.

"Do ye think she needs me?" she asked him, not for the first time.

"Would you care to check on her? Would it make you feel better?"

"I think so."

He started to stand, but she waved him away. "I should do this alone."

"Are you certain?"

She nodded, gathering her skirts around her, but he rested his hand on hers, stopping her. "I only hope your friend knows what she is doing."

That was so far from the truth. Davina was so deeply ensnared by Alexander, she had forsaken all common sense. "A woman in love seldom does."

She hurried up the spiral staircase. At the end of the hall, the torch outside the bedchamber she shared with Davina sputtered and sent the light dancing erratically across the wall. Gilli and Taran stood at the open door, Gilli peeking inside the room and Taran against the wall, his head bowed in concentration. Cait moved as quickly as she could.

Gilli giggled, then whispered, "His breeks are down around his ankles. I can see his bare arse."

"What are they doing?" Taran asked, his brow drawn in hard lines. "It sounds like he's hurting her."

Cait pulled Gilli from the door. She peeked through the crack and sucked in her breath. Davina lay on the bed with her skirts pushed above her hips, and Alexander stood between her legs disrobed from the waist down. Cait swallowed uncomfortably, then soundlessly shut the door.

"Why are you two spying?" She tried to get the image of them together out of her head, but it hung there like an oil painting nailed to a wall.

Taran lifted his chin in her direction. "Ye have me spying all the time. Now ye dinnae want me to?"

"Not on Davina!"

"Well, she's more fun to spy on than yer drunken sot of a friend Captain Campbell," he argued, his blond curls bouncing with assurance.

"He's nae my friend, and ye know that good and well, Taran Matheson." She shook her head and wagged her finger at Gilli. "And you? Why were ye spying on Davina?"

Gilli sidled closer to Taran so they were shoulder to shoulder. "We hadn't come to spy. We came to see if wee Sawney was up so we could play with him, but the nursemaid took him away. Then Davina arrived with that soldier."

Gilli clasped her hands behind her skirts, then tilted her head to the side. "What is she doing with that man, anyway?"

Cait wasn't sure how to answer the question. She hadn't expected to see what she had. Or perhaps she did.

She tried to erase the image of Alexander moving between Davina's legs, his fingers pressed into her thighs, the muscles in his backside tensed. But what she couldn't forget even more was the look on Davina's face. Her eyes closed and mouth open in complete surrender. There was no turning back for Davina.

Cait tousled Taran's hair. "I heard that Lilas made ginger cake. *Aran cridhe*."

Gilli grabbed Taran's hand and led him to the stairs, then they vanished behind the curved wall.

Chapter 9

Alexander tugged on his breeches, then straightened the hair that had partially escaped his ribbon during his tumble with the blonde wench.

"I cannae believe we finally found each other," she said, whatever her name was.

"'Tis a miracle."

"That's what I believe. Divine intervention," she said, her voice serious.

He hadn't meant it literally. He would've rolled his eyes, but she was watching him intently.

He stared at himself in the looking glass situated on the dresser to adjust the lace at his throat. It needed to be washed, the fabric now grey with wear. He turned to ask the lass if she would take care of it for him but noticed she did not have the dry red hands of a laundress. He glanced down at her lying on the bed, her blonde hair splayed across the pillow, her gown crumpled. How did he know her? He couldn't deny he'd met her before. He remembered snippets of their past together, but she'd looked slightly different back then, less worn. In time, she had thickened around the middle, but her face was still fair, save for a few lines etched in the corners of her eyes. He recalled that she used to wear her hair carefully pinned up. It was shiny and soft back then, but now it was dull and like something a rat would nest in.

"Ye seem lost in thought. What are ye thinking about?" she asked.

His least favourite question. Clearly, she did not want an honest, exact answer, so he gave her the one that would promise him future release between her thighs, at least until the snow melted and they could finally deploy. "You, of course."

She sighed, satiated. "To hear yer voice again . . ."

He forced a smile as he buttoned his coat. "'And yours. 'Tis like nourishment for the soul."

"Ye were always so poetic. I think that's what drew me towards ye."

"Was it?" Women were so easy. A few kind words, a compliment, and their skirts lifted as if by the power of a sorcerer. "Ask me no more whither doth haste the nightingale when May is past. For in your sweet dividing throat, she winters and keeps warm her note."

"Are ye saying my voice is like the nightingale's song?" she asked, now propped up on her elbows.

He leaned down and kissed her with as much tenderness as he could gather. "I am."

She giggled.

He took one last glance at himself in the looking glass. *None the worse for wear.* His stomach grumbled. "I need something to eat." He moved towards the door to listen for music and frolicking below, signaling that the festivities hadn't ended.

She sat up, her eyes dreamy. "Wouldn't ye rather stay with me up here?"

He considered it, but he wasn't sure his cock would agree that she was worth the prolonged hunger. "Of course I would . . ." If he could only remember her name. In as loving a tone as he could muster, he said, "But if we stay in here much longer, we risk being seen, and your reputation would then be tarnished."

She frowned. "My reputation? That was tarnished the day ye left."

That was undoubtedly true. *But where? Where did I leave you?* He needed information. "I would hope that you remember the date."

"Of course! The twenty-second of April, not two years past."

Two years? He was in Scotland then, near the border. No, north. Heading to Fort William.

"I believe it was the twenty-third," he said. That sounded good, like he had some real semblance of what she was referring to.

She shook her head confidently. "Ye left Glenorchy on the twenty-second."

Glenorchy! Of course! Now that their meeting place was established, his memory started to return. His father had just been imprisoned in the Tower, and—at Father's urging—his mother had given him no choice but to enter into service to the king, the very one to which Father had turned traitor. Those were not good times. He was angry and resentful then and may have taken his frustration out on a few women as he marched north. He did things others likely wouldn't approve of, but most people were far too judgemental anyway.

THE TACKSMAN'S DAUGHTER

He hadn't behaved poorly with this lass, though, as evidenced in her desire to see him again. And if he remembered correctly, she'd warmed his bed many times, making his stay in Glenorchy somewhat tolerable. "Make yourself more presentable so we can go downstairs and join the others. I'm famished."

She seemed disappointed, but he couldn't address it at the moment. She was wasting precious time pouting and lounging while the feast below dwindled.

She slipped off the bed and stood in front of him, her palms resting on his chest. "I was hoping that we could talk. Ye could tell me how ye spent the last two years we've been apart."

He definitely wouldn't do that. Most likely she wouldn't approve of tales about the whores he'd had or some of his more questionable practices with them. He could lie, of course. "There is plenty of time for that. We are not leaving until the snow melts from the passes."

"Then I'll pray for more winter storms."

She said it with a smile on her face, but there was nothing pleasant about it. He wasn't sure how much more of Scotland and this rough living he could endure. His stomach growled. He was growing impatient. "The skies look promising. We will likely depart in a matter of days."

"So ye will leave me once more?" she asked. Her chin dropped to her chest. She was too weak for him. He preferred women with more fight. Fire.

"'Tis sad, but a soldier's life is lonely, I am afraid." Until they could forge their way through the pass, he would take his fill of her and never look back. He moved towards the door, then gripped the handle. "Are you joining me or not, sweeting?"

He was angry. Damned angry. The only food left was smoked herring.

"Pour me more," he said, unable to look at the blonde wench beside him. It was her fault that he had nothing to eat. If she hadn't delayed him with her foolish talk upstairs, he'd have a gut full of salt beef or blood sausage.

"More?" she asked, her voice annoyingly high-pitched.

"The Claret. The wine," he answered impatiently.

"Would ye care for a bannock?" she asked, a small piece in her outstretched hand. What the hell was her name?

"I would not." He'd had enough of the damned bread in the last eight days—or was it nine? Either way, it felt like an eternity.

She set the bannock on the table, then placed her hand on his forearm. It was a gesture undoubtedly meant to soothe him, but it only infuriated him more. She said something else, but he ignored it.

She spoke again. "Well . . . can we?"

He finished the last of his wine in one long gulp. Sadly, it wasn't in his mouth long enough for him to taste it. He wriggled his finger towards the bottle next to her, indicating for her to pass it to him. She did, and he poured himself another glass. "Can we what?"

"Discuss an important matter."

She always seemed to be talking in riddles. "At this moment?"

She nodded with uncertainty.

He took another sip, this time allowing its sweet cherry finish to linger on his tongue.

"Not in here." She glanced around at all the kitchen wenches. Some bustled about with curious stares, and others were too involved in concentrating on placing one foot in front of the other to notice their presence at all. "Come."

Reluctantly, he followed her out of the kitchens, but not without grabbing the half-empty bottle of wine first.

She led him to the same alcove where Edward had hit him earlier. Someone had lit the torch in the sconce on the wall. A quick burst of air entered briefly, painting the stones with frenetic light.

He stood there silently waiting for her to speak, thankful for the company of the wine. She picked at her fingers for a good amount of time before she took a deep breath and faced him squarely. "We haven't discussed how we spent our time while apart. But I think we should."

Was she going to admit to having taken a lover? He should probably save her the trouble of her confession and let her know that he truly couldn't care less. He finished his glass and poured himself another. "Go on."

"I know ye may have fancied other women while on campaign. Ye may have even shared a kiss with one or two . . ."

If she only knew. Thank God the wine had mellowed him somewhat or he would have told her how many women's throats his cock had become acquainted with.

"But I never took notice of another man. When ye left, ye took my heart with ye." She played with the folds in her gown, picking and smoothing, picking and smoothing. A tear traced down her cheek, hesitating for a second before it plunged to her breast.

They were the words he'd prayed to hear from Berenice. She'd never said anything that had suggested her devotion, but she had agreed to marriage, so it would have come eventually, had Edward not interfered.

Frankly, he'd never had a lass profess her love to him before. Never. His trysts usually ended badly, the wench bitter and inflamed for some reason or another. This was an interesting change. He wondered how it could work to his advantage, outside of the obvious.

THE TACKSMAN'S DAUGHTER

She wiped away her tear. "But . . . ye left me with something to remember ye by."

What had he left behind? A kerchief? A ribbon? A ring? If it was something of value, he wanted it back.

By the way she was breathing and fiddling with her gown, one would think she'd stolen this item instead.

"Why are you so nervous?" he asked. If she'd acquired the pox, it was certainly not from him. He had expertly managed to escape its clutches—as far as he knew.

"Yer right. I needn't be nervous. I'm just going to say it." She exhaled a deep loud breath. "We have a son."

His hand froze in midair, his wineglass poised for another sip just in front of his chin. His heart paused as well. "A son?"

"Are ye nac happy?" She looked pathetic, her dark eyes begging.

How many times had he been in this predicament? Three now? Four? "How do I know the child is mine? He could be anyone's bastard."

Her face melted. She looked like she was about to crumble, her voice thin and fading with every word. "I named him after you. Sandaidh. 'Tis Alexander in Gaelic. But I call him Sawney."

"That hardly proves anything." He finished his wine in one gulp and paced in the alcove's tight space. "And what kind of name is Sawney?"

"You would probably call him Sandy. At least that's the English way."

"Sawney, Sandy. He is not mine." He ran his hand over his hair, grasping his queue and giving it a little tug. "If you are searching for an inheritance, you should know that it might never happen. The king is considering attainder—"

"What are ye saying?" Her face twisted inward. "I care naught for an inheritance. I . . . I . . . thought you'd be happy."

"Happy? Why would I be happy?" This lass had to be mad. No sane woman would expect a man to be happy about having to feed another mouth, especially an illegitimate one.

She stumbled over her words. "I . . . We . . . could be a family now."

His face flooded with heat. "A family? I do not even remember your name."

Chapter 10

No one had asked Taran to spy. Not Cait. Not MacIain. Not John or Alasdair Og. He had decided to do it on his own.

He had the gift of sight. Not the kind everyone had—although he could see light and dark shadows and forms—but the kind only a seer has. No one, not even Gilli, knew that besides his grandda. That was a secret better kept than shared, Grandda had said, for it could bring him more trouble than blessings.

He'd sensed things lately, nothing he could quite put a name to, but he hadn't felt settled since the soldiers arrived at Alt Na Munde. Not because he'd heard something that might bring about strife or because Cait had fed him all her doubts, but because deep in his gut, he knew something wasn't right.

That first night, ten days past, he dreamed of a face drenched in blood. He'd startled awake, his skin blanketed in sweat from head to toe, the light from the full moon washing his vision in a glowing haze. He'd kicked off his wool covers, trembling from the memory. Although he only knew what MacIain looked like from the descriptions Gilli told him, he was sure it was him. Then as days passed and the clan chief remained unharmed, he'd started to doubt the dream had meant anything.

But this very morning, the cows broke from the byre at the foot of the brae and ran up the glen east of Black Mount, their lowing loud and painful to his ears. The crunch of the wood fence and their pounding hooves in the mud sent shivers up his spine. No one knew what had spooked them—except for him.

He headed outside when he heard the commotion. Everyone was shouting and giving orders, but it sounded as if no one knew what they were doing.

THE TACKSMAN'S DAUGHTER

His head snapped to the sound of MacIain's voice. "Who did this? What happened?"

Niven Whitson, the stable hand, answered, his voice quaking like he'd seen a ghost. "I never saw what did it. Not a wolf or fox was anywhere nearby. I swear it!"

MacIain's voice boomed. "Then what did ye see, lad?"

Niven sounded nervous. "Some of the kine started swishing their tails, their heads up and ears perked. Then all of a sudden, they burst through the fence."

Beasties could sense things the way Taran could. They too knew trouble was brewing. What kind remained to be seen, but there was no denying that feeling that hovered over him like a storm cloud that wouldn't blow away.

MacIain started shouting orders into the frosty morning air. "Some of ye will go fetch the missing kine. The others will stay here to mend the byre."

Vibrations of chaos surrounded Taran, and the smell of men covered in the kind of sweat that comes with worry wafted towards him. He hurried back to the manor, not at all interested in getting in the way of the men racing about.

"These things happen for a reason," his grandda said. Taran knew that to be true and realized his dream about MacIain had meaning. He wasn't sure what exactly, but it had to have something to do with that man Drummond who'd arrived in Glencoe that morning just after the cows had broken from the byre. The soldier had been asking about Glenlyon's whereabouts since breakfast, but no one seemed to know where he was.

It was late afternoon when Taran caught the slow drawl of Drummond's voice again not too far from where he was sitting. "I would be much obliged, sir, if you would direct me to Captain Campbell."

Taran straightened in his seat. What was so important for this man to spend all day searching for that glaikit fool?

One of the men answered, his voice unfamiliar. "I dinnae know where he is now, but you'll find him at Inverrigan's tonight. Just up the glen."

Something about Drummond tied Taran's belly in a knot. He had a voice that sounded confident and fearful at the same time, something Taran had never heard before. It was almost as if the words he wasn't saying were more important than the words he was. He obviously had something to tell Glenlyon, and Taran wanted to be there when he said it.

He could never venture to Inverrigan's on his own, so when John and Alasdair Og mentioned they were headed up the glen, Taran asked if he could join them. It had taken a bit of convincing, but eventually they agreed.

He slipped on some icy patches a few times on the way there, his breeks soaked when they finally arrived. It didn't matter, though. It gave him a good excuse to stand with his back to the fire close to where Glenlyon sat, the bampot's words already slurred with drink.

By the time Taran's breeks were dry, Drummond entered smelling of smoke and spices. He stood next to Taran, brushing his sleeve roughly and flicking cold droplets onto Taran's head and neck as he spoke. "Captain Campbell?"

"Aye," Glenlyon answered sloppily.

"Captain Drummond at your service."

Glenlyon's chair creaked when he shifted. "Ye braved the weather to join us for some cards, have ye?"

"I'm not here for cards, sir," Drummond answered, followed by the sound of crinkling paper and his boot scuffing the floor. "I have orders from Major Duncanson for you."

The other men in the room suddenly stopped speaking. The wind howled outside and rattled the door as it grew louder.

Glenlyon grunted a few times, the paper crinkling every now and again. Then he fell silent except for the sound of his fingers dryly running across the parchment. "Our orders have come to move on. We've burdened ye long enough. We march against Glengarry at dawn."

It was news that should've set Taran at ease, but it made his back more rigid. He tried to shake it off, but that hard feeling remained steadfast from his shoulders to his hips.

Glenlyon's chair scraped across the floor, the clump of his boots heavy and slow on the wood planks as he settled on his feet.

"Then we bid ye a good night and a farewell," John said.

"Ye have hosted many men here, sharing yer whisky and food," Glenlyon said, a sadness in his voice that pricked the back of Taran's neck. Glenlyon shuffled to the door and opened it, allowing a burst of cold air heavy with the stinking fug of smoke from wet peat to fill the room. He exhaled loudly. "I want to thank ye for yer kindness. *Tapadh leibh.*"

The door closed behind him, and John patted Taran roughly on the shoulder. "We should head back to Alt Na Munde. It sounds like the wind's starting to fuss. If we dinnae leave now, we'll be forced to sleep here on the floor overnight. Grab yer bonnet, Taran."

Taran felt the ledge of the hearth for his bonnet, the wool now dry and warm from the fire. They said their goodbyes and stepped outside into the cold. The brothers started walking, but Taran stopped to listen to the voices in the dark.

"These folks have hosted us for almost a fortnight. How can I—" Glenlyon's voice shook.

Drummond angrily whispered, "You will do as you are told!"

THE TACKSMAN'S DAUGHTER

    Grandda always said Taran's hearing was better than a bat's. Another mixed blessing. The hesitation in a man's breath and words or the rapid tapping of his fingers on a table told Taran more than he needed to know about the man's state of mind. After listening to the two soldiers' nervous whispering nearby, he was sure that whatever was written in those orders had slipped a noose around Glenlyon's conscience.

Chapter 11

"Wake, Edward!"

Edward shook awake with the rousing hand that prodded his shoulder. "What the devil?"

Alexander shoved his dagger and pistol at him. "Rouse the others."

Edward set his weapons beside him on the floor. Not a single shred of light shone through the window. "'Tis not yet dawn."

"Major Duncanson sent orders. You need to help me muster the men." Alexander kicked at the other soldiers sleeping in the room, the tip of his boot jabbing into their sides. Two men grunted angrily at the affront, and another swatted him away as if he were a gnat. Alexander slapped the back of the man's scruffy head with his gloves. "Get up, you imbecile!"

Edward stood, rubbing his face brusquely. "What is the hurry? What did the orders say?"

Alexander's face glowed with excitement and daring. "We are to attack at five of the clock."

"Attack whom?" Edward asked, thoroughly confused. The wind howling outside was almost loud enough to drown out his words.

"The MacDonalds."

Had he heard right? Edward grabbed Alexander by the collar, heat flooding his chest and neck. "What are you saying, brother?"

Alexander smacked his hand away. "We are ordered to fall upon the rebels and put all to sword under seventy. Most especially MacIain and his sons."

"Rebels?" This had to be a mistake. "Duncanson ordered this?"

THE TACKSMAN'S DAUGHTER

"He did. Glenlyon received the orders at Inverrigan's last night," Alexander answered a little too joyously. He fastened his leather belt over his shoulder, setting his ammunition pouch on his right hip. "Hurry! You are wasting time!"

"This makes no sense! For what purpose?" Edward asked, his shoulders buzzing with alarm.

"Are you questioning the major's orders?" Alexander tugged at his lace cuffs. "You are a soldier. You do as you are told."

"You want me to slaughter the very men who have granted us warm beds and sufficient food for the last ten . . . twelve days, without question?"

"And women. Anyone under seventy."

"This is outrageous!"

"You are so weak, Edward." Alexander shook his head in disgust. "Where is your sense of duty?"

"Where is your sense of loyalty?" he snapped. This was forever the problem with Alexander. If an opportunity arose that promised excitement, he would choose it over doing what was right.

Alexander speared him with a glare, his jaw clenched tight. "My loyalty lies with King William, and the MacDonalds have been traitors."

Edward's jaw dropped. "Traitors? MacIain swore his Oath of Allegiance in January."

Alexander finished buttoning his coat. "Five days late. The deadline was the thirty-first of December."

Cait had told him the whole story, how MacIain had traveled north to Fort William instead of south to Inveraray, delayed even further by the severe storms. But he had given his word on behalf of his MacDonald clan nonetheless. "The man pledged his loyalty to the king. He was sincere in his submission."

Alexander snickered. "And to whom have you pledged your loyalty, brother? The MacDonalds? Or that little Scottish whore of yours? Is *that* not why you are reluctant to follow orders? Has the comfort of her bed made you turn against your king?"

Edward shoved him against the wall, his whole body quaking in rage. He wanted to pummel him, to make him trade a tooth for every ill word. "Have some respect, brother."

The others in the room stared, frozen, mouths hanging open in shock. Alexander laughed wryly. "Go ahead, Edward. Do it in front of all these men."

Edward wanted to. He didn't care if he was brought before a court and tried. But he had to stop this attack on the MacDonalds first. "You are well aware that my loyalty is with King William. I believe him to be a righteous man, incapable of approving such a heinous act. 'Tis dishonourable. This must be Glenlyon's doing."

A sudden wave of guilt for having spent all this time trying to convince Cait the old man was harmless, burned in his chest.

"I will not deny that the old cur must consider this order a gift. 'Tis his opportunity, after all, to get vengeance for all his petty issues. But this is not his doing. You will see. Major Duncanson and his troops will soon be here to assist."

"You know this to be true?"

"I read the orders myself," he answered flippantly.

Edward couldn't take another moment of Alexander's smug voice. He rummaged in his coat for his pocket watch, a gift from his father when he turned twenty, one of the last gifts he ever gave him before he was sent to the Tower. He shrugged on his coat and strapped his weapons to his side, stepping over the one prone body still lying on the floor blocking his way to the door. He had only sixteen minutes to get to Cait and the others to warn them.

Edward scaled two stairs at a time, desperate to get to Cait. The icy wind slipped through the cross-shaped arrowslit windows in the stairwell, keening eerily like a wailing old woman. He stopped briefly to peer through the dim morning light at the wave of red and tartan pushing through the village, a thick layer of snowflakes distorting his view. Some of the men held torches aloft, their flames blowing sideways in the gusts. He took a hard breath to steady his nerves, the frosty air burning his throat. His guilt for having chastised Cait for her doubts about the soldiers' presence weighed heavily on his mind. He would never have thought his regiment and the others with him would turn so viciously on their gracious hosts. His stomach churned just thinking about it.

At the top of the stairs, he reached for a torch, then reconsidered, realizing it would only draw the soldiers to them like a beacon in the dark.

He hurried down the corridor through the darkness, one hand tracing the wall, and found the third door on the right. He jerked the handle, but it was locked, so he pounded on the door. "Cait!" His heart hammered in his chest. "Cait, please! Open up!"

He thumped harder, and the door creaked open. Cait stared wide-eyed at him, her hair in a long, messy plait. "Are ye mad? Banging on my door at this hour?"

He pushed his way inside. Davina and Gilli jolted upright, the sheets pulled up to their necks, their eyes wide with shock in the poor light.

"You need to leave," he said. He yanked the bedclothes down, then grabbed Gilli's arm, making her scream.

THE TACKSMAN'S DAUGHTER

Cait snatched his hand. "What has bedeviled ye, man? Ye cannae come barging in here and put a fright into all of us. At the very least, 'tis most indecent of ye to—"

Edward grasped her forearms, forcing her to look into his eyes. "Listen to me, Cait. You need to hide. You are all in grave danger."

He felt her stiffen.

"Is there someplace you can go? Someplace safe?" he asked.

He darted to the window and squinted through the wavy glass, his face now covered in sweat. He could see very little, so he inched it open, the cold air washing over his face instantly. A few men in the distance stood in quiet groups, listening to the orders from their commanders, the light from their torches blowing erratically in the wind. The betraying hiss of swords being pulled from their scabbards sliced through the storm.

Cait joined him and spoke in almost a whisper. "What is it, Edward? What is happening?"

He didn't want to tell her, but he had to. "Orders have come . . ." He swallowed hard. "To put all MacDonalds of Glencoe to the sword."

She and Davina both had MacDonald blood running through their veins, so he knew their surnames wouldn't spare them.

She stared at him in a way he'd never forget, even if he lived to be one hundred. "Orders?"

It was only a matter of minutes before the clock struck five. His heart raced. "We have no time. You must go now!"

"My parents! They've gone back home." Cait grabbed his coat at both shoulders. "You must warn them!"

"I shall, but I'll see you to safety first." He unstrapped his pistol and dagger from his belt and handed them to her. "Take these. You might need to defend yourself."

She passed the pistol to Davina and strapped the dagger around her waist. She reached under a pillow and pulled out her black knife with one hand and scooted Gilli out with the other. "We have to go, Gilli."

"But I'm tired," she whined, punctuating it with a loud yawn.

"I know ye are, lassie, but you need to listen," Cait said as she fastened her black knife to her leg.

Davina grabbed a gown that was draped over a wooden chair. "We need to dress first."

"There's no time for that. You need to go now. The brewhouse? The dovecote?"

With shaking hands, Davina dropped her gown and lifted Sawney from a cradle on the floor. She tightened the blanket around him, then wrapped him in her arms, her face heavy with grief and fear.

Cait shook her head. "'Tis too cold out there for the wee ones. I know a better place."

He held them back while he peered into the darkness of the hall. In the distance soldiers' voices echoed through the manor. He urged them out the door and followed them to the stairs, his heart pounding angrily. Cait stopped on the landing and opened a hidden hatch.

He glanced down into the darkness and breathed a sigh of relief. They would be safe in this hidden room.

Davina climbed down first, and he handed her Sawney. Then he guided Gilli down. Outside, the crunch of boots in the snow and the clicking of muskets broke the silence.

"You'll go to my parents?" Cait asked in a heated whisper.

Her parents lived halfway up the glen. He wasn't sure he would reach them in time to warn them, but he would try. "I promise you, Cait. And then I'll return for you."

In a daring move, he pulled her close and kissed her hard. She weakened briefly in his arms, then hurried down the ladder into the secret room.

Edward checked his pocket watch. Three minutes to spare.

He scrambled down the rest of the stairs in search of his men. Perhaps he could talk some sense into them, make them see the dishonour in what they were about to do. If he could convince them to refuse to take up arms, he could save those at Alt Na Munde from slaughter, but it would delay him from getting to Cait's parents. If he ran to warn them first, his men would begin the attack in and around the manor where the majority of Glencoe's residents lived. He ran his hands roughly through his hair. He had no time to waste.

He ran outside, the earthy smell of burning peat lingering in the frigid air, the snow blowing fiercely into his eyes and ears. He leaned into the wind, the sting of the icy blasts burning his cheeks and making it difficult to see. A flash of red appeared, and he shuffled towards it. He seized the soldier's coat and spun him around. "Where is Leftenant Gage?"

He shrugged.

Edward shook him. "And Leftenant Lindsay?"

The soldier lifted a lazy finger and pointed back in the direction of Alt Na Munde, where Lindsay now stood at the door speaking with a servant. It was beginning.

THE TACKSMAN'S DAUGHTER

Edward dashed back to MacIain's home and through the entrance. MacIain yelled from within, "Get the officer a dram while I ready myself to bid him a proper farewell."

The servant slipped by Edward, then Lindsay appeared, adjusting his periwig. He started for MacIain's bedchambers.

"What are you doing?" Edward asked, trailing behind him. He hurried in front of him to block his way. "This is madness! You must reconsider!"

Lindsay nodded at a group of soldiers, and Edward was suddenly forced back, hands tightly gripping his shoulders and arms, one over his mouth. He fought to break free, but it only landed him a sharp jab to his ribs. He arched his back, gritting his teeth to fight the pain.

Lindsay pushed open MacIain's door to reveal the clan chief pulling on his trews, then leveled his pistol at the old man. Edward stiffened. The leftenant steadied his aim, then shot MacIain through the back of his head, sending bits of brain and flesh onto the bedstead and wall.

Lady Glencoe screamed and ran to his side. Edward inhaled sharply, unable to believe what had just happened. Lindsay's betrayal struck him like a punch to his gut. He was living a nightmare—one he knew to be real.

Another soldier Edward had played cards with many times, shot MacIain once more in the back. Edward twisted to break free, but the three grenadiers holding him remained as steadfast as granite.

A flood of soldiers entered the room, their bayonets poised.

"God save the king!" Lindsay shouted, grappling with his ammunition pouch.

"God save the king!" repeated his men.

Lindsay reloaded his pistol. "Take him out into the snow and leave him where the dogs can feast on his bones."

Two men grabbed MacIain's legs and dragged the chief out by his heels. Lady Glencoe collapsed on top of him, her wails piercing Edward's chest.

"Get out of our way!" they barked, roughly shoving her aside.

She clawed at the soldier's legs to stop him, her fists white-knuckled and locked onto his stockings. He wrenched her nightshift over her head, the embroidered seams splitting as easily as a pea pod, then kicked the long, lean arch of her back. Lady Glencoe lay there naked, gasping for breath, her palm slapping the grey flagstones. A cold slick of dread slipped down Edward's spine. He would go to hell for this—they all would.

The soldiers holding Edward loosened their grasp at the sight of her, and he broke free. He rushed to help her, but they pinned back his arms before he could reach her. "Let me go!" he shouted.

"Get her rings!" one demanded.

A rat-faced soldier with beady eyes and a pointed nose snatched her wrist and tried to pry off her bejeweled rings but couldn't.

"Leave her be!" Edward struggled to pull free, but another set of meaty hands clamped down hard on his shoulders.

Lady Glencoe screamed as the soldier at her side bent to bite her rings from her fingers. Edward kicked him in the ribs, a satisfactory crunching sound stopping his pursuit, allowing her to crawl away and disappear.

Someone punched Edward in the face, catching him unawares. The men holding him dragged him to the door, heaved at once, and tossed him into the snow face down. His head hit hard, and flashes of the horror he had just seen played in his eyes.

"Where are your weapons?" It was his brother's voice. A not-so-gentle nudge from a boot met with Edward's hip.

Edward struggled to sit. He brushed the snow from his face and hair, his left cheek throbbing in pain.

Alexander stood over him, a half-pike in one hand and a musket in the other. "Get up."

Edward slowly stood, his ears ringing. "This is murder under trust!"

"A martyr, are you? 'Tis quite unbecoming, brother."

A musket shot rang out in the distance, and someone screamed. Edward's head snapped to his right where the glen, dotted with MacDonald homes, stretched far into the darkness.

Soldiers ran between the crofts, muskets in hand, shooting inside windows and doors. An elderly man ran into the snow in his nightshirt, the wind whipping it in all directions. Then a shot blasted and he fell, a bloom of red spreading across his back.

"Stop! Put your weapons down!" Edward grabbed a soldier, a Scot, and dragged him to the ground. He snatched his pistol and hurled it aside, his chest burning in anger. Then a hand grasped his shoulder and spun him around.

"Sergeant Gage!" Farquhar' pressed his bonnet to his head, his face ruddy with cold.

Kennedy stood behind him, his plaid stretched snugly over his shoulders. They were both soldiers he'd played cards with over the last week. "Who gave these orders? They cannae be right!"

Edward shielded his eyes from the wind. "Help me stop them!"

Farquhar shouted above the wind. "We've tried! No one is listening!"

Edward's throat knotted tight. He couldn't waste more time. He left them and ran up the glen, his heartbeat thundering in his ears. He had to find Cait's parents. Ahead, Alexander's voice broke through the chaos, his words crisp and spirited. "Set their roofs aflame. It will force the savages to run out, and then you will have a good clean shot."

Edward watched helplessly while pine torches were thrown onto a nearby thatch-roofed dwelling, the twigs sparking instantly. They crackled at first, then roared as the fire caught, the heat of the blaze radiating outward and instantly melting the snow circling the croft. Floating ashes mingled with the snowflakes, swirling wildly in the wind. Within minutes, more than twenty homes stretching up the glen went up in flames, the sparks floating into the night sky like winter fireflies.

He ran up the brae and scanned the darkness for the Cameron's cottage, the pop of gunshots and women and children screaming scattered through the glen. His gaze passed over the small crofts until he spotted their home burning to the ground like all the others.

Chapter 12

Cait stood atop a crate to peek out of the small opening of the laird's lug into the entrance hall of MacIain's house. A mass of soldiers in red coats and tartan scrambled inside, pistols, muskets, and dirks drawn, their boots scraping and clomping on the stone floor. Some wore masks of hate and others looked indifferent, their faces expressionless. Cait steadied her breath, her hands clutching the ledge of the opening jutting from the wall.

"What do ye see?" Davina asked softly.

Cait waved her hand to hold her off. She couldn't speak. It was too dangerous, and she wasn't sure if it was physically possible with her throat knotted tight.

A shot rang out, and she tensed. Then another, and a loud commotion ensued with arguing, shuffling, scattering. Sawney began to wail. Cait glanced back at Davina, her heart pounding, desperately signaling Davina to put the child to her breast. Davina stared at her blankly. Cait silently prayed Davina would do it.

"Why bother?" Davina whispered.

Since the evening she'd spent with Alexander, Davina had only been an empty shell, her face drawn, her movements lethargic and purposeless.

Cait squeezed her fists tight, her hands shaking uncontrollably. "Please, Davina," she said, holding her breath.

Davina gazed down at Sawney, then slowly pressed his mouth to her breast, and Cait exhaled.

Davina's voice came softer than a whisper. "I havenae milk, but I dinnae think he cares."

THE TACKSMAN'S DAUGHTER

A group of soldiers in the hall, some cradling silver platters, cups, and candlesticks, parted to make way for two Redcoats dragging a man's body across the floor, hauling him away like a cow's carcass on its way to the offal heap. Cait squinted to get a good look at the dead man, his long white hair mixed with blood trailing behind him, his face blown away, unrecognizable. Lady Glencoe, covered in blood and her face red and puffy, stumbled after him naked, howling in grief. Cait's throat jumped as she squeezed back a cry. MacIain!

Seconds later, another scuffle occurred, and four Redcoats wrangled their way to the door, one struggling to get free of the others. "Let me go!" he shouted.

Her heart stopped. It was Edward. She stretched to get a better look, the tiny bars blocking the window in her way. She choked back tears and pressed her palms to her temples. Her legs started to weaken. It looked like he'd been beaten. Within an instant, the men threw him out the open door and into the cold. She rocked back and forth, her mind spinning. How could he save her parents now?

Cait slumped off the crate, her throat tight. "They've killed MacIain, and Edward is powerless."

Davina slowly twirled one of Sawney's curls around her finger and spoke calmly, her face soaked with tears. Sawney stirred, his tiny hand closing into a fist and finding its place in the crook of Davina's neck. "Then we shall die here."

Cait brushed aside Davina's hair from her cheek, then turned up her chin. "We willnae die here, Davina."

Cait wasn't sure how they would survive, but she wasn't going to surrender so easily. As long as they remained hidden, they would be fine. She hoped. They simply had to stay quiet, and then they would wait until the soldiers left. She glanced around the room. Only a small pot of honey, some whisky, and an old book sat on some shelves behind the ladder. Nothing else. But they could easily last a day or two without food until the soldiers marched on.

After a few minutes, the shouting stopped, and the hall was eerily silent. Cait held her breath as she listened for footsteps on the other side of the wall. Nothing. She stepped back onto the crate and peered at the dark entrance, now empty except for the body of a servant and the pool of blood beneath him. The smell of gunpowder stung her nose and burned her eyes. She rubbed wildly at her nostrils, eager to remove the sting.

Frantic footsteps with heavy breathing and female voices pierced the silence. Lilas and three kitchen maids dressed in their nightshifts and wrapped in blankets shuffled into the entrance.

"Lilas?" Cait whispered. The cook's head spun, twisting side to side, searching for the voice that called her. "'Tis I, Caitriona Cameron. Up here." She stuck her fingers through the bars in the small opening, wriggling them up and down to get her attention.

Lilas spotted her fingers and panicked. "Leave at once, lass! The beasts have set the house ablaze!"

Cait froze. It wasn't gunpowder that she smelled but smoke.

Lilas and the other women crowded out the front door, clinging to one another in desperation. A series of shots blasted forth, and Cait's stomach clenched. Blood spattered backwards into the hall, one woman's shoe left just inside the threshold, the bottom half of her leg visible from the laird's lug.

Cait jumped off the crate and grabbed Gilli, who was curled in the corner underneath the ladder. Gilli pulled away, saying something unintelligible. Cait shook her roughly. "Ye must come, Gilli. We have to leave."

Cait turned to Davina, her insides quaking. "I'll climb the ladder first to make sure 'tis safe. Then Gilli. You follow with Sawney. Understand?"

Davina blinked absently. Cait hurried up the ladder, pushed open the hatch slowly, and paused to check her surroundings. Smoke curled along the ceiling. They had to get out fast.

She listened for footsteps or voices, but the halls were silent, so she clambered onto the landing and helped pull up Gilli. She glanced down into the hidden space to see what was taking Davina so long and found her still seated on a stool, rocking Sawney back and forth in her lap, the pistol lying across her knees, balancing precariously.

"Quickly, Davina!" she begged, her fingers briefly touching the dirk at her waist and the *sgian dubh* strapped to her leg.

Davina made no move to come.

"Ye need to listen to me, lass. Ye may want to give up yer life for a man who isnae worth it, and that's fine if that's what ye truly want. But 'tisnae fair to wee Sawney. He deserves a future."

Davina hugged him close, tears streaming down her cheeks. Finally, she looked up at Cait, her gaze watery and hesitant.

Cait leaned into the hole, her heart pounding. "Alexander isnae a good man. 'Tis a blessing that he's no longer in yer life."

Davina stood, and the pistol clanked at her feet. Cait silently willed her to move towards the ladder. Flames were visible through the arrowslit in the stairwell, their orange glow growing with each second. They had to move quickly.

"Sawney needs his mother to give him the life he deserves. Now come."

THE TACKSMAN'S DAUGHTER

Davina glanced down at him, then up at her. Cait's heart pounded, her arms reaching. Finally, Davina passed him to Cait, then climbed the ladder. At the top, Cait led her by the crook of her arm onto the landing, then shut the hatch. They fled down the stairs, Gilli clinging to Cait like a vine.

They ran through the great hall and down a long corridor to a wooden postern door barred with a rusted latch.

"Help me with this, Davina!"

Davina handed her son to Gilli and tugged back on the bar with Cait. It wouldn't budge.

"Wait here." Cait ran back down the hall and into the kitchens. It was noticeably hotter than the back of the manor, the exposed skin on her neck and chest prickling with the heat. Thick black smoke floated across the ceiling. She coughed, unable to take a full breath, the smoke dipping lower. She sank to her hands and knees, searching for the basket where Lilas kept the mallet she used to pound the meat when it was too tough. She crawled past the hearth, her hands groping blindly in the dark. Her fingertips met the basket's rough weave, and she reached in. The metal of the mallet was still cool to the touch. She snatched it, her eyes bleary and burning, and rushed back down the passage to where Davina, Gilli, and Sawney waited. "Stand back!"

She pounded the end of the iron bar, bits of rust flaking off with each blow. She prayed the roaring fire would muffle the clanging. After the sixth strike, it gave an inch with a high-pitched shriek. Cait reared back and gave it another good hit, her chest opening with hope as it budged a little more. Gilli bounced up and down, her hands clasped together in prayer. Cait gritted her teeth and flung the mallet once more, sending the iron bar flying onto the floor with a great clang. She lifted the latch and pushed everyone out into the night, her body shaking from head to toe in release.

It took only seconds for her to realize she'd made a mistake. A Scots soldier grabbed the sleeve of her nightshift and spun her to face him, a pistol pointed at her chest. He cocked the hammer, and it clicked into place, his lips curling into a smile. Before he could pull the trigger, she slid the dirk from its sheath at her waist and pierced his gut. His eyes widened in shock, his smile fading quickly, then he slouched, his weight pressing down on her arm. She withdrew her blade and stepped to the side to allow him to fall in a crumpled heap.

She'd never killed a man before. She glared down at the bloody knife in her shaking hand. The sound of a single shot stirred her out of her thoughts, and she ran into the brae behind Alt Na Munde.

She stared into the black alders and pines. She didn't see Davina or the wee ones, their white nightshifts barely discernible in the snowstorm, but it was the only place they would've gone. She was glad the snow made it difficult to be spotted, but the sun would rise soon enough, and they would no longer be able to rely on the dark for cover.

She hiked up the hill, the hem of her nightshift occasionally getting stuck on a half-buried branch. Her feet were frozen, no longer able to feel the pricks and pokes of the rocks beneath the snow.

"Over here," Davina whispered loudly.

Cait trudged towards her voice, the crackling of Alt Na Munde's roof sharp in the eerie silence. She found the three of them huddled tightly together, partly protected by two large granite rocks at their backs.

"I'm so c-c-cold," Gilli said through chattering teeth. She sat tucked underneath Davina's arm and around Sawney, who slept buried inside his wool blanket. "W-w-when can we go back?"

Cait settled beside her and drew her close. In the distance, a dozen or so cottages and bothies were still burning, the smoke now evident in the increasing light. She rubbed Gilli's frozen feet between her palms. "When 'tis safe."

She didn't know if it would ever be safe again. If Glencoe would ever be the same.

"Where is T-T-Taran?" Gilli asked.

Cait didn't know what to say. She hoped they were able to escape, that maybe Edward had the time to alert him and his grandfather too, but her chest squeezed tight knowing it was unlikely.

"There's blood on yer knife." Davina motioned towards it with a small jerk of her head. Edward's blade lay unsheathed at Cait's side.

Cait shook her head, begging her not to ask further questions. She didn't want Gilli to know that she had killed a man. She wiped off the blood in the snow, then returned it to its sheath.

The wind blew hard, the snowflakes so thick now she couldn't see farther than the clump of bracken at her feet. Her clothing—all their clothing—was soaked through. If the storm didn't stop or the soldiers didn't leave the glen soon, she wasn't sure how much longer they'd survive.

She squeezed her eyes shut to erase the mad thoughts filling her head. How could this have happened? Why had she listened to Davina and Edward and let down her guard? Where *was* Edward? Had he made it in time to warn her parents? She pressed her lips together and said a silent prayer for them. Were they also hiding in the braes, wondering if she and Gilli were safe?

Would Edward come for her as he promised? Or was he lying like so many others, dead in the cold, reduced to a bloodied mound of snow?

She couldn't imagine it. Didn't want to imagine it. He had kissed her before he left. She could still feel the warmth of his lips pressed to hers, the stubble from his chin scratchy on her skin. It had happened quickly. Too quickly. She didn't want to think she'd never see him again.

Cait's stomach grumbled. They'd been shivering in the cold for hours now, the sun completely hidden by the grey cloud cover. The snow hadn't stopped for even a second, the gusts churning it up in great swirls before the huge flakes found a place to rest.

Cait's head burned as if her crown were being branded with a hot iron. Her hands and feet were no longer part of her body, completely unable to bend or feel. Gilli lay shivering uncontrollably in her lap, the tips of her fingers and toes discoloured to a dark violet. Cait shoved Gilli's feet between her knees and her hands in the folds of her nightshift. Gilli moaned with the sudden movement.

"Do ye think we should stay here?" Davina's voice was weak, breathy.

"I'm feart to move," Cait said. "There are some caves and corries up the brae about a mile from here, but I dinnae think we can make it without being seen or without dying first from the cold."

"I'm nae sure I can brave another night, Cait. And the bairn needs to eat."

Cait smiled sadly at the dark tuft of hair peeking out from under the blanket. The laddie was either too cold or too weak to fuss about his hunger. It broke Cait's heart, but if they could just endure one more night, she was sure the soldiers would leave the glen. From what she could see, they had destroyed the entire village, so there was no place left for them to shelter. Even Alt Na Munde couldn't offer them protection, its roof gone and its contents likely a smoldering heap of rubble.

"Eat some more snow. It will keep us alive until we can search for survivors or forage for food." Cait scooped a handful of snow in her frozen hand and offered it to Davina, but she turned her head.

"One night, Cait, then I'm going back down to the village to feed my bairn. Someone must still be there." Davina pressed Sawney's head to her cheek and closed her eyes.

Men's voices woke Cait the next morning. They were Scots, not Englishmen, their burrs trilling from their tongues easily. She was afraid to move, afraid they were Campbells come to finish their slaughter with three lasses and a bairn. She crouched low over Gilli, pressing into the rock behind her, wishing she could sink inside of it and disappear.

Her whole body ached as if she'd been wielding her father's claymore for days on end. She arched her back and winced. The cold had bitten into her like a sharp-toothed beast. She wondered if the blood was still running through her veins or if it had frozen like the rest of her.

The snap of branches signaled them coming closer. She carefully shifted her weight to reach for the dirk at her side, sending a searing pain into her hip and legs. She waited for the sharp tingling to stop, wiggling her toes as best she could. She jostled Gilli in the process, but it didn't wake her.

One spoke. She couldn't make out what he said, but she knew his voice. It was Alasdair Og.

"Alasdair!" Her cry sounded more like a croak than his name, so she cleared her throat and tried again. "Alasdair!"

The crunching footsteps stopped, waited. "Who calls?"

Cait swallowed, her throat on fire with the effort, her lips splitting with each word. "Caitriona Cameron. We need help."

In a rush of stomps and crackling twigs, he and his older brother, John, approached, fear and concern etched in their faces.

"Can ye help us?" she asked, her jaw frozen stiff. Tears spilled down her cheeks uncontrollably.

John kneeled beside her and wrapped her hand in his. "Have ye been out here all day and night? Since . . ."

She cleared her throat again. She gestured with her chin towards Davina and Sawney, then down at Gilli. "Aye."

They stared at her with pity in their eyes. But she didn't need their pity, she needed their strength—their help to guide them to a spot beside a fire and get them some warm porridge.

John removed his plaid and wrapped it over her shoulders, shielding both her and Gilli. Alasdair did the same for Davina, the muscles in his jaw flexing. "We can get ye somewhere warm. Somewhere safe."

A fresh rush of tears rained down her cheeks.

John avoided her gaze and reached tentatively to smooth Gilli's hair.

"Come, Gilli. 'Tis time to go now." She shook her sister gently, but she didn't stir. "Gilli, please. Ye need to wake. We're going to find shelter, but I'll need ye to get off me and walk on yer own."

Alasdair shared a quick glance with his brother, who bit his lip uncomfortably. "Cait." He paused, his voice soft and solemn. "Gilli's gone. She's with the angels, lass."

Cait wiped her cheek with the back of her hand, her wrist frozen at an odd angle. She couldn't believe it. She wouldn't believe it. She brushed Gilli's hair away from her forehead with a crooked, icy finger and stared at her sister's beautiful pale face. Her blue lips. "Gilli. Ye must wake. Please, Gilli!"

But she didn't move.

THE TACKSMAN'S DAUGHTER

Alasdair rested his hand on Cait's shoulder. She shrugged it off, her throat tight with grief. John reached to take Gilli, but Cait gripped her lifeless body closer. One last time.

Part Two

Chapter 13

February 13, 1692
Glencoe, Scotland

Smoke and ashes no longer clouded the air. Snow had started to accumulate on top of mounds of burnt rubble left from the fires. It was as if God was trying to hide the terrible crime that had just been committed under a pure white blanket.

Edward squeezed his eyes shut to try to erase the image of Alt Na Munde aflame, the roof collapsing inward, sending a great plume of smoke and sparks into the grey morning sky. He would've never agreed to Cait hiding in there had he known they were going to set the manor ablaze. It was his fault if she hadn't made it out in time. He wished he had stayed with her and the others until after the attack and he could've seen them to safety. He buried his face in his hands, regret flooding his chest.

Cloaked only by the fierce snow, he wove through the trees that framed the glen searching for her, his head throbbing and hands frozen. He couldn't call out her name with soldiers still sprinkled about Glencoe, their accusations of his traitorous deeds ringing throughout the glen. He could almost smell their need to teach him a lesson in every venomous claim. He hunkered behind fallen trees or scree, his stomach clenching every time one ran his bayonet through a body that lay on the ground, waiting until they ventured farther up the glen.

Once they were gone, he hurried to Alt Na Munde. Beside it, the door to the dovecote lay open, a handful of pigeons scattered in front, pecking at the snow. He peeked inside, remembering that he'd suggested they escape there. He wished Cait had listened, but its only inhabitants were the pigeons roosting in the tiny alcoves, clumps of them huddled together for warmth. The only other building left standing was the granary, but she wasn't there either.

He wandered into the clump of pines that dotted the brae behind the manor, combing the hillside for a sign of her. After a fruitless search, he returned to the glen to hide inside her parents' home, or what was left of it. Her father's body lay partly outside the door, charred but for the blade still clutched in his hand. Her mother—identifiable only by the large blue stone that hung from her necklace—had been reduced to a pile of black bones and ashes. Their fates were clear. It was Cait's that remained in question. Edward could only pray that she had managed to escape from the hidden room beneath the stairs to safety before Alt Na Munde burned to the ground.

He carefully stepped between scorched cups and pots to Cait's mother, dipped his head in prayer, then removed the blue stone from around her neck that the looters had somehow missed. It came loose with no effort, the fine chain charred and in clumps, then he tucked it inside his shirt, hoping he'd one day be able to present it to Cait.

A voice broke the silence, and he froze.

"He tied them up and gagged them. Eight of Inverrigan's servants all in their nightclothes."

Edward crouched low in the burnt-out cottage, carefully making his way to a windowsill. Nearby, Drummond spoke, his chest swollen and cheeks rosy with excitement.

Campbell stood next to him, staring straight ahead, his face expressionless. "I took them out to the byre and shot Inverrigan in the chest."

"Then ran your bayonet through the hearts of the servants one by one. Is that not so, Campbell?" Drummond asked enthusiastically.

No one seemed bothered by the account but Edward. The story twisted in his gut like gnarled roots. He steeled his stomach to hold back the bile that was building in his throat.

Drummond rambled on about the slaying, his arm draped roughly around Campbell who remained stoic—seemingly neither proud nor ashamed of what he'd done, the cold-hearted dastard.

In the distance, a wash of soldiers appeared at the mouth of the glen. Drummond climbed upon a wall surrounding a destroyed cottage and turned to watch their approach. "Major Duncanson's regiments have arrived. A bit late, I might add."

Edward recalled Alexander telling him the major's troops were supposed to act as reinforcements that morning. Something about them arriving several hours after the attack niggled his thoughts. Why would the major have set the time of the attack at five in the morning if he wasn't going to be there until hours afterward? The storm couldn't have delayed them. It wasn't until just after midnight that it had started to snow lightly, but not enough to slow the men's progress, especially if they had ferried in on boats from the narrows at North Ballachulish—where they were stationed not three miles away—then marched directly into Glencoe. The real storm hadn't started until right before the attack. Edward frowned at the oncoming soldiers. Poor timing was not a mistake that a major in the king's army would typically make.

He stayed crouched until they left, then sidled around the burnt ruins to the crumbling wall enclosing the home, hesitating as loud voices approached.

"He should be hanged a traitor!" someone shouted nearby. "He tried to stop us. Grabbed my hand, he did, and kept me from firing."

Edward stiffened. That voice was referring to him.

"He did the same to me," another voice said. "Threw me to the ground and kicked the pistol right out of my hand!"

"And you are certain 'twas Sergeant Gage?" Alexander asked, his voice clear, his tone both curious and pleased at the same time.

"'Twas your brother, Leftenant. He was but an arm's distance away when he attacked me. I saw his face plain as day."

Edward waited to hear how Alexander would respond. Would he dismiss these charges? If Edward were accused of treason—like Father—the king might build a stronger case against him and undoubtedly choose to attaint. That would destroy Alexander's future. His titles. His fortune.

On the other hand, Alexander could use him as a pawn, turning him in as a traitor to demonstrate the extent and breadth of the loyalty he bore for William. Alexander could get rid of him and possibly elevate his standing with the king at the same time. Only a true servant of His Majesty would turn in his own brother for treason, after all. But would Alexander betray him like that?

There was a lot that lay between them—a history that Edward wasn't proud of—and Alexander would likely make this more personal. His brother had spent his lifetime stewing over Father's preference for Edward. And although it had been years since Edward's dalliance with Berenice, he knew Alexander yet burned over it. Edward was but the bastard brother—turning him in as a traitor would no doubt be Alexander's sweetest revenge to settle the score.

Edward laughed sardonically to himself. He knew his brother too well.

He edged along the stone wall, then hopped over. Cait had told him there were small caves in the brae of the northern ridge, just below the Pap of Glencoe. Supposedly, only the local villagers knew about them, and for the time being, they seemed the best place for him to hide. Dare he hope to find Cait there too?

He looked back once at the grouping of soldiers surrounding his brother. They still held their pikes and swords at the ready. Edward's heart thumped hard as he remembered what so many of them had done the morning of the massacre. Shooting children who were clinging to their mothers' legs. Running their swords through old men and women in their nightclothes as they hobbled from their burning homes. It seemed implausible that they'd killed the very same people who had poured their drinks and lit their hearths only a day earlier.

"Cockards. Every one of them," he said to himself.

He hid behind a tree, waiting for them to take direction. Alexander stood with his hands on his hips, as smug as ever, his voice filled with cunning and vengeance. "We cannot allow a traitor to escape his due punishment."

His words were no surprise. Edward stared at the snow at his feet, concentrating on his brother's voice.

"'Tis our duty to obey the king's orders and punish all traitors and rebels to the utmost extremity of the law. In the same vein that we took down the MacDonalds, we must take down all traitors. Even if that traitor is my own brother. We shall find him, and when we do, we will present him to the king to be hanged."

The men grunted in assent, all seemingly satisfied with Alexander's pathetic speech. One of them spoke, but Edward couldn't hear him clearly over the howling wind. Edward cautiously peeked around the tree.

"We shall begin our search east. He has likely headed out of the glen." Alexander waved his men to follow.

That was good. While they marched east, Edward would head north into the brae in search of a cave.

In the moonless sky, darkness descended on the village, and Edward could no longer continue his search. He scaled the jagged rocks near the base of Aonach Eagach, where Cait had mentioned there were hidden caves, barely able to feel his feet inside his boots, his neck frozen from the snow that had found its way into his collar. He slipped on the granite scree, his hands groping the rocks' sharp edges that covered the slope. Inevitably, he banged his knees numerous times, but the freezing wind numbed him sufficiently to prevent the assured sting of pain.

Eventually, he found a depression in the ridge large enough to protect him from the violent wind. It wasn't as deep as a cave, but he settled against the rock, relieved to have a place to rest. He winced as his feet came to life, the sting starting in his ankles then traveling to his toes. As he shivered in his boots and wool uniform, he remembered how he hurried Cait, Davina, and the children out of their bedchamber shoeless and in their nightclothes. He squeezed his eyes shut, ashamed that he not only hadn't considered that there may be a need to escape the manor and head for safety elsewhere, but he'd told them there was no time to dress. If they had fled during the fire, it was his fault they would not be able to escape the driving snow and freezing temperatures too.

The army was comprised of a band of murderers, liars, and thieves—his brother included. And to think he had joined the king's forces, believing that being a soldier was the most honourable thing to do to support his mother. When he'd been commissioned as a sergeant, he'd assumed his elevated status as an officer would sway the king to reconsider Father's imprisonment in the Tower. He recalled the sinister look on Alexander's face and his snide laugh when Edward had disclosed his desire to see their father freed. Alexander cared nothing about their father's incarceration as long as the king didn't pursue attainder. But Edward couldn't imagine his father—the same man who'd seen to his tutelage and care, who'd taught him to ride a horse, who'd beamed with pride when Edward shot his first stag, who'd told him that he was a miracle born—rotting away in a London dungeon until the swing of the axe or a noose ended his life.

"Oh, Father. I made a poor decision." He was referring to his choice to join this unscrupulous army, but after he'd said it, he wondered if what he really meant was his decision to turn traitor. His father's fate would be sealed as soon as Alexander reported Edward's seditious behaviour to King William. But he breathed easier, knowing his father would say, *honour before everything.*

He peered out the cave at the narrow crooked path leading into Glencoe. All regiments moved east together like red and brown ants in a messy line, the grenadiers easily spotted by their fur caps and the battalions in their blue bonnets. Mixed in were the goats, sheep, and shaggy-haired cattle that they were taking as the spoils.

Edward fell back against the granite wall, a heavy, dull drumbeat starting in his chest. Nothing would be left for the MacDonald survivors—if there were any. Their homes were gone, their families, friends, and now their food.

Cait stood at the entrance to the cave, dressed in a magnificent blue gown trimmed in lace, her black tresses hanging to her waist. She glowed, bright and beautiful. He desperately wanted to touch her.

"How did you find me?" he asked.

"Where else would ye be?" she replied, one corner of her mouth turned up.

"Your parents were already gone. I . . . I tried—"

"I'm sure ye did." Her eyes bore into him. *"And did ye come back for me?"*

"I did." He sat up and stretched his hand across the space separating them. *"I never wanted to leave you, but—"*

"Did ye know that the soldiers would set the village ablaze?" she asked, taking a few steps nearer. She smelled of smoke and whisky, and as she grew closer, he noticed the hem of her gown was smoldering.

"Of course not. I thought I would be able to return to you and help you escape after the soldiers had left. We would be together."

She laughed. *"Together?"*

He nodded.

She lifted her skirts to her knees, unbothered by the burning hem, and he stared at the fawn-coloured stockings covering her legs. He wanted to touch them, but she was still too far.

"Come to me, Edward. I have something for ye."

He slowly stood and closed the distance between them, desperate to feel her touch, perhaps her palm caressing his cheek. He waited, ready for whatever she offered.

She reached into her skirt and pulled out a knife, the gleam of the moon shining on its flat surface.

He wasn't afraid. *"And yet you draw your blade?"*

"Aye. I do." She lifted it to his chest, pulled back her arm, and thrust.

Edward jerked awake, his breath ragged. He sat up, the stone at his back damp and cold, and stared into the blackness.

Chapter 14

Davina sat on a shaky stool in Cait's aunt's tiny cottage, hugging Sawney tight to her chest. He'd been tossing and turning for more than an hour, his little hands curled into fists under his chin. His breath came jagged and shallow as it often did in a fitful sleep. She rubbed her cheek against his forehead. She wouldn't let what happened to Gilli happen to her sweet son.

Cait hadn't spoken since Alasdair and John had rescued them two days earlier. Before they left the forest, John had hidden Gilli's body beneath a cairn of stones to mark her grave. It was then that he had mentioned his mother, Lady Glencoe, had also frozen to death in the hills that night, three of her fingers chewed almost to the bone by the soldiers in an effort to free her of her rings. The thought of that poor woman suffering so, turned Davina's stomach.

He'd promised Cait that he would return as soon as the weather eased and give Gilli and his dear mother a proper burial on Eilean Munde, the MacDonald burial island in Loch Leven. Cait had reluctantly agreed. She'd sat and gently rocked her sister, whispering the words to *Griogal Cridhe* in her ear. It had bothered Davina to hear it, the story of how a century earlier the Campbells had murdered the MacGregor chief in front of his wife and child. It was clear why Cait had chosen that lullaby to sing to Gilli, each tear dropping from her lashes a vow to avenge Campbell. It pained Davina to see her dear friend so distraught. And determined.

A day later, Alasdair had found a batward from Ballachulish to ferry them on his boat east to Kinlochbeg in Argyll, where Cait had an elderly aunt and two cousins. Davina had desperately wanted to leave Glencoe, the image of the buzzards circling overhead, their sharp beaks pulling bits of flesh from the dead bodies that lay exposed in the melting snow, disturbed her every thought. With the village three miles away, the ride took only a few hours and was peaceful, the banks of the loch sheeted in ice and snow.

Now, settled in the cottage, Davina rocked Sawney in her lap with soothing movements, her breath visible in the frigid air.

"I'm going to get more kindling for the fire," Finnean said. Cait's cousin brushed his buttercream-coloured hair across his forehead as he adjusted his wool bonnet. His eyes like bilberries, small and a dull dark blue, barely glanced in her direction.

Davina nodded, still too afraid to speak. She didn't want to pretend to be happy or relieved. None of them knew if the killings had stopped and if they were truly safe. Even Alasdair had taken his wife into hiding, afraid there was more to come. It was there that a friend of Alasdair's wife gave her and Cait a couple of old gowns when she saw them dressed only in their nightclothes. Davina nervously rubbed the knee of her borrowed gown, the green wool well-worn and dotted with moth holes. She shifted on the wooden stool, and its uneven legs rocked unsteadily.

Sionn, Finnean's older brother, entered the room. "Did ye see where they were headed?"

Davina turned to face him. He stood by the window, his index finger pulling back the leather curtain an inch or so. Strands of his brown hair hung messily over his eyes.

"The soldiers?" she asked.

He looked at her sideways. "Are ye daft? Who else would I be talking about?"

Davina's stomach clenched. They had only been at their cottage for a few days, but she already knew that there was nothing decent about these two lads. They hadn't said a kind word to her or Cait since they'd arrived. "I dinnae know their whereabouts."

"It would've been helpful if you'd paid attention to that wee detail before ye left." He shook his head in disgust, then faced the window, mumbling obscenities under his breath.

The details meant nothing to her. If anything, she wanted to *forget* the details of what she'd seen—Duncan Rankin's body floating in the loch, already bloated with four bullet holes in his back. Lilas and the kitchen maids tangled in their bloodied clothing at the entrance to Alt Na Munde. And although she hadn't seen MacIain, Cait had told her that his face had been blown apart, unrecognizable except for his great height and mane of white hair matted with blood. Once she'd boarded that boat, she never turned back to look.

THE TACKSMAN'S DAUGHTER

Sawney stirred, a soft moan escaping his lips. "There ye go, laddie," she said, patting his back.

Sionn snapped, "If he's going to start fussing, I willnae have it."

She stiffened at his tone, then bounced her son gently. "I think he's hungry." She hoped Auntie Meg wouldn't mind if she searched her cupboards for something for Sawney to eat. "I'll make him some porridge or oatmeal brose." She thought her soft tone would calm Sionn, force him to lower his own voice, but it didn't.

"Dinnae take more than yer share." He grabbed the rifle leaning against the wall beside the door and stepped outside, his angry words trailing behind him.

She breathed a sigh of relief when he was gone. She had to convince Cait that they needed to leave, that they weren't welcome, and it was simply a matter of time before the cousins' aggression manifested into more than just foul speech.

Cait pushed aside the deer pelt hanging in the doorway, one hand brushing her stomach as she shuffled out of the back chamber. "Have ye seen my dirk?"

Davina glanced at Cait's faded blue gown. It was the first time since they'd left Glencoe that the blade Edward had given her was not strapped to her waist. "Ye used it at the burn, the last I remember."

Cait rubbed her forehead and glanced sleepily around the small room. She'd been living in a fog for days now, and Davina wondered if she'd ever come back to life.

Cait brushed her hand down her face. "Where are the others?"

"Yer auntie is at a croft nearby. She said one of the townsfolk—I forgot her name—would likely be willing to spare some blood sausage. The woman has more than she needs since her husband died of a sudden fright in January."

Cait yawned once. "And my cousins?"

"Finnean is fetching more firewood. Sionn left with his rifle, so . . ." Davina hoped they left never to return, but that was a farfetched wish.

She stood clumsily with Sawney bundled in her arms and inched aside a sackcloth curtain to peek into the first of the two rough-hewn cupboards. She winced at the strong acrid stench that affronted her. Only a small sack of salt and a smattering of mouse droppings occupied the shelf. She turned her head to the side to clear the smell from her nostrils. This time she stood back a bit before opening the second cupboard. Inside she found a bag of oats, some barley, and a block of sheep's milk cheese wrapped in cloth.

"Can ye hold my wee one?" she asked Cait. "I'll make us some porridge."

Cait blinked twice as if considering the question, her bottom lip quivering. She hadn't wanted anything to do with Sawney after Gilli had died. Davina hadn't taken it to heart, though. She knew Cait was suffering in a way only someone who has truly loved and lost knows how to.

"Come now, lass. Ye must be famished." Davina stepped closer to her, and with one hand, stroked her pallid cheek.

"I cannae hold him," Cait said in barely more than a whisper, her eyes full of panic. "It reminds me too much . . ."

Davina's heart cracked apart. Cait was clearly stuck back in that moment when she'd cradled her sister in her arms, unable to will her to take another breath. They had both suffered so much heartache and loss in the last week, it was hard to move forward. Hard to believe in anything anymore. "I know ye can hold him. The same as you've done many times before."

Cait shook her head, the tears now falling.

"Sit over here on the stool by the hearth where you'll be warm, and I'll put him in yer arms." Davina nudged her and settled her on the stool. Slowly, she handed over Sawney, his eyes heavy-lidded and his pale lips slightly parted. Cait frowned down at him, despair and angst in her wan features.

Davina brushed aside a lock of his hair. "Just hold him there while I put on some water to boil."

"But what if—"

"He'll be fine."

"But . . ."

Davina bent to wrap her arm around her. If it weren't for Cait's insistence that they escape from Alt Na Munde when they did, she and Sawney would be dead like all the others. Although it was difficult, considering all she'd seen and heard, she had to be strong for Cait. She and Sawney might be all she had left. "Wheesht, lass. Nothing will happen to the laddie while yer holding him."

"But I was holding Gilli . . . I didn't know . . . What will my parents think of me?"

"They will say ye did the best ye could. That it wasn't yer lack of effort or concern that took Gilli's life. 'Twas God's desire." Davina's pulse pounded in her ears. She couldn't take much more of this pain. This sorrow. She wanted to be strong enough for both of them, but she wasn't sure she could be. She pressed Cait's hand in hers. "'Twas a gift that Gilli died peacefully in yer arms. 'Twas yer embrace that let her know how much ye loved her right up to the moment she took her last breath."

Cait stared at Sawney, her eyes filled with tears. "I willnae forget it, Davina. Never."

Davina knew that. She'd heard the determination in Cait's voice when she sang that lullaby to Gilli. She wouldn't forget what happened. The loss. The betrayal. Or the man behind it all. Glenlyon would pay.

THE TACKSMAN'S DAUGHTER

They were so different. Davina wanted to forget everything.

Three weeks passed and Davina thought she'd rather trudge through the snow on foot back to her home in Glenorchy than stay another day in Kinlochbeg. Sionn and Finnean had started looking at her strangely, a sharpness to their stares, a tightness in their jaws. She kept Sawney in her arms when they were in the cottage and only let him toddle free when they left. Cait's auntie Meg couldn't have been more different, though. There was a sadness to her, present in her eyes and in the way her mouth naturally turned down in discontent. But she couldn't have been sweeter, insisting that Davina call her 'auntie,' too, and offering milk and a bit of bannock with jam every chance she got. That is, every time her sons left in search of food.

For Davina, the days were bad, but the nights were worse. That's when the memories came back in the form of dreams. Many nights, they'd left her out of breath and in a terrible sweat, but she'd managed to reach out for Sawney and touch his soft chubby hand or round belly, and the fear would melt away instantly. And then there were some memories that had nothing to do with the attack but were just as heart-wrenching.

She could not have predicted what happened between her and Alex. The night they finally found each other should've been magical, something that would've awakened every faery, every spirit in the Highlands with its vast power. He'd looked so charming in the candlelight, so tall and assured in his uniform. Even with that tiny trickle of blood escaping the corner of his mouth, he'd seemed like a warrior, a true soldier too brave and poised to be concerned over a minor injury. As she'd stood there in the alcove, her heart pounded so hard, she was sure he'd heard it. The way he'd pressed her hand to his cheek then gently guided her away, reminded her of their days in Glenorchy.

She hadn't wanted to go up to her bedchamber to talk, but he'd insisted it was the best location for privacy. She'd agreed, of course. After all, there were no pretenses, no boundaries between them. They had shared a bed many times before.

They'd managed to climb the stairs unseen, the noise from the evening's festivities below drowning out the sound of his boots on the stones. She'd ushered him into her room, and he shut the door quietly.

She'd wanted to cry, to let out all the sadness and hope and fear that she'd felt over the last two years, but she didn't.

"So here we are alone," he'd said, one eyebrow raised in question.

She knew what he wanted. But it was all too fast. She needed to tell him about Sawney and know his intentions first. And why he left Glenorchy without telling her or giving her any inkling of where he was headed or when he'd return.

"Are we playing a game? Do you wish for me to come after you?" he'd asked as he loosened the lace at his throat.

He seemed so relaxed. So casual. And she was wound so tight.

"No game. I only wish to speak with ye." She'd hid her trembling hands in the folds of her skirt.

He threw his coat on the bed and crossed the room to where she was standing. "Why must we talk first? I find that so . . . tiring."

She wanted to pull away, to make him listen to her, but she couldn't resist the smell of him, the velvety sound of his voice. He kissed her hard and long, and before she knew it, his hands were beneath her skirts and between her thighs, probing and pushing. But his fingers were a little too rough, and she couldn't stop thinking about all the unanswered questions swimming in her head. When she hadn't responded the way he wanted her to, he'd grabbed her hand and pressed it to the front of his breeks. He was ready for her, but she wasn't ready herself. She tried to pull away, but he threw her to the bed and covered her in bites and kisses until she could no longer think straight.

She'd been in this position with him before—a position of defeat and surrender. The first time they'd been together, he had been insistent, rough, and she hadn't been ready. It was not a memory she cared to recall, but it had happened nonetheless. She couldn't erase it. She'd heard that pain was inevitable the first time, so she'd thought it part of the act. And then in Glencoe that night, it felt the same. Of course, she had already lost her maidenhead to him, so the pain and shock of it all were a little different. But it was still unpleasant. Not loving and not gentle. Looking back, she realized it wasn't what she'd thought it was. It was impersonal, as if she could've been anyone. And much of it hurt, but she didn't fight back—not like the first time. She'd played her part, letting him continue to squeeze and push until he found his release and finally rolled off her.

It wasn't as if he was unkind at first. He'd whispered sweetly in her ear and spoke tenderly like he had when they first met. The poetry, the adoring words. After the first time they were together in Glenorchy, he'd sought her out every day to steal away with her in dark corners in hidden places, encouraging her back into his arms. But now, knowing he didn't think of her as she did him—didn't even know her name—she knew what she was to him. A village whore. A harlot to be taken at will.

Had he known that night what he was bound to do? That he would plunge his sword into the hearts of the men and women who'd hosted him and his men?

THE TACKSMAN'S DAUGHTER

As she remembered the sounds of that early morning—the shouts, gunshots, roaring flames, cries for help--it was as if a fog had lifted and she could see clearly all the way to the sharp horizon. He hadn't been the man she'd thought he was. Her mind had turned him into what she desired, wanted at the time. Need had clouded her judgement and made her a fool.

But if all of this were true, why did she still yearn for him? She ran her fingers through Sawney's brown curls. His wee face turned up with her touch, and she knew.

Chapter 15

"Yer a fine seamstress, Cait."

Cait glanced down at her crooked stitches and wondered how much whisky her aunt had already managed to pour down her gullet. It was only noon, but Auntie Meg's glassy eyes danced in their sockets, and her face was flushed. "Thank ye, Auntie, but I'm nae so sure my hands were meant for delicate work."

Auntie Meg smiled, her nose a hearty pink. "You'll make a good wife someday. My Sionn could use a sonsie lass like you to warm his bed at night. He's four and twenty, ye know, and is quite the hunter. You'll never go hungry with him as yer husband."

First of all, *Finnean* was four and twenty. *Sionn* was six and twenty. And secondly, he wasn't a hunter. He was a cattle reiver. A thief.

Auntie Meg's wrist peeked out from her sleeve, a dark violet bruise encircling half of it. Cait wondered which of Auntie's sons had done that to her. "I dinnae have a marriage mind right now. He'll have to find a wife in someone else."

"All lasses have a marriage mind." Her face soured with a disapproving look. "'Tis what God gave ye life for—to find a man, grow heavy with his seed, and bring forth his children. A woman needs a man to provide her with a home, and a man needs a woman to provide him with a family."

It was hard to believe this woman was her mother's kinfolk. They shared the same father, but Auntie Meg was a child born of his first wife, and her mother was the daughter of his second wife. Plainly, they were raised differently. Cait's mother had been taught that a good marriage should not stem from necessity but from the heart.

"I'll keep that in mind, Auntie."

The door flung open, bringing in the cold wet air with it, then Davina entered with Sawney in tow. "I have yer ladle, Auntie. The tinker said to pay ye thanks for the salt beef ye sent him."

Auntie Meg tried to stand but must've thought better of it when she teetered. Instead, she plopped back into her chair. "Did he fix it, then?"

"Aye." Davina passed her the ladle, the handle firmly affixed to the scoop. "Ye see what a nice job he did with the welding?"

Sionn burst through the door, his boots muddy almost up to his leather trews. His dark hair was wet and messy, and he had a rifle in one hand and Edward's dirk strapped to his side. Cait had thought she had lost it somewhere between the river and Auntie's and had agonized over it for weeks.

"Yer wearing my dirk," she said, meeting his steely gaze.

He rested his hand on the hilt as if it had belonged to him always, his fingernails rimmed with filth. "A woman has no need for such a weapon."

"Ye stole it from me."

He shrugged one shoulder. "Do ye wish to try to take it back?"

Heat crept up Cait's neck. "Are ye challenging me, then?"

He took a step closer, and Auntie reached out her hand to stop him. "What is it that ye want, Sionn? We're busy."

"Busy? Yer sitting about clucking like hens in a roost when there's work to be done." He turned to Cait and asked in a gruff voice, "Is my sark mended?"

Cait tossed him the shirt she had stitched, and he caught it in one hand. "Ye might speak to us with a kinder tone and nae like ye have thorns up yer arse."

In a flash, he grabbed her arm, squeezing until she thought she might collapse from the pain. Her knees started to buckle. Auntie Meg stood but remained quiet, one hand on her chair to steady herself. Davina grabbed Sawney and pushed him behind her skirts. Cait tried to speak, to shout, but no sound came from her throat.

"Ye dinnae speak to me like a common whore! You'll watch yer tongue, or I'll cut it out!" He grabbed the handle of Edward's dirk. "And I've the perfect blade to do it."

In one motion, he let go of her arm and thrust her against the wall. She hit it with a thud, a shooting pain traveling down from her shoulder and into her hand. She fell to the floor and instinctively felt for the *sgian dubh* strapped to her thigh. She wanted to hold it to his neck and press its tip into the little indentation at the bottom of his throat, but the sadness in Auntie Meg's eyes kept her from doing it, silently telling her that she loved the lout, even though he was a brute and an awful disappointment.

Auntie Meg skirted behind her chair, the ladle gripped tight in her hand, and shakily removed a pannikin from beside the hearth. She forced it into Davina's hand. "Go fill this with milk for the brose pudding. Make haste, lass."

Cait tried to steady her breath and shared a quick glance with Davina to assure her she was fine. Davina took the small pot, then left clutching Sawney tightly to her hip.

Auntie Meg rubbed her hands down the side of her skirt and looked everywhere but at Sionn. "Tell yer brother supper will be ready in an hour." She tucked a loose strand of grey hair back in her kertch with trembling fingers. "He's at the Leven north of the faeries dun. He's taken the boat, but I'm sure he'll be back by now."

He stared at Cait, his shoulders heaving in anger, one hand on the hilt of Edward's dirk. "Remember what I said."

"We should leave here." Davina set another egg gently into the basket.

Cait stuck her hand under the warm belly of a hen and extracted an egg with only a small cluck of disapproval from its caretaker. The roof of the henhouse was just tall enough for her to stand in, but Davina had to stoop to keep her head from knocking into the rotting wooden rafters.

Cait set the egg in Davina's basket. "We dinnae know if the soldiers have left the glen. We need to wait to get word if 'tis safe first."

She wondered why Alasdair hadn't sent a letter or a messenger. He was supposed to let her know where her parents were and when she could return, but he hadn't. She didn't know what to make of that. Could it be that Alasdair hadn't found them yet? Even so, he would've sent a messenger by now to tell her one way or the other.

Sawney cupped an egg in both palms and offered it to Davina. She bent to let him put it in the basket himself. "It's been a month since the . . . since we left. Surely they've gone on their way."

Had it been a month already? Cait's heart pinched at the thought that Gilli had been gone that long. She wanted to visit her grave on Eilean Munde and read the words engraved on her throuch. To pray and ask for forgiveness. To explain that she'd never be forgotten. And she wanted to see her parents and thank Edward for helping them. But he likely left with his regiment. She pressed her lips together, remembering their kiss.

As much as she wanted to go back, she was afraid of what she'd see.

"If 'tis Sionn and Finnean yer troubled over, ye needn't be. I can handle those two sumphs. They dinnae scare me." But that wasn't exactly true. She had to admit, she was a little surprised when Sionn had grabbed and pushed her. She hadn't seen it coming. If Auntie hadn't been there, she would've pulled her blade to defend herself. It would've been the time to show him that she would never let him get away with that again.

Sionn and Finnean were strange lads, full of mystery and fire. It was hard to tell what would fan their flames at any given moment. It could be a tangled piece of hemp rope or a rat in the cupboard. Sometimes she could sense their blood boiling and other times their tempers would flare suddenly. Either way, the aftermath was unpleasant.

A few days earlier, she'd asked after the letter Alasdair was supposed to send, and Sionn turned on her as if she'd struck him.

"Ye think yer so special because yer the tacksman's daughter? So ye can read. No one cares," he shouted, his face red and twisted with hate.

She hadn't bothered to defend herself. All children of tacksmen were given an education, and one of the things she learned was not to boast about it to an angry clod like him.

She tried to stay out of her cousins' way, but the cottage was small, and they always seemed to be lurking nearby when she was doing her chores. She didn't care for the way they looked at her when she was alone feeding the chickens or at the burn fetching water. She'd caught them a few times hiding behind an oak or the corner of a bothy to watch her, but they'd always slunk away without saying a word. "The truth is . . . I wish to return to Glencoe, too."

"Then we shouldn't tarry."

"And if we go back and no one is there?"

Davina half-smiled. "Better alone than in ill company."

The door banged open, and a burst of light shone in the henhouse, blocked by a dark figure. The hens squawked at the intrusion, their wings flapping angrily. Cait squinted at the light, where tiny feathers and dust motes swirled in the disturbed winter air.

"How long does it take for you two babblers to gather a few eggs?" It was Finnean. He stooped in the doorway, his hair the colour of dirty white foam.

"We'll be done in a bit," Cait said.

"Make haste about it, then. I'm hungry." He stared at them through slanted eyes for a few seconds, then ducked back out of the threshold and disappeared in the bright light.

Davina spoke up, a slight quaking in her voice. "Ye cannae tell me that lad doesn't put a fright into ye. And his brother's worse."

Cait could only imagine what Auntie Meg's life was like before they arrived. Poor woman stayed top-heavy with drink day in and day out simply to cope. Neither of her boys lifted a finger to help, always too busy searching for someone's kine to steal or drinking whisky on the banks of Loch Leven. She'd spotted them there several times with their feet propped up on the side of their boat, half-drunk and smacking each other with the backs of their hands while they laughed. But by the time they returned home, they were ornery and looking for a stramash. That was why Auntie was always mentioning marriage. She needed someone to share her chores and deflect their anger. Although Cait had never seen either of them strike her, she knew it was being done with regularity, for she saw the evidence of it on her back and shoulders when she removed her gown to wash.

Cait was caught between waiting to hear from Alasdair and leaving her sweet auntie to deal with her sons on her own. "Let's give it one more week. We should be fine until then."

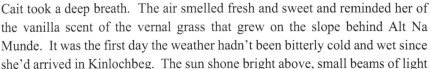

Cait took a deep breath. The air smelled fresh and sweet and reminded her of the vanilla scent of the vernal grass that grew on the slope behind Alt Na Munde. It was the first day the weather hadn't been bitterly cold and wet since she'd arrived in Kinlochbeg. The sun shone bright above, small beams of light streaming through the trees onto the celandine, its yellow star-like blossoms peeking out of sparse patches of green brush. Cait plucked one and rubbed its soft petals on her chin and cheek. The first real sign of spring.

She sat by the burn and carefully scraped the edge of her *sgian dubh* along a flat rock, back and forth until the blade was glistening and sharp. With the stem of the flower held between her forefinger and thumb, she grazed it along the blade, splitting it in two with no effort. Pleased, she twirled her knife a few times between her fingers, then slid it back into its sheath at the top of her stocking.

Two thrushes with spotted bellies hopped on branches above her head, their grey-brown feathers ruffling in the gentle breeze. One flitted down and stood at the edge of the burn opposite her. With tentative steps, it tested the water, then dipped in its beak for a quick sip. It hopped twice and sank in up to its belly, washing its feathers with rapid, tiny splashes. Cait stilled, afraid to disturb its morning ablutions.

It was late March and more than a month since her life in Glencoe had changed forever. Gilli was gone, her parents were likely in hiding, and Edward was, well, she didn't know. Would she ever see him again? Or had he marched on?

The little thrush flew back up to the branch, its companion hopping closer in greeting. Cait picked another flower and twirled it between her thumb and forefinger, watching it spin in a blur of yellow. She brushed the celandine bloom across her lips, closed her eyes, and thought about the last time she'd seen Edward. He had kissed her. She assumed he did it in a moment of confusion, for she never gave him an invitation to behave in such a way. But she hadn't pulled away either. It had been quick and strong, and she wondered how that kiss would have changed had they not been in such horrible circumstances. Would it have been slow and soft? Would she have wrapped her arms around his neck and kissed him back?

Her mind had fallen into a state of mindless trance when birds squawked above, breaking the silence, the little thrushes flying away. She peered up into the canopy, and a small flock of previously hidden birds suddenly scattered in different directions.

She held her breath, knowing they'd flown away for a reason. She sat straight and paused to listen, warmth creeping into her nape, her fingers inching towards her blade.

A twig snapped, and she jumped to her feet, her *sgian dubh* firmly in her grasp. Sionn stood not ten feet behind her, his legs braced apart, one side of his mouth curled up. He had a strange look on his face—danger mixed with pleasure.

He took a step forward, and she stumbled back, ankle-deep into the cold water of the burn. "What is it that ye want, Sionn?"

Her heart hammered and her pulse thrummed in her ears.

He moved closer and she took another step back, soaking the hem of her gown past her ankles. She scanned the trees to the right and left of him, looking to see if his brother was anywhere nearby, but she saw no one. Her right palm tightened around the hilt of her *sgian dubh*.

He stared at her through squinty eyes, fingers twitching. He edged nearer, his hands now curling into fists. His silence unnerved her.

She pointed her knife at him. She could throw it, but he was only a few feet away, too close for it to spin and stick. She would have to stab him directly. She didn't want to, but she wouldn't risk what happened to her the last time she had to defend herself. "Take one step closer and I'll give ye a taste of my blade."

"No, ye won't." He licked his bottom lip and sneered. "I saw the way ye cowered when I pushed ye. Ye willnae fight me."

"The only reason I didn't draw blood then was because I didn't want to do it in front of yer mother. But she's nae here now." She didn't want to hurt him. He was kin after all, and it would break her auntie's heart.

"'Tis true. But ye cannae do much harm with that wee thing." He jerked his head, indicating her knife.

"Take another step closer and you'll discover if that's true." Her pulsed raced, but with the bogwood handle of her blade set firmly in her grip, she reminded herself that her da had taught her well how to use it. And unlike years ago, this time she had only one man to fight, giving her a much better chance.

Sionn tilted his head to the side and scratched the scruff of his neck as if he was thinking of retreating. "Yer right. I've heard about yer skill with a blade," he said, his head nodding slightly.

Cait exhaled. She remembered when Edward had said almost those same words to her a little more than a month before. Her shoulders relaxed, and her fingers loosened around the handle.

He brushed a thumb across his lip contemplatively and started to turn away. Suddenly, his arm swung out and hit her outstretched hand, knocking her blade into the air and several feet to her right. She lunged for it, but he caught her arm and flung her to the ground like a sack of flour, the back of her head banging on the hard-packed earth. Pain bloomed through her skull, and her vision blurred. He climbed on top of her, and he clamped his hand on her jaw, his palm damp and reeking of manure.

She tried to twist and buck him off, but he pressed his weight into her, making her immobile. She grabbed his sark and jerked it hard to the side. "Get off of me, ye son of the devil!"

Her own voice rang sharply in her ears, and she winced.

"Ye think ye can come into my home and thrash me like ye do?" Spittle flew from his mouth as he spoke, spraying her face.

"Perhaps 'tis time someone told ye to speak to yer mother with respect," she said through clenched teeth.

He jammed her head into the ground, then lowered his mouth to her ear, his breath rancid, smelling of raw onions and whisky. "Seems to me that *you* should be treating *me* with a bit more respect. 'Tis *my* home yer eating and sleeping in."

"Let go of me, ye smelly dunderheid." She reached down to his hip to pull his dirk from its sheath, but it was pressed snugly between them.

His grip tightened on her jaw. "Ye dinnae seem to know yer place. A wee *galla* like you."

She dragged her fingernails down his cheek. With a grunt, he jerked his head back, then flipped her over on her stomach and shoved her face into the dry grass. She squirmed to get free, but his weight pinned her solidly to the ground.

Her heart hammered desperately, images of the soldiers years earlier flashing behind her eyelids. She squeezed her eyes shut, blinking rapidly to force out the dirt and clear her vision. A little farther than an arm's length away, the gleam of her blade poking through the scant grass caught her attention. If she could wriggle a little to her right, she could reach it.

THE TACKSMAN'S DAUGHTER

"I've seen the way ye look at me and Finnean. Like yer better than us. Yer father being MacIain's tacksman. You and yer friend filling my mother's head with lies."

She had no idea what he was talking about. She had only spoken to Auntie about her life back in Glencoe. Her family. Their meals together. Their home and the land where their tenants lived.

She had to get her knife. With one hard push, she bucked and jolted to the right, and his left hip slipped off her, releasing his weight just enough for her to spin onto her back. He grabbed her face hard, his fingers pressing the inside of her cheeks into her teeth. She tasted blood, metallic and sharp coating her tongue. She groped for her knife, her fingers frantically reaching over the dead pine needles and through the cold damp grass. She touched the handle with her fingertips, inching it closer until it was firmly in her grip. In one swift move, she sliced it across his neck.

"Bitch!' he yelled, clamping his hand to his wound.

She rolled out from under him and snatched up a rock as big as her palm, then used a nearby alder to help her stand and regain her balance. He stumbled towards her, and with as much strength as she could muster, she smashed the rock over his head. He landed hard on his knees, then toppled over face first. When he hit the ground, his hand slipped from his neck, a smear of blood across his palm.

Her heart leapt into her throat. She wasn't sure if she killed him. And she wasn't about to move closer to check.

With her knife in hand, she ran back to the cottage, crushing the yellow celandine at her feet.

Chapter 16

Davina sat in front of the cottage, washing a bundle of green onions while Sawney frolicked about in front of her, hitting an acorn with a stick. He missed most of the time, and she wondered if he'd gotten the idea from watching the men play *camanachd* at Alt Na Munde. Would he remember such a thing?

Her fingers carefully stroked the long green stems to free them of dirt. She held them away from her nose, their sharp, biting scent too strong for her liking. She was taking more time than she needed to clean them, but it was so beautiful outside—cold yet sunny—she wanted to prolong her stay outdoors as long as she could.

Sawney had lost sight of the acorn and was spinning in circles looking for it.

Davina pointed to the edge of the grass. "'Tis over there, laddie."

He smiled with recognition and ran after the nut. Something moved in the copse of pines behind him. She set the pail of onions aside and stood, her hand shielding her eyes from the sun.

Cait burst out of the trees, running like she was being chased by the devil.

"Where is Finnean?" Cait asked, out of breath.

"Why are ye running?"

"Where is he?" Cait wiped her brow, her black knife grasped firmly in her palm. It wasn't like Cait to expose her blade unless she was twirling it between her fingers. Or defending herself.

"He went to the blacksmith's at the base of the hill."

Cait's shoulders heaved as she caught her breath. "Good. That will give us time to leave."

THE TACKSMAN'S DAUGHTER

Davina stared at the blade, its edge laced with blood. "Why are ye baring yer knife?" she asked, hoping she'd used it to skin a rabbit but suspecting otherwise.

Cait glowered at the blade in her hand as if she had forgotten it was there. After a few silent seconds, she bent and wiped it on the grass. "Is Auntie inside?"

Davina nodded, still confused. Clearly, something wretched had happened.

"Grab Sawney." Cait slipped her knife into the top of her stocking. "We must leave."

Sawney, still playing with his stick and acorn, looked up at having heard his name. "Mama?"

Davina waved at him and smiled halfheartedly, then turned around to question Cait, but she had already disappeared inside the cottage. She tossed aside Sawney's stick, then grabbed his hand.

"Mama!" he cried, pointing to the acorn lying in the dirt. Davina snatched him up, his body tensing and his legs kicking furiously to escape her grasp. "Down!"

Sawney pitched back, almost flinging himself from her arms. She glanced quickly at the trees, but saw nothing, their leaves flickering in the breeze and catching the light. By the time she entered the cottage, Cait and Auntie were deep in discussion, Auntie sitting in her chair by the hearth and Cait kneeling at her feet.

"I left him at the burn," Cait said, her voice soft and steady.

"The burn?" Auntie pressed her lips together, her chin wrinkled and trembling.

Cait nodded. "I dinnae know if he's dead."

Davina sucked in her breath. What had Cait done?

Auntie sat quietly, her hands folded in her lap over the stocking she was mending. "I'll no ask why ye did it as I dinnae wish to know the answer. But I am nae fool, lass. I am too familiar with the poison that runs through my sons' veins, and I can only imagine that ye did what ye felt ye needed to do." She wiped away a tear that fell from the wrinkled outer corner of her eye. "I only pray that if death has taken him, God has forgiven him for all of his sins."

Since Finnean was at the blacksmith's, they had to be talking about Sionn. Heat crept into Davina's chest and neck. Could Cait truly have killed him?

Cait rested her hand gently on her aunt's. "We must leave. All of us. I cannae promise ye that there's a home to return to, or safety, for that matter. But I can guarantee ye that 'tisnae safe to stay here."

Auntie's brow crinkled, and she eyed her warily. Davina was surprised at how calmly she had taken the news, how it hadn't sent her into fits. Resolution settled on Auntie's face. "I cannae leave. 'Tis my home. My family—"

"I've seen the purple marks on yer neck and arms. Ye cannae tell me ye feel safe here," Cait said, her eyes pleading.

"They're my sons. I willnae leave them." She set aside her sewing, then stood, readjusting her kertch. "Ye said he's at the burn?"

Cait nodded and stood with her.

"Then I need to go to him. Ye should be on yer way. Take the boat."

Cait started to speak, but there was a catch in her breath. She started over. "Will ye forgive me, then?"

Auntie Meg didn't look at her. She stared down at her hand, where her fingers played with the edge of her bodice. "There's naught to forgive. Now go on."

The ride on Loch Leven was quiet except for the sound of the oars dipping and splashing in the water.

"What did he do?" Davina asked, breaking the silence.

Cait pulled back the oars half a dozen times before she answered, barely audible. "'Tisnae what *he* did. 'Tis what *I* did."

Davina hugged Sawney tighter to her breast and shuddered, imagining.

Cait shook her head, indicating her refusal to speak. After that, Davina prodded her no further.

The west-flowing current had eased their journey, and they arrived at the shores of Glencoe while the sun was still high against a canvas of deep blue. Cait guided the boat to a sandy spot, then jumped out, soaking her skirts to her knees. Still asleep, Sawney lay heavy in Davina's lap. She shifted him higher on her chest and climbed out, the shock of the icy water jolting her alert.

She glanced at the glen in the distance and the notched ridge along the northern edge. Not a soul could be seen. Not a fisherman nor hunter. "We need to go farther into the glen."

Sawney squirmed in Davina's arms, mewling a protest at being carried. Davina set him down on the muddy riverbank. "It willnae be easy with this one stopping every time he spies a peculiar stone."

"We'll take turns carrying him." Cait bent down to him. "Would ye like that, laddie?"

It had taken Cait almost a month to warm to the idea of holding Sawney. At first, he had been the one to crawl into her arms and rest his head on her chest, but lately she had started inviting him into her embrace. Davina didn't think for one second Cait had forgotten her last moments with Gillian, but at least it seemed she was moving closer to forgiving herself for the lass's death.

Before he could protest, Cait swooped him up onto her hip and started walking along the twists and bends of the River Coe, humming softly near his ear.

Davina was happy for the reprieve. Carrying him gave her sharp pains in her back at the end of the day. She knew he was at an age where she should stop, but lately she needed the closeness of his smooth skin and plump cheeks more than he needed her to transport him from spot to spot. She watched his mouth move as he admired a stone, cooing and hooting randomly. His dark curls blew softly in the breeze, his tiny ears pink with the cold. If only Alex had met his son, she was sure he wouldn't have turned them away.

Guilt filled her chest, knowing he could have participated in the slaughter of the good people of Glencoe. But he was a soldier following orders. He would've never hurt her. Perhaps he never raised his sword, or if he had, he'd done it reluctantly. She could only pray that that was the case—for Sawney's sake. Either way, she'd never speak of her stubborn affection for him to Cait. How could she? It would only prove her to be the fool she knew she was.

They were a short distance from Alt Na Munde when Davina couldn't take another step. She dipped her hands into the river and brought the cold, fresh water to her lips, then drank. "I dinnae think I can go any farther, Cait." She leaned against a large flat rock and kicked off her wet shoes. They'd given her blisters on the back of her heels which were now a bloody mess.

Cait set Sawney on the grass, then stretched her back. "'Tisnae that far. Ye can see Alt Na Munde from here."

Davina searched the base of Aonach Eagach, where they had huddled together after the raid. MacIain's home cowered in the distance, a dark blotch against a barren background. Nothing grand remained. The windows and roof were gone, and the stones were mottled with black smears. "Ye willnae find anyone there."

Cait took a deep breath. "I need to see that for myself. Wait here."

Cait trudged across the glen, looping her knife between her fingers like she always did when she sat idle or was agitated. Davina watched her follow the path of the river until she was but a small blue dot in the distance. Sawney kept himself busy rubbing a stone between his palms and trying to balance it on his head, surprised every time it fell to the ground. He looked so much like his father. Would she ever see Alex again? Would she get the chance to introduce him to his son? She knew that whatever ill will lurked in his heart, meeting his son would change him.

Davina unwrapped the cloth filled with cheese and three wedges of a bannock that she'd taken from Auntie Meg's. Sawney, now thoroughly bored with his stone, rushed to her, slamming all his weight into her knees. "Hungry, are ye?"

She broke off some bread and slipped a small piece into his open mouth. Her stomach growled, and she ate some too. If they didn't find someone to take them in soon, they would run out of food quickly. It was almost dusk, and in a matter of an hour or so, the sky would be washed with pink.

Cait's face was red with exhaustion as she approached. "I looked everywhere. We're the only ones here." She wiped the sweat from her brow with the sleeve of her forearm. "'Tis hard to look at, Davina."

Davina's stomach tightened. "Do ye mean to say—"

"Ruins. All of it. The dovecote and the granary yet stand with no roofs, mind ye, but the washhouse and brewhouse are naught but a heap of ashes next to Alt Na Munde."

"And did ye see anyone?" Davina asked, hoping Cait understood that she meant live folk.

Cait shook her head. "There isnae a cottage or bothy left standing."

"So yer home—"

She shook her head again. "We'll need to find shelter for tonight."

Davina wasn't sure what to say. If her parents' home was destroyed, then her parents . . .

Cait stared off into the distance, her chin set. "There were no bones in the home. They must've escaped."

Davina held her breath. She prayed Cait was right. "And MacIain's croft at the other end—"

"Burned. Did ye no believe me when I said naught is left?" Cait waved off the bannock and cheese Davina offered her.

"Aye, but I was hoping ye were exaggerating a bit." Davina pushed a small bite of cheese into Sawney's mouth. He took it happily, his head now resting on her lap. "We could go to the old kirk on Eilean Munde. Surely the soldiers wouldn't have desecrated that holy land."

Cait hmphed. "Do ye think they suddenly found their morality, then?" she asked sarcastically. "If the isle is untouched, 'tis because they were too fat and lazy from eating our food and drinking our whisky and wine to ferry over boats."

Even sitting in the middle of the glen, knowing piles of burnt rubble and debris littered the land, Davina still found it hard to believe those men had turned on them.

THE TACKSMAN'S DAUGHTER

She wrapped up what was left of the food. "We can sleep in the chapel, then in the morning we'll leave."

Chapter 17

They rowed the boat to Eilean Munde and left it on the rocky bank at the MacDonald Port of the Dead. With little daylight left, they hurried to the kirkyard where fresh burial mounds lay scattered over previously smooth land. Some mounds had stones at one end, and others remained unmarked.

"There are so many new graves." Cait stood with her hands planted firmly on her hips, fighting back an eruption of anger. She scanned the hilly land that stretched from one end of the isle to the other. "How are we to find Gilli?"

Davina held her arms out and wiggled her fingers at her son. "Come, Sawney. Up ye go." She settled him on her hip, then with her chin, pointed east. "I'll look over there."

"Fine. I'll search here." Cait watched the two of them go, Davina's head bowed and Sawney pressed to her breast.

Cait waded through the graves, some old and covered in lichen, the words on their throuches dulled by years of wind and rain. So many MacDonalds. Stewarts and Camerons too. But mostly MacDonalds.

Part of her didn't want to find Gilli's grave. It would seem too real then, too final. In the last month, every time she'd thought of Gilli, her sister was smiling or laughing, round green eyes alight with excitement or curiosity—not with blue lips and eyes frosted shut like on the morning of her death.

The day her sister was born, deep lines had creased her mother's forehead, and a damp patch of sweat spread between her breasts. She was babbling with worry that this bairn wouldn't live past the first week. The three between Cait and Gilli—all boys—had died only days after their birth. But somehow, Cait knew this one would live.

THE TACKSMAN'S DAUGHTER

She'd stood by the little boxbed where Ma lay, while the midwife crouched between Ma's legs. It was summer, but the peat fire was still lit, its grey smoke floating up through the small opening in the cottage's roof. Ma was mostly quiet until the final push, when a high-pitched shriek escaped, her face pinched in anguish. Cait had wanted to cry out too, afraid of her mother's pain. But then, Gilli was born, pink and mewling like a lambkin, and Cait's urge to scream disappeared. The midwife wiped Gilli clean and handed her to Ma, whose face was now slack from exhaustion.

"This bairn will survive, Ma," Cait said, brushing the tiny tuft of black hair on Gilli's crown with the tips of her fingers.

Ma's head slowly lolled towards her. "How do ye know that, lassie?"

Cait wrapped her thumb and index finger around Gilli's ankle, and with the vigor of a spirited goat, she kicked her hand away. Cait smiled. "Because she's strong. Like me."

But now, staring out over the fresh mounds on Eilean Munde, she realized that Gilli's strength didn't matter. Even MacIain, the most powerful of them all, couldn't prevent his own death.

She wasn't sure how she was going to tell her parents about what happened to their beautiful daughter. Would they blame her? Probably not. But she would always blame herself.

She was careful not to step too close to the mounds, afraid of walking upon someone's grave and disturbing its spirit from slumber. Eventually, she found a smaller grave near a lonely black alder, its branches still bare except for a handful of tiny green buds sprinkled about. She knelt on the fresh spring grass and squinted at the lettering on the stone. "Davina!"

Davina returned to her side out of breath and dropped to her knees, plopping Sawney beside her. In a whisper, she read, "Gillian Cameron."

There was no date of birth or death, but Cait knew it had to be her sister. The stone was not covered in moss and lichen like the older ones. The letters of Gilli's name were crooked, and the engraving was rough, clearly not fashioned by a stonemason.

Cait stared at the grave, blinking to chase away the tears. She swiped at her cheeks, her breath jagged and throaty. Davina squeezed her hand, but it offered little comfort. The little mound before her held her sister's body. She ran her fingers over the letters of her name, angry at herself, at the men who attacked their village, at Glenlyon. At God.

She turned away and tried to steady her breath, Gilli's death solidified in the stone at her knees. She pressed her eyelids shut with her fingertips, then opened her eyes, waiting for her vision to clear. To her right were two pieces of slate with the same uneven lettering. Cait gasped. Anne and Malcolm Cameron. Her parents.

"What is it, Cait?" Davina asked, panicked.

Davina's gaze followed Cait's, and her breath caught.

Cait gripped Davina's hand hard and spoke with effort. "Be this soul on Thine arm, O Christ, Thou King of the City of Heaven, Amen . . ."

Together they recited the *Beannachadh Bais*, the realization that Cait had lost her whole family burning like hot embers in her chest.

Cait lay prone between her parents and Gilli's graves, the damp grass cool on her cheek. She'd sent Davina and Sawney away, yearning for some time to be alone with her family. Her fingers absentmindedly played with the grass on top of the mounds, caressing and stroking. As each minute passed, it became easier to breathe. Not because she accepted their deaths—she didn't think she'd ever be able to do that—but because she had no choice. She had to keep going, keep moving.

She flipped onto her back and stared at the sky. It was still blue, but only for a little while longer when it would eventually transform into a striking shade of pink and orange. She wanted to watch it turn with her sister and parents. Could they see it too? Could they see her? The world instantly seemed huge and empty, a frightening place for an unmarried woman with no family. She belonged to no one now. She still had Auntie Meg, but she wouldn't dare return to Kinlochbeg after what happened. She had Davina, of course, but Davina was barely welcome in her own home, so a woman of no relation from another village would scarcely be welcome either.

She pulled her *sgian dubh* from her stocking and twirled it between her fingers, the weight of it familiar and comforting. It was something she could do without thinking. Years ago, she'd had to concentrate fiercely on not stabbing herself, but now the movement and the rhythm came naturally. It flipped back and forth, sunlight glistening off its edge as it spun.

Minutes later, a clump of clouds glided in front of the sun, their shade bringing even colder breezes with it. Cait shivered. Was it because of the wind or because of her loss? Perhaps it was both. She listened to the sound of her own breath, now steady and shallow. She closed her eyes and stared at the faint red impression of the clouds framed by the black nothingness on the inside of her lids. Suddenly, the brilliant sun made its appearance again, streaming through the naked branches of the alder tree and turning the insides of her eyelids a bright red.

She opened her eyes and whispered, "Why are ye shining? Dinnae ye know what happened?"

THE TACKSMAN'S DAUGHTER

There was too much to think about, too much uncertainty. And then she remembered Edward. Her heart twisted at the thought of him reaching her parents too late. Had he even carried out his pledge? What if it was a lie and just an excuse to soften her so he could steal a kiss? But he'd seemed so earnest as he said it. He'd also promised to return for her, but he hadn't done that either. Could he be one of the turncoats? He was an Englishman and a soldier, after all. But then why would he have warned her?

Tired of thinking, she stabbed her blade into the ground, closed her eyes, and drifted off to sleep.

"Ye need to come into the chapel before 'tis too dark. If ye wait much longer, ye willnae be able to find yer way." Davina stood above her, the sky now a deep purple.

Cait missed the sunset. She sat up and took a deep breath. "What will become of me, do ye think? What should I do?"

A slight breeze whistled through the trees. "You'll do what I did." Davina kneeled beside her. "You'll hold yer head high and believe that somehow this is part of God's plan."

"Do ye think He knows what He's doing?" It was a blasphemous question, but Cait didn't care. What else could He do to her? Strike her dead? That might be a relief. A blessing.

Davina's eyes widened. "Ye shouldn't say that, lass."

Cait wrapped her arms around her knees, her throat tight. "Then what should I say, Davina? He watched while my whole family died. Did He smite the attackers? Nay. He let them safely leave the glen with their hands wiped clean."

"Yer wrong. Their hands are nae wiped clean. They're filthy with sin. And they will be punished on Judgement Day."

Would that be enough? Cait didn't think so. That was why she had to get to Glenlyon first. Then she could punish him and send him to his own day of judgement sooner. "How can ye have such faith?"

"Are ye saying ye have none?"

"'Tis hard for me right now, mind ye, with my sister's dead body to my right and my parents' bodies to my left." Cait knew she sounded sarcastic, but she couldn't help it. She didn't feel like listening to the catechism.

"Listen to me, Cait." Davina reached for her hand. "Right now, it seems as if all hope is lost. That God has forsaken ye. But heed my words. Yer heart will heal."

The last of the sun sank below the horizon, allowing the first stars to make their appearance. Cait rubbed her arms to warm them in the chilly night air.

Davina continued, "Do ye remember saying almost those same words to me but a month or so ago?"

Davina was right. Cait had said something similar the morning of the attack while they hid in the laird's lug at Alt Na Munde and Davina hadn't wanted to leave, still heartbroken over Alexander. But being disappointed about a lover was different from being the only family survivor of a brutal attack. She patted the back of Davina's hand, then plucked her blade from the earth. "I know ye mean well, but there is only one way my heart will heal. And that will be with the death of Glenlyon."

Chapter 18

This was the last trip Edward would make to Eilean Munde. He brushed the dead branches from the bow of the small boat he'd found shortly after the soldiers left the glen and pulled it from its hiding place near the shore. It was daybreak, and he was ready to finally move on. To where, he didn't know, but he had to leave Glencoe. Too many ghosts.

He waded through a small field of flowers—their dangling purple bells and bright yellow petals too cheerful—and shoved the boat into the water. The short row to the small island was easy with the agreeable current urging him along and without the extra weight of a body or two to slow his progress. He no longer needed the spade he'd fashioned from a sturdy branch and some blackened iron he'd found in the ruins of the smithy farther up the glen. There was no one left to bury.

He drifted to the shore and jumped out, soaking his boots through. The icy water didn't bother him, though, now that he was used to it. He'd been coming to the burial island every day for more than a month, and having cold feet was just part of the routine. He tethered the boat to a wooden spike he'd set upon his first trip here.

He remembered that day clearly. He'd climbed down the brae and spent the daylight hours searching for Cait and the others, the cold wind at his back finding its way into a tear on his sleeve. He had been just about to give up and return to safety when two large Highlanders appeared behind Alt Na Munde, carrying bodies. Edward had hidden behind the dovecote and watched, his nerves pricked, while the men loaded them into a wagon. He couldn't be sure how they would receive him, considering he still wore the scarlet coat of one of the king's soldiers, so he'd stayed safely tucked behind the small stone wall of the dovecote until they started carting the bodies to the shore.

He'd followed them, his footsteps muffled by the squeaking wagon wheels and the crunch of the stones as they made their way down the glen. The Highlanders leaned into the biting wind, wearing the MacDonald tartan, their belted plaids draped around them like cloaks hiding their identities. He skirted behind trees to avoid being seen, but it hadn't mattered since they never glanced back. While they'd loaded their boat, he'd waited patiently on shore until they reached Eilean Munde, then rowed over himself, circumventing their path to get to the other end of the tiny island. He'd hidden in a small structure that must have once been a place of prayer. The icy drizzle had dripped through the holes in the thatch roof and onto the dirt-covered stones, creating a muddy mess at his feet.

The Highlanders had removed the plaids from around their faces, and that was when Edward recognized them as MacIain's sons, John and Alasdair Og. Part of him felt relieved that they had survived the slaughter, but part of him feared their vengeance—should he be discovered—would be vicious.

They'd lifted the bodies out of the wagon and set them gently on the frozen ground. One figure was larger than the other, but both were female, their long white nightshifts flapping angrily in the harsh wind. The brothers drove their picks and shovels into the earth—vigorously at first and then slower as the sun dipped lower in the sky—until they were satisfied that the graves were deep enough.

Edward had crept out of the chapel to get a better view, his gut turning with fear that one of the lasses was Cait. He'd inched closer, dodging behind trees and clumps of bracken until he had a clear view of their pale faces. The larger woman had the mature features of one in her later years and wore a long silver braid, her nightshift stained dark crimson from her neck to knees. The other one was small, too small to be Cait. A child. Edward exhaled in bitter relief.

But then Alasdair Og had lifted the child, her raven hair hanging to his knees as he cradled her. He lowered her body into the ground. Edward swallowed hard, the weight of her death like lead in his stomach. It was Gillian.

He'd disappeared back into the chapel and collapsed in the corner, praying for her soul, hating himself for being one of the king's men and not being able to stop that horrible morning's events.

The next morning, he woke and found a small slab of slate on the west side of the tiny island. In it, he chiseled her name as best as he could, using an old nail he'd plucked out of a broken stool left abandoned in the chapel and the heel of his boot as a hammer.

THE TACKSMAN'S DAUGHTER

But now, upon his final visit to Eilean Munde, there were no more bodies to bury and no more names to mark. This trip to the island was merely a farewell.

"Grant unto them, we beseech Thee, Thy mercy and everlasting peace."

Edward lifted his head to the blue sky, the sun burning bright just above the horizon, its orange glow remaining in his sight long after he turned away. With Cait's family's graves at his feet, he'd said his last prayer for Gillian and all the people he'd met during his short billet in Glencoe who now lay buried on the island.

He would make every one of the soldiers pay. Especially his brother. He wasn't sure how, but he would do it. They would undoubtedly find each other at some point, and Edward would be damned if he'd let that sorry cur strike first.

Out of the corner of his eye, he noticed a pale blue form appear in front of the sun, slowly growing larger each second. He blinked to focus, but dark red spots remained blocking his vision. He instinctively reached for his dagger, but his hand landed on the empty strap that used to hold it there.

The blue grew sharper and took on the form of a woman, her dark hair in a long plait over one shoulder. He blinked twice, three times. His heart thundered in his chest. Cait?

She inched closer, a blade in one hand, a glint of light flashing as she edged towards him. She looked almost as she had in the dream he'd had over and over since it all happened. But something was different. He cursed the spots before his eyes and squinted, straining to see her clearly.

The figure froze. Her face came into focus. His chest burned. It was Cait, a sadness in her eyes that hadn't been there before. Long black wisps of loose hair from her plait floated in the breeze around her head like a wild halo.

The bubble of despair that had lived inside him for more than a month burst. He tentatively reached out for her, his hand shaking.

She clutched the knife tighter, pointing it directly at his chest.

Cait stilled, glaring at him as if she'd never seen him before.

"Cait? What is it?" Edward asked, afraid of her answer.

Her fingers readjusted their grip, her words barely louder than a whisper. "'Tis hard to look at ye wearing the scarlet coat of a traitor."

"I have not betrayed you, Cait. I tried . . . I did everything I could . . ." He said nothing further, unconvinced she wasn't a simulacrum formed by his cruel imagination. As he stared at the blade in her hand, the steady thumping of his heart thundered in his chest with each passing second. He was ready for whatever she would do. He supposed he deserved a knife through the heart.

A tear slid down her cheek. "Everyone's gone."

"I tried, Cait. But there was only one of me and an army of them. I had no chance."

Her lips tightened, but her expression remained stoic.

"And when I saw Alt Na Munde go up in flames, I thought . . . I thought the worst." His throat burned at the memory of the roof ablaze, sparks flying high above into the angry blizzard. "I—" His voice broke off, and he cleared his throat. "I searched for you. I never stopped. I came here every day, burying bodies." His chest ached as he remembered the people he'd supped with. Entire families he'd grown to know. "There were so many. And every evening, I left thankful that I had not yet found yours."

She lowered her hand, her blade loosely held at her side. "My parents?"

He nodded slowly. "But John and Alasdair Og buried your sister."

Her chin trembled, and the wind tossed about a few wayward strands of her hair.

He took a deep breath. "I fashioned a shovel to dig the graves and marked them—"

"So *you* were the one who engraved her name on her throuch?" She brushed away the hair that had blown across her cheek.

"And your parents' as well. Some of the others too. MacIain. The ones whose names I knew." Edward fought the need to pull her close, to hold her in his arms again.

"Lilas?" she asked, taking a step closer.

He nodded.

"Taran?"

He shook his head. "But that doesn't mean he's not . . ."

She dropped her knife and fell into his arms, her head pressed against his chest and her hands tightly gripping the back of his coat. He ran his fingers over the folds at her waist. The blue wool was rough and thick and real between his fingertips. A light flutter of her skirts swept across his boots at the ankles, and his breath slowed. She was no ghost. Nor a vision.

He rested his cheek on top of her head, rocking her gently in his arms, her tears now falling freely. He held her tight, praying this meant she'd forgiven him for wearing the red coat of a king's soldier, for being a part of something that stole her family away from her. Her shoulders quaked with each sob, her grip eventually loosening as the moments passed. He could have held her like that forever, but she pulled away.

THE TACKSMAN'S DAUGHTER

She wiped the tears from her cheeks and faced the chapel. "Ye can come out now, Davina. 'Tis safe," she yelled half-heartedly.

Relief washed over him as Davina emerged from the chapel with her son at her side, her steps slow and measured. He understood her wariness. Wearing the bedraggled uniform of a soldier and an unkempt beard, he probably looked like the beast she imagined him to be.

"'Tis Edward. He's alone." Cait turned back to face him and spoke softly. "Where are the others? Yer regiment?"

"I'm afraid I know not. But they're no longer here in Glencoe. I saw them leave shortly after . . . that day."

"And ye didn't go with them?"

He shook his head. "I couldn't. I wouldn't."

Her brow crinkled in question.

"I'm a deserter. A traitor, if you will."

Davina joined them, and he told them how he watched Leftenant Lindsay shoot MacIain in the back of his head while he pulled on his trews and offered them a farewell drink. How he tried to stop the soldiers from carrying out their orders. And how he ran to her parents' cottage to find it aflame. "By the time I got there, there was nothing I could do."

He reached for Cait's hand, and she allowed it. Her skin was cold and dry but soft under his calloused palms. "I almost forgot." He reached into his coat, pulled out her mother's stone, and handed it to her.

She gasped, then brought her hand to her lips. "Her sapphire."

He nodded. "I thought you might want it."

Her bottom lip began to tremble. "I . . ."

Her tears came quickly. He took the chance and pulled her close, his chin resting on top of her head, her face buried in his neck. She shook as he held her, one hand clutching the stone and the other resting on his chest. He wanted her to stay wrapped in his arms for as long as she needed, but the one thing they didn't have was time. "I cannot promise that there aren't other soldiers nearby searching for survivors or for me, so we need to leave." He held her at arm's length to study her face. Glencoe was her home. The only one she'd ever known, so he understood he was asking a lot of her. "Will you come, lass?"

She glanced down at her sister and parents' graves, then nodded solemnly.

"I'll bring you back when 'tis safe." His heart sank as she broke from his grip.

"Safe," she repeated as if saying it would make it possible, make it happen.

Davina touched his sleeve to get his attention, her son clutching her skirts. "We can go to Glenorchy."

He turned to Cait. "Is that what you wish?"

She nodded tentatively.

Davina lifted Sawney onto her hip. "My uncle is there, and he needs to be told what has happened."

He probably already knew. In the time since the massacre, those who'd escaped must have spread word of the events that had unfolded.

"Her uncle is the Earl of Breadalbane," Cait offered, staring at her mother's treasured sapphire. "He should know what Glenlyon has done."

Edward jerked back. Had he heard her right? "You wish to report the crimes of Robert *Campbell* to John *Campbell?*"

Davina waved her hand in an airy gesture. "Aye, but he's nae a friend to Glenlyon. Ever since he shamed himself by becoming a drunk and a debtor, he's fallen out of favour with my uncle. Breadalbane finds him an embarrassment to the clan. I heard him say so myself when I saw him last in December."

He shook his head with doubt. "I'll take you there, but don't expect him to react as you wish. Your uncle is likely embroiled in the mess."

"Why would ye say that?" Davina asked, incredulous.

"Because the orders would've had to go through several hands before they arrived in Glenlyon's. And they just might've gone through Breadalbane's." Although he had no proof that Breadalbane was involved, he suspected there was a lot more to the machinations behind the massacre than any of them knew. "Your complaints may fall on deaf ears."

Cait turned to Davina. "Do ye think yer uncle could be behind it?"

Davina balked. "He wants nothing to do with anything that old bawheid Glenlyon is involved in. I promise ye that."

"The truth is, we have nowhere else to go. If he doesn't listen, at least we'll have a roof over our heads until we figure out what to do," Cait said assuredly, tucking the stone inside her bodice.

"Very well," he agreed hesitantly.

He led them back to the chapel to gather their meager belongings and spotted Cait's knife in the grass. He bent to pick it up, but she snatched it first.

She spun it once between her fingers, then stuck it in its sheath in her stocking. In a low voice full of regret, she said, "Ye should know I lost the dirk ye gave me."

His dagger. He'd given them his dagger and pistol that night for protection. Both of which would not have saved them from burning alive inside Alt Na Munde. He remembered Alexander asking where his weapons were, why he was unarmed.

It was a strange confession to hear from her. After all that had happened, all that he had done—or not done—she thought he'd care about his blade? He pressed her palm to his lips, finding that safer than trying to say all that he couldn't. For the first time, he noticed a dark red scar bisecting her palm. He traced his finger over it. "What happened?"

She withdrew her hand immediately and closed it into a fist. "English soldiers. 'Tis an old wound."

Her reticence told him not to press the issue further, but now he understood her fear and suspicion when he and his regiment arrived in Glencoe. Guilt engulfed his chest. She'd been right.

They walked in silence down the slope to their boats and chose to take his back since it was large enough to fit all four of them inside. They settled in, and he jabbed one oar into the rocky bottom, then pushed away from the island.

"There are a couple of horses that graze along the river farther up the glen that I might be able to gather," he said. "It shouldn't take more than a few days' ride from here, barring any unforeseen mishaps."

"Is it safe?" Cait asked, her head tilted to the side in question.

He tugged hard on the oars, his coat snug on his biceps and back. "Well, we'll follow the river east through the glen to avoid any mountainous passes, so—"

"I mean, is it safe for *you?*"

He shrugged, then answered between strokes. "As long as I am not caught."

It was as simple an answer as it was true. What else could he say? If they stayed out of sight of the regiments, especially his brother's, he would be fine. If not, then he would meet his fate on a gibbet.

Cait, Davina, and Sawney sat by the river while Edward tried to tease the horses into his grasp. They clearly belonged to someone in the glen who had not returned to claim them. Edward had watched them feed on the spring grass over the past few weeks, knowing he would one day ride one of them out of Glencoe to someplace where he wouldn't be recognized. He couldn't head south to his home in England because the army would undoubtedly search for him there first, and he couldn't head north to Fort William out of fear the soldiers bunking at the garrison would turn him in. If he headed east, he'd have to travel through large towns where his brother would surely have soldiers ready to pounce the moment they spotted him.

He caught the smaller of the two horses—a garron—rather quickly, his piebald coat still thick from winter, and led him to Davina. The stallion was a bit less willing.

Edward clicked his tongue while edging closer to the huge bay. Over and over, he got close enough to lead him by the neck, but the horse jolted out of his grasp. By the time he caught the stallion, the sun hovered high above in the cloudless sky.

He led the bay by his crest to the women, then filled his flask with fresh water from the river and passed it to each of them. "Not as good as whisky, but it will do."

Cait smiled at him, and he instantly warmed. Would they ever return to what they had? Or at least what they almost had?

He took a quick sip, then tucked it back into his coat. "I suppose we can now add horse theft to my treason charge."

Davina brushed something out of Sawneys hair. "Dinnae fash. 'Tisnae stealing. We're kin to the MacDonalds. Yer fears should flit away like dandelion seeds in a strong breeze." She wriggled her fingers in the air, her gaze still fixed on her son.

But that offered him no comfort. The ghost of a coarse rope remained circling his throat.

"Right now, looking as bedraggled as ye are, ye appear the horse thief. But we're with ye, so . . ." Cait shrugged one shoulder in nonchalance.

"I hope you're more convincing with my executioner," he said.

She gripped the mane of the huge bay firmly with one hand and stroked its muzzle with the other, then smiled. "If I'm not, then I hope ye can run fast."

He laughed. The sound of it, the feel of it, startled him. It had been such a long time since he felt anything but anger and disgust. He turned to Davina. "Can you ride without a harness?"

Davina shot him a nervous glance. "I dinnae think I can manage it safely with Sawney in my lap."

"I can take Sawney," he offered. He had planned to ride with Cait, two on each horse, but this would work too. "You and Cait can ride together."

"I'd like to keep the laddie with me." She nudged her chin at the stallion. "That's MacIain's horse. A bit unruly, that one."

He helped Cait up on the smaller horse first, then hoisted Davina behind her. Cait patted the garron's neck gently, and his piebald head bowed in submission as if she'd ridden him a thousand times.

"He seems fond of you," he said.

"He's quite gentle, but I dinnae know his name." She ran her hand over his crest, her gaze averted. "He belongs to Angus MacDonald, MacIain's other tacksman."

Edward's chest tightened. In the short time he'd billeted in Glencoe, he learned there were only two men elevated to that status—one of them Cait's father.

THE TACKSMAN'S DAUGHTER

Edward lifted Sawney, wedging him between his mother and Cait, then grabbed a handful of the stallion's mane just above his withers and swung himself onto his back. The horse danced nervously in place. "And do you know this one's name?"

"Och. That's *Cuthach.*"

"*Cuthach?* Fury?" The horse jerked his neck back twice in disagreement to Edward's firm grip.

Cait shrugged. "He earned that name, mind ye. But you'll find that out yerself soon enough."

Chapter 19

Alexander had scoured every crevice, every copse of trees from Glencoe to Fort William. He'd asked every ratty Scot along the way if they had seen any stray English soldiers, had even shown them the picture of his brother that Jameson had sketched for him, but not a single soul knew anything. No one had spotted his brother or the other two traitors—all three officers in service to the king.

Two soldiers in his regiment—Francis Farquhar and Gilbert Kennedy—needed to be caught and brought to justice. But not simply because they'd snapped their swords, but because they would prove the perfect trophies to present to King William, who would no doubt applaud Alexander's valiant efforts and loyalty. He didn't care if they were hanged or set free as long as the king rewarded him for their capture and dropped his notion of attainder.

As for Edward, that was personal. He wouldn't mind if Edward was punished for his self-righteous ways and found his head and limbs on the end of a pike. It would serve him right. His demise would put an end to Father's devotion to his bastard, who thought himself better than his noble counterparts.

"Do you wish for us to search further, Leftenant?" Private Mulliken asked, standing in front of Alexander's desk at the garrison, the sketches of all three deserters' faces in his grasp.

Alexander leaned closer in his chair. "Have you heard me say otherwise?" Why was it that every soldier serving under him proved a simpleton?

"No, sir." Mulliken turned to leave and dropped the sketches in the process, sending them floating about the room in every direction. He scrambled to pick them up and partially tore one when it got stuck under the corner of the desk.

THE TACKSMAN'S DAUGHTER

Alexander took a deep breath to steady his nerves and control his anger. "Leave my sight."

"Of course, sir." Mulliken bowed as he shut the door behind him.

It had been two months since the attack. Where could they have gone? Were they traveling together? As far as Alexander knew, none of them had guns, swords, or daggers, so if they were approached by troops, they would not be able to sufficiently defend themselves. That was good. But he couldn't be sure that the local villagers wouldn't arm them—especially if they were Jacobite clansmen—in support of their refusal to attack the MacDonalds. Even then, they might have the chance to fire a shot or engage in some combat, but it shouldn't cost Alexander more than a few casualties in his regiment.

A knock on the door pulled him out of his reverie.

"Enter!"

Two blue eyes partially covered by a mop of brown curls peeked around the door.

"What is it?"

A lad with barely a hair on his chin stepped inside, a messenger bag hanging over his shoulder. "A letter, sir. The sentinel at the top of the stairs directed me here." He nervously shuffled his feet.

"You may approach."

The boy advanced cautiously and handed him a sealed letter. It was not the orders Alexander was waiting for from Major Duncanson. He could tell by the size of the small red seal on the back. It was from his mother. "That will do."

The messenger paused, his mouth working nervously.

"Is there something else?" Alexander asked impatiently.

The lad stuck out his hand, palm up, and Alexander swatted it away. "How dare you come in here like a beggar."

"I was only hoping for a penny, sir," he whimpered.

"You and everyone else. Now leave!"

The lad scooted out the door, and Alexander slammed it behind him. Money. Everyone wanted it. Everyone wanted *his*. He had no doubt his mother had written to tell him that she had not received the stipend he'd promised to send her from his pay. The truth was, she hadn't received it because he hadn't sent it. He couldn't understand how she was unable to make do with his father's fortune, however diminished it was. The king had imposed exorbitant fines on them when he was sent to the Tower, but surely what was left over had to be enough to run a household and maintain the servants. Besides, he needed his money to pay for the occasional whore or bottle of Claret.

He tossed the letter on his desk and felt for the small pouch of sterling tucked inside his coat. Six shillings, three pence. Enough to entertain him for a while. He moved in front of the looking glass and studied his reflection. He could use a shave and perhaps have his hair trimmed. A good bath was in order now that the weather had started to warm up. There was a bawdy house just outside the garrison in Maryburgh that offered those services in addition to more pleasurable ones.

He pressed down his coat, which was starting to look more ruddy-brown than red, then straightened his cuffs and collar, both of which needed some mending and a good washing as well. The day he could turn all of it into a heap of ashes couldn't come soon enough. But for now, his frayed grey cuffs and faded coat gave him the look of a well-seasoned soldier and not a nobleman with riches to spare, just the impression he wanted to make. Perfect for where he was going.

"Caroline is busy. But I have a new girl I think ye might like." Sterling Struana—as all her customers referred to her—spoke in a Lowland accent much like his soldiers from Edinburgh.

She called over a young lass with blonde hair and dimples, who wore a green glass bauble around her neck and a faded gown that must have been golden at one point but was now the colour of pale butter. "This is Lorna."

"Yer an officer, right?" Lorna's eye lit up as she spotted his waist sash and the gold lace on his coat cuffs and vest. He could almost see her counting the coin that came along with that distinction. Another one with her hands already in his pockets.

"How astute you are."

She cuddled up to him, her head tilted in a highly practiced, coquettish manner. She was attractive enough with a sweet smile, but at the moment he had a taste for someone a little less kittenish. He turned back to the madam of the brothel. "I'd like a petite brunette this time. A bit of a tiger, if you will." He couldn't stop thinking about that Scottish whore with whom his brother kept company. One who looked like her might do.

Lorna's mouth turned down in a pout. "But I can please ye any way ye wish. I'm nae timid like some of the other lasses."

That could come in handy perhaps another time, but now he had other ideas. "I will most definitely keep that in mind, Lorna."

Sterling Struana dismissed her immediately. Tapping her top lip with her forefinger, she scanned the room. The boot-shaped mole situated in the outer corner of her eye crinkled into the shape of a heart when she squinted. "Wait here. I think I have the perfect lass for ye."

THE TACKSMAN'S DAUGHTER

Alexander studied the crowd. Most of the women were already entertaining men, their breasts exposed and skirts hitched up to their knees. He recognized one of the men as Corporal Lyon, a thick-middled officer in his late thirties with a ring of brown hair starting at one ear and ending at the other. He was wedged between two buxom whores, his hands roughly gripping each of their arses.

A diminutive girl with long brown tresses approached with Struana, a defiant smirk on her face that excited Alexander.

"I'm Wynda," she said, her hands resting lazily on her hips. "If 'tis swiving ye want, then—"

"She's a bit pricier than the other lasses," Struana interjected.

Of course she is. He liked her saucy nature, though. Her body was hard and tight, and she looked like she would give him a good fight if he provoked her enough.

Struana draped her arm around Wynda. "For a bob and two ye can have her for one hour."

It was then that he realized why her customers called her Sterling Struana. She was an expert at prying the sterling from men's pockets. "You are not from Stirling, are you?"

She shook her head. "Edinburgh."

"Just as I thought." If he wasn't in need of a good release, he'd walk away. "I will give you a shilling and not a penny more."

Struana seemed to consider his offer. "A bob and two. But I'll get ye that bath and shave ye asked for."

This whore had better be good. He turned his back to both of them and extracted a shilling and two pennies from his pouch. He dropped the coins in Struana's outstretched palm, then climbed the stairs with Wynda.

"Ye never told me yer name," she said, her hand gripping the door handle.

"'Tis . . . Edward."

"Unbind me or I'll scream!"

He had Wynda's hands tied behind her back with her hair ribbon. Her chest and face were pressed against the mattress. Her legs kicked helplessly as he stood behind her, his fingers probing between her tensed cheeks. Tiny drops of water smelling of lavender dripped from his newly washed hair onto her buttocks. "You need to be taught a lesson," he said calmly.

When he found what he was looking for, she wriggled and bucked under his grip. "This was nae part of the deal," she cried, her words muffled by the bedclothes and mattress. "There are other lasses who will agree to this!"

"A virgin, are you?" He liked that. And he liked the occasional well-landed kick that brought him a little pain. "If you hold still it will not hurt as much."

"Ye mangy bugger!" She bucked, then emitted a brief whelp, her mouth remaining agape long after the sound had died.

Immediately, he lost himself in memories, images, anger. All the times Edward had bested him with women, in battle, with Father. But most of all, with Berenice. He had no idea of how much time had passed when he finally heard the whore speak.

"Please stop." Wynda's plea emerged as a whimper, breathy and small, urging him out of his trance.

"You should have never chosen my brother." He twisted his hand in her hair, then wrapped it around his wrist and pulled. "As punishment, you will do as I wish."

"What are ye saying? Yer brother?" Tears streaked their way down her cheeks and onto the bed.

With one final push, he collapsed on top of her, his limbs weak and filled with relief. After a few moments he rolled to the side and slid on his breeches. Wynda made no effort to move.

He tugged his shirt over his head while she lay inert like a slender bundle of wheat, her expressionless brown eyes blinking slowly.

He adjusted the lace at his throat and buttoned his coat. "You played your part well. This is for you." He tossed a penny on the bed, and it landed just in front of her nose.

He waited for her to thank him, but she didn't. Everyone was ungrateful these days. Even Scottish whores.

He leaned over her to untie her hands. Her arms flopped to her sides, but she didn't move. He dropped her yellow hair ribbon in a neat little pile beside her. "Much obliged for the bath and shave."

He shook his head at her unwillingness to acknowledge his departure. Stubborn. He turned the doorknob and her warbling voice followed him out. "I'll not forget this, Edward."

Alexander returned to the garrison just after nightfall. He set the torch in the sconce by the door, then plopped onto his chair behind his desk, inhaling the scent of lavender yet on his skin. *What a night.*

The moon slid from behind a cloud and cast a ribbon of blue light across his desk, illuminating his mother's letter. As much as he didn't care to read it, he knew he would have to sooner or later, so he ripped open the seal and held it up to the moonlight.

My Dearest Alexander,

THE TACKSMAN'S DAUGHTER

Circumstances here are becoming dire by the moment. Word has come from court that the Earl of Manchester has been openly expressing interest in our properties to the Earl of Portland. The nerve of that man! I am sure you are aware of the breadth of affection that the king has for Portland. The two are practically inseparable, which leads me to believe that Portland has conveyed Manchester's desires for our landholdings and estates to His Majesty.

To make matters worse, the king has not replied to any of my pleas for leniency. It has been three months since I sent the last letter begging for his mercy, and I have heretofore received no correspondence. I worry that Manchester's push for our property will inspire the king to attaint and leave us as paupers.

I will do my part and continue to write to the king to try to instill us in his good graces. I will also run our estates as best I can using the mere pittance I have been left with since your father's imprisonment. But it is your duty to form alliances with those who can help our cause. Surely, you have not squandered your time in the king's service, engaging in debauchery and dishonour, or have you? 'Tis time you change your ways and prove yourself worthy of your titles and inheritance. Remember, I am not the only one whose livelihood lies in peril. You have a great deal to lose as well. So, I am appealing to the selfishness that I know pervades your heart. If you care nothing for me, I know you will do what you must to at least save yourself.

I have yet to receive the funds you promised.

Your most devoted mother,

Elizabeth

Could she not spare the barbs in a single letter?

At least this time she was careful not to mention Father's support for King James. After all, he and his mother had been denying it since the rumours leaked out, and putting it in writing was a dangerous mistake. Of course, they weren't exactly rumours, but until now, there was little proof except for that single intercepted letter and one drunken night when his father had spoken of his Jacobite allegiance a little too loudly at a tavern in York.

Alexander folded up the letter and shoved it into his coat. He had to find Edward and the two other deserters soon.

Chapter 20

Cait stretched her back and legs, her muscles sore and pinched from three days of riding. They had crossed through Rannoch Moor, a boggy barren area that offered little to no shelter from the early spring winds, then camped beside the River Orchy, which would eventually lead them to Kilchurn Castle. A sudden chill ran up her spine. They were now on Campbell lands.

On the grassy bank, Edward crouched to start a fire with little Sawney by his side. "If you take two flint rocks like these and strike them together, you can make a fire. Watch." He scraped the stones repeatedly, holding them close to a small pile of dry branches, and finally, they caught. Sawney's mouth popped open in wonder, his big brown eyes wide and smiling.

This man in his red coat had saved her mother's sapphire. He'd etched her family's names in stone. He'd taken her, Davina, and Sawney into his care, offering them his protection. He'd given up his comforts—his warm wool coat for them to sleep under—while he froze each night on the cold side of the fire. Everything he did was unselfish and from his heart, and it made her own heart ache.

None of it made sense. He was an Englishman, and unfortunately, she was plenty aware of what they were capable of.

He pierced three trout with sharp sticks and placed them over the fire, then held his flask to Sawney's lips, helping him tilt it up, a small trail of water dripping down his chin.

Cait and Davina finished hobbling the horses, using pieces of their petticoats they had torn into strips. The horses didn't seem to mind it. Angus and MacIain had probably hobbled them on their journeys when they traveled with her father to collect the rents over the years.

The four of them sat around the fire, watching the horses graze. Sawney nestled between Edward's knees, and Cait and Davina huddled together under his coat. A thin plume of smoke rose from the flames, then danced wildly with the breeze.

"What do ye plan to do when we arrive at Kilchurn, Edward?" Cait asked.

"Shortly before, I'll need to leave you two to enter on your own." Edward turned the fish over the fire. The juicy drips popped and sizzled as they landed in the flames. "I'm an outlaw. If I were seen, my fate wouldn't be any better than this fish's."

Davina shivered. "My uncle will be sympathetic to your—"

"Sympathetic?" he asked, one eyebrow arched with skepticism. Almost hidden by his shaggy beard, his mouth curled into a wry smile.

She nodded half-heartedly.

He shook his head and laughed. "At best, Breadalbane has a reputation for being . . . unpredictable."

Cait knew what he really meant but was hesitant to say in front of Davina. Her uncle was not known to be the most scrupulous man. Cait's father had told her that Breadalbane had stolen money bestowed upon him by the government that was supposed to be given to several Highland chiefs in return for their promise not to rebel against King William. So, if Edward was truly wanted, there was likely a reward for his capture, and Breadalbane would certainly be tempted to claim it—even if his own niece begged him not to.

The bushes behind them rustled, and Cait snatched her *sgian dubh,* her heart pounding. Edward held up a hand of caution. They listened to the silence for a moment, Cait ready for a wolf or boar to burst forth from the trees. Edward stood slowly, his body blocking Cait, Davina, and Sawney from whatever was in approach. He reached back, his hand groping the air in her direction. Cait slipped him her knife, her heart hammering steadily in her chest.

She instantly felt helpless without its smooth handle in her grip. If it was a beast of any kind, she could strike it square in its heart with one quick toss of her blade.

Edward took a cautious step and waited. One of the fish fell into the fire, the sizzling and spitting alarmingly loud.

The bushes to their left shook, and Cait stood, hoisting Davina and Sawney up with her. They needed to be ready to run.

Out of the darkness, two men emerged still partially shaded, blades in their hands. The muscles in the back of Edward's neck flexed. "Who goes there?"

One of the men, draped in the dull green plaid, grey breeks, and yellow hose of a soldier, inched closer.

Cait held her breath. Could they be there to turn him in for desertion? She wished she hadn't surrendered her knife.

As the man approached, the firelight flickered over the features of his face, his hazel eyes and red beard now visible. She recognized him from Glencoe as one of the officers Edward often played cards with, but they'd never been properly introduced.

Edward straightened, his voice hopeful. "Farquhar, is that you?"

"Aye." The man raised his brow in question. "Sergeant Gage?"

The other man, also a foot soldier, moved into the moonlight, his face haggard and covered with a layer of grime. He sheathed his blade, then glanced behind Edward at Cait and Davina and smiled, his white teeth a stark contrast to his filthy skin. "Always the lucky one with the lassies, Sergeant, aye?"

Edward laughed, and Cait's shoulders loosened, but she refused to let her guard down.

Farquhar stuck his knife into the base of the flames and flicked the trout out of the embers. "Ye almost lost your supper. Would you happen to have a spare fish for two deserters?"

―――――― ⁘ ――――――

Farquhar and Kennedy recounted how they'd broken their swords, rendering them useless the morning they were told to turn on their hosts. They'd been seen by a young private who was pissing next to the brewhouse just after the orders were given, but at the time, they didn't care. They had only minutes before they were to order their men to attack and had to act quickly.

"We couldn't do it. We had supped with Angus MacDonald that night, and I was expected to run him through six hours later?" Kennedy grunted with loathing, then wiped a trail of juice running down his chin with the back of his wrist.

Cait shivered from the memory. She hadn't considered other soldiers refused to act. "Who gave ye the orders?"

Kennedy briskly scratched the crown of his scraggly head, bits of grass and twigs sprinkled throughout. "Glenlyon, 'twas. We were billeted in Inverrigan not a stone's throw from Angus's home, where Glenlyon was resting his head at night."

She knew it. This was not what Edward had told her it was—an order from someone much higher up in the chain of command. This was Campbell's doing.

THE TACKSMAN'S DAUGHTER

As if Edward could see her blood boiling, he set his hand gently on her forearm. "He was doing as he was told. His orders came from Major Duncanson."

Cait pulled her arm away. "Did ye see those orders yerself, then?"

Edward pressed his lips together in a clear effort to stay calm. "I did not, but I was told that they came from him."

"And who told ye such a tale?" Cait asked, trying hard to keep her voice level, but it was impossible. With Sawney cradled asleep in her lap, Davina shot her an annoyed look.

He hesitated, and she knew whatever he was going to say was going to help her prove her point. "My brother."

"Well, well," she said, renewed with vigor. "Yer dear brother. The same conniving houghmegander who has placed yer head on a platter. The one who—"

"So yer brother reported ye?" Kennedy shook his head in disgust. "I cannae say I'm surprised."

"I made it clear I wanted no part of it, and then he saw me without my weapons. His plan is to have me hanged." He said it calmly and plainly, as if he were explaining the process of gutting a rabbit. He swept his hand out at their campsite. "So here we are."

"Well, I didn't think ye were sitting here in the dark with two bonnie lassies because the army gave ye leave to do as ye pleased," Farquhar said, wiping his hands on his breeks.

Edward slipped a bite of fish into his mouth then licked his fingers. "Well then, now that we know we all have a price on our heads, what are we going to do about it?"

They set out the next morning for Kilchurn Castle, Farquhar and Kennedy on foot behind them. A heavy mist hung low and damp, hiding drooping tree branches and rocky obstructions, forcing them to move at a slow pace. Edward rode in front, now in complete control over *Cuthach*, who'd lived up to his name and tried to throw him off the first day.

Upon their approach to Dalmally, a small village with a parish kirk just off the river, they decided that the men would stay back and set up camp while Cait and Davina continued on the short ride to the castle. That way, anyone who saw their horse in approach would assume she and Davina were alone, quelling any air of suspicion. And if word *had* reached Glenorchy that the army was in search of three traitors or if Argyll's regiment was nearby, Cait could ride out to alert them in time, and then they could escape on one of the footpaths leading south or east.

She and Davina waited patiently while the sure-footed but senseless garron they rode paused to consider how he was going to get around a felled trunk. When he turned his head back to suggest he needed help, Cait tugged his mane to the left to guide him along. "Ye think yer uncle will punish Glenlyon?"

Davina's answer came after a slight hesitation. "When I tell him what happened, he'll feel compassion for us."

Breadalbane compassionate? That didn't sound like the Breadalbane she'd heard about. The only compassion the man probably ever had was for his henchman, who could be trusted to report if one of his servants took an extra piece of bread from his stores. Greed was what defined the man—certainly not compassion.

The sun burned brighter, warming Cait's shoulders, and the mist started to pull away as if urging them onward. The horse snorted at the change in weather, then lifted his head with confidence at the clear path ahead of him. Cait could now see the arcs and slopes of the river, its gentle waterfalls curving over smooth rocks into deep pools framed by weeds and bracken.

Behind her, tiny fingers played with her hair, tugging and twirling, something she had learned over the past four days that Sawney did to soothe himself enough to fall asleep. He lay cuddled between her and his mother, his warm, chubby body pressed against the small of Cait's back.

Cait pictured the two of them nestled together behind her and suddenly felt overcome with sadness. Everyone she had ever loved was dead. She was alone—without a home, without a family. She had never traveled farther than Kinlochbeg—a place she had no desire to return to—and suddenly felt helpless, a feeling she rarely experienced. She was an outsider, a vagabond. She blinked away the tears that threatened to fall.

"There 'tis!" Davina said in an excited whisper, Sawney snoring peacefully in her lap.

Kilchurn Castle loomed at the end of a promontory that overlooked a great loch. Smoke rose into the cloudless sky from chimneys that peeked over the trees like jagged teeth, and a bevy of workers surrounded the north end.

"Why is it so busy?" Cait asked. So many people meant far too many eyes. She sank, relieved that the men stayed back.

"My uncle is adding barracks."

"For soldiers?"

"I believe so. He wishes to convert it into a garrison. 'Twas even busier in December when I lodged here on my way to Glencoe."

There was little doubt that the coin he kept from the chiefs was paying for his expansion. "But the king has Inverlochy. I mean Fort William," Cait corrected herself.

"Aye, but that's a *wooden* garrison. My uncle thinks the king will choose Kilchurn as the new stronghold for the Highlands."

So he was looking to draw favour from the king. And likely some sort of monetary compensation too. "Are we going to be welcome here, Davina?"

"Of course!"

"Well . . . I remember ye told me that yer uncle threatened to flog ye for keeping Sawney's father's name a secret."

"Aye. But that was two years past." She said it nonchalantly, but Cait remembered the stories others had told about how Davina cried and begged her uncle to spare her the public embarrassment. "He's warmed to me since then."

Cait wished she could see Davina's face, to read what she was really thinking. "He sent ye away."

"'Tisnae as if he banished me. I was living at Kilchurn when it happened. He merely sent me back to my parents when 'twas obvious I was with child."

"And then they turned ye away nae a year later. Is that nae why ye came to Glencoe? To be with yer mother's kin?"

"What are ye getting at, Cait?" Davina's tone had hardened. She shifted, her hips sliding farther onto the horse's rump, the pressure of Sawney's weight lessening on Cait's back.

The spot between Cait's shoulder blades tingled. "I'm only saying that there's a good chance we willnae be welcome here."

Chapter 21

They left the horses in the care of the stable boy and were greeted by a guard posted at the front gate. After a brief explanation of who Davina was, he let them pass. The castle had changed quite a bit since she'd left it months earlier. What was once only a knee-high wall on the north end was now a structure two storeys high with plenty more room to grow. Her uncle had mentioned once that he planned on housing over two hundred troops in the new section, making it a third the size of Fort William but much stronger, considering its walls were built of stone. It was useless now, though. Davina shook her head at the stone piles and hordes of porters, stonemasons, and carpenters that crowded the small courtyard.

A gentleman Davina didn't recognize, wearing trews made of the Campbell tartan and a matching blue velvet coat, pointed at the stairs with a flourish of his hand. "If ye wish to see the earl, I will escort ye to his apartments."

Davina hiked Sawney higher in her arms and climbed the spiral staircase to the earl's private chambers, Cait trailing behind. Nothing had changed since Davina had been there in December. The same blue, green, and red pastoral tapestries hung on the walls to hide the cracks in the mortar that allowed cold air to seep thorough. Her uncle sat on the far side of the hearth in his favourite chair, hand-carved and covered in gold and green damask, a glass of spirits in his hand—a position she'd seen him in many times before. Lady Glenorchy sat nearby, working a bright orange thread into a needlepoint design in her lap. A rush of heat spread through Davina's chest as the memory of the last time they spoke—or squabbled—swirled angrily in her head. She'd set off for

Glencoe that day in tears, shaking from the obvious contempt they showed for wee Sawney.

"I dinnae recall summoning you, Davina. Have ye forgotten yer place, lass?" Lady Glenorchy was not her aunt and made that perfectly clear each time they saw one another. Davina's mother's half-sister was Breadalbane's first wife and Lady Mary Campbell was his current. The countess often reminded her that she would do well to remember that.

"And I see ye brought yer bastard with ye," Breadalbane said with a sour look.

"His name is Sandaidh, and he's my *son*." Davina pressed him harder to her chest. "I didn't come to quarrel, Uncle. I came to tell ye of a terrible crime that has been committed against Clan Donald of Glencoe."

Her uncle's perfectly coiffed brown periwig hung almost to his elbows, his thin lips turned downwards in disdain. He pinched the bridge of his long straight nose, then picked at something under the fingernail of his little finger, before gesturing indifferently for her to sit.

She moved towards a bench not far from the hearth when Lady Glenorchy stopped her. "Are ye going to introduce the lass, or are we to guess her name?"

She was so bound by their presence, Davina had almost forgotten Cait was with her. "Lord John Campbell, Earl of Breadalbane, and Chief of Glenorchy . . . Lady Glenorchy, Countess of Breadalbane, this is Caitriona Cameron."

Cait offered a quick curtsy, then straightened. Davina noticed her knuckles were white from gripping the folds in her skirt so tightly. Lady Glenorchy nodded at the bench, and they sat.

"If you've come to tell me that the MacDonalds of Glencoe have been punished for their insubordination to the king, I already know," her uncle said, unamused.

"Punished?" That was not the word she would have used. "They were slaughtered, Uncle."

He chuckled. "MacIain was late giving his Oath of Allegiance. His lack of concern for meeting the deadline was a perfect display of his disloyalty. And his people suffered for it." Whatever was stuck under his fingernail seemed to be of great interest to her uncle, as his gaze hadn't moved from it once.

Her chest grew tight. "Dozens of people were killed, many in their beds, some burned. Even children—"

"Dozens? That cannae be." He finished his drink in one pull and leaned forward in his chair, suddenly interested in the conversation. "There are hundreds of MacDonalds in Glencoe."

Davina sensed Cait's agitation and restraint, her knee bobbing up and down rapidly.

"Many more died while hiding from the soldiers in the cold. We were fortunate to survive." She glanced briefly in Cait's direction. "But Cait's sister and parents were not."

Her uncle stood and leaned one graceful arm along the fireplace mantel. "Well, as long as MacIain paid with his life, that is all that matters, I suppose. He's been a thorn in my side for as long as I can remember. Raiding my lands and reiving my cattle."

Inspired, he continued. "Did ye know that he refused to cooperate at our meeting in July? I needed him to help me garner support for William, and he refused! He sat right where you are." He pointed at Cait with a crooked, angry finger. "And then he stormed out, promising to thwart my efforts with the other Highland chiefs. I'm glad he's dead!"

Davina started shaking, and Sawney stirred. She patted his back briskly. "You . . . I . . ." She had to gather her thoughts, but she found it difficult to clear her head of the anger that filled it. "What they did goes against all the rules of Highland hospitality! Did ye know that the soldiers were billeted throughout the glen? They were fed and given MacIain's best whisky and wine. They were entertained each night by pipers and bards. They—"

Cait reached out her hand to stop her, giving her wrist a good squeeze before she spoke, her eyes defiant. "I think he knows, lass. I think he knows."

They settled in a small room which had been a servant's when Davina lived there, no larger than the henhouse at Alt Na Munde and with a similar smell. The three of them lay on a thin pallet, Davina against the wall with Sawney beside her and Cait on his other side. With no hearth and no window, it was like lying underground in a cold coffin.

"I cannae believe he said those things about MacIain." Davina spoke into the dark, mostly to herself but hoping Cait had heard. "He was a good man. Good to his clan and good to those soldiers too."

Cait exhaled a long breath. "Well, apparently there was no love lost between him and yer uncle."

That was certainly true, at least on her uncle's part. "So what do ye think about Uncle's claims that he was nae loyal to the king?"

The little pallet filled with straw crunched when Cait's shoulder lifted in a shrug. "I dinnae know what to think. Could be true."

Davina had heard about support growing in the Highlands for King James to return to the throne and wondered if MacIain was one of his followers, a Jacobite.

"Either way," said Cait, "we should get some rest so we can head out early in the morning."

THE TACKSMAN'S DAUGHTER

Davina stiffened. "We just arrived. Why would we leave?"

Cait turned on her side to face her. "First, I didn't get that feeling of compassion that ye mentioned from yer uncle nor his wife, so I'm thinking they might have our horse ready at the yett by dawn whether we like it or no. And second, judging by the disappointed look on yer uncle's face when ye told him only a few dozen were killed, he willnae punish Glenlyon for his crimes, so our complaints are falling on deaf ears."

That may have been so, but at least her uncle hadn't turned her away. He had even invited them to join them in the dining room for their morning meal the next day. She hadn't had an appetite, however, the strong aromas of the castle food arriving at the table long before the actual food had, sending her stomach into turmoil. But it was nice to have received the invitation nonetheless. Despite Lady Glenorchy's unmasked disdain for her, it was the closest she'd come to feeling like part of a family again. She had Cait and Sawney and her kinsfolk all under the same roof. She couldn't leave. "But we finally have a decent place to sleep."

"Decent?"

Perhaps that wasn't the right choice of word. Davina turned on her side to face Cait and rested her hand on Sawney's round belly. "We need to stay. I cannae let it rain on my wee laddie another night. He needs to be safe and warm and fed properly. Sleeping in bogs and on riverbanks with only a soldier's coat to cover us isnae good for him." Her heart ached at the thought of him shivering at her breast. "Ye understand that, don't ye, Cait?"

"Aye," she whispered. "*You* should stay here with yer bairn. *I'll* leave."

"Ye cannae do that!" she said, shocked. "Ye cannae travel alone. 'Tisnae safe."

"I willnae be alone. I'll be with Edward and the others."

"Have ye gone mad, lass? Ye cannae travel with three men into the woods."

"Are ye suggesting that Edward would be anything but honourable?"

She thought about it. He had done so much for them until now and had never made advances on her—or Cait, as far as she knew. But then again, she wondered if he had and Cait had permitted it. "What about the other two?"

"Do ye really think Edward would allow it? And I can defend myself, ye know."

That she knew, and she didn't want to be reminded of it. Twice in the last month or so, she'd seen Cait holding a bloody knife with only a vague explanation of how the blood had got there. "Where will ye go?"

"To wherever Glenlyon is. If no one else will punish that pawkie Campbell for what he's done, I will."

Davina sighed. There was no point in arguing with her. She wouldn't listen. "I dinnae think I could bear to be apart from ye. Yer like my sister."

Cait said nothing in return, but her hand found Davina's in the dark.

"The arrangements have been made. You will serve Lady Glenorchy and see to her needs, and I will allow yer bastard to stay. At the first sign of trouble from either you or him, I will have ye thrown out of here. Understand?" Breadalbane shoved a hunk of black pudding into his mouth, his eyes boring into Davina as she sat at his table.

Heat flooded her cheeks. She was both grateful and humiliated all at once. "I understand, Uncle."

Lady Glenorchy speared a herring and held it precariously above her plate. "I'll arrange for a nurse for yer bairn, but *you* will care for him when yer no needed. Do ye understand?"

"Aye, milady." Davina didn't dare take a bite of the food on her plate, worried she would have a mouthful the next time they expected her to respond to one of their reprimands or threats. "And I will do my best to keep Sawney out of yer way."

"What ye mean is, out of our *sight,*" Lady Glenorchy said, reaching for a bannock.

"Of course." From the corner of her eye, she saw Cait shake her head slightly in judgement.

Her uncle stared at her over the rim of his pewter mug. "And ye need to stay clear of the labourers. They dinnae need the distraction of a willing lass when there's so much work to be done."

A willing lass? Davina took a deep breath. Her past would forever follow her. It wasn't that she was willing. It was that she was in love. And at the time, she thought he was too. "Of course, Uncle."

He held a mouthful of ale in his inflated cheeks for a few seconds before he swallowed it. He stared at his wife, who was busy chewing, her mouth twitching and nibbling like a rat's. "Are ye planning to take provisions to the kirk today, Wife?"

She finished nipping at her bannock, then dabbed her mouth with her napkin. "I am. The vicar has mentioned need of food for the poor. I thought I'd bring him some turnips and onions and perhaps some—"

"As long as ye dinnae take my wine." Breadalbane flipped an uninterested hand in her direction. "Or my whisky."

She bowed her head in assent, but Davina watched her roll her eyes behind lowered lids.

THE TACKSMAN'S DAUGHTER

Her uncle helped himself to another slice of blood pudding. "Take a few men with ye. The two traitors have recently been spotted nearby. They're likely dangerous." He lifted his index finger in the air. "A man who defies orders lives without honour."

Davina shared a quick glance with Cait. If the men were presumed dangerous, then those searching for them would shoot upon sight and not capture them for a trial.

"They were last seen in Black Mount. Close enough to be concerned," he clarified.

That news was clearly at least a day old. If they only knew how close they really were. At least it sounded as if no one had seen Edward. Yet.

"I'll take some men with me," his wife answered obediently.

He spoke while chewing. "I'll see to it that they're well-armed."

Chapter 22

Cait waited until the castle was still and all its inhabitants were snoring in their chambers. She slipped out of the bed she shared with Sawney and Davina and hurried down to the stables, the sky still dark and sprinkled with stars. When she entered, her sweet little piebald garron turned his head in acknowledgement. She held her finger to her lips. "Wheesht."

The bridles and rope she'd hidden under the straw in the back of his stall were still there with the dirk, pistol, powder horn, and shot she'd stolen earlier from Breadalbane's weapons case in the castle armoury. She fitted her horse with one of the bridles, tossed everything else in a feed sack she found hanging on the wall, then strapped it to her waist with the rope. With her hand steadying the heavy bag as it banged against her thigh with each step, she led her horse out of his stall.

He shook his head as they approached the stable doors, jingling and clanking the tack and breaking the night silence. A stable hand stirred in the loft, and she startled, the thump of his body turning over on his pallet. She held her breath, her hand tight on her horse's reins. She concentrated on the space above, listening for the slightest sound. Confident he was once again asleep, she quietly urged her mount out of the stable and into the courtyard, her heart racing. She had to get to Edward and warn him that word had reached Glenorchy that Farquhar and Kennedy had been spotted in Black Mount.

Two door wards stood at the entrance of the castle, flanking the great wooden gate. Both were armed and wearing sleepy scowls on their faces. Cait inhaled deeply, taking in the cool night air, then feigned the best smile she could muster so early in the morning. Her heart thumped loudly, causing her breath to hitch. She wasn't sure if leaving the castle grounds would require the same sort of attention entering would, but she was about to find out.

"*Beannachd Dhia dhuit.*" She hoped the benevolent greeting would encourage them to let her pass. "Will ye be so kind to open the gate for me?"

The one on the left scratched his crotch with tenacious intent, then stopped abruptly upon realizing he was being observed. Quickly, his hand emerged from under his plaid. "The gates dinnae open before dawn unless the laird commands it."

"I told him last night at supper that I'd be leaving early in the morn. Perhaps he forgot to inform ye two fine gentlemen to open the gate."

The left guard straightened as the other one came to life. "Ye dined with the laird?"

"Aye. With Himself and Lady Glenorchy." She swallowed hard while they scrutinized her from top to bottom. She realized her worn gown—once a faded blue but now approaching grey—wasn't of the quality expected of someone who would have such close contact with a laird. She hoped it wouldn't trigger suspicion.

"What do ye think, Graham? Do we let the mistress pass?"

The right guard, Graham, stepped closer with a knitted brow, his gaze fixed on her bedraggled gown. "We need to inform the laird."

Her stomach tossed. "I wouldn't do that."

Graham walked around her horse, one hand gliding over the black and white spots on his withers and back. "And why is that?"

"Ye obviously haven't heard about the incident at his castle in Perth. Castle Balloch?"

"What incident?" they asked in unison.

Cait struggled to remember the information Davina had told her over the past few months about her uncle, but it only came to her piecemeal. "The laird had told his door wards there the same thing—not to open the gates until dawn or without his permission. Sure enough, one night one of his guests was delivered a message of an urgent nature and had to leave in the wee hours of the morn. The guards argued with the man that they couldn't open the gate, then finally agreed that they would wake the laird to get his consent."

Graham came from around the horse and faced her, his eyes sparked with curiosity. "Did the laird give the command to open it?"

"He gave the command, he did," she said. "But the door wards were both whipped to a hair's breadth of their lives for waking him from a deep slumber."

They shuffled uncomfortably, the left guard now busy scratching his head. "'Tis the truth?"

"Aye. Ye know how Breadalbane can be. He didn't become laird for being soft, mind ye." She had no idea if anything like that had ever happened, but he did have a castle in Perth so there was enough of the truth mixed in to make them believe it. She hoped she got the name of it right.

They seemed to consider what she said, undoubtedly drawing on their own encounters with the tyrant and other infamous tales. Graham rubbed the back of his neck, his gaze flitting back and forth to the tower house where the earl was unquestionably sleeping.

She huffed, her nape prickled with sweat, and started to turn the garron around. "Fine. I'll let the laird know myself, but dinnae say I didn't warn ye."

"Wait," one called after her. She gripped the reins firmly, pausing while they whispered anxiously to each other, her knees growing weaker with every second. Finally, they unbolted the inner door, then the outer, and let her through. She recited a silent prayer of thanks, then started to lead the garron with the reins firmly in her grasp when Graham stopped her. "Wait!"

Her heart rattled in her chest. He plodded over to her, gripping the hilt of the sword strapped to his waist, his expression serious. She assumed he was going to ask her what was in her sack, so her mind scrambled to think of ways to avoid opening it. Hit him with it and run? Faint as a distraction? Flirt and promise all sorts of sordid things if he would just let her pass?

"Here." He bent low and cupped his hands, his fingers intertwined a couple of feet off the ground. He jerked his hands at her legs. He was offering to help her mount her horse. "Go on, then."

She smiled shakily, then stepped into his palms. *"Tapadh leibh."*

She rode the better part of an hour at a leisurely pace so as not to draw attention should anyone be foolish enough to be awake this early. Her shoulders loosened now that she was away from the castle and Breadalbane. She took the path that she'd previously taken with Davina, scattered crofts and bothies partially hidden by trees on both sides, traces of smoke trickling out of their chimneys.

It was still early enough for her to make it to the kirk and say a prayer for her family before any congregants showed. There would be no questions to answer, a sure way to evade telling the truth—or a lie, for that matter.

The sun peeked from behind the ridge when she reached the kirkyard. A sparse number of graves dotted with leaning throuches glowed pink in the low light. She dismounted, and the garron stared at her inquisitively with his big brown eyes. She wondered if he missed his master, Angus MacDonald, the way she missed her family. She combed his white forelock with her fingers. "Ye need a name. What should I call ye?"

THE TACKSMAN'S DAUGHTER

He blinked slowly once, then nudged her hand upwards with his black and white muzzle. He had the solemn expression of an old man who had traveled far and cared for many. "What do ye think of *Cìobair?* Shepherd."

Cìobair lowered his head in acquiescence.

"Ye like it, then. It suits ye." She removed the rope from around her waist and hobbled his legs. "Although sometimes *I* feel like the shepherd and yer one of my lost sheep, ye poor senseless beastie."

She hid her sack of contraband behind a throuch dotted with lichen, the name Wallace MacGregor engraved on it. Should anyone come upon her, she could always claim she had no idea where it came from. She patted *Cìobair's* neck. "Wait for me, aye?"

The nave was dark except for one row of lit candles set on a stone ledge near the entrance. She shivered in the cold, dark space and sat on a timeworn wooden pew in the back. She closed her eyes, her mother's sapphire warm against her skin, and prayed for everyone—her sister and parents, Edward, Davina and Sawney, Taran and his grandda, Lilas, Auntie Meg, and herself. She prayed for every single inhabitant of the land that now lay charred and broken and those who were only visiting when the soldiers took up their swords. She even prayed for Sionn's soul. Whether he was alive or dead, it certainly needed mending.

A scratching noise forced her to turn to her right. A tiny grey mouse edged along the wall, stopping and sniffing along the way, then disappeared into the center of a rolled-up tapestry. It was a cozy little home. Safe and probably warm.

"May I help you, my dear?"

She spun to find a tall thin clergyman standing behind her in a black cassock, his hands folded neatly at his waist.

She stood, flustered. "I was only praying."

He smiled. "Well, then, dinnae let me disturb ye."

He grabbed a candle from the ledge, then glided to the altar, his robes dragging on the floor behind him. He set it beneath a painting of the Blessed Virgin in a blue robe, cradling her bairn in her lap. Her face glowed in the candlelight. He stepped back, his head tilted to the side and lips turned up in a gentle smile. Cait's own heartbeat slowed just watching him. He stood that way, silent and still, for several minutes.

"Reverend?"

He startled out of his trance. She instantly regretted disturbing him. "Och. Forgive me."

"Come here, child." He waved her over, and she joined him, facing the painting. "What do you think? 'Tis lovely, aye?"

It was beautiful. The look of love between mother and child was serene and strong and full of truth. Suddenly, something inside of her broke, and her throat tightened up. She nodded clumsily, then let out a strangled sob, her breath ragged. "Reverend, I—I . . ." Her voice trailed off into tears.

He folded her into his arms and let her cry until she finally settled into a state of surrender, her sobs now mostly silent.

She sniffled and wiped at her nose. "When the village burned . . . Glencoe . . . everything I know burned in the flames."

"Ah. Glencoe." He took a moment before continuing. "Have ye lost yer way, then?"

She blinked away her tears. "My way?"

He nodded, then released her gently. "Have ye forgotten that all the strength ye need is in the Lord's hands? Look to the mercy of God, child."

She hadn't seen much of God lately. Where was He when those soldiers killed her parents or when Gilli died in her arms? Or when Sionn attacked her in the woods? "Aye. I have lost my way."

With his thumb and forefinger, he tipped her chin up and smiled sadly. "Then my heart breaks for ye, for you will never find peace until ye give yerself to the Lord."

"I want to feel at peace, Reverend," she said earnestly.

"Then ye know what ye need to do." He guided her to the door. "St. Conan's Well is but up the road a wee bit. Go there and have a drink. Bathe yer face in it. I think it might help ye settle yer heart and find what yer looking for."

She left the kirk, retrieved her bag, then led *Cìobair* down the road just past a small bend. A narrow trail snaked out of the woods and led to the river. The sound of water rushing and the wind blowing through the leaves put her at ease. She left *Cìobair* to graze on the soft grass at his feet, then meandered through the trees until she found the well. A small stone wall surrounded it on three sides, allowing water to cascade over a ragged lip on the edge. She dipped her hands into the frigid water and splashed it on her face. Rivulets ran down her neck and into her bodice, and she shivered. She pressed her fingers to the spot between her breasts where her mother's sapphire lay safely tucked. Golden plovers whistled to one another cheerily overhead, but she didn't feel happy. She hadn't felt happy in a long time.

The trees shuddered above, whispering to themselves, their new green leaves flipping and twisting in the wind. The morning sunlight shifted left and right between branches. On the opposite riverbank, a fat brown otter rolled back and forth in the grass, grooming his fur. Cait bent over the well and washed her face again with the cold water, this time scrubbing her cheeks with her palms and dousing her sleeves in the process. She waited for the saint's spirit to wash over her, to take away her pain and replace it with something quiet, peaceful. But nothing happened. She sat on the edge of the well and stared up at the canopy of branches, beams of light piercing through the leaves and blinding her. It made her think of Glencoe and the faery pool Gilli liked to go to, disappointed every time she returned having not caught a faery. Cait had joined her at times, watching the orbs of light dance on the leaves and grass, Gilli hopping around, trying to catch one in her palm. Cait almost smiled at the memory.

The crunch of footsteps approached, jolting her out of her reverie. She scanned the trees, but after looking into the light, all she could see were spots before her eyes. She held still, waiting and listening to determine if the footsteps were coming closer. She blinked rapidly, trying to clear away the blindness, then stood, her pulse racing as a dark figure appeared in the distance. It moved closer, so she inched her way around to the other side of the well, her hand fumbling for her *sgian dubh*. "Stay where ye are!"

Suddenly the footsteps stopped, but her pulse still thrummed in her ears.

The figure began moving unsteadily, injured, she thought. Perhaps limping. Her eyes started to clear, and she focused intently on the nearing shape. It inched closer, and she sucked in her breath. "Dear God!"

Chapter 23

"Taran!" It was Cait's voice. The patter of her feet in the grass grew louder as her dark shape approached. Her skirts brushed against his legs as she fell to her knees. She hugged him tightly around his waist. "I thought ye were dead," she cried.

Taran dropped his cane and hugged her back. It felt so good to have someone to hold again, someone to hold him. He didn't know what to say. He'd heard lots of chatter about the killings that day. Everyone who survived had a story to tell about the attack and their escape.

She sighed, then led him to sit. "Is yer grandda here too?"

His throat burned at the thought of the last time he'd felt the grip of Grandda's hand on his. He shook his head. "I dinnae know where Grandda is. The morning of . . . the fires, he woke me from my sleep, and we ran out of Alt Na Munde together. But then something happened, and he let go of my hand. I fell. There were people screaming and shots in the air, and I called out for him, but he probably couldn't hear me through all the others."

She rested her hand on his and gave it a little squeeze. It was warm and soft, and he hoped she'd keep it there for a while. "Then how did ye get here?"

"A giant lifted me off the ground and carried me away. Later, I was told 'twas Big Henderson."

"And he brought ye here?" she asked.

"Nay. He handed me to Rinalda. Ye remember her? A washerwoman at Alt Na Munde?"

"Aye." The bounce of Cait's head shook his shoulder.

THE TACKSMAN'S DAUGHTER

"She was escaping on the footpath that passes by MacIain's croft. Ye know the one?"

"I do."

"We hid in the woods until they said the soldiers left, then walked to Etive to stay with people there."

Her hand pressed his firmly. "Those are Campbell lands, laddie."

He heard the doubt in her voice. "Aye, but when we told them what Glenlyon and his troops did, they were outraged. So they let us stay for a bit."

"Is that so?"

"Och, aye. At first, they didn't believe us, but then ye could hear them gasp and huff in disgust." He felt for a blade of grass, plucked it with his free hand, then stuck it between his teeth. It was cold and sweet and smelled like spring. "Ye sound like Cait, but ye dinnae smell the same."

She laughed and held him at arm's length, her hands tight on his shoulders. "Is that so?"

He leaned into her again to sniff her hair, then inhaled deeper, just to be certain. "Well, ye dinnae smell the way all the women at Alt Na Munde smelled."

She ruffled his hair. "What did we smell like, then?"

"Lavender. And other things too. Lilas smelled like baking bread and lavender."

"That's because the washerwomen used to put wee bits of lavender in the buckwash after they boiled it. But I'm no wearing my own clothes. That's why ye dinnae smell it."

It was one of the things that reminded him of home back on the Isle of Harris. Everyone there smelled the same—sweet and lemony like bog myrtle. But it didn't have anything to do with the wash. It was because they rubbed the leaves on their arms and necks to keep away the midges.

He nodded. Gilli smelled like lavender too. "But ye do still smell like heather honey."

The back of her hand caressed his cheek, and heat crept into his face. He bowed his head. "'Tis the way I remember ye. The way I remember everybody."

"Of course it is, laddie." She pushed his cane back into his hand. For a moment, his heart stopped, afraid she was saying farewell, but then she led him closer to the river and they sat next to one another, their backs against the cold stone wall he'd grown to know very well over the last couple of months, her arm draped over his shoulders.

"I come here a lot when I can sneak away," he said. "'Tis supposed to be a good praying well, but it doesn't work, ye know."

"Well, my prayers were just answered." She kissed the top of his head tenderly.

He knew that she hadn't prayed for him to come traipsing up to her at this very moment, but he liked the kiss just the same. A horse snorted nearby, then shifted in the grass, the clomp of his hooves soft and cushioned.

"What do ye pray for, laddie?" she asked.

Ever since the women at the kirk had told him about the well, he came as often as he could to pray that he'd wake one morning able to see. But after months had passed with no change, he only prayed for his sight to improve—just enough to see the shape of something small, someone's face or a rabbit or faery. It seemed like less to ask of God, so he'd thought he'd try it. "Nothing important."

He plucked another piece of grass for Cait and handed it to her. She took it with a little puff of breath and thanked him between clenched teeth.

"I know what happened to Gilli and to yer Ma and Da." Tears pricked behind his eyes, and he tried to blink them away.

She stiffened beside him. "And how do ye know that?"

"Word travels. Every Sunday, the vicar announces another name or two. Usually MacDonalds, but sometimes others." He remembered the day, the moment, he'd said *Gillian Cameron*. He'd felt as if his heart were cleaved in two. He remembered her soft hair and the way she giggled and how she used to thread her arm through his when they walked amongst crowds in the great hall. He would do anything to have those moments back. "I was going to marry Gilli."

He spit out the grass and leaned into Cait, unable to hold back the tears he'd held for so long. She wrapped her arms around him and pulled him close, her own warm tears raining on his shoulder.

They walked along the river, and Cait let Taran guide the horse by his reins. It made him feel useful again. The people in Dalmally were nice but treated him like he was sickly. "Do ye think I can ride him?"

"He's a good horse, but he doesn't have much sense, ye know." She touched his sleeve gently. "We need to get to Edward first, and then I'll let ye try later. Perhaps on the way back."

His stomach churned, and he was suddenly thirsty. "I'm no going back. I'm staying with you and Edward."

She stopped, and he stopped with her. "Ye need to go back before anyone starts fashing over ye."

"I willnae go."

"We're going to be traveling, laddie. If I have to ride all the way to London to tell the king what Glenlyon has done, so be it."

"I'll go to London with ye. I'll tell him that even Glenlyon's own kin are ashamed of him."

"I appreciate ye wanting to help, but ye need to go back to the people who are caring for ye."

"They're no my kin or even my friends. But you are," he argued, a tingling spreading through his chest. He couldn't go back. They never let him do anything, just sit in one place peeling onions or shelling peas. "I willnae be a bother. And I can help."

"I know how helpful ye are, laddie. Ye were the best spy I ever had." She draped her arm around him, the familiar weight of it somewhat soothing. "But we're going to be traveling far, and yer grandda could be looking for ye. Ye need to stay put in one place so he can find ye."

"He's no coming." He didn't want to cry again in front of Cait, so he squeezed his lids shut and faced the ground, his hair falling over his eyes. It had been more than a month now, and he hadn't found him yet. And the truth was that judging from the piercing screams and the rain of gunshots that morning, he knew it was unlikely Grandda had survived. But he didn't want to think about that.

They resumed their walk, skirting rocks and dodging low-hanging tree branches. Every once in a while, one would catch Taran by surprise and thwack him in the head, but after getting hit a couple of times, he learned to follow the horse's cue and duck when he did. Never once did Cait try to take the reins away from him.

"Taran!" It was Edward's voice. His dark shape grew larger in approach. "Thank God!"

Taran's chest swelled with happiness. He brought *Ciobair* to a halt. Edward cradled his head between both hands. "'Tis good to see you, lad." Then he pulled him into a strong hug, much tighter than Cait's or Grandda's. He wondered if that was what a father's hug would feel like.

"I'm coming with ye to London," he said, hoping Edward would go along with his plan.

Cait set her hand on his shoulder with a consoling pat. "Wait a second there. That hasn't been decided yet."

"What is this about?" Edward asked.

"Cait said yer going to ride all the way to London to tell King William what Glenlyon has done, and I'm going with ye." He'd said it in a burst as if every word was connected to the next, confident and ready.

"London?" Edward sounded confused.

Taran could feel them looking at one another, their silence making his heart pound.

"He has people here caring for him," Cait said. He sensed her sending signals to Edward with her eyes.

He felt he was losing ground and started to panic. "But I dinnae wish to go back. And forbye, I can help."

"Can you?" Edward asked, but not skeptically. It sounded like he simply wanted to know how he could help, and that gave Taran hope.

"Aye. Look." He reached into his shirt and pulled out a piece of paper he had hidden there. He held it out, and someone took it.

The paper crackled as it unfolded, then it was quiet for a moment. Taran tried to steady his breath. What would they think?

"Where did you get this?" Edward asked.

"'Twas posted on the wall outside the parish kirk. Some women were blethering on about it and said yer name, so when everyone had gone inside, I pickered it."

"What is it?" Cait asked, her voice now close.

"A warrant with my portrait," Edward said, unamused. "Apparently, I'm a traitor and a malefactor worth one hundred pounds."

"Let me see." The paper crackled between them. She hmphed. "'Tis remarkable. Looks as if ye sat for it. Before the beard, mind ye."

Somewhere nearby, the grass rustled. It wasn't something small like a squirrel or rabbit. Taran concentrated on the cadence of the steps to figure out if it was a four-legged beast or a two-legged one. There were four steps, but not rhythmic like those of a cow or horse. He reached out for the closest arm. "Someone is coming."

After a pause, Edward said, "I don't see anyone."

But Taran knew the sound of footsteps. "They're near."

Cait pulled him close, and he felt her hands busy with the paper, folding and shoving it at Edward. Above Taran's head, she spoke nervously. "Ye should hide. There's a narrow crossing a wee bit—"

Men's voices traveled through the trees, stopping Cait midsentence. The rustling of grass grew louder. Taran waited for someone to move. Cait's grip on his shoulder loosened.

"'Tis only Kennedy and Farquhar," Edward said, sounding relieved.

Taran had no idea who they were, but if Edward wasn't worried, he wouldn't be either. As the footsteps grew louder and more pronounced, Edward leaned down to Taran with one arm around his shoulder. "I believe you'll prove very useful. Well done, lad."

Chapter 24

"You will have to go without me." Edward ripped his portrait into tiny shreds and threw it into the river. He turned to Cait, who was sitting with Taran by the horses and smiling at something the lad had said. "I won't leave her."

Farquhar shook his head. "Ye could be putting her in danger. What will the army do to a lass who is caught with a traitor?"

Edward would never allow Cait to be caught. If he anticipated them in approach, he would send her and Taran away. "She is safer traveling with me than without me."

"Suit yerself," Kennedy said, defeated. "But I think ye should convince the lass that Glenlyon will never be punished. To surrender her quest for justice."

He obviously didn't know Cait. "'Tisn't in her nature to simply do as she's told."

"A willard lass, have ye?" Kennedy asked, a smirk on his lips. "Are ye certain ye dinnae wish to come with us?"

Edward glanced back at her again. She and Taran were lying in the grass with their heads together, Cait's hands moving in wide arcs as she spoke, her long black hair spilling over the ground behind her. "I'm certain."

When he turned back, Kennedy was staring at him through narrowed eyes, grinning. "I see."

And so did Edward. There was something about her that made him want to stay close. Something that drew him and others to her. Her strength? Her beauty? Her resilience?

Out of the corner of his eye, he saw her stand and ease her blade from under her skirts. He stilled, his hand searching his hip for the weapon that wasn't there. He held his breath as he scanned the terrain in front of her, but he saw no sign of a threat. She drew her arm back slowly, then whipped it out, releasing her knife in a flash of movement. Kennedy grabbed his arm, his grip tight and eyes wide, but Edward had seen her cast her blade like this many times before. There was no fear in her face. Only concentration. Immediately, she raced to a spot a dozen or so yards away, crouched low, then rose with a hare raised high in one hand. "Supper!"

His shoulders loosened, and he exhaled a hard breath. Beaming, she returned to Taran, then tossed her catch into the sack beside them. He shared a quick smile with her, his hands still pulsing steadily.

"Where will you two go? You cannot return to Black Mount now that you've been spotted there," Edward said, knowing they also couldn't return to their families and risk capture.

Farquhar shrugged one shoulder. "North. Or to one of the isles. 'Tis better if ye dinnae exactly know."

"Of course." If caught and tortured, the less information he had, the less likely he'd be able to betray his friends.

Kennedy knelt on the riverbank and splashed his face with water. "You'll need to stay clear of Edinburgh. Argyll's officers have marched there."

Cait turned abruptly, her attention now drawn to what they were saying.

Farquhar added, "And dinnae go to Fort William. Hill's regiment is there. Everyone will know ye."

So that is where Alexander is. Edward patted them on the back, truly grateful for the information. "Well, that leaves me little choice but to head out of the glen and into the wood. Until we meet again, gentlemen."

They crossed the river and disappeared into the thick copse of pines, their tartans the same earthy colours as the landscape surrounding them. Edward prayed they wouldn't get caught. They were good men, now forced to leave everyone they cared for behind. And he was going to have to do the same. He could never return to his mother in Boroughbridge. It was going to break her heart.

He pulled off his scarlet coat, rolled it into a ball, then shoved it in the notch between two rocks.

"What are ye doing?" Cait asked, brushing bits of grass and leaves from her clothes.

"I'm becoming Edward MacKinnon."

"What?"

"If we are going to travel, I'll need to take on a different identity, and that coat marks me as a soldier."

THE TACKSMAN'S DAUGHTER

"The beard and the long hair will help," she offered. She stared at him with her hands planted firmly on her hips. "Well, regardless of who ye are, yer going to need these."

She grabbed a feedbag that rested against the tree where her horse was happily grazing and brought it to him. He peeked inside and found a small arsenal of weapons and a bridle. He pulled out the dagger and pistol, both fancy and emblazoned in silver with the Earl of Breadalbane's family crest. His muscles tensed. "Would I be foolish to presume that the earl gave you these?"

"Aye. Ye would be foolish to presume that," she said resolutely.

"So, you are equipping me with stolen weapons?" He turned the dagger over in his hand, its sheath so intricately engraved, it looked like it could have belonged to King William himself. "I imagine the reward for my capture has just increased by another hundred pounds."

"I'm giving ye weapons you'll need to defend yerself with. There's a powder horn and shot in there too." She crossed her arms in front of her. "Are ye complaining, then?"

He couldn't help but smile. "Not complaining. Simply surprised." He strapped them on using his own leather belts and waved his arm over his newly acquired bedecked weapons. "How do I look?"

She studied him with a crooked finger curving over her lips, her head tilted to the side, the corner of her mouth edging up. "Like a disheveled soldier wearing stolen weapons."

"That's not the look I was hoping for."

"Well, ye dinnae look like Edward *MacKinnon. He* would be wearing a plaid and sporran and wielding a broadsword above his head like a true warrior," she said, grinning.

"I suppose you're right. A MacKinnon would look like a MacKinnon."

"And he'd sound like one too." She tapped Taran on his shoulder, and he followed her back to her horse. Edward helped her up first, then the lad. She grabbed the reins and smiled. "That's why you'll be practicing the Gaelic of a *real* Scot."

They rode east, Cait and Taran teaching Edward indecent phrases in Gaelic, some with which he was already familiar, but many with which he was not. Naturally, they were the one thing his mother hadn't taught him growing up, and with no other children having Scottish heritage nearby, he hadn't learned them. If anything, it was an entertaining way to pass the time.

Taran said, "And if yer friend has embarrassed ye in front of a lass, ye say, '*S i an aon tè a dheocas bod nas fheàrr na do mhàthair, do bhràmair.*'"

"Taran! Where did ye learn such a thing?" Cait seemed clearly shocked but pleased all the same.

Edward laughed. The only word that was unfamiliar was '*bod,*' and it was fairly clear what that meant from the rest of the sentence.

"Och. 'Tisnae so bad." Taran turned in Edward's direction. "It means, 'The only person who sucks cock better than yer mum is yer lassie.'"

Edward tried to stifle his laughter, but it was impossible. "I figured that, lad."

After a while, they seemed to run out of offensive phrases and talked about other things—horses, Taran's home on the Isle of Harris, food. The weather had been fair most of the ride with only soft white clouds in the distance. It would mean they would reach the bend in the river before dusk, when they'd turn off and head for Tyndale.

"So, when do ye think we'll arrive in Edinburgh?" Cait asked, her face turned up to the sun, eyes half-closed.

Fury shook his head, jangling his tack. He hadn't been too keen when Edward fitted him with his bridle, having not worn one for quite some time, he guessed. But after a short battle of wills and a good, hard bump to his shoulder, Edward managed to maneuver the bit into his mouth. "We're not going to Edinburgh. Argyll's regiment is there."

"Even better," she said nonchalantly. "Glenlyon will be there."

"Have you forgotten that if we go anywhere near there, I will likely be recognized and hanged from a gibbet?" He wished he had a flask full of whisky. It would make the idea sound less terrifying.

"Then how will I report him to someone in command?" she asked, her voice newly sharp with displeasure.

"You did that with Breadalbane, and he hadn't cared, so why should anyone else?" From what Edward understood, the earl was high in command of this particular siege. And from what Cait had told him, it sounded like he condoned the actions of the regiment.

"I'll tell someone else. Someone with greater authority."

"They know what he's done. Campbell could not have carried out those orders without someone else commanding him to do so. I already told you that."

She shook her head obstinately. "I dinnae believe the king would allow such a thing. This was Glenlyon's doing. He was all too happy to enact revenge for a few missing kine."

"Do you truly think the man would slaughter your clan over stolen cattle?"

"I do." She cursed under her breath in Gaelic, and Taran giggled.

THE TACKSMAN'S DAUGHTER

Edward tried not to laugh, but it was impossible. There was something rather appealing about hearing her swear such vulgarities. "Well, Glenlyon may or may not be a 'swiving son of a whore' as you say, but either way, you cannot confront him. Not in Edinburgh nor anywhere else."

"And why is that?" she asked defiantly.

"Because unless you would like to see me hanged, I cannot be there when you do it. And since I expect your little meeting is not going to go over nicely, you might need my help. Without me, you could be putting yourself in grave danger."

"You've forgotten I have a reputation."

He paused, unsure about what she was referring to, then he remembered. "Your reputation with a black knife. Of course."

"I'm just as talented with a dirk." As she rode past him, she stared at him with cold eyes. "Ye cannae deprive me of this, Edward. The man will pay for what he's done. I'll understand if ye choose to leave, for I would not wish ye harm. But I ride to Edinburgh."

He wasn't going to challenge her. It would do no good anyway.

He struggled to think of a single person to whom Cait could convey her complaints, but the only two people ranked higher than Breadalbane were the king and Dalrymple, and as far as he knew, they were likely both in London.

They rode mostly in silence, then stopped at dusk along the River Lochy across from a salmon stair. A series of small waterfalls descended into a clear, shallow pool. While the horses dipped their lazy heads to drink, Edward removed his weapons, shoes, and stockings. He inhaled sharply with the shock of cold as he dipped his feet into the icy water, then plodded farther in until it was knee-high. With one hand submerged, he guddled for a fish, still and ready, waiting for it to swim within his grasp. It took only minutes for him to catch one as long as his forearm, wriggling its slimy body back and forth and splashing him with frigid drops. He carried it back to the grassy bank and speared it through to place it on the fire Cait and Taran had built. For good measure, he caught another four, all of which he shoved in the feed sack for later meals.

Cait sat combing her fingers through Taran's blond curls, occasionally picking out a stray burr or piece of grass from the tangles, all of which he objected to with angry grunts.

Edward settled next to her, his mind full of uncertainty but his heart filled with none. "For now, we'll head into the woodland glen east of here. It will provide us with shelter until we know 'tis safe to continue on to Edinburgh."

Cait's hands stilled. "Does that mean—"

"We shall stay together." He offered her his flask like he had so many times before, but this time, he was offering her much more. She reached for it, and he wrapped his hand over hers, his thumb tracing over her soft skin. "I left you before, but I'll not leave you again."

She stared up at him, her pale green eyes brimming with tears. He wanted to kiss her but wasn't sure if she would allow it. He leaned in slowly, his eyes fixed on hers, his heart pounding with hope. She inched closer, trusting, her lips slightly parted. The kiss was soft and warm and fixed something inside of him that he knew was broken. She had forgiven him for not saving her parents, for not protecting her and the others. And it freed him from his own shame.

She spoke, their lips still touching. "I'll be leading ye into danger."

He brushed her cheek with the back of his hand. "We both have quite a bit to lose, but we've come this far."

"We've come this far *together.*" Her lips met his again, soft and trusting.

He leaned closer for more, then felt a smack on his arm. Taran made a disapproving sound, his nose wrinkled in distaste. "Someone's coming, so ye best stop yer kissing."

He was right. But this time it sounded like a larger group too close to avoid. He swept his weapons closer to his side, hoping they weren't soldiers.

"What should we do?" Cait asked, her face full of worry.

Edward pulled the fish from the flames and cut it into pieces, steam rising from its flesh. He set each piece of salmon on a rock to cool. "'Tis too late to hide. Stay put as if nothing is amiss."

From the edge of the tree line, three drovers approached, leaving a dozen Highland cattle to graze in the fading pink light, their shaggy goldish-brown heads bent idly. The largest of the men was a giant with red hair fastened in a queue, and the other two were of average height and older with long grey beards and hair—one stout with a droopy eye, and the other thin like a reed. Edward greeted them in Gaelic. He scanned the small cache of weapons they wore. From what he could see, they all carried swords and dirks, but he was fairly certain—considering the rotundity of the giant and the others' advanced ages—they didn't pose a threat. "*Beannachd Dhia dhuit.*"

"Do ye have any of that left for us, *caraid?*" the stout older man asked.

"Plenty." Edward reached into the feedbag, pulled out two more fish, and set them over the flames.

They joined them around the fire, the giant sighing heavily as he sat, his gut jiggling with the effort like Christmastide custard. "I need to rest my weary body. Been traveling for over a fortnight now."

"May I ask where you are headed?" Edward realized his mistake the moment the words left his mouth. They were too formal, too English.

"An Englishman with the Gaelic?" the giant asked, eyes narrowed.

"Lived in England for a while," he said, hoping that would end the discussion.

"Och. Ye should try to lose that foul tongue if ye can." The giant laughed, exposing at least half a dozen missing teeth, the remaining ones brown and rotting. His grey-haired companions joined him in his folly, the thin one possessing no teeth at all.

Edward forced a smile, flipping the fish with a steadied hand.

"Ye here for the *cruinneachadh?*" asked the stout fellow with the droopy eye.

"There's a gathering?" Edward asked.

The old drover glanced at the others, then at Edward. "What did ye say yer name was?"

Cait shot Edward a nervous look.

"I didn't, but 'tis MacKinnon. Edward MacKinnon."

The drover waved at the giant with a flourish of his hand. "Duncan here is a MacKinnon."

Edward nodded in his direction to acknowledge the coincidence, unease creeping into his neck and shoulders. "You said there's a meeting?"

The three drovers' gazes flitted back and forth between them, Duncan scratching his jaw and sending all sorts of unspoken signals. Suspicion pricked at Edward, his limbs tightening in response. They were hiding something, but he didn't know what.

It was Duncan who decided to answer. "Well, Edward *MacKinnon*. Where are ye from?"

His stomach clenched. Was Duncan trying to set a trap? He poked a stick into the embers, careful not to engage anyone in eye contact. "Skye."

"Och." Duncan slapped his knee but without humour. "I'm from Skye."

Cait slowly closed her eyes and bowed her head, hiding her mouth behind her hand.

"Do ye know Callum and Morogh MacKinnon of Torrin?"

Edward dug into the recesses of his memory. He knew no one by those names, but his mother had mentioned Torrin before. And then it struck him. "My grandmother was from Torrin. Her name was Peigi MacKinnon. My grandfather, Brian, was from Kilbride."

The giant's face lit up, and he scooted closer. "Brian MacKinnon of Kilbride? He lived but a shout away from *Tobar na h-Annait.*"

The Well of Annat, the river goddess who looked after young maidens. His mother had told him many stories about how his grandparents would watch the new brides parade past their cottage to drench themselves in the sacred well in order to become fruitful. He breathed a sigh of relief. "You knew my grandfather?"

He shook his head. "My father did. He said after yer grandmother gave birth to her fourteenth bairn, yer grandda wanted to have the well holed up."

Edward smiled. His mother had told him the same.

"Well, seeing as yer a MacKinnon of Skye, I suppose we can tell ye what the meeting is about." He pulled a flask from his belted plaid, took a long pull, then handed it to Edward.

He held it up in salute, relieved and happily anticipating the sweet burn of whisky. *"Slàinte!"* He closed his eyes as he drank, savoring the fire of it in his mouth before he swallowed.

The giant leaned in, his expression suddenly staid. "We're Jacobites. And we're here to discuss King William."

Chapter 25

Alexander's head pounded. How much complaining could a man do? The only reason he'd welcomed the colonel into his quarters was because he thought he had good news about the search for the traitors. And now he was stuck listening to the old man gripe about nonsense.

"And all of their livestock is running amok in the recreation yard, destroying my vegetable garden and trampling over the graves nearby." Colonel John Hill paced back and forth from the window to the door in Alexander's small quarters. "They haunt me all day and night, reminding me of what we have done."

Alexander massaged his temple with his thumb. "They are not here to haunt you. They are the spoils of war."

"War? There was no war! 'Twas slaughter." His face faded to white as he dropped into a chair and rested his head in his hands. "We have ruined Glencoe, their goods prey to our soldiers and their homes to fire."

Alexander rolled his eyes. Sympathy and regret were not appealing traits in an officer. How had he ever become governor? "We followed orders."

"I should have never listened to Dalrymple. I should have employed my own sense of morality, for God's sake, and stopped this nonsense!" Hill threw up his hand dramatically and knocked his grey periwig back, exposing wispy white hairs sparsely sprinkled on his shiny scalp. "The man is the devil! As is Hamilton! And Breadalbane! They are the ruin of me."

Alexander checked his pocket watch. Hill had been in his quarters for over an hour now, and in another minute, Alexander was going to toss him out the window. "It did the job, though, did it not?"

Hill readjusted his wig, his fingers dancing nervously over his brow. "Did the job?"

Alexander leaned back in his chair and sighed. "Taught the Highlanders a lesson."

Hill's mouth fell open, and his brow lifted in shock.

"Come now, Colonel. How many chiefs have since submitted to the king's mercy and pledged their oaths of allegiance? A dozen? Perhaps more?" Alexander waited for a response, something to indicate the dolt had heard him, but he remained mute as if apoplectic. "Is that not what we set out to accomplish?"

Finally, Hill came to life. "Do you know what they are saying about us in Edinburgh?"

Alexander shrugged. "That we are noble, loyal subjects?"

Hill leaned forward in his chair, a look of horror on his face. "That my officers and I exceeded orders and carried out the attack without sanction."

Alexander scoffed at that. "I did as I was told. Major Duncanson sent orders to Captain Drummond, and he relayed them to us."

"But they are saying that the king hadn't sanctioned the attack. And Dalrymple is now denying his part too."

That didn't sound likely. Dalrymple made it no secret that he despised Highlanders and their thieving ways. If anything, he undoubtedly toasted himself in celebration of the orders being carried out. "I can only say I have no remorse for what I have done. We are soldiers. We do as we are told. And we were told to take down MacIain, his sons, and all his miscreant clansmen. And that is what we did."

Hill returned to the window, his distraught face reflected in the glass pane. "You forget. His sons escaped that morning."

He'd heard that. Apparently, they were last seen gathering arms for survivors and positioning them throughout the hills and glens of Dalness and Glen Duror. But that was a while ago. What harm could they possibly do now? "Do you still have your scouts out there?"

Hill rubbed his forehead. "I do, but there is very little news except that the Camerons are incensed and ready to cut down any *Redcoat* patrol in the area. They could incite others to join them."

Alexander yawned behind his fist. "Let them. We will run them through like we did their bandit brothers."

Hill turned and faced him, his features drawn and haggard. He opened his mouth to speak, then closed it and exited the room with no farewell or explanation. He was an odd man. Too conscientious and brooding for his own good.

THE TACKSMAN'S DAUGHTER

At least the old fool was gone. Now he could tend to more pressing matters.

That whore from Sterling Struana's had complained to the bullyboy there that she'd been sodomized against her will by an officer named Edward residing at the fort. As a result, the beast came with his fists clenched and his mouth tight in search of this *horrid* person. Of course, since there were no officers named Edward in residence, he was sent away and told to keep his distance from the garrison. Alexander had watched the entire exchange from his window. It was not as if he hadn't paid the doxy for services rendered—and handsomely, he might add. In any case, that was not his problem at the moment.

He needed to find a new woman to satisfy him, and since he couldn't return to Struana's and didn't care to take any of the toothless whores parading their distasteful wares on High Street, he needed to look elsewhere. And that was why the invitation to dine at Inverlochy Castle at Lady Lilith Gordon's request was rather enticing. There had to be a woman or two there in need of a good prigging.

Alexander quickly washed, tied his hair back in a ribbon, and gave a thorough brushing to his coat, freeing it from a month's worth of dust. Although he was attending as Baron Mansfield, his uniform betrayed his identity as a soldier, albeit an officer, but nonetheless a man not living the leisurely life he was meant to live. All because of his father, the damned fool.

He arrived on horseback at Inverlochy Castle as the sun set over River Lochy. Servants were busy lighting torches along the path leading up to the arched entrance for any future latecomers. He handed the reins to a stable hand who could not have weighed more than seven stone or so, judging from his height and gangly limbs. Alexander's borrowed horse was aged, though, and unlikely to cause a struggle for the lad. Not that he really cared. It was simply that, should anyone be looking, it would draw attention to the fact that he'd arrived on an old draught horse and not a destrier.

He followed the insufferable cacophony of the pipers into an entry where dozens of people milled about. The women wore velvets and tartan, some with necks adorned with jewels and others bare. More were Scot than English, but it didn't matter. With his eyes closed, he couldn't tell the difference between a Scottish cunny and an English one.

He made his way to the great hall and found a seat on a bench at one of four long tables. The only chairs were the six upon a rostrum in the front of the hall for the laird and his family. Alexander took a deep breath to combat his revulsion at the unsophisticated—almost barbaric—accommodations.

"Fàilte!" The laird stood, red-faced and too jolly for Alexander's taste. Lady Lilith stood beside him, resting one delicate hand on his wrist. "We are honoured to have you as our guests this evening!"

He gave a short speech about something or other, then signaled for supper to be served. Part of it was unrecognizable and encased in a yellow membrane, but roasted venison and pheasant were also served, much to his liking, so it wasn't entirely miserable. The wine was plentiful and similarly wonderful with a bouquet of vanilla and spice, and dare he say, a hint of mushroom?

The auburn-haired woman seated to his right seemed to be enjoying her wine as much as he was. Her gown was in need of updating, the gold lace trim framing her décolletage a bit frayed and faded, but her breasts were nicely displayed and practically begging to be released from their confines. Although she did not seem to have the wealth he preferred in a lover, he listened to her introduce herself, happy to note she was English. He smiled politely while she explained her acquaintance with the laird to the man next to her. Her voice was lively, not soft and comforting. It showed no sweetness nor sincerity. Not like Berenice's. *Her* voice was like velvet, her lips silk, her words . . . well, her words had been a poultice for his heart. She would be hard to replace in that regard. In every regard.

"And how do you know the laird, Baron Mansfield?" the woman asked, summoning him from his thoughts. The gentleman seated between them belched, then excused himself from the table. Alexander waved away the stench he left behind.

"He visits the garrison often to meet with the governor, who was kind enough to make the introduction." Alexander loathed this part of the game. He would act the courteous, charming baron who laughed politely at all her witless remarks, and she would believe that his compliments were genuine and there was actually a match being made. "And you, Miss Raeburn? How does a woman as lovely as you come to find herself here in Scotland?"

She tilted her head coquettishly. "Do you promise not to tell?"

He placed his hand over his heart. "You have my word."

She scooted closer to him on the bench, filling the empty space so that her thigh pressed against his. "I am here with Viscount Campden." Sitting this close, he could see a small spray of freckles sprinkled across the bridge of her nose and onto her cheeks. She placed her finger over her lips and grinned. "As his mistress."

"Viscount Campden?"

She nodded, then pointed to a corpulent man on the other side of the room by the hearth, his green woolen coat straining to close over his protruding gut. His face was fleshy and loose, and his jowls wobbled as he spoke.

THE TACKSMAN'S DAUGHTER

"He must be at least thirty years your senior," he remarked, surprised.

She finished the rest of her wine in two large gulps. "Thirty-three, to be exact, and a bore in bed."

Something warm and wonderful blossomed in Alexander's chest. She was perfectly ripe for the picking. He reached for her hand, kissed her palm, then placed it over his cock. "'Tis a crime to have a boring bed partner."

He pressed her up against a tree, her legs wrapped around his hips as he pounded into her. With each thrust, her large breasts bounced while her head banged into the trunk. He didn't care how hard she pulled his hair or how fierce her teeth bit into his neck. He liked the pain. It brought him closer to release.

He plunged into her one last time, his hips ramming hers with as much force as he could muster. She uttered one final squeal, then sank into him, her head resting on his shoulder.

They stayed silent while they caught their breath, the cool night breeze refreshing on Alexander's damp skin. He pulled out of her and stumbled a bit, surprised by his weakness.

"That was quite a performance." She kissed his mouth hungrily, greedily. "I have a mind to leave that old gundigut for you."

Warning bells sounded in his head. The last thing he needed right now with all his money problems was a mistress to support.

She traced her fingers over the silver buttons on his open coat. "A baron and an officer in the king's army. Quite impressive."

If she only knew his title could be rescinded at any moment, she'd hardly be impressed.

"So how many men are under your command?" she asked.

He wiped the sweat off his face with his sleeve. "Fifty. Or sixty, perhaps."

She tucked her breasts back into her bodice. He was sorry to see them go. "All foot soldiers?"

"They are."

"You must be a powerful man, Mansfield." She tugged at her skirts, straightening the pleats and brushing down the fabric. "Are there other officers there with you?"

"Of course." He tucked the hem of his shirt back into his breeches. "A dozen at least."

She stood on her tiptoes to bite his bottom lip. "How long will your regiment be at Fort William?"

Laughter sounded nearby. He glanced at the river and spied a small group of revelers seated on the bank, torchlight dancing on the water. "You are awfully inquisitive, Miss Raeburn."

"After what we did, you may call me Jenny."

"Very well, Jenny." He buttoned the front of his breeches, then retied his hair ribbon. "Why all the questions?"

"'Tis simple." She grabbed the front of his shirt with both hands. "I want to know about the man who scandalously occupied the last twenty minutes of my life."

He liked her sauciness. And the fact she fucked like a whore but was free. "Then you should know my name is Alexander."

"When will I see you again, Alexander?"

"That depends."

"On?"

He pressed her hand to his cock. "How quickly you can make me hard again."

She unfastened his breeches and cupped him in her hand, stroking gently at first and then firmer. "It seems to be working."

She bit his nipple through his shirt, and he moaned. With her free hand, she pushed his shirt out of her way and moved her mouth lower, nibbling her way down. He leaned back against the tree, afraid his legs might give out.

"'Tis definitely working." He could feel her lips arc into a smile on his skin just below his navel.

She took him in her mouth, and he sucked in his breath.

"Baron Mansfield?" A man's voice addressed him in the darkness.

Alexander glanced in his direction briefly but saw only a small dark shape in approach. "What is it?"

Jenny lifted her head, freeing him from the warmth of her mouth, the cold air chilling him. He grabbed a handful of her auburn hair and forced her head back down. "Don't stop."

The man cleared his throat, averting his gaze from the obvious transgression occurring at Alexander's hips. "The Earl of Breadalbane has summoned you to Kilchurn Castle. You are expected to leave in the early morning hours."

Jenny stilled, and Alexander groaned.

The messenger thrust a letter into his hand. "The details, sir."

Part Three

Chapter 26

Late April, 1692
The Highlands of Scotland

It was well past dusk, and not a single star could be seen through the heavy clouds in the night sky. The giant, Duncan, leaned into the fire on his haunches, rubbing his palms together as he spoke, the flickering firelight illuminating his face in orange and yellow. Cait was both exhilarated and frightened by what he said, her arms tingly as though a light frost covered her skin.

Duncan's face puckered as if he'd bit into an unripe cherry. "Incestuous, lawless thieves? That's what he thinks of us?"

"And dinnae forget cannibals," added Broc, the drover with the droopy eye.

Cait inhaled sharply. Was what they were saying true? Could King William really believe Highlanders were all those horrid things?

"How are we supposed to respect a man who thinks of us as beasts?" asked Ronan, the tall, reed-like drover with no teeth, his words spewing forth in a series of airy whistles.

Duncan shifted his weight, lifting his plaid and exposing a little more of his thigh than Cait cared to see. "And they plan to slay all of the nonjurors. They've already done so to Glencoe."

Edward stared at Duncan sideways. "They slew the man, but MacIain wasn't a nonjuror. He gave his oath of allegiance to William."

The three drovers shared a look of surprise. Ronan's mouth hung agape, his lips curling in over his gums. The fire crackled and popped, marking the silence. Cait leaned into its heat, but it did nothing to soothe the turmoil in her mind, the memory of MacIain's bloodied face and torso being dragged across the floor still crisp and clear.

"I hadn't heard that." Duncan bowed his head and sighed heavily. "So he was slain for naught."

"It wasn't for naught. They wanted to make an example out of him." Edward paused, then shot Cait a quick apologetic glance. "The army was going to punish Glengarry for not swearing his oath by the first of the year, but the storms prevented us from getting there, so we billeted in Glencoe."

"We?" Duncan asked, his tone accusatory. "You were one of them?"

Cait's stomach clenched. "He was one of the soldiers, but he never—"

Edward rested his hand on her wrist to stop her. "I had no notion that we were being sent to slaughter anyone."

"Then what did ye think ye were there to do?"

Edward tossed the bones of his fish in the fire. "Honestly, I thought the mere presence of my regiment with Argyll's and those waiting at Fort William were meant to frighten Glengarry into declaring his loyalty to William. Eight hundred soldiers could do that, I believe."

Ronan and Broc swung their heads in Duncan's direction, waiting for him to respond. Duncan laughed derisively. "That attack was planned long ago, *caraid*. And I would stake my life on it that William penned his name at the bottom of the orders."

―――――◆―◆―◆―――――

Edward returned with an armful of twigs and inserted them into the pyre one by one. All three drovers lay snoring on their backs, their feet splayed apart and their hands resting on the dirks at their hips. Taran lay curled up next to Cait, his soft breathing soothing to her ears. Even still, she couldn't sleep.

What the men had said about the king nibbled at her like summer midges. It was dangerous talk, and she wasn't sure if she believed it or not. Either way, she didn't think it was safe to be seen around them. If they were being followed, she, Edward, and Taran would all be accused of being Jacobites. She lay on her back, the damp, mossy ground beneath her giving way each time she twisted or turned.

Edward edged nearer, his body close enough that she felt the warmth emanating from his skin.

"I dinnae know what to make of Duncan's accusations," she admitted, trying to find a comfortable position to settle in for the night.

"Is that what has you restless?" he asked, his voice low.

"Aye," she answered faintly. She stared into the dark above at the canopy of trees, their thick leaves a blanket shielding her from the night sky.

THE TACKSMAN'S DAUGHTER

"You needn't let his babble keep you from your sleep." He turned on his side to face her. "'Tis Jacobite sentiment meant to rally more support."

That may have been so, but it didn't mean it wasn't true. And if it was, what chance did any of them have if the king thought of them as less than human? Complaining to him that a Campbell led an attack against a MacDonald—one Scot against another—would only confirm his belief that they were all unruly reprobates. How could she ever approach him with her complaint? He would probably laugh and send her away. "Do all the English think that of us, Edward?"

"That you are incestuous cannibals?" He laughed softly. "Well, *I* don't. If I did, then I would have to believe I am one too—or at least half of one."

She smiled. She'd momentarily forgotten he was not fully English, his speech so even without the songlike expression and trilled burr of a Scot. But there was definitely something about him that made her feel safe and protected, something strong and unforgiving that betrayed him as being as much a part of Scotland as she was.

"You may rest well knowing I don't think of you that way. If I did, I would've slept with one eye open these past weeks," he added teasingly.

"Does that mean all of these nights, ye weren't watching over us?" she asked, a little surprised. "All the while ye were merely snoring away yer cares, I suppose."

"Did anything happen to you?"

"Not yet," she whispered. "But we have guests tonight."

"Well, then, if you don't mind, I'd like to drape my arm over you to ensure our guests don't throw you on the back of one of their cows and drag you off."

"I'd put up an awfully good fight."

"I don't doubt that. But just the same, it will allow me to keep both eyes closed."

It had been more than two months since the attack, and she hadn't slept through the night even once. She could still smell the smoke from the burning cottages, its acrid taste caught in her throat and on her tongue. The vision of the charred bodies dusted lightly with new snowfall and scattered throughout the village haunted her dreams.

The days were easier, though. With Edward near, she had moments when her heart calmed and her thoughts weren't blanketed by death and betrayal. Those moments were fleeting, but she was grateful for the little respite they offered. She realized she needed him close by—at the very least, within sight. His presence soothed her like a gentle fire or lullaby.

She turned over on her side, facing away from him, granting him permission to move closer. "Very well, do as ye must."

His hand brushed her hip, then moved higher and around her waist, the weight of his arm settling gently around her.

She watched as sparks floated up from the fire and disappeared into the darkness above. Her mind raced from memory to memory, the good and the bad, all forming who she'd become. She wasn't sure if her father would be proud of every decision she'd made in the last few months, but he'd commend her for remaining strong after all that had happened.

She tapped the back of Edward's hand lightly. "Do ye remember when we were on our way to Kilchurn and we heard someone in approach?"

"I do," he whispered, scooting in closer to match his body to hers.

"You beckoned for my knife."

He nodded, his cheek brushing against the back of her head.

"I could've defended us."

"I know that quite well." He wrapped her more firmly in his arms, his warm breath mingling with her hair. "If it hadn't been Farquhar and Kennedy, but people who would have harmed us, you would've thrown your blade. I will not let you have a man's death on your conscience. Murder is a heavy burden to bear. Even in self-defense."

She closed her eyes to try to erase the images of the soldier who had a pistol aimed at her chest when she'd escaped from Alt Na Munde and of Sionn as he fell to the ground, his neck slit ear to ear. As horrid as he was, she hadn't meant to kill him.

Edward shifted, and she intertwined her fingers with his. "Edward?"

He squeezed her hand once in response.

She gripped it firmly, her confession overdue. Tears pricked her eyes. "I know the burden well."

The rise and fall of his chest against her back suddenly stopped. She held her own breath, waiting for him to say something. Anything.

His breathing resumed, strong and steady against her neck. He kissed the back of her ear, her hair, her cheek, then whispered, "Sleep, lass."

She inhaled deeply and settled into his embrace, pulling his arm tighter before she closed her eyes.

Morning came without incident. By the time Cait woke, Taran was already resting against a tree, whittling away at his walking stick, one hand carving while the other rubbed and tested the newly smooth surface. Cait brushed away the dew that had settled on her clothes overnight and smiled to herself at how soundly she'd slept in Edward's arms. They hadn't spoken any further after her admission, and he hadn't pushed for more information. He had simply wrapped her in an embrace that told her he would not judge her for what she'd done, now or ever.

He stood at the edge of the woods, bidding the drovers a farewell. Like obedient dogs, their cattle stood by their sides, their big black eyes peeking from behind their shaggy golden fur. Broc and Ronan stood with their arms crossed, nodding in agreement to whatever was being said. Curious, Cait moved closer to listen.

Duncan adjusted the strap holding his deerskin sporran and eyed Edward closely. "It seems to me that ye might not be such a loyal subject after all."

Edward started to speak, but Duncan held up his hand to stop him. "Ye needn't reply. If yer so inclined, ye may wish to join us at the gathering. 'Tis only a week's ride or so to Stirling. You'll pass through there on yer way to Edinburgh."

Edward eyed him warily. Cait expected him to decline the offer, but instead, Edward nodded once before heading over to the horses.

She joined Duncan, who fiddled with his sporran and plaid. Ronan stepped away to piss against a tree. She turned back once to check that Edward remained busy unhobbling the horses before she spoke. "Do ye believe with yer heart that William ordered the attack?"

"I'm as certain as I am that blood runs through these veins." With a clenched fist, Duncan extended his arm to display a ropy green vein that traveled from his elbow down to his wrist.

"I lost my entire family." Her heart raced as she choked out the words.

He tapped his sporran, then reached in to inch out a letter, its paper crinkled and dirty from passing through what must have been many hands. His gaze bore into her fiercely. "Rest assured, lassie. I have something here that will give the king his due."

She closed her eyes, picturing the three graves, the ground above them still swollen from the recent burials. If the king signed those orders . . . She swallowed the lump that formed in her throat. "Then I wish ye God speed."

As soon as the three drovers left and Taran was out of earshot, she turned to Edward. "Ye nodded when Duncan told ye of the *cruinneachadh*. Do ye plan to join them?"

"Of course not. But do you think it would've been better to refuse his offer and cast suspicion on us as Williamites?" Edward leaned in close. "He just confessed to an act of high treason. Do you think he would have let us go on our merry way knowing we could identify him as a traitor?"

She hadn't thought of that. Either way—attending a Jacobite gathering or expressing no desire to attend—would add more danger to their already full plate. Edward was playing the middle of the road.

"'Tisnae that I'm nae curious as to what they would say, mind ye. I'd like to know. There seems to be some truth in their words." She couldn't deny that they'd created some real doubt in her mind about King William and his motives. "Do ye think the king knows about these gatherings?"

Edward scratched the side of his nose, then shrugged. "Well, I can promise you this—he knows his last defeat of the Jacobites at the River Boyne was short-lived, and although many men were killed, the Jacobite sentiment remains."

That was almost two years earlier in Ireland, a world away. She'd only heard bits and pieces about the battle. More than a thousand Jacobites had died. Not as many casualties in William's army. Could that have been why MacIain was targeted by the soldiers? Could he have been a Jacobite? She remembered the day in February that the soldiers entered the glen and MacIain had referred to the garrison as Inverlochy, then quickly corrected himself and called it Fort William. And she also remembered that Breadalbane claimed MacIain's tardiness to pledge his oath demonstrated his disloyalty to the king.

Edward hmphed, tearing her away from her thoughts. "'Tis much easier to kill a man than it is to kill an idea."

"'Tis true." She'd heard talk about the Jacobite cause in Glencoe, a stray word here or there, but it was always hushed and stopped by the time she was able to ask what the chatter was about. "I've never been included in the talk until now."

Edward seemed uncomfortable with what she was saying. She sensed it in his stiffness and unwillingness to look directly at her while she spoke. He peered into the distance, his blue eyes focused on something far away.

"What has ye so bothered?" she asked.

He glanced at her briefly, then looked away. "There's something I haven't told you."

The tone of his voice was somber, serious. Her heart thumped in anticipation of something horrible.

"'Tis about my father."

The only thing she knew about his father was that he was an Englishman of noble birth who'd fallen in love with his mother when he was already betrothed to his current wife. Apparently, he'd begged to retract the marriage agreement between both families so he could marry Edward's mother, but Edward's grandfather had denied his request. Edward had put it lightly, but Cait would wager that his grandfather did more than simply *deny* his appeal to marry a Scottish commoner.

She reached for his hand. "Tell me."

THE TACKSMAN'S DAUGHTER

In a torrent of confession, he told her that his father was taken to the Tower of London three years earlier when he was arrested as a Jacobite and how this had affected him and his mother.

"We were both heartbroken," he admitted sadly.

"Ye were close with yer father." Even now, Edward seemed tortured talking about him, his head bowed and his mind far away.

"As close as an illegitimate son can be. He lived a day's ride from us but spent more time at our home than he did at the one he shared with his wife."

She didn't doubt that was why Alexander resented him so much.

He continued, "He's a good man who was drawn into the rebellion. 'Tis that simple."

And that dangerous. She'd heard about the Tower and all its torture devices.

"When Father went to prison, the countess stopped his payments for our upkeep. My mother worried about how she would manage, so with the little influence he had left, Father arranged for me to be commissioned as an officer in the king's army to help support her. The same was done for Alexander." He paused, rubbing his brow slowly. "But more importantly, joining would help clear our name and hopefully lead the king to forgive my father and release him."

"I suppose Alexander thinks the same."

"Not exactly," he said sardonically. He took a deep breath before continuing. "He joined the king's forces to prove his own loyalty but not to have Father released."

"I dinnae understand."

With a little more vigor in his voice, he explained, "Alexander doesn't give the hair on a rat's arse if Father is freed. The only thing he cares about is his inheritance. And if the king chooses to pursue attainder, all of Father's lands and estates will be forfeited to the crown, and Alexander will lose his hereditary titles and properties. 'Tis the idea that there is a corruption of blood in the family name, starting with our father and continuing on forever."

It was astonishing how different the brothers were, one with a pure heart and the other with a heart as black and empty as a cavern.

"I've always wondered if Father was right. If King James is the better king." He reached for her hand, his eyes finally fixed on hers. "But even with all my doubt about William, I cannot engage in a rebellion against him. For my father's sake. You understand?"

Her throat closed. She understood his desire to stay away from the Jacobites, but her situation was different. Her parents and sister lay in the cold ground, their corpses withering away as each day passed. If William had ordered the attack, his hands were covered with their blood. "I do understand. But I cannae say I feel the same."

They bridled the horses, ready to leave when Taran pulled Cait close, his bottom lip caught between his teeth.

"What is it, laddie?" She stroked his head and twirled one golden curl in a spiral.

Taran's voice came to her in a whisper. "There's something ye should know."

She shot Edward a quick concerned glance, and he joined them. Edward settled his hand firmly on Taran's shoulder. "Go on."

"That man. Duncan . . ." Taran paused, the knuckles on his hand white from gripping his cane tightly.

"What of him?" Edward asked.

The little vein on the side of Taran's neck pulsed steadily. "He's going to choke to death on his own blood."

Cait froze. It was a strange assertion, to say the least.

"What are ye saying, lad?" Edward asked, his brow drawn together in concern.

"I'm saying . . ." Taran's hands worked nervously over the top of his cane. "I have the second sight. *Taibhsearachd.* I'm a seer."

Chapter 27

Alexander took a boat from Fort William to Glenorchy the morning after Lady Lilith Gordon's dinner party. For two days, he'd been forced to sit amongst four large crates filled with hens and various other squawking, stinking fowl, the ferryman smelling no better than his feathered cargo. He'd left irritably, reluctant to leave his amorous new lady friend, Jenny Raeburn, who showed great potential for keeping him sexually satiated. But then he'd received word that all three traitors—including his pathetic brother—were seen near Dalmally, but a half hour's ride from Kilchurn Castle, and his spirits lifted. After some confusion as to whether or not he should be traveling with his regiment, Colonel Hill insisted that he travel alone as Breadalbane's request to see him was of a personal nature and not one with military purpose.

Midafternoon on the second day, the ferryman rowed him up the River Awe until it was no longer possible due to the shallow passes. They pulled up to the shore, the hull of the boat scraping the rocky bottom.

"What do you expect me to do?" Alexander asked, already resenting the answer.

"You'll have to walk. The castle's not far from here. You'll be there well before dusk."

He disembarked angrily, rocking the boat and soaking his right shoe as he stepped in the icy water to catch his balance. Although he was glad to be free of the stench and constant clucking, he was not thrilled that he would have to spend the next hour or so walking along the bank with no escort or batman to carry his bag. Every few minutes, he cursed the colonel for not providing him with at least one soldier to accompany him and carry his valise, his right shoulder inevitably rubbed raw from the leather strap.

To make matters worse, he was held at the gate to await Breadalbane's permission to enter. He stared at the two imbecile door wards, thinking he might slice off both of their heads for that show of disrespect. Did they really think that he, standing there in the uniform of a leftenant for the king's army, posed a threat? And why hadn't the guards been informed of his impending arrival? He hoped the trip was worth all this aggravation.

He was escorted into the earl's apartments by a tall, solid man—much like himself—wearing a fine blue velvet coat and a well-coiffed white periwig. Alexander had never met him before, but everything about the servant bothered him—his coat was as nice as any Alexander had back in England, his hands were clean and uncalloused, his shoes buffed. The servant knocked on the salon door, the gleam of his green beryl ring mocking Alexander. Finally, the door opened, and he was instantly greeted by Breadalbane, standing beneath a huge wall tapestry depicting his coat of arms.

"Leftenant Gage. 'Tis a pleasure to see ye again." His eyes scanned Alexander's bedraggled clothes down to his muddied shoe. With long manicured fingers, he plucked a stray feather from Alexander's sleeve. "Rough trip, was it?"

Alexander forced a smile. "Not the most pleasant, but worth making your acquaintance, I assure you."

Breadalbane directed him to sit in the chair opposite, separated by a table plated with fish and cheese. The last time Alexander had been at the castle, the earl had made him wait more than an hour before he offered him some food. It was his way of posturing, making sure everyone in his presence understood he was the cock in a room full of capons. This time would likely be no different.

"Good to hear." Breadalbane took a moment to stuff a herring into his mouth before continuing. "I summoned ye for good reason."

He certainly hoped so. "I must say I am baffled as to why I am here without my regiment. Does it have anything to do with the deserters?"

Breadalbane waved a hand dismissively. "They're likely long gone by now."

Damn! Without them, his plea to the king wouldn't have a backbone. "When were they last seen in Glenorchy?"

Breadalbane shrugged, clearly unconcerned. "A week ago, perhaps."

"Were they spotted on foot?" It was unlikely that anyone nearby was wealthy enough to provide a few horses to some soldiers with whom they sympathized. But it was certainly possible. He eyed the food, hoping to silently convey to the old gasbag that he should invite him to eat.

THE TACKSMAN'S DAUGHTER

Breadalbane shoved a hunk of cheese into his mouth, then wiggled his fingers over his plate to free the crumbs. "I believe so."

His indifference was infuriating. "In which direction were they last headed?"

"Really, Leftenant. I have no idea." He drank what was left of his wine, then signaled for more with the snap of his fingers in the direction of his glass. "There are more pressing matters right now, and I need yer help."

"Of course, milord." He took a deep breath, aggravated by the earl's lack of concern. "How may I be of service?"

Breadalbane drummed his fingers on the table impatiently as the servant poured him more wine. As if suddenly satisfied that he'd made Alexander wait long enough for food or drink, the earl mumbled something to another servant, who within seconds, returned with a glass, handed it to Alexander, and poured him some Claret.

Breadalbane motioned for the man to leave the decanter on the table, then dismissed him with the sweep of his hand. Once the door was safely shut, he spoke. "It appears that a copy of Major Duncanson's letter is circulating throughout the Lowlands and England, as far south as London. And now there is talk of an investigation of the *incident* at Glencoe."

Alexander drank half his wine in the time it took the earl to state his concern, his body joyously warming from the inside out. "Major Duncanson's letter? Which—"

"The one that details our plans to kill MacIain and his sons," he answered impatiently.

"And why is this a problem?" Alexander sent him another silent signal with his eyes to offer him to partake in the food, but the old goat kept babbling instead.

"It also states that they were to put all under seventy to the sword. Essentially, to slay all of Glencoe. Women. Children."

"I see."

"Do ye?" Breadalbane asked, his long brown periwig precariously brushing the rim of his wineglass. "Duncanson's letter states they should begin the attack at five of the clock, but Hamilton's orders to him were to begin at seven."

Alexander remembered that although Duncanson had promised reinforcements, his regiment didn't reach Glencoe until hours after the attack. He'd likely changed the time in order to avoid participation in the slaughter, keeping himself out of trouble—should any arise. "So, we are now Duncanson's scapegoats."

"Precisely. But most importantly, *my* name will be brought into the conversation." Breadalbane lifted a herring from the plate. "But I want ye to know, when I met with Stair in London this past winter, all matters regarding this incident were agreed upon *before* I came along."

Alexander was no fool. He knew the earl was heavily enmeshed in the attack on the MacDonalds. Many people believed the reason he was reinforcing his castle was to thwart the constant attacks by other clans—especially those by the MacDonalds. He had an axe to grind, and this was the perfect way to do it. And John Dalrymple, Master of Stair, knew it and was undoubtedly thrilled he had a partner who agreed the Highland clans must be put in their place. Starting with Clan Donald was unquestionably a mutually agreed upon choice.

"Are you concerned you might be implicated in the investigation should there be one?" Alexander asked.

Breadalbane popped the herring into his mouth, then absently motioned for Alexander to take one with an incoherent grumble. Finally. "Have ye forgotten that my surname is Campbell?"

That was definitely problematic for the earl. Not only was everyone aware of the long-standing feuds between the two clans, but Breadalbane had assigned his very own cousin, Robert Campbell, to lead the attack, narrowing the gap between the earl and the orders. His reputation was also in the balance ever since he was unable to get the local Highland chieftains to agree to swear allegiance to King William. All of this—in addition to the missing fifteen thousand pounds that were meant to go to the chiefs as encouragement—led the king's advisors to have strong suspicions regarding Breadalbane's fidelity. That money likely remained in the earl's pocket. Alexander would bet his title on it.

Starving, Alexander quickly ate two herrings and a piece of cheese before he answered. "So, what is it, exactly, that you would like me to do?"

With a heavy exhale, the earl refilled both of their glasses. "I'd like ye to deliver a letter to the Earl of Mar in Edinburgh."

"Does he not reside in Stirling?"

"Aye, but he's meeting with an architect there to discuss designs for Alloa Tower."

"You want me to go to Edinburgh to deliver a letter? Surely, you have a servant who can transport it." Alexander simmered with frustration. This errand would only take him away from his search for his brother.

"This is far too important." Breadalbane smothered a fishy belch behind his fist. "I need to know it willnae be intercepted by anyone before it reaches the recipient. And you, as one of the king's soldiers and an officer, would never allow that to happen, would ye?"

Alexander peered at him through narrowed eyes. "You know I would not."

THE TACKSMAN'S DAUGHTER

Breadalbane strode over to his desk to retrieve the letter to the earl along with a quill and ink and set them in front of Alexander.

"Sign yer name at the bottom there, if ye will." Breadalbane pointed to an empty space at the foot of the letter.

Alexander stared at the writing, all unintelligible and written in Gaelic. "Why would I sign this? I have no idea what it says."

Breadalbane dismissed his concern with a wave that ended in a reach for the quill, then handed it to him. "'Tis explaining the events in Glencoe. And Mar willnae receive it unless it has two signatures on the bottom. One from me and one from a witness."

Alexander thought it strange but signed it nonetheless. He left enough space for Breadalbane to sign his name above his, then wiped at a smudge of ink on his forefinger.

"More wine?" Breadalbane refreshed both of their glasses and reached for the letter. "Now, where were we?"

Alexander pulled it from his grasp. "You were telling me how you wish for me to travel all the way to Edinburgh to deliver this letter for you. I imagine you will be supplying me with a proper steed?"

Breadalbane nodded slowly, his hand now settled in his lap. He finished his wine in three large gulps, his eyes fixed on the letter. "Of course. Shouldn't take ye more than a fortnight to ride there."

A fortnight sleeping on boggy ground and eating whatever he could catch. "That servant of yours . . . the one who showed me to your apartments?"

The earl raised one eyebrow. "Aye. What of him?"

Alexander slid the letter across the table. "Send him in. I find his blue velvet coat rather alluring. It would look so much better on me. Don't you agree?"

Alexander appeared that evening at supper freshly bathed and wearing the coat. The servant who'd grudgingly surrendered it stood at the door with a dour expression, wearing a brown wool coat that was pilled on the elbows and cuffs.

Breadalbane nodded at a servant who offered him wine, then turned to Alexander. "We will begin once my niece arrives."

"Your niece, milord?" Alexander asked, newly interested in the evening ahead.

Between sips, the earl answered. "Davina. A relation of my first wife."

Lady Glenorchy rolled her eyes, then sauntered away.

Davina. He knew that name. *Dear God, could it be . . . ? Breadalbane's niece?* How could he not have known that? He could conjure up an excuse, perhaps pretend a debility or colic. Or say he forgot something back in his chambers and never return.

Just as he decided to bend over in false agony, she entered the room out of breath, her blonde waves slightly tousled and hanging limp like leaves after a hard rain. "Please forgive my lateness, Uncle. My son . . ."

Her voice trailed off the moment she spotted Alexander. His heart pounded in anticipation that she would slander him in front of the earl and his wife. He held his breath and waited for the insults—and his ruin. He had to do something.

Breadalbane led her to him by her elbow. "Leftenant Gage, this is my niece—"

"Davina." Alexander feigned enchantment, hoping he sounded genuine enough that she would put their latest encounter aside and refrain from spearing him with sharp affronts.

At the sound of her name, her mouth slowly lifted into a smile—genuine, not sardonic—and the heat escaped his chest. She raised her hand for him to kiss, and as he bent to oblige her, she whispered, "Ye *do* remember me."

She probably mistook his flushed face as a sign that he was excited to see her, but as long as it kept her from creating a scene, he didn't care.

They didn't speak much to each other during the meal, Davina sending him uncertain glances every now and then. Alexander found her reaction to his presence rather interesting—instead of being incensed, she seemed pleased—and cautiously let down his guard. During the course of the evening, Alexander's shoulders were pulled as tight as a bowstring while he waited for her to divulge the true nature of their relationship to the earl. But once dessert was served, he relaxed as not a single word was said, both of them careful to act like polite strangers. Alexander assumed she must have been trying to protect him from the earl's wrath should her claims as to his identity as her son's father be known.

At the close of the evening, he turned to the earl. "I would be delighted to escort your niece back to her room, milord. A lass as lovely as she should never be alone with all of those workers traipsing about."

"Very well." Breadalbane waved a disinterested hand in her direction. "I only hope they finish the barracks soon. I'm tired of dodging falling bits of mortar every time I step into the courtyard."

Afterward, in the dark hallway that led to her chamber, she spoke in a whisper. "How did ye know I was here?"

Poor, pathetic thing. She thought he'd searched for her after the attack. "Where else would you be, Davina? Glenorchy is your home." He used her name again, just to reinforce that he knew it.

THE TACKSMAN'S DAUGHTER

"I thought ye meant what ye said the last time we were together. That ye didn't remember me." The torchlight cast unflattering shadows on her face as she spoke. "That ye didn't wish to be together."

"Did I say that?" He took both of her hands in his. "It must have been the wine. If I recall, I had far too much with little to eat. Forgive me, sweeting."

"I knew ye couldn't have meant it." She looked up at him through her lashes. "Would ye care to meet yer son, then?"

Oh. That. He'd almost forgotten. His stomach roiled. He was thankful to be veiled mostly in shadow, able to hide his displeasure. He answered her in a singsong voice. "Lead the way."

They moved quietly down the corridor to her room, uncomfortably close to Lady Glencoe's chambers. While they walked, Davina had mentioned that she was quite pleased with her new quarters, the old ones when she had first arrived being dismal.

Slowly, she opened the door, revealing a sparsely furnished chamber barely large enough for both of them to be in at the same time. Alexander was taken aback. He thought the earl would've allotted her a room worthy of a family member, but this mousehole was likely selected by his newest wife, who clearly didn't care much for the girl. At least there was a hearth.

A small crate containing a meager pallet lay on the floor on one side of her bed, and on top was a lumpy mix of blankets and limbs. Davina bent to readjust the covers so that the child's head could be seen. He was dark-haired like Alexander, but with only a marginal amount of light coming in from the small window, he couldn't see his features. Truly, the child could belong to anyone.

"Is he nae beautiful?" she asked.

"He looks like an angel," he cooed, hopefully convincingly.

It was the right thing to say because she locked her door and led him to the bed, her face glowing with hope and affection.

"I must ask ye a question," she said, her eyes boring into his. "Did ye . . . Were ye part of the attack?"

Could she be serious? Did she think he sat aside and watched it all happen?

"I need to know," she added.

"As an officer, I instructed my men to follow orders as they were given to me."

"But did ye raise yer sword?"

He realized if he answered her truthfully, she would not share her bed with him, and his groin was already aching with anticipation. "I cannot claim to be innocent. I *did* allow the attack to take place." That part was true, and it made him sound remorseful. "But I did not take part in the killing."

In truth, he'd only killed four people. All men. He would never kill a woman or child. Only a beast would do something like that.

She exhaled with what sounded like relief. "I knew it. I knew ye were nae capable of such a thing."

"Of course not." He climbed on top of her, trying to loosen her bodice. In an effort to sound sincere, he whispered, "We should keep our love for one another a secret from your uncle for now."

"Why? I want to tell him that you've returned for me and Sawney."

How was he going to get himself out of this mess? Why did she have to be the earl's niece, for God's sake? And at this point, he wasn't sure if that could work for or against him. The earl could force him to marry her or destroy him for not marrying her. If he did marry her, he could leave her in Scotland, appeasing the earl while maintaining his freedom in England. But since she was clearly not a favourite, he would receive no benefit of properties from the marriage.

And then there was the matter of his father's attainder. Would the earl push for it as punishment if he didn't marry Davina? At the very least, he had to bide his time.

With one hard tug on her bodice strings, it came loose. He lowered his mouth to her breast. "I wish to be in your uncle's good graces before I tell him about our relationship. He could send me away in anger, after all."

"If ye think that best."

He answered with her nipple between his teeth. "I do."

The next day, he received a note from Davina asking him to meet her in the castle armoury before supper. It was a peculiar place to have a rendezvous, but if he was going to be away from civilization and any possibility of sharing a bed with a town whore for an entire fortnight, he figured he should comply.

He wound down several flights of narrow stairs and through a small passage that led to a thick wooden door. It was quiet except for the occasional scratching from some sort of rodent in the nearby granary. He looked both ways before entering, the heavy door squeaking loudly as it opened. Davina stood inside, a silly grin on her face, looking like she'd just stuck her finger in a pie.

He started to unbutton his breeches. "We only have a few minutes before supper, so—"

"I brought ye a surprise."

His fingers steadied on the final button. Davina's bastard appeared from behind her skirts, leaning into her with one hand wrapped around her leg and the other tugging on a curl.

THE TACKSMAN'S DAUGHTER

"Yer son. Sandaidh." She scooted him forward.

He hurriedly re-buttoned his breeches, his cock having lost interest in a dalliance. The child moved closer with a few nudges to his back.

"Go on. Pick him up. He likes that," she offered.

He had absolutely no desire to touch the child in any manner. "I am dressed for supper, Davina. Surely you do not expect me to ruffle my clothing."

She lifted the child and shoved him at his chest. "Only for a second."

Alexander gritted his teeth and took the bastard from her arms. At that very moment, Breadalbane appeared, a powder horn in his hand. Alexander hurriedly dropped the child on the floor, barely keeping him upright in the process.

Breadalbane stared at them, his gaze hopping curiously between Alexander and the bastard. He narrowed his eyes and glared. "What is this?"

"Your niece was introducing me to her son." Alexander straightened his velvet coat, tugging at the hem.

Davina perceptibly deflated. She bowed her head and stared at her fingers that were now playing nervously in her bastard's hair.

"Ye are to keep the bairn tucked away. Do ye understand?" Breadalbane grabbed a bag of gunpowder, tightening the tie around its throat.

"I was only—" she started.

His fingers stilled, his eyes spearing her with authority. "Not another word."

Alexander held his breath, waiting for the earl to put the pieces of the puzzle together and bring down the axe, but Breadalbane simply held his gaze for a second longer than necessary, then exited the room without glancing back.

Davina stared at him, clearly hoping he would say something soothing or promising about the encounter, but if he spoke, it would only be to tell her what a fool she was for revealing the truth of their past.

Only a few minutes later, they stood in the dining room, awaiting the earl's entrance. Alexander wondered if he would mention their brief encounter or ignore it altogether. At his urging, Davina stood on the other side of the room to dissuade the earl from suspecting anything untoward going on between them. The fire burned low in the hearth as he waited, the flames barely visible above the ashen logs.

Finally, the earl entered and pulled Alexander aside, his eyes boring into him. "I heard the king is considering an Act of Attainder on yer father. I imagine that must weigh heavily on yer mind."

It was a strange way to start a conversation, especially considering Alexander had never mentioned that fact to him. But news of a peer possibly being attainted would likely travel fast between nobles. "Naturally."

He shrugged nonchalantly. "I can help ye."

He pulled a sealed letter from inside his coat and handed it to him. "I just received word that His Majesty is headed to Edinburgh. Since ye will already be there, this will give ye the gift of an audience with the king. Ye will have his ear for as long as it takes ye to place the letter in his hands."

"And in return?" he asked, certain Breadalbane wasn't offering him an opportunity to speak with the king out of the goodness of his heart.

"One good turn deserves another."

And there it is. A favour.

Breadalbane lifted a glass of wine offered by a servant from a silver tray. "Ye will speak well of me. Let him know that I had no interest in harming the good people of Glencoe outside of my desire to see MacIain punished for his disloyalty to the crown. I could plead my innocence, but it would be much more effective if someone else vouched for my character. Someone of rank who was there and *knows* I had no hand in it. Are we clear?"

Speak well of John Campbell, Earl of Breadalbane? If he did, he'd be the first to do it.

Chapter 28

It had been almost three months since Davina had seen him. Three long, torturous months that had sent her thoughts whirling through her mind like snowflakes in a blizzard. *This* was the Alex she remembered—loving, kind, polite. Not that rake who crushed her under his boot with his harsh words. She should've known something was amiss when he'd told her he didn't remember her or want to be a family. It simply wasn't like him. It had to be the wine that turned him sour.

She'd seen the effects of drink before, making the wisest men fools at times. Even her own father had been known to embarrass himself after being too cup-shot to utter a single coherent word. Once he'd even woken from a drunken stupor, complaining that the ghost of his deceased mother had been pulling his toes. It made no sense, but her mother had explained his visions as one of the evils of partaking in spirits. No one had slept well that night, worried that there might have been some truth to his claims and that the old woman's ghost would give their toes a good tug when they were fast asleep.

She couldn't wait to tell Cait that it had all been a misunderstanding. But when would she ever see her again? She missed their sisterhood. At Kilchurn, none of the women spoke to her, all whispering in each other's ears when she entered a room. The only woman who smiled in her direction or dared speak to her was the nursemaid who cared for Sawney during the day. She was kindhearted and loving, but mostly to him, not her. The countess wanted Davina to pay for her crime—as she'd put it—and understand that no one would befriend a depraved woman. Her pointed words often sent Davina into tears, longing for the comfort of Cait. It had only been a couple of weeks since her dear friend had left Kilchurn, but it felt like years.

The last few days with Alex hadn't offered her the reassurance she'd hoped for either. He insisted that their relationship remain secret, promising her it wouldn't be long before he disclosed the truth. He was going to have to explain away the last two years to her uncle, but he said he wanted to earn her uncle's praises first. Each day, he either rode into Dalmally with him or lounged in his apartments with the other visitors staying at the castle, laughing and drinking. It seemed as if Uncle enjoyed his company, so she thought he might be moving closer to gaining his approval. But as far as she knew, he hadn't revealed the true nature of their acquaintance to him as of yet.

During the day, they spent very little time together. Alex worried that others might see them and their ruse would be exposed. But at night, he crept into her room and loved her fully, his hands gently cupping her chin as they kissed, sweet whispers of devotion traveling down her neck to her breasts. He'd called her "his lady" over and over, his eyes closed, words intent. Those were the moments that reminded her of who she knew him to be. She only wished they came more often.

Tonight was his fourth night at the castle. She placed another log on the fire to warm the room before his visit. She bent to tuck Sawney's blankets around him when a woman's laugh in the hallway broke the silence. With the door inched open just enough for her head to peek out, she looked both ways but saw nothing. A few minutes later, Alex tapped on her door and slipped inside, his blue velvet coat open and his lace cravat untied.

He turned the key in the lock behind him, and she stared at his disheveled state. Never had she seen him with his clothes unbuttoned or untidy outside of her bedchamber. "Where were you?" she asked, her arms crossed in front of her. "Were ye with that woman?"

He swiped his hand across his mouth and chin, his face screwed up in question. "What woman?"

"I heard a woman. In the hall." Her face grew hotter with every second he didn't respond.

"Oh. That woman." He sat on the edge of her bed and yanked off his shoes, his back to her. "Of course not."

She didn't want to sound jealous, but it was hard to control the accusation in her voice. "Then why is yer clothing undone?"

He shrugged off his coat and tugged his shirt over his head. "I loosened my clothes as I climbed the stairs, fully aware that I would be in your chamber within seconds." He turned to her and sighed. "This interrogation is truly unbecoming. Shall I sleep in my own quarters?"

THE TACKSMAN'S DAUGHTER

He was right. She sounded like a shrew. Why would he be with another woman when he had her? Sawney whimpered lightly, reminding her that she had to lower her voice. "Forgive me. I dinnae know why I thought that . . . ye wouldn't be faithful."

He swung his legs under the bedclothes, not having removed his breeks. "I accept your apology."

She unraveled her braid and let her hair fall over her shoulders and down her back, just the way he liked it, then climbed under the covers. He flipped on his side, his back to her. She'd upset him. With a tentative hand, she reached for his shoulder.

"When will ye go to my uncle?" It was the wrong thing to ask, but she was unable to stop herself.

"Soon enough," he mumbled.

"How soon?"

He turned his head to face her and answered in a tone of displeasure. "Must we go through this again?"

"If you'd only give me clear answers, I wouldn't fash over it." She sank back into her pillow.

"I have no answers. You will simply need to trust me."

She wanted to, but the last time she trusted him, he'd left her without notice and carrying his child. "I need more."

He jerked up the coverlet and yawned.

Time was running out. He'd told her about the letter Uncle had entrusted him to deliver to the king, so she knew he was bound to depart at any moment. She stared at the light and shadows that danced on the ceiling. "When does he want ye to leave?"

"In a few days' time. I need to be there before the king arrives," he mumbled sleepily.

She sat up, the sheet sliding to her waist. "Take me with ye."

"To Edinburgh?"

"Ye said Argyll's regiment is there, aye?"

"Mmhmm," he answered, disinterested.

"And Glenlyon is the captain of that regiment?"

"Mmhmm."

"Then I want to join ye. Cait will be there."

"That is why you wish to go?"

"Her being there makes it easier to leave."

"But why would you want to leave?"

"I dinnae feel safe here." She'd told him several times she wasn't happy at the castle, but that wasn't what she was talking about. She'd overheard too much while in residence, and it concerned her. "Once the king discovers everything, he will most likely sequester Kilchurn Castle from my uncle."

"What will the king discover? You are speaking in riddles." He flipped onto his back, one arm resting lazily behind his head, his muscles flexing with every slight move.

She knew she wasn't making sense. She took a deep breath to steady her nerves. "There's something about my uncle that . . . well . . ."

"Go on."

"I heard him speaking with a man. It was late at night, and I hadn't meant to eavesdrop, but it had grown too cold to leave the window open, and when I went to close it, I heard them talking below." She noticed she was moving her hands too much, waving and pointing unnecessarily, so she folded them in her lap. "I dinnae know his name or where he came from, but he had come to bring news of King James."

Alex sat up, suddenly very interested. "What did he say?"

"He told Uncle that the king—James, not William—was trying to convince King Louis of France to launch an invasion."

Alex's brows lifted. "This man, whoever he was, was warning your uncle that an invasion was possible?"

She shook her head. "He wasn't *warning* him, exactly. He was *informing* him."

"What are you saying?"

"Well, Uncle was *pleased* with the information. He said that if King Louis gave James the strength of his army and fleet, he would provide whatever support he could."

Alex's mouth fell open, then eventually curled into a smile. "So the old goat is a Jacobite."

They left the castle five days later without disclosing their relationship to her uncle and without Sawney. It tore her heart from her chest when she bid him farewell, smothering him in kisses and drenching him with her tears. She knew the nursemaid would take very good care of him, but she worried about the king's guard coming for her uncle if his true allegiances were discovered. What would happen to Sawney? Alex promised her that they would hear of the king's intentions before anyone ever reached Kilchurn, and they would send for Sawney immediately. But it still ripped her apart to leave him, his dark eyes smiling and unaware that she might not return for months.

She was also disappointed that Alex hadn't confronted Uncle with an intent to marry her and legitimize their bairn. But Alex had said that her uncle wasn't quite ripe enough to offer his blessing, so he didn't want to push it. However, he *was* ripe enough to hand her over to Alex when he offered to take her with him to Edinburgh. There had been no questions, no fuss, no mention of the obvious impropriety of a man riding alone for weeks with an unchaperoned, unmarried woman. Uncle had merely muttered a comment about her already being ruined, then handed her over as if she were a soiled, discarded old stocking.

The horses he'd provided them with were fine—a stallion and a palfrey—which pleased Alex. As long as they weren't long in the tooth, Davina didn't care if they were draught horses. But it somehow lifted Alex's spirits, making him more pleasurable to be with than he'd been the last few days.

They reached Tyndrum the first night and set up camp at the edge of a small wood of birches and oaks. Alex built a tent barely large enough for the two of them while she set their food on the wool blanket they would later use as the night grew cold.

"I only wish Sawney were with us," she said.

Alex bent to light the fire, repeatedly striking a small piece of metal against a flint rock. "'Tis too cold and damp. I told you he is better off in the castle where he can sleep next to a warm hearth."

"I know, I know. But I miss him." She wanted him to drape his arm around her, comfort her, but he stayed in front of the fire, fanning it with his hand. "Don't you?"

"What?"

"Miss him."

He stood and swiped his hands together, freeing them of debris. "I barely know him."

Her heart panged. That was not the response she'd hoped for. "Yer his father. Ye must feel something."

"Fathers rarely feel affection for their sons."

"'Tisnae true." She didn't have a brother, but she was sure that if she did, her father would've loved him fiercely. "What has soured ye so?"

He set his hands on his hips and stared into the fire. "What I meant to say was that fathers play favourites. As mine did."

"Surely he loved ye. He simply may have shown it in odd ways, the way fathers often do."

He inhaled deeply, his broad shoulders rising with the breath, then shook his head. "My father reserved his love for my brother only."

It wasn't that she didn't believe him. She did. Love was a fickle thing, after all. At least it was for her. As fickle as the moon. It could be strong and sure one moment, then wane to almost nothing the next. She understood what he was saying. Her own parents had disavowed their love when they learned she was with child.

"But he must've—"

"I heard him. I was only ten. 'Twas my birthday." He bit his bottom lip and looked up at the night sky. "He and my mother had no idea I was standing outside the door. They were arguing because Father wanted to leave that morning for Boroughbridge where his . . . his whore and her bastard lived. Mother carried on about the day being special, urging him to leave the next day instead."

Davina stood and reached for his hand, but he pulled away.

"They called each other a few choice names, as I recall." He shrugged one shoulder, his fingers fitfully tapping the side of his thigh. "Nothing unusual. But it was what he said before he stormed out the door that day. He said, 'If only I had married Morag, then Edward would be my legitimate heir, and this would not be a matter for discussion.'"

Davina took a deep breath. Clearly, he was still holding a grudge, carrying the pain deep within his heart. If only he could let it go, it might free him to love easier. Love her. Love Sawney. "Ye should make amends with him when we arrive in Edinburgh."

He looked at her, incredulous. "My father? He's in London, not Edinburgh."

"Nay. Yer brother. He's with Cait."

He stared at her, little flecks of firelight dancing on the dark hair above his brow, and one side of his mouth lifted into a smile.

Chapter 29

"We can stop here for the night." Edward helped Cait down from her horse, tired from the long day of riding.

A few days back, Taran had decided to ride with him on Fury, insisting it was more of a man's horse than Cait's. He and Cait had shared a smile when he'd said it, knowing that Taran had taken to him during their travels, sticking closely to him like a burr on stockings.

Edward placed both sets of reins in Taran's hand. "Lead the horses to the river to drink. Can you do that, lad?"

He silently agreed, likely happy he had been trusted with an important task.

Edward smiled at this little family they had formed. Though neither Taran nor Cait shared his blood, they had something more solid and sure. Loyalty. And need. It bound them together.

Each night, they curled together tightly, sometimes with Taran between them, his feet or knees pressed against their legs. On those occasions when the lad slept on the other side of Cait, Edward would keep Cait close until, at some point, she would roll away during her sleep. In the early morning hours, Edward would wake with the sudden weight of her head once again resting on his shoulder, and he held her as if she belonged to him.

There was so much he wanted to tell her. How he finally felt he had a purpose, one he understood clearly and was grateful for. One she had given him. He wasn't proud of the way it came about, but he believed finding one another after the massacre was God's way of offering him a second chance to correct the wrongs of his fellow countrymen and the Scots who'd followed their lead. He would also do what he could to find the answers to the questions she had. He hoped one day they would bring her peace, but he feared that might be impossible. He leaned closer to her, breathing in her scent—mildly sweet like heather honey.

She looked up at him over her shoulder. "Smelling me, are ye? Yer just like Taran."

"I shall take that as a compliment. He's—"

"Careful, laddie!" Cait shrieked, startling him into disquiet. She turned to face him, her grip on his wrist tight. "He's too close to the bank. He could fall in, and I dinnae think he knows how to swim."

Taran stood a few feet from the water's edge, seemingly out of harm's way. Edward patted her hand which now held a fistful of his shirt in it. "Even if he falls, the water is no deeper than a foot or two. I think he'll be fine."

"But the current. He could lose his footing and—"

He spoke softly. "The current is gentle. And we're here to watch him."

He positioned himself on the grass and motioned for her to join him. They settled close, shoulders touching, and in silence, watched Taran test the ground before him with his cane.

He nudged her. "You see? He's being cautious."

Cait exhaled a long breath. "I suppose he is."

One of the horses whinnied, and Taran searched with his hand to rub its neck. "Hold yer wheesht."

Edward laughed. "And he's good with the beasts."

She sighed. "He needs us, though."

He grabbed her hand and squeezed it, then let go. "You needn't worry. We shall watch over him until we receive word of his grandfather's whereabouts."

"Do you think he's still alive?" With her right thumb, she rubbed the scar on the palm of her left hand—something he noticed she did out of habit when she was deep in thought.

"There's a chance, but I imagine it to be small."

"He'll want him back."

"That he will," he agreed.

"I'm nae certain I want him to leave." She tilted her head and stared at him. Tiny flecks of silver shone in her pale green eyes.

"We cannot force him to stay. It wouldn't be right." He understood that Taran filled the hole her sister had left behind. He saw the comfort the child brought her, the smiles and laughter that were no longer possible with Gilli.

She rested her cheek against his shoulder, and he kissed the top of her head. "What are we to each other?" he whispered.

"What do ye mean?" She pulled away, her face blank except for a lingering sadness in the corners of her eyes.

THE TACKSMAN'S DAUGHTER

"I mean, what *are* we to each other?" He waited for her to say something, anything. But she remained quiet.

Finally, she stammered, "I . . . we . . . I dinnae know, Edward." Her thumb traced over her scar with a bit more vigor. "I've lost everyone I've ever held dear to my heart. You and Taran are all I have left."

"Are you worried that something might happen to us?"

She stared down at her hands. "I couldn't bear it."

With a price on his head, something could very well happen to him, and the closer they got to Edinburgh and the Earl of Argyll's regiment, that likelihood increased. He watched the breeze send a few loose strands of her hair dancing in its wake and realized that although he wanted to promise he would be with her as long as it took to bring to justice those responsible for her parents and sister's deaths, he couldn't.

It was midafternoon when they reached Stirling, the sun making only brief appearances between showers the entire journey, leaving them cold and damp most of the time. It was almost June, but summer weather hadn't seemed to find its way into Scotland.

They tied the horses to a hitching post in a small village at the base of Stirling Castle, which sat perched high above them on a rocky bluff in the distance. Edward had been there only once before, when he and Alexander had lived in the barracks awaiting orders from their senior commanders. Neither the castle nor the village had changed much since then. It was still a market town bustling with merchants selling their wares, costermongers and victualers shouting from the back of wagons or inside tents, their colourful displays of fruit and vegetables piled artistically behind them.

Except for the occasional rabbit or grouse, they hadn't eaten anything in the last couple of weeks besides fish. And then once, just outside of Tyndrum, they'd found raspberry bushes laden with fruit, some already ripe enough to eat. Edward remembered that day fondly. Cait had made a game of feeding him, tossing berries at his mouth for him to catch. On occasion, he would miss purposely just to hear her laugh.

Taran elbowed him, joyous wonder in his face. "I smell gooseberries."

Edward rested his hand on Taran's shoulder. He didn't have a single coin to purchase anything. His pouch with his winnings from playing cards had burned in the fire at Alt Na Munde. "I have no coin to offer you, lad."

"No need to fash." Taran moved into an empty spot between two merchants. "Sometimes when Grandda and I traveled, we'd go to villages where no one knew us, and he'd let me tell fortunes for a penny."

"You tell fortunes?"

"Well, no exactly *fortunes*. I use my ability as a seer."

Ever since Taran had confessed he had the sight, a hint of discomfort remained in Edward's shoulders. "I'm not certain I want you to do this."

He waved his hand at him, unconcerned. "Some of the time, I dinnae see anything, but sometimes I do. If I see misfortune, I dinnae tell them. I'll tell a wee whid instead. A good one, though."

"It could bring trouble." He leaned down to Taran. "If someone should catch onto your game—"

"Och. Most of the time, what I say is true. And forbye, everyone believes a blind lad. Especially one as braw as me." He flashed a dimpled smile, his grey eyes staring straight ahead.

Edward turned to discuss Taran's idea with Cait, but she was on the far side of the square, watching a juggler entertain a small crowd of people.

"Fortunes! Have yer fortunes told!" Taran shouted in a practiced voice. "A penny for yer fortune!"

Edward stood back and watched as Taran attracted one person and then another wishing to have their fortunes told. Some left smiling and others left praying, their gazes lifted to the heavens, but everyone seemed to leave happy.

Satisfied the lad knew what he was doing, he wandered over to a weaver's tent where tartans of all patterns were displayed. He ran his hand over the heavy wool and thought if Taran collected enough sterling, he might be able to buy a blanket for all of them to huddle under on cold nights along their journey.

He roamed aimlessly from stall to stall, noticing that even with the barracks so close, only a smattering of soldiers wandered about the market, their scarlet coats easily spotted in the sea of drab browns, greens, and greys. Although Edward still wore the grey breeches of his regiment, they blended in nicely in the densely packed crowd. He purposefully bumped into one of the soldiers, stared directly into his face, and mumbled the greeting, '*Beannachd Dhia dhuit, a duine.*' He did it not only to identify himself as a Scot, but to see if he showed any signs of recognition. The soldier merely shoved away with a grunt, leaving Edward satisfied that either the news of three traitors hadn't yet reached Stirling, or his heavy beard and use of Gaelic rendered him unrecognizable.

Standing a little straighter, he turned to join Cait, but a tap on his shoulder forced him to stop. Duncan, Ronan, and Broc stood behind him, their faces lit up as if the four of them were old friends. Edward tried to smile in greeting but couldn't.

"So ye came," Duncan said, his thumbs tucked into the leather belt holding his sporran.

Edward scrambled for something to say that would keep him in neutral territory. "Are there many of you here?"

THE TACKSMAN'S DAUGHTER

Duncan leaned in. "This is a large showing for the market, if ye understand my meaning."

Edward did. He scanned the crowd, wondering who was truly there for the gathering and who was there for the goods. It was hard to say, but now that he thought about it, there were scores of men standing around with their heads bowed together.

"Will we see ye tonight?" Duncan asked.

"Where will you be?" It was the most noncommittal response Edward could think of.

"There's an almshouse right behind the Kirk of the Holy Rude. We meet after sundown."

Edward nodded once, and the three drovers vanished into the crowd.

That night as Taran sat on their new tartan blanket counting his remaining coins, his face blank while his fingers rubbed the markings on both sides, Edward told Cait about his chance meeting with Duncan.

"They're gathering not far from here. At the almshouse," he said.

"Do ye think 'tis dangerous for us to be here?"

That's exactly what he was thinking. If William's guards got word of a Jacobite rally, Edward didn't want to risk being rounded up with the others. "We should leave first thing in the morning."

He slept fretfully that night, Cait curled up next to him, and Taran nestled close on her other side. If it hadn't been so late and they hadn't ridden all day, he would've suggested they leave immediately, but the horses needed to rest, and so did they. As it turned out, the night passed without incident, and they were on the way to Edinburgh just before dawn.

They traveled east at a casual pace, the weather again cold and drizzly. Cait wore the tartan draped over her head to keep her warm. Although Edward suggested Taran ride with her to stay dry under the blanket, he'd refused, insisting a little rain didn't bother him.

Not ten minutes into their ride, Edward spotted three piles of rags on the side of the trail. He rode closer, the brown heaps slowly taking the forms of men. With no alternative but to remain on the path, he silently signaled for Cait to stay behind, one hand on the dagger at his waist. Fury sidestepped, unhappy with Edward's command to move closer.

"I smell blood," Taran whispered. "What is it?"

Edward edged nearer, spotting a dark pool girdling one of the men. Fury took a few more cautious steps until Edward could clearly see the face of the first man. Duncan. Ronan and Broc lay nearby, all dead.

A chill ran through Edward's veins. "'Tis Duncan and the others."

Edward felt Taran's body stiffen. "How were they killed?"

Edward stared at the blood staining the backs of both of the older drovers' plaids. "Ronan and Broc were run through, it seems."

"And Duncan?"

A clean gash spread across Duncan's neck, a trail of blood leading out of his mouth. He'd died just as Taran had predicted. "Throat slit."

"I told ye so."

Chapter 30

Cait sidled up next to the bodies in the road.

"What are you doing?" Edward called from his horse.

She dismounted to take a closer look. Duncan's throat had been slit ear to ear. "I want to pay my respects."

From behind, she heard Edward grumble his dissent, but she bent down anyway, blocking his view of what she was really doing. "A quick prayer. 'Twill only be but a second."

Duncan lay on his back, his arms and legs splayed apart. Strands of his red hair were stuck to his cheeks, and his eyes were frozen open, staring past Cait through big black pupils. They no longer looked glassy but had a strange flatness to them, telling her his soul had already abandoned his body. His deerskin sporran lay twisted at his side, tied shut with a rough piece of twine.

Cait said a quick prayer, unwound the twine with trembling fingers, then reached into his sporran for the letter he'd shown her only days earlier. She held her breath as she slid it out—the *Earl of Mar, Edinburgh*, written on top—and slipped it into a pocket tied beneath her skirt.

Cait didn't mind riding all day to Falkirk. The farther she got away from Stirling, the better. But the danger remained with her, this time tucked inside of her gown and pressed closely against her thigh. She knew she was taking a risk that could get her killed, but would it matter? Her family was dead, their croft burned to the ground, and the only place she'd known as home was changed forever. If she were caught yet the king were removed from the throne for his hand in the massacre, her death would be a small price to pay. But she couldn't let Edward and Taran become embroiled in her decision to help the Jacobites. They were far too precious, so she vowed to keep the letter a secret.

When it began to rain, she slipped it into the bag tied to her waist, shoving it to the bottom to keep it dry. It drizzled most of the ride, bringing a chill to her skin that she welcomed, for it allowed her to concentrate on staying warm and not on the danger that lay ahead.

Edward had told her that Falkirk was even bigger than Stirling, but she couldn't imagine it. She had never seen so many people all at once, shuffling around and bumping each other in the market square. Certainly not in Glencoe. If her village had three hundred crofters, she'd be surprised. But in Stirling, there were at least that many squeezed into the square alone and dozens more milling about. She'd been jostled herself as she stood watching the juggler toss pieces of fruit in the air, then catch them behind his back or in his mouth. She'd never seen anything like that before. But that was the difference between townsfolk and Highland villagers. Townsfolk could waste their days throwing fruit about, but in the Highlands, where working the land and tending to the beasts kept everyone busy from dawn until dusk, there was no time for such nonsense.

The sun dipped behind the horizon just as the weather cleared, and they found a nice spot near the river to water the horses and sleep for the night. Taran had fallen asleep quickly by the fire, only his curls peeking out from under their new wool blanket. He was such a good lad, mindful and sweet. She liked having him with her yet wondered if Edward was wrong and his grandda had escaped the slaughter and was sick with worry over him. But how would she find out? Would he have dared return to Glencoe? Or was he back on the Isle of Harris?

Edward reappeared from washing in the river, wearing only his breeks. The rest of his clothing was draped over one arm. He approached, rubbing his face with his cravat. As he moved closer, the broad planes of his chest and the muscles of his stomach were accentuated by the firelight. He was a beautiful man, strong and confident, and with only a smile, he could awaken unfamiliar feelings within her.

She enjoyed their closeness. The certainty of him. And she didn't mind the kisses she'd shared with him in the past. But Davina had fallen from grace for allowing similar feelings to get the better of her. Cait didn't want to pay the same price. Not that she would ever be so weak as to allow a man to take her in such a way and then abandon her. She supposed she couldn't force a man to stay, but she had to trust her instincts. She was certain Edward was different from his brother. She'd seen evidence of it so many times over the past few months. As he grew closer, she settled into the thought that she might be falling in love.

She wondered if Davina had felt the same, confident that she had found a man who would never betray her. She suddenly felt guilty for any judgement she may have had about her.

She watched as Edward stopped briefly to stretch Taran's blanket over an exposed ankle, then stand over him with the glimmer of a smile on his lips. It was as if he did it without thought, the most natural thing that came to him at that moment. It was the way he cared for her too. As if she was all that mattered and was a large part of his heart.

They were her family. Her home. It may not last long, but it was all she had.

"The water is frightfully cold." He jammed two sticks into the ground, balanced his cravat over them to dry, then stood close to the fire, briskly rubbing his hands together. After a few seconds, he tipped his head back and sighed. "Much better."

Cait dropped another branch on the fire and joined him. His arms folded around her, and she melted into the warmth of his skin.

Her breath slowed as she stared into the flames. Orange and yellow tendrils flicked upward, sending sparks floating away into the darkness. "I've been thinking about what ye asked me the other day."

"About?"

"Us."

His cheek rested on top of her head, his heartbeat strong and steady on her back.

She took a few deep breaths before speaking. "I dinnae know how to say what I feel."

She felt his stomach clench, then his arms loosened around her. "You needn't say anything, Cait. I understand."

"Ye do?" She was embarrassed and relieved all at once. She didn't want to have to tell him her feelings. But he wasn't reacting the way she'd hoped he would.

"I believe so," he answered somberly.

"Come sit." Confused by his lack of a reaction, she led him over to the opposite side of the fire from Taran, where they sat, Edward with his arms wrapped around his knees, his mouth stern. She touched his arm lightly, and he turned to her, half his face illuminated by the fire. Her stomach shuddered nervously. She knew what she wanted to say but wasn't sure she could do it.

Instead, she took his face in her hands and kissed him. At first, he didn't respond, so she nudged him closer, and his lips grew soft and interested.

He drew away from her slightly, his brow crinkled. "I thought you were going to tell me . . ."

His words trailed off when she nibbled his bottom lip. She pulled back to look at him, to study him. "We . . . are all we have. And when we get to Edinburgh . . . it could all be over."

He was silent, gazing at her as if he'd heard her speak for the first time. He brushed his thumb over her cheek, his eyes sad.

She leaned into him and kissed him hard, allowing every feeling to pour out of her in a storm of emotion. Her fingers got lost deep in his hair as her mind went blank. She wanted him, needed him, and she prayed he felt the same.

He eased her onto her back and kissed her neck and the hollow of her throat, his mouth teasing and fervent. Through her bodice, she felt his heartbeat pound against her own. She closed her eyes as his lips moved lower to her breasts, sending fluttering sensations low in her belly. He edged one leg between hers, his hands moving, his mouth wandering.

He lifted his head and stared at her, his chest rising and falling rapidly. "Would you like me to stop?"

Would she? She stared into his eyes. She knew if it were daylight, they'd be burning blue the way they always were when he was excited, but with only the stars above, she couldn't see their colour. She whispered, her mouth close to his. "I want ye to know how I feel about ye. I may be damned for it, but I want ye to know."

"Are you sure, lass?"

"I am."

With one hand, he fumbled with the buttons on his breeks. He pulled up her skirts, then stilled. "I hope you know, Cait, that I—"

She pressed a finger to his lips. "Wheesht. I want this, Edward."

There was no one left to judge or reprimand her for what she was about to do. Tears welled in her eyes, not from fear, but from the knowledge that she was moving forward, accepting a new life—for however long—with him.

He moved slowly, carefully. She held her breath, eager to feel every part of his skin that touched her. They were joined in body, their past, and their uncertain future.

Afterwards, they lay in each other's arms, his fingers playing with her hair. She melted into the warmth of his chest, her cheek resting above his heart.

He was the first to break the silence. "I have never been in love before. You've changed me."

He'd whispered he loved her only minutes earlier but hearing him say it again shaped it into something firm and solid. "It felt nice to have ye so close."

"Did it?" His chest vibrated with the words. "No regrets?"

THE TACKSMAN'S DAUGHTER

"None."

The firelight cast a warm glow over his skin and dark hair. She ran a finger over his lips. "What have ye done to me? You and yer smile. Yer crooked, drunken, English smile."

He tipped up her chin with one finger. "When we met and you told me your father fell in love with your mother over her smile, you said you would never fall so easily."

She kissed him softly. "That was before I met *you*."

"Are we going into town today, then?" Taran asked between shrieks. Cait pulled her fingers through his curls, attempting to rake through his morning tangles.

"Stop yer fussing. If ye would do this yerself every once in a while, it wouldn't hurt so much when I finally get to ye." Cait unraveled a small twig from a knot and tossed it aside. Out of the corner of her eye, she watched Edward fiddle with the fire. After a few seconds, his gaze caught hers, and he smiled. They hadn't spoken about what transpired between them the night before, but they didn't have to. It was part of who they were now, and the thought of that settled warmly in Cait's heart.

Edward handed Taran a stick with a trout pierced on it. "What's the hurry, lad?"

Taran bit off some fish. "Ever since I had those gooseberries in Stirling, I've had a hankering for more."

"Eating like a fat rich man pleases ye, does it?" Cait asked. She brushed her fingers through his hair one last time, then handed him his cane. "Like a cow that's grazed all summer, you'll be plump and ready for market."

Taran stood, his eyes staring straight with alarm. "Ye dinnae mean to get rid of me, do ye?"

Edward patted him on the shoulder. "Nay, lad. You needn't worry about such things. Where I go, you go. Understood?"

Taran seemed to melt with Edward's words, his face once again filling with lightness. But Cait wondered if what Edward said was true. Not that she didn't trust he believed what he'd said, but she wondered if some day Taran's grandda would return for him.

He wandered off to the horses, nibbling at his fish as he waved his cane through the grass ahead of him. His blond curls glistened in the sunlight, giving him the appearance of an angel. Was it wrong of her not to want his grandda to reclaim him? They were like a patchwork quilt, the three of them. All from separate cloths of different colours, but once stitched together, the pattern seemed to make perfect sense.

"I know what you're thinking." Edward settled on the grass beside her. "I feel the same."

"If only Gilli had lived, she would be here with us." She slowly braided her hair while she watched Taran bend to pick something out of the grass.

Edward kissed her right above her ear, summoning her out of her reverie, then stared at her busy hands, his eyes narrowed with curiosity. "How did you get that scar? Not from all that twirling you do with your blade."

She stilled, and the fingers of her left hand instinctively closed over her palm. "Nay. 'Tis a memory I wish to forget."

He reached for her hand and turned it palm up, his thumb tracing over its center. The scar was red, perfectly straight, and slightly raised, starting between her thumb and forefinger and stretching across her palm. "Will you not share it? With me?"

She could either refuse to tell him or explain what had turned her into such a chary woman. As much as she didn't care to revisit the ghosts of the soldiers that haunted her every time she looked at her scar, she knew what he was asking for was more than the telling of a tale. He was asking her to share herself, her past, with him.

She took a deep breath, allowing her mind to return to the time it happened.

A regiment from Inverlochy had ferried into Loch Leven to camp just outside of Glencoe in Ballachulish. She was fourteen at the time and had never met an Englishman before. But she'd heard tales of the English over the years, none of them good.

Time and again over a period of a few weeks, soldiers entered Glencoe, looking to speak to MacIain or her father about routes north to the garrison or east to Kinlochbeg. Other times, they'd wandered into the village soused with drink and searching for more, and it was one of those times that they had come upon her unexpectedly.

She'd been in the brewhouse fetching the pipe her da had left there, when two soldiers stumbled in, their breath stinking of whisky and their faces covered in sweat. At first, she hadn't thought much of them, but when their expressions sobered upon seeing her, a chill ran through her bones.

The older one had a dark beard that covered most of his face. He nudged the younger one and spoke in a clipped English accent. "I believe this lass was waitin' for us in here. Weren't you, lass?"

The younger soldier laughed falsely, more out of obligation than humour, it seemed.

She tried to sidle around them to the door, but the older one blocked her way. "Where do you think you're goin'?"

THE TACKSMAN'S DAUGHTER

Her throat tightened, forcing her to squeeze out the words. "My da is probably looking for me. He should be here any moment." It wasn't the truth, but only a man who was either mad or didn't know her father would dare take that chance.

"Your da?" He smacked the younger one on the chest with the back of his hand. "Did you hear that, Pratt? Her *da* is comin'."

This time, Pratt looked as if he wasn't sure if he should laugh or not. Instead, he snorted, then glanced behind him.

"I don't think your *da* is comin'." With dirty fingers, the older one touched her hair. She stepped back, her heel slipping into the catch basin. "And that means you have plenty of time to entertain us."

She glanced past Pratt at the brewhouse entrance, her heart racing at the thought no one was coming to save her. Panicked, she kicked his shin, sending him hopping and stumbling just enough for her to leap to the door. The moment she grasped the handle, a large arm curled around her waist, lifted her off the floor, then forced her against the wall. She fought as Pratt pinned her arms and the older one pulled up her skirts.

"Let go of me!" she yelled.

With his breeks down around his ankles, the bearded man shoved himself between her thighs. Haphazardly, he pumped into her, jabbing her everywhere but where it mattered. He didn't seem to notice, his eyes glassy and his grunts coming faster. His beefy hands tugged at her bodice and ripped it, exposing one of her breasts. Then his mouth came down on her hard, his tongue and teeth sliding over her skin.

Bile rose in her throat, and she retched all over the shoulder of his scarlet coat. He pulled back immediately, and while he stared at the mess in shock, she gave him a sharp kick to the groin, sending him into a curled heap on the floor.

Horrified, Pratt jumped back, letting go of her arms. Freed, she skirted past him and ran for the door.

"Get her!" yelled the bearded soldier.

Pratt came up behind her, spun her around, and jabbed his blade at her stomach. She deflected it with her hand, its sharp edge slicing through her palm. At first, she felt no pain, but after she managed to free her other hand from his grip and wrestle his blade from him, the sting burned through her palm and up her arm.

As if the devil had entered her body, she thrust the knife as hard as she could into Pratt's chest. It struck bone and stuck straight out, a tiny stream of blood slowly making its way down the front of his soiled white shirt. Pratt froze, his eyes wide with disbelief. Before either soldier could move, she ran out and never saw them again.

Edward shook his head once, his mouth in a tight line. "That was not the account I was expecting."

"Did ye think I was going to say I sliced it spreading jam on a bannock?" She tried to make light of it, but her voice came out shaky.

"I'm not certain what I thought." He pressed her palm to his lips. "So now I understand all the suspicion towards the soldiers. The distrust."

The image of all the fresh graves on Eilean Munde flashed before her. "'Twas justified, as it turns out."

"It was," he acquiesced somberly.

"And now ye know why my da taught me how to defend myself."

He nodded, his eyes narrowed, his gaze looking inward. She had obviously stirred something inside of him. Something dangerous. He kissed her palm once again and spoke with a velvet voice that didn't match his stern features. "You're a brave lass, Cait. *Mo chaileag uain'-shùileach chalma.* My brave green-eyed lass."

"Ye needn't ever fash over me, Edward. As long as I have my blade, I can take care of myself."

He smiled at her. "I know that well, indeed."

Chapter 31

If she would only. Stop. Talking.

One more word, and Alexander would tie Davina to a tree and leave her for the wolves. Why had he agreed to take her with him? At first, it seemed like a good idea, having her there for the prigging. It was a long journey, after all. And then there was the fact that bringing her would remove her from Breadalbane's presence, rendering her incapable of disclosing that he was responsible for her ruin. There was no doubt the old man would've forced him into a marriage with her to legitimize her bastard. But now with her incessant questions and arguing, he wanted to return to that moment when he'd agreed and take it all back.

They had at least another week—perhaps two if the terrain was boggy—before they'd arrive in Edinburgh, where he could happily leave her with Edward's Scottish whore and go about his business of having his brother hanged for treason. Killing two birds with one stone, as it were.

As he sat there listening to Davina's inane chatter, he forced his mind to travel to a place of comfort. He settled his hands on the pommel of his saddle and inhaled deeply, remembering the scent of lilac that gently blanketed Berenice's flawless skin.

He'd never find another woman like her. Her confidence. The firm yet gentle way her hand rested on his forearm as she stood beside him in the presence of greater peers.

He'd met her just after Father had been taken to the Tower and his mother sent him away to beg Father's cronies for funds to tide them over until the whole matter regarding his treachery was resolved. He'd ridden to Lancaster reluctantly, the only saving grace being that the city was far from the gossip surrounding the Gage family name.

He'd only been there a few days before the newly widowed Berenice smiled in his direction. From then on, he was grateful he'd made the journey. At first, he'd considered only bedding her, but in a matter of a few weeks, his heart had opened in a way it never had before. It was an unfamiliar feeling. Shocking even. She'd looked at him as if he was the most important man in the room. Not flirtatiously, but with admiration. It was a look he hadn't seen since he was a child and still in his mother's good graces. She spoke kindly, adoringly. She praised his intelligence, strength, charm, noble manner. She saw all the value in him that his father never managed to see, parading him around Lancaster, proud to have him as her escort.

Even after he told her about his family's misfortune, her affection had never wavered. Her words had lifted him to what he'd been before his mother had treated him as a regrettable disappointment. Berenice had promised they would overcome "the small matter" of his family name being tarnished as long as they were together. She'd spoken of marriage, but she needed his name to be cleared by the king. Most of all, she'd promised to write a letter to her late husband's uncle about him.

"He is presently at court, so surely he could put in a good word with William," she'd said, a kiss marking her sincerity.

But then Edward arrived, and soon after, those approving looks became glances barely acknowledging Alexander's presence. Before long, there was nothing he could say or do to fully capture her attention. With marriage no longer of interest to her, Berenice suddenly lost the desire to write that letter.

"I'd like to purchase a trinket for Sawney when we arrive in Stirling." Davina's declaration returned him to the present. She rode behind him on a chestnut palfrey, the high-pitched squeak of her saddle more soothing than her voice. Had she always trilled her Rs that much?

"A *tr-r-r-rinket?*" He couldn't help but mock her ridiculous speech.

"A bauble. Something for him to enjoy."

"I know what a trinket is." That was one of the problems with her. She didn't even recognize an insult when it was being hurled her way. If she had, she would shut her mouth for a change and remove her hands from his purse. "What you mean to say is you would like *me* to purchase a trinket for him."

"Ye said there was a market there."

Again, she missed the point. It was going to be a long week, indeed.

He turned briefly in his saddle to face her. "Shall we wait until we arrive before you spend all of my coin?"

THE TACKSMAN'S DAUGHTER

If she had only caught him in the stairwell with that woman back at Kilchurn Castle, he would be riding alone peacefully with no one prattling in his ear. He shouldn't have lied about it. He should have said, *As a matter of fact, I was with that woman you heard laughing in the hall. And although it was akin to fucking a bowl of clear broth, at least she didn't babble through it like you do.*

"I'm also considering a new ribbon for my hair," she added.

He rolled his eyes. "Some things are meant to be thoughts, *sweeting*. Not spoken aloud."

Alexander wasn't *completely* miserable during the journey. There were actually several wonderful things about being sent to do Breadalbane's bidding. The first was that it allowed him to leave Fort William and escape his mother's frequent letters replete with her financial woes. They would all likely pile up on his desk there now, her complaints and demands unread. The second was the very nature of Breadalbane's request, for it placed Alexander in the king's presence—a feat he wouldn't have been able to accomplish easily on his own. But with Breadalbane's importance in the Scottish Privy Council and role in the events in Glencoe, the king would undoubtedly receive him as the earl's messenger.

But the best part of it all was that although Breadalbane considered Alexander to be *his* pawn in this pursuit, his eavesdropping niece had made him *Alexander's* pawn. The knowledge that Breadalbane was secretly a Jacobite could only work to his advantage. He could either report the earl's disloyalty to King William and be heralded as a hero, or he could blackmail Breadalbane with it, forcing him to convince the king to surrender his pursuit to attaint his father. Either way, Alexander would be rewarded.

That would all be well and good, of course, but if he were able to gift Edward to the king in shackles, it would make it that much sweeter. His cock grew hard just thinking about it.

Davina stood by her horse, feeding him a handful of grass. Alexander adjusted his breeches, now tight with his enthusiasm. "You do realize he can graze on his own?"

She laughed. "But his mouth is so soft and tickly."

The horse nibbled from her palm, his lips reaching and grabbing sloppily. She giggled again and bent to pick more grass. Alexander admired her from behind and instantly grew inspired.

"Leave him and come to me."

"But I was—"

"I said leave him."

As she approached, she brushed her palms on her skirts, freeing them of any remaining grass. She was an attractive woman. Not as attractive as she'd once been before she birthed that misbegotten child of hers, but nevertheless she was worth the effort of removing his breeches.

When she was within reach, he pulled her closer and spun her around.

"What are ye doing?" she asked coquettishly.

With his hand on her back, he guided her to a tree and bent her over, setting her hands on its trunk for support. "Spread your legs."

She tried to turn to face him, but he grabbed her hands and replaced them on the tree. "Stay like that."

She obeyed, naturally, and he threw up her skirts over her buttocks.

"Alex—"

"No talking." He hated when she called him that, reducing his name to something that sounded so plebeian. Peasant-like. Only one woman was permitted to do it, and because of Edward, he would never hear his name uttered from her perfect lips again. He released himself from his breeches and entered her hard.

She cried out in a breathy moan. He liked that. It excited him.

He had never taken her from behind and wondered if that was what made her seem so boring to him. She'd never suggested it—or anything else out of the ordinary, for that matter. But this felt good, and he liked to watch her hands struggle to grip the tree, slipping and clawing as he thrust into her and made her lose her balance.

He concentrated on the feel of her, wet and warm around him. With her face hidden from view, she could be any one of the multitudes of women he'd had in his past. That whore, Wynda. Jenny from Inverlochy Castle. Or the harlot in the stairwell, whatever her name was. Or she could be the one he hadn't yet had. Cait.

He grabbed her hips and plunged as deep as he could, emptying himself into her. For a few seconds, his mind went numb and his thoughts jumbled, sending him to a place of only physical experience. When the last pulse of release left his body, the fog in his head lifted, and he sadly remembered that the woman he had been with all along was Davina.

In what felt like two years but was only two weeks later, Alexander rode directly up to Stirling Castle with Davina trailing behind him. Crowds of people parted to clear a path for them up the hill, some with suspicious eyes and others indifferent to their presence. It was obvious he was headed for the castle, considering he wore the uniform of an officer and the barracks were there, yet still some stared, questioning his arrival.

THE TACKSMAN'S DAUGHTER

Hopefully, he would be able to acquire a proper meal and lodging for a couple of nights. Where they would put Davina, he didn't know or care as long as it would provide him with some peace and quiet.

A bevy of ragged-clothed sutlers stood outside the castle walls, selling their wares on upturned crates under makeshift tents. Alexander helped Davina off her horse, took her reins, and started to walk to the gate.

"I'll wait here," she announced. "I want to see what they're selling."

Of course you do.

He led their horses through the gate and inner courtyard over to the stables and released them to the stable hands.

"Well, look who it is," said a teasing, familiar voice.

Alexander spun to see to whom it belonged, his loins warming with hope. And there she stood, Jenny Raeburn, her auburn hair tied up prettily, the tops of her breasts pouring out of her bodice.

With a wide smile, she sidled up to him. "Remember me?"

Alexander looked past the courtyard to the gate to make sure Davina hadn't entered. "Remember you?"

"Perhaps you need a reminder." She took his finger and stuck it in her mouth, sucked, then pressed his hand to her breast.

He hadn't needed the reminder. Although their evening together at Inverlochy Castle was a month or so earlier, it was still fresh in his memory. He ran his thumb inside her bodice over her nipple. "What a lovely coincidence. Here with Viscount Campden, I presume?"

She lifted her eyebrows in acknowledgement. "Boring me to tears."

"What would he have to do with the garrison?"

"He has no business *here."* She ran her fingers down the row of silver buttons on his coat. "He's at the earl's—an old friend, I believe. I told him I wanted to see what the victualers were selling, so I left him there discussing things I care little about."

"The earl?"

"Argyll. We are staying with him at his lodgings—in case you were wondering."

"I *was* wondering." The earl's home was next to the castle, only a few hundred yards from the gate. Very convenient.

"So when will I see you?" She glanced around them. "Alone?"

"Make it happen."

She sauntered away, turning once to make sure he was watching.

"Who was that woman?" Davina touched his sleeve from behind, and he turned to face her.

"I have no idea. She was asking for directions to the chapel."

She smiled, apparently satisfied with his answer. She held out her hand, palm up. "Well, there's a sutler who's selling plums outside the gate. Three for a penny."

An invitation to Argyll's lodgings arrived that night, just as he'd expected. He had explained to Davina that it wasn't a social visit but a military meeting of sorts that was not meant for civilian ears. Reluctantly, she bid him farewell, then returned to her quarters located in the old part of the castle, the king's house, leaving him free to rendezvous with Jenny.

Just after nightfall, he took a brief walk down the cobblestone road and arrived at Argyll's estate. He wore the blue velvet coat taken from Breadalbane's servant, happy to be free of his musty uniform. An elegant supper was served, the first meal he'd had since leaving Kilchurn Castle that didn't require him to catch it first.

Alexander sat at the long dining table across from Jenny and her hound-faced paramour. Argyll sat at the head with his wife at his side, one hand affectionately placed on top of hers for most of the meal. His periwig was parted neatly down the middle, the long brown curls hanging freely over his chest. "What brings ye here to Stirling, Mansfield?"

Alexander set down his wine. "I have been asked to deliver letters from the Earl of Breadalbane. One to His Majesty and the other to the Earl of Mar. Stirling is merely a necessary stop on the way to Edinburgh."

Campden's pudgy face lit up. "We are headed there ourselves. Perhaps you would like to join our convoy. We could use one of the king's men to protect us along the way. You do have your uniform with you, do you not?"

"Of course." Out of the corner of his eye, he saw Jenny smile behind her wineglass. "It would be my honour to escort you. When do you plan to leave?"

"In a few days' time, I hope." His jowls jiggled as he spoke. "I do not wish to be around this Jacobite nonsense any longer."

"Yer fears are unwarranted, Campden." Argyll speared a perfectly prepared piece of mutton on his plate. "I believe the orchestrators of that gathering were dealt with appropriately. They no longer pose a threat."

"Pardon me, milords, but what exactly are you talking about?" Alexander felt a soft stockinged foot stroke his own, then climb farther up his shin. He glanced across the table briefly at Jenny, a conspiratorial smile on her lips.

Argyll swallowed the last of his mutton. "There was a Jacobite rally held nearby recently, and now fingers are being pointed in all directions. Campden here doesn't wish to get caught in the net."

THE TACKSMAN'S DAUGHTER

"I am *no* Jacobite," Campden asserted, one hand raised firmly. "And if it weren't for Jenny's insistence that we stop in Stirling to visit the market, I would be nowhere near this rebellious behaviour."

"Everyone knows you are a loyal subject to King William, my pet," Jenny said, her foot finding its way farther up Alexander's leg. "But Stirling is such a lovely town, and I thought I'd find something that might please you in the market square. You should really go there, Leftenant. 'Tis a remarkable place of wonders."

She was throwing him bait, and he was happy to bite. "Perhaps I will. When would you suggest I go?"

"Although the afternoons are crowded, that is when the most *extraordinary* things seem to happen."

"I appreciate the advice, Miss Raeburn." He ran his hand over the bridge of her foot that had managed to travel to the lower part of his thigh, his breeches now thoroughly snug.

Campden shoved a piece of meat in his mouth and mumbled a warning between bites. "Beware of the Jacobites, Mansfield. You do not want to be seen in association with any of them. Wear your uniform. That should keep them away."

Jenny turned to Argyll. "Couldn't you send in one of your regiments, milord, to frighten them off?"

Argyll shook his head. "I have only a nominal appointment as the head of those regiments. I dinnae interfere with their tactics."

Lady Elizabeth finally spoke for the first time that evening since introductions. "The king is sending soldiers. They should arrive any day now."

That was why Alexander had received strange looks from the townspeople as he approached the castle. They thought he was arriving on behalf of the king to capture and punish traitors.

"Will they?" Jenny asked. There was something peculiar in her tone that made Alexander study her. But then she winked at him, and warmth spread throughout his loins, pulling his thoughts elsewhere.

Chapter 32

"I heard some of what she said." Taran sat on the wool blanket with Edward, his hand searching the grass beside it for twigs. One after the other, he tossed them towards the smoldering fire and missed, but Edward didn't have the heart to tell him that.

"I don't think she meant for you to hear it." Edward draped his arm around Taran's shoulder. Cait had told the story of her scar that morning, and Taran had been quiet since.

"Those men tried to rape her," Taran said with confidence.

"A lad of nine needn't know of such things."

"Rape?" Taran crinkled his brow. "My grandda told me. Said that was what killed my father."

Rape killed his father? "I think you misunderstood things, lad."

"Nay. Grandda said some men raped my mother before they killed her, and my da went after them. He came upon them in a field, and they speared him with a pitchfork."

Edward had never known where Taran's father was. He hadn't even been certain he was dead. But now he knew and wished he didn't.

Taran picked at the grass beside the blanket. "It happened before I was old enough to remember him."

Poor little lad. "It sounds like your father was a brave man."

"Och, aye. The bravest." Taran sniffled, his little chest quivering with the effort to hold back his tears.

Edward pulled him close and rocked him gently, whispering the words of a poem his mother used to sing to him as a boy. His mother speaking Gaelic had

THE TACKSMAN'S DAUGHTER

always soothed him, the words strange and their meanings mysterious. It hadn't mattered that he didn't understand most of it back then. It was her voice that had pulled him away from his sadness. "*Is mi am suidhe air an tulach . . .*"

He couldn't imagine not having his mother as a child. She had been his place of comfort and stability. She was part of every childhood memory. And that made him think. If he were a lad as young as Taran and had gone missing, it would've killed his mother not to know his whereabouts. What had happened.

If Taran's grandfather was still alive, he had to be told where Taran was. That he was safe. And as much as Edward didn't want to give him up, he had no right to keep him if there was someone else out there who needed him more.

As the flames flickered steadily, Taran fell asleep. Edward laid him down on the blanket, brushed the hair out of his face, and walked down the slope to the river where Cait was washing.

It was dusk, a slight breeze blowing but not enough to ripple the grass or stir the trees. Halfway down the slope, he noticed Cait's blue gown folded neatly on top of a rock on the bank. An abrupt splash ahead drew his attention to where she stood by the river dressed only in her shift, the wet skin on her arms reflecting the pink light of the evening sky. She bent to wash her face, and golden droplets of water sparkled in the waning sunlight. He took his time before joining her, happy to revel in the simplicity of her beauty bathed in rose.

A weight had lifted off him since she confessed her feelings and they had shared the night together. She touched him freely now, sometimes the action as little as a brush over his cheek, fingers tucking back hair that had escaped his queue. Other times, she embraced him, her weight comfortably pressed against his chest. He did the same with no reservation, unafraid of her reaction, knowing that sort of intimacy was possessed only by those who shared an understanding that they belonged together. That they were a part of something that could not be broken.

She was the woman he wanted. The woman he loved. And she belonged to him. It was all quite simple.

She stood with her back to him, now only a few paces away. "Were you watching me bathe?" she asked, clearly having sensed his presence.

"And if I was?" He joined her and tucked her close, breathing in the sweet scent of her hair and rubbing her skin that was covered in gooseflesh.

She took her time before she smiled up at him and answered. "I dinnae think I mind it."

He kissed the droplets of water from her lips and cheeks, then dipped his flask in the river and offered it to her. "Are you not cold? That water is freezing."

She shrugged in his embrace. "I'm warm now."

He smiled. "The fire still burns. Come with me. I have something to discuss with you."

He grabbed her gown and boots, and they walked back up the hill to their camp, now moonlit. Taran lay asleep, the blanket bundled tightly around him. He set her clothes near the fire and waited while she warmed herself.

She spread out her fingers near the flames, her naked silhouette in shadow beneath her shift. "What is it ye have on yer mind, then?"

He studied her for a few seconds before answering. "Knowing we could lose everything when we arrive in Edinburgh, let's hold on to what we have right now."

"I dinnae understand."

He ran his fingers over her bare shoulder to push back a few strands of wet hair. "I'd like to find a minister in Edinburgh who will marry us."

She stiffened, then spun to face him. "Are ye proposing marriage?"

He'd never considered marriage before. The women in his past may have been beauties too, yet they'd held no power over him. His relationships were fleeting and devoid of feeling for the most part, except for the physical intimacy between them. There had been no promises of love. No overtures of a future together. He'd never cared to make any of those women his. He *wanted* them to return to their husbands or lovers after he'd gone. They left no indelible mark. But Cait's imprint remained with him since the evening they'd met and she'd so clumsily explained her talents with her little black knife. Her face, her voice, every move she made had stayed with him since then, filling his mind at all hours of the day and night. It was impossible not to care for her, love her, and imagine her next to him for the rest of his life. "If you'll have me."

"If I'll have ye?" she asked.

"Well, I am an illegitimate Englishman who is wanted for treason, which, by the way, is the same charge that has placed my father in the Tower thereby leaving me with no inheritance." He nudged his head in the direction of their two horses. "I am presently also a horse thief and the possessor of stolen goods belonging to an earl of great importance, I might add. I have no money to speak of, and my only sibling is a half-brother who would like to see me swing from a gibbet. So, I would understand if you would prefer to wait for a better match." Hearing the truth spill out of his mouth all at once, he was suddenly nervous about her response.

THE TACKSMAN'S DAUGHTER

She hmphed. "So, ye want to know if a woman with no home or family and nae a cow or sheep to offer as tocher, wearing borrowed clothing on her back—well, nae at the moment—" she said, casting a quick glance at her gown drying by the fire, "—who's the one responsible for stealing the items ye mentioned and committing other unspeakable acts, will accept yer offer of marriage? 'Tis either a bout of lunacy or pity that brings ye to propose because—"

"I'm proposing because I love you, Cait. And although the circumstances surrounding our acquaintance were not the most pleasant, they have nonetheless brought you to me." He pulled her close and spoke from his heart. "For that, I am most grateful."

She shrugged out of his embrace. "The circumstances."

"There must be a reason for what happened." He kissed the curve of her shoulder. "I am your family now. I have been for some time."

"Aye." A single tear glistening silver escaped the corner of her eye and vanished into her dark tresses. She reached for his hands and their fingers entwined. "Ye *are* my family, Edward."

"Go without me. All of those people make me feel like a pigeon crammed in a dovecote." Cait waved him away with the flick of her hand, her forefinger poised on the edge of the handle of her blade. She speared it at a tree at least twenty paces away, and it stuck. She rushed to release it, then returned to her spot, this time facing the opposite direction. Edward watched as she spun and once again flung her knife, hitting the tree dead center in its trunk. She practiced her aim almost every day, challenging herself in different ways and impressing him more each time.

As much as he didn't like the idea of her staying behind, he understood her discomfort in being around crowds of people. She'd spent her entire life in Glencoe, seeing the same faces day after day and being perfectly content with that. But he had to go into Falkirk, not only for provisions, but to get word of any news that might affect their departure to Edinburgh the next day.

And to write and post a letter that would cleave his heart—and hers—in two.

"Then Taran will stay with you."

"Are ye going to find me some shoon?" Taran asked, wiggling his foot in Edward's direction.

Edward knelt beside him, then slipped off the torn leather shoe wrapped around it. "Set your foot here."

He placed Taran's foot along his forearm to measure the length of it. His toe stopped right at the curve of a vein below Edward's elbow. "I'll get you some if they have them."

"Are ye not worried you'll be recognized?" Cait asked, pausing her practice.

"With this beard?" He stood, one hand on Taran's shoulder. "The best place to hide is in plain sight."

It was certainly possible that a sketch with his likeness had reached as far as Falkirk—especially since Argyll's regiment was stationed in Edinburgh only a few days' ride away—but he hoped the crowds in the market would be too distracted by the chaos around them to notice him.

He winked at Cait and gave Taran's shoulder a little squeeze. "I'm counting on you, lad, to take good care of Cait while I'm gone. Can you do that for me?"

"Och, aye. I can hear trouble before it arrives."

"I know you can. That's why I'm trusting you with something so precious."

Cait smiled and stood on tiptoe to give him a kiss. "Hasty back."

He mounted Fury and took one more look at the two of them standing at the edge of the wood, Cait's hand resting protectively on Taran's shoulder. His family.

He inhaled deeply and forced a smile. Their bond, their closeness, was going to make sending out a letter to find Taran's grandfather—something he knew he had to do—that much harder.

Chapter 33

"Ye needed it, laddie."

Taran slipped his sark over his shoulders, unhappy with the scrubbing Cait had just given him. Drops of cold water rained down on his back from his hair, still dripping from dunking his head in the river. "My grandda only made me bathe twice a year. Once in the spring and once in autumn before the weather changed."

Cait handed him his shoes. "Well, I think ye missed yer last washing. Ye smelled like a goat after a few days of hard rain."

He slipped the worn leather over his feet and wiggled his toes, the big ones sticking out the ends. "There was no point in washing my feet, aye? My toes will only get slaisterie again as soon as I start walking."

"Do ye wish to put clarty feet in yer new shoon?" she asked, handing him his cane and urging him ahead with her hand on his back.

"Do ye think he'll get them for me?" He hadn't had new shoes since Grandda had given him some at Hogmanay two years past. It was the same day he'd eaten three servings of cranachan heavy with whisky and slept through the evening festivities. Grandda had laughed, saying he couldn't handle his spirits like a true Matheson, so the next day, he'd sat him down and served him a good pour and a lesson. When he remained able to stand without teetering, Grandda slapped him on the back and handed him his new shoes.

"If there's a souter there, he'll get them," she said.

They walked back up the hill to where *Cìobair* was hobbled and nickering softly nearby. Cait had told him that he was a fine gelding—not as tall and fierce as Edward's stallion but just as strong and brave. All Taran could see, though, was a blur of black and white movement where the sound was coming from. He imagined his shiny, spotted coat, soft if he rubbed it one way and prickly if he rubbed it the other.

Cait handed him a chunk of cheese they'd purchased in Stirling, and Taran stuck it in his mouth. She always seemed to know when he was hungry or thirsty. He chewed with his mouth closed and swallowed before he spoke, something he'd been practicing since Cait told him he ate like a cow chewing cud. "I should've gone into Falkirk with Edward. I could tell fortunes and make us some more coin."

"We have enough for now," she said, patting his shoulder conciliatorily.

"Then I'll do it in Edinburgh. Edward says the streets are crowded with goldit fools ready to have their coin plucked from their pockets."

"I doubt he said that," she said, her tone reprimanding.

Taran's face flushed with heat. "Och. Well, he did say that we'd see more people in one day in Edinburgh than we'd see in our whole lives in the Highlands. I could make a king's ransom."

"Ye need to take heed with that. City folk may no take a liking to a lad who claims he can see a person's fortunes or misfortunes, or what have ye, before God wills them to happen."

"I told ye I only tell the good visions as I see them. The rest is all a bunch of havering," he insisted.

"Just the same," she said, setting her *sgian dubh* in his hand, "'Tis time ye learned how to throw a blade."

Taran swallowed. Grandda only ever let him hold a knife when he was whittling. "I can do it."

"I know ye can, laddie." She straightened the knife in his palm. "Feel the weight of it. The handle is heavier, so ye want to hold it by the blade."

He flipped the knife so the handle pointed outward.

"Be sure the dull side is what lies across yer palm." Her hands reset the knife. "Yer cack-handed so ye want to keep yer left leg back."

Taran stepped out with his right foot. "How far is the tree?"

"Only a few paces away, so ye needn't throw too hard, mind ye."

He nodded.

"Keep yer arm level with the ground, aye? But bend yer forearm back and—"

The crack of a snapped twig not far off in the distance made him freeze. "Someone's coming."

Cait's skirts brushed across his legs as she skirted past him. She took back her knife. "Drovers. Perhaps we should hide."

THE TACKSMAN'S DAUGHTER

She untied *Ciobair,* and they moved deeper into the trees. Taran listened carefully to the male voices and the clomp of hooves on the soft ground. One man farted and another laughed. "There's at least two of them. They have the Gaelic."

Cait pressed her hand to his chest, holding him still as she peeked around him. "Aye. Highlanders. And at least two dozen kine."

"Do ye think they're Jacobites?" he asked, his heart racing. Wherever those Jacobites went, there always seemed to be trouble, and without Edward there . . . well, he wished Edward was with them.

"Wheesht," she whispered.

He listened as the sounds grew clearer in their approach. Suddenly, Cait drew in a sharp breath and her hand clamped onto his sark. He froze, afraid if he said a word, they were close enough to hear it. Cait sounded like she was holding her breath, and it had to be a minute or so before she finally exhaled. His own stomach clenched in anticipation.

The drovers finally passed, their footsteps fading into the distance. Finally, her grip on his sark loosened.

"What happened?" he asked.

"I dinnae believe it," she answered, fear in her voice.

"What?" His legs felt like they might buckle.

"He's alive. And here."

"Who?" Whoever *he* was, his presence made her uneasy.

Cait hesitated, then swallowed deep enough for him to hear. "My cousin. Sionn."

"Why cannae we say anything about seeing yer cousin?" Taran asked.

"Because I'd like to forget about it if ye dinnae mind," Cait said, the frustration in her voice clear. "Forbye, he's gone. No need to think about him any further."

Taran didn't understand her. If one of his kin showed up in the middle of the woods far from home, he'd greet them with a hug and pray they'd stay. Instead of being happy, she was all out of sorts. "Fine, then. I suppose ye dinnae want to teach me to throw yer knife now, do ye?"

She puffed out a long breath. "I'm a bit . . . Forgive me, laddie, but I cannae concentrate on that now. Ye need a steady mind and a steady hand to manage a blade, and I have neither."

Gilli had been like that too. Fine one minute and prickly the next. The last time was when Lilas had given them a big slice of *aran cridhe* to share and he had taken the last piece. He'd quickly learned that it had been the wrong thing to do.

But this time was different. He hadn't done anything wrong to turn Cait so brittle.

He spent the afternoon whittling until the clank of a horse's tack signaled Edward's return.

Cait squeezed Taran's arm once. "Remember what I said, laddie."

He hadn't forgotten, but he still didn't understand it.

Edward ruffled his hair, then hugged him close. He smelled like the spices and smoke of the market. "Did ye get them?"

Edward slipped the shoes tied together with a silky ribbon into Taran's hands. He ran his fingers over the smooth leather. They felt much sturdier than his *cuaran* shoes made of deer hide, and these had real soles.

"The ribbon is for Cait, but the shoes are for you. The leather is waxed so your feet shan't get wet." Edward wriggled his ear playfully.

He sat against a tree and slipped them on, wiggling his toes freely. They were the finest shoes he ever owned.

"Everything good while I was gone?" Edward asked, a smile in his voice.

Taran bowed his head, pretending he hadn't heard.

"Aye." Cait's voice seemed a bit too cheery. "Perfectly fine day."

Taran bristled. He'd never heard her lie to Edward before.

Chapter 34

Alexander scanned the market throng for Jenny. It was late in the afternoon, and he hoped he hadn't missed his opportunity for their rendezvous. If he had, it was all Davina's fault. He probably shouldn't have admitted that he was going to the market without her. But she hadn't needed to cause a scene over it back at the castle. A gaggle of busybodies had come to her side in rescue, consoling and petting her as if she were the family cat. He'd had to placate her with kind words and false promises while the meddlesome horde stood by and watched disapprovingly, their narrowed glares judging every word he said and how he said it.

"Will ye bring back something for wee Sawney?" she'd asked, tears welling.

"Of course. If there is something suitable."

She hadn't liked that response, and neither had the women surrounding her. But he didn't give them a chance to protest. He merely bowed and exited the castle courtyard as quickly as he could.

Now, even amidst hundreds of people milling about, pushing and jostling, he felt free, unfettered. Shouts in all directions came from rag hucksters, fishmongers, and even a bonesetter promising to set dislocated fingers and toes. A chaunter singing ballads for a penny on top of an upturned crate also fought to have his voice heard. But the cacophony was all a welcome reprieve from Davina's niggling complaints that were always accompanied by eyes teeming with blame.

He listened to the chaunter croon a ballad about a fair young maid who swore her growing belly was due to an admiring pasteler feeding her pastries and not his sausage. It actually made Alexander smile while he searched the walls of the neighbouring buildings for broadsheets announcing rewards for Edward and the other two traitors. But his smile eventually faded when he found not a single one. He'd had Jameson draw a dozen copies of each soldier's likeness and given half of them to Glenlyon before he left with Argyll's regiment. Why hadn't the imbecile posted at least one in Stirling? Edward had to have passed through on his way to Edinburgh.

As he ambled around the fair, people skirted by him like water rushing past rocks in a riverbed, avoiding his gaze. He wore his uniform just as the earl had suggested the evening before, but instead of feeling superior like he usually did, he felt somewhat ill at ease.

"Lookin' for a sweet piece of fruit, officer?" a trilly voice asked.

Alexander turned around to find a diminutive man wearing an apron that hung past his knees, an open basket of ripe plums cradled in his arms.

Alexander slipped a penny from his purse and held it out to the man, then snatched it back. "Tell me first, have you heard anything about three traitors from Glencoe who may have traveled through here? All officers in the king's army?"

The fruit peddler's face blanched. "If I had, I wouldn't speak of it to anyone."

"And why is that? 'Tis your duty as a loyal subject to report rebels who have been engaged in treasonous acts—"

"Treason?" the peddler asked. "Who was treasonous? The soldiers who refused to turn their swords on their winter hosts or those who did?"

Alexander's jaw tightened. If he wasn't in the midst of so many people, he would draw his dagger and hold it to the man's throat. He leaned into the peddler's face, sending a few plums tumbling out of his basket and onto the hard-packed dirt. "How dare you question the actions of the king's army!"

"I . . . I meant no disrespect, officer. But I heard that the attack was done without the king's consent. That there was a letter."

"What letter?"

Sweat beaded on the peddler's brow. "Something that said all MacDonalds under seventy should be put to the sword. *All*—even women and children. The king hadn't signed it."

That had to be the letter that Hill and Breadalbane had mentioned. The one Major Duncanson wrote to Drummond. He pushed the peddler aside, toppling over his basket and sending plums in all directions. The little man scrambled to gather them up.

Alexander wanted to tell the peddler and all of those who stood staring at the man on his hands and knees in the dirt that those orders were sent from the king, but he didn't. With all the reported Jacobites around, he couldn't take the chance that it would start a rebellion, and William would discover that Alexander was at the crux of it. He threw the penny at the peddler and fought his way back through the crowd to leave.

"There you are." Jenny caught his arm. "I've been looking all over for you."

He shook his head. "Not now."

He twisted away, but she pulled him back. "What has you so feverish, Mansfield?"

"You wouldn't understand."

"Perhaps I would."

He stared at her. She was a lot like him—smart, hungry, deserving of something better. But most importantly, her future like his hung in the balance. A puppeteer controlled each of their fates. For her, it was the earl. For him, it was the king. With one commanding cut of the string, both of them could be left powerless. Destitute.

He led her out of the market and between two buildings to a small grove of trees. He took a deep breath to try to calm his boiling temper. "This place is brimming with Jacobites. I can feel it."

"What?"

He paced, his thoughts spinning in all different directions. Colonel Hill was right. This was a bigger problem than he'd originally thought. "Word has spread that William did not sanction those orders. But he did! Now it is turning people against us—against the king!"

"What orders?"

"The orders for us to attack those MacDonald savages. In Glencoe."

"Ah. Glencoe. So I've heard." She reached out her hand to stop his pacing. "Are you certain the king knew about them?"

"Of course! I read the orders myself," he insisted.

"The king's signature was at the bottom?" she asked intently, her eyes fixed on his.

"The letter was written on his behalf by one of our officers."

"Oh." She seemed deflated by his response. She glanced away and shrugged, speaking in a disinterested tone. "You are merely a minion. Someone to carry out the deeds of another. You will not be held responsible for what was done. That blame goes to whomever ordained the act."

That made him think. *Would* he be held culpable as an officer should an inquiry be conducted? Or would the blame go to those higher up—Hill, Breadalbane, Dalrymple? The king?

Her voice pulled him from his thoughts. "Did you ever see the king's signature on anything ordering the attack?"

He shook his head. "If he had placed anything in writing, it would have gone to the Master of Stair or Breadalbane." But as he thought about it, Breadalbane had made it sound as if the king had no knowledge of it or was at least questioning who did. After all, the earl wanted Alexander to argue his innocence to the king. "Dalrymple, most likely."

"Master of Stair?"

He nodded.

"I see." She bit her bottom lip in concentration. Then after a second, she kissed him fleetingly on the cheek. "I really must be going. Campden will undoubtedly be wondering what has taken me so long."

She turned to go, but he gripped her by the elbow and held her back. "Have you been asking me these questions for yourself or someone else?"

"I don't know what you mean," she answered, brow crinkled and smiling.

There was something about their exchange that bothered him, but he couldn't quite put a finger on it. "Lie down."

"Truly, I must leave."

"I said lie down."

"Alexander." She spoke in an exasperated tone, her head tilted to the side.

He grabbed her arm and jerked her to the ground. She let out a sharp yelp as she stumbled and fell backwards. "I don't have time for this!"

"You told me to meet you here. Did you not?" He climbed on top of her, flung up her skirts, then released himself from the confines of his breeches.

Her legs scrabbled beneath him. "You would have me like this?"

He seized her wrists and held them firmly in his grip on either side of her head. She struggled fervently, and a renewed vigor spread through his groin. "Are you going to fight me?"

She glared up at him, her nostrils flaring, her face red. Her chest heaved with each breath, then suddenly her body relaxed, and she spread her legs and smiled.

Chapter 35

In part, Davina appreciated Alex's concern about her safety, but were the Jacobites so dangerous that she couldn't go to the market with him?

The eldest woman in the room, Mistress Livingstone, patted her once on the back of her hand, her blue eyes milky with age. "He'll return with a bauble for yer wee one. You'll see."

But would he? She was trying so hard to create a love between Alex and Sawney, but he seemed resistant, afraid to risk the kind of heartache he'd experienced with his father. That wasn't exactly what he'd said, but she was a good reader of people and could plainly see the struggle within his heart.

"I'm going." All heads turned in her direction.

"To the market?"

She nodded and swung her shawl around her shoulders.

"Ye cannae go unescorted."

"I'll be fine. 'Tis a short walk, and there are far too many people on the street for anything to happen." She didn't wait for their approval. She left the king's house and strolled right outside the castle gate.

The walk down to the market was steep, her leather slippers sliding on the cobblestones. People smiled and nodded in her direction as she passed, but once when she turned back, she noticed two women carrying baskets point at her and snicker. Davina walked on, newly embarrassed by her green gown, the bodice now stretched uncomfortably over her waist. She'd had it since arriving in Kinlochbeg in February and hadn't given it a thought since, but now it seemed that the sun shone brightly on the frayed neckline and cuffs, the stray threads poking out of the split seams in the waist highlighted.

She hurried her step, head down, following the shouts and laughter that grew louder the closer she came to the market. The same sutler who had been just outside the castle walls the day before stood on a crate near the front. "Delicious plums! Three for a penny!"

Her mouth watered, the thought of their sweet juice rolling over her tongue driving her towards the peddler. But when she looked in his basket, the plums were covered in dirt and badly bruised. They had looked so lovely earlier—shiny and dark purple. Why hadn't Alex purchased them then?

She wandered through the crowd, delighted by the lively spirit of the townsfolk. They seemed happy, busy, engaged in all that was around them. Was the market always like this? New faces and bright coloured fruit in red, orange, and yellow. Smells both tangy and sweet wafting on the breeze. She inhaled deeply and scanned the booths, taking in all that she had never seen before.

Glenorchy suddenly seemed so small. There was no market, no crowd, no fiddler, no chaunter. Even the peddlers who occasionally approached the castle gates had little to offer. Perhaps some onions, dyed wool, or capons and partridges hanging from a line. But nothing that flooded her heart and senses like the Stirling market.

"Freshwater cockles! Picked today! Finest in Stirling!"

Davina peeked inside three barrels at the cockles sitting at the bottom, their brown and white shells with deep ridges coated in a fine layer of bubbles.

"Have a taste, lass." With a sharp blade, the huckster scooped under a small lump of orange meat to loosen it and handed her the open shell. "Go on. Tell me 'tisnae the best cockle ye ever tasted."

She turned up the shell and chewed. It was cold and slightly sweet like river water. She thought she could eat a dozen.

"Will that be a bushel for ye, then?" the huckster asked, wiping his hands on his hips.

She held up one finger while she swallowed the cockle. "They're quite good, but I need to find my . . ."

What *was* Alex? He wasn't her husband. At least not yet. He was her lover, but she couldn't tell the man that. "I'll return with some money."

The huckster sighed. "Tasting my cockles for free, are ye? I'll give ye cockles to taste." He shooed her away with his hand, and she shuffled down the aisle, her cheeks aflame. Where was Alex? He said he was going to the market, but she didn't see a single red coat anywhere.

Two stalls down, next to a tallow chandler, a dish turner displayed all sizes of wooden bowls and dishes. But that's not what gained Davina's attention. It was the small ball and cup toy that sat beside a stack of expertly crafted wares. Perfect for Sawney.

"Is that for sale?" she asked the old woman seated on a small stool behind the table, her hands gnarled with age.

With one crooked finger, the woman shakily pointed at a pile of rags behind her, one shaggy mop of red hair peeking from underneath. "That's wee Niall's. I dinnae think he'll wish to part with it."

Davina nodded dejectedly and turned to leave, but the old woman's voice stopped her.

"Unless, of course, ye are willing to pay . . . thruppence for it."

Three pence? That was a lot of money for a child's trinket, and although she knew Sawney would love it, she couldn't take a toy away from that little boy. "Keep it for wee Niall. I'll find another."

"Pshht." The old woman jerked her head in the sleeping child's direction. "His grandsire will fashion him another in a trice."

"Are ye certain, then?" Sawney had never had a real toy, and it would be fitting if the first one he had was given to him by his father.

"Aye."

"Then I'll find my . . . husband . . . and we'll return." She felt proud saying that, even if it wasn't true.

Davina searched the crowd again for Alexander's red coat but couldn't find him anywhere. She stopped two young women. "Have ye seen a soldier here? Tall, dark, and wearing the red coat of the king's army?"

Both shook their heads and hurried away. She asked another woman with three small children trailing behind her clutching her skirt. "Beg pardon, but have ye seen any soldiers hereabouts?"

"Soldiers? Are the soldiers here?" she asked nervously.

"My husband. I'm looking for my husband."

"Ye from the garrison?"

"Aye."

"Have the regiments arrived, then?"

"Regiments?"

"I heard the king is sending soldiers to the garrison." The woman's children stared up at her with dirty faces.

"I know naught of that. I'm only looking for my . . ."

The woman gathered up her children in front of her. "Come now."

She left Davina wondering why everyone seemed so afraid of the soldiers. It was ridiculous, though. They were the ones who were going to protect everyone from the Jacobites.

She decided to find a shady spot and wait for Alex to appear. Perhaps he'd visited with the Earl of Argyll before going to the market. He'd said they had military matters to discuss the night before, so he might be finishing up any unsettled business. It was a lovely day, cool and breezy, rain clouds far off in the distance posing no immediate threat, so she'd happily wait.

She passed a vendor selling beautiful wool cloth, at least half a dozen tartan patterns rolled into large bolts on a patch of grass. The MacNab tartan was in the back, the warp and weft of the fabric as tight and fine as she'd ever seen. When she finally found Alex, she would ask him if he would purchase a length of the cloth for her to make a new gown, for it wouldn't be long before she'd outgrow the one she wore.

She meandered between two buildings to find the perfect respite, the thought of purchasing some cloth and the ball and cup on her mind. At the back corner of one of the buildings, three little boys huddled together giggling, one with his hand covering his smiling mouth. It made her heart ache for Sawney.

She joined them and leaned down to their height. "What has ye so giddy, laddies?" she asked, smiling.

They pointed at a nearby copse of alders, the bright green oval leaves dancing in the wind. She stared but didn't see anything. "What is it?"

They tittered again, then ran off into the crowded market.

She glanced back at the trees and was about to walk away when she spotted a flash of red in the tall grass. She moved a little closer, the skin on the nape of her neck prickling with discomfort. Could it be Alex? Before she could finish her thought, his dark hair emerged briefly then sank back down, cloaked by the grass. She inched ahead, her legs heavy as if they were shrouded in lead. For a second, she thought he might be hurt, but then she heard moans that sounded much like her own when they were together. And she knew.

Why she continued her approach, she had no idea. Her heart hammered in her chest with each step. Her throat tightened. The woman's moans continued, burning Davina's ears and bringing tears to her eyes.

She crossed through the grass until she reached the edge of the trees. In front of her lay the father of her son and the woman she remembered seeing at the castle who he'd said had asked him for directions. His hips moved angrily between her thighs, but the woman beneath him didn't seem bothered. Her eyes were half-closed in rapture, her pale white hands suddenly freed from his grasp gripping his buttocks, pulling him into her. Davina opened her mouth to speak, but her trembling bottom lip and constricted throat prevented the words from coming out.

THE TACKSMAN'S DAUGHTER

The woman's eyes flitted open and caught sight of Davina. Instantly, her legs clamped hard around Alex's hips, stopping him abruptly.

"What is it? You want it harder?" he asked, his voice husky and arrogant, his mouth finding one of her large, exposed breasts.

Davina could almost feel the graze of his teeth on her own skin as he fastened on the woman's nipple.

She caught her breath, wiped the tears from her cheeks, and regained her composure. That familiar flutter low in her belly made her clutch her stomach. The first time she felt it was not a week earlier, when she'd dismissed it as a touch of colic. Just before they'd reached the castle, she felt it again and knew what it was.

She ran her hand over her belly, not yet round but hard from the child growing inside of her. She turned to the side and retched in the grass.

Part Four

়

Chapter 36

June, 1692
Edinburgh, Scotland

They arrived in Edinburgh in the late afternoon just as the clouds parted, allowing the sun to finally make its appearance. Cait pressed a hand to her quaking stomach. Although Edward had described the city many times, she wasn't prepared for the sheer size of it. Massive stone buildings lined the streets, wagons and carts filled with barrels and crates bumped along the cobbles, and men and women strolled about wearing velvets and heavy satins in bright blues, greens, and orange. People appeared from every direction.

She stared into their faces, searching for clues that might expose them as Jacobite or supporters of King William. But nothing gave them away. Not the hint of a treacherous smile or the glint of a mischievous gaze. There was no way to tell where their loyalties lay.

She raised the bag that hung from her waist into her lap, hugging the letter to the Earl of Mar closer. How would she ever find him without drawing suspicion? Was he a known Jacobite? Would the mere mention of his name send the king's guards to arrest her? Her stomach turned at the thought that Edward and Taran could be accused of being Jacobites because of her. She had to keep them out of it. But she couldn't let the king get away with the slaughter. So, if this letter somehow forced William off the throne, then she would do her part to deliver it.

Edward edged his horse in front of hers to fit through a narrow vennel shaded by tall buildings on either side. She wondered if keeping the secret about seeing Sionn in Falkirk had been a good idea. She'd done it to spare him the worry, hoping her cousins were well on their way to England, where they were sure to fetch higher prices for their beasts—a scenario she preferred. But now she wondered if they had been heading to Edinburgh and were hidden amongst the masses.

As the horses entered a crossroad and the sun emerged once more, she took a deep breath. The city was a lot to absorb all at once, and it filled Cait's chest with a strange heaviness.

"'Tis too large. Too busy. Too . . ." Her throat tightened as she spoke. There was so much to look at.

"We haven't even entered the heart of the city yet, *mo gràdh.*" Edward stopped his horse. "We'll look for lodgings here. I'd like to avoid Argyll's regiment if I can, and if we travel farther up, we'll be too near the garrison."

Cait was happy to stay far from the castle as well. Too many soldiers. But she knew she was going to have to go there eventually if she was to find Glenlyon.

They dismounted and wandered about, asking people for directions to the nearest inn, but everyone seemed to be from somewhere else, knowing very little about the city. They led their horses farther down where shops dotted both sides of the thoroughfare.

"They should be able to direct us to an inn," Edward said, handing her his reins. Two men on the opposite side of the street stood in front of an apothecary, the one wearing a long apron clearly the chirurgeon who worked there. "Wait here."

Cait watched as he hurried across, dodging a rag-filled cart pulled by a sad-looking donkey. With her hand on Taran's shoulder, she waited while Edward spoke to the men, one shaking his head and the other pointing in multiple directions.

After a few minutes, Cait decided to ask the fair-haired woman standing on the corner. She wore a bright green gown with bows on the shoulders and down the front of her bodice, purple fuzzy balls peeking out from her low neckline and cuffs. Cait had never seen such a fanciful trim on a gown before, especially not one resembling blooms on a thistle. The woman smiled and batted her eyes, her face powdered white and her cheeks and lips rouged the colour of a ripe raspberry.

THE TACKSMAN'S DAUGHTER

"Beg pardon, mistress. We're looking for some lodging. Do ye know of any?"

The woman glanced at her and Taran, flipped her hand in their direction, then took a few steps away. "Yer scaring away my customers."

Confused by her response, Cait asked again. "Do ye know of an alehouse that might offer lodging or an inn—"

Exasperated, she barked, "Don't ye see those three men over there?"

Cait turned to look at Edward and the two strangers.

A glimmer of sunlight touched the woman's cheek, highlighting its coarse texture. She waved a white handkerchief at them to get their attention, but none of them looked in her direction, so she dropped her hand to her side, frustrated. "I'll wager at least one of them is flush in the pocket, but I'll never see a penny of it if you and the laddie dinnae make yerselves scarce."

A lump rose in Cait's throat at the realization of what the woman was selling. "Well, the tall one belongs to me, and I can tell ye he doesn't have a penny to his name."

The woman glimpsed down at Taran and then at his cane, a hint of pity in her dark brown eyes. "If yer man doesn't have a penny to speak of, as ye say, ye should go to the church up the road a bit. But if he does, as I expect he might—or ye wouldn't be asking after an inn—ye should go to the White Horse." She pointed to an archway in the middle of a building near the end of the street. "Ye need to go to Ord's Close through that pend over there and walk through the back court. That's where you'll find it."

The woman sauntered away, her hips swinging in a manner that made Cait glad Taran couldn't see.

Ord's Close was but a hundred paces away from Holyrood Palace, the royal household for the king. Her stomach tightened at the thought he might be living there, his feet next to a fire and a glass of Claret in his hand. She gritted her teeth to prevent the words she wished to mutter about his demise from escaping.

They entered the hidden courtyard and found the White Horse Inn in the back corner. Edward handed both reins to a stable boy who looked no older than Taran, then they all stepped inside a dark parlour smelling of leather and freshly cut wood. Several mismatched upholstered chairs dotted the room, and a small hearth sat at one end.

Edward spoke quietly to a slender, elderly man in a white periwig and tartan trews. Cait couldn't hear everything they said, but when Edward pointed in her direction and said the words 'my family,' she heard it clearly. She liked the way it sounded coming out of his mouth. He hadn't faltered on the phrase, letting it roll off his tongue as if it were the most perfectly natural thing to say.

She wandered farther into the room and stared at a portrait of a young woman who had the same tired brown eyes as Davina. She was attractive yet plain, with a similar kind, closed smile Cait had seen on Davina's face many times. It made her wonder what she and Sawney were doing at that very moment. Walking the grounds of Kilchurn Castle? Throwing stones into the murky grey waters of Loch Awe? Watching the otters slither onto the grassy banks?

Edward finished with the innkeeper and joined her and Taran by the hearth. "We have enough money to stay here three nights. We'll need what is left for food."

"Och. Ye needn't fash. I'll tell fortunes," Taran offered.

Edward patted him on the back. "Not necessary, lad. I'm going to see if there is a card game nearby where I might be able to earn some winnings."

Although she didn't like the idea of Edward chancing what coin they had left on a game of cards, what could she do? They needed more money, and she didn't want Taran to take the risk of upsetting someone and getting hurt.

Edward had told her that one of the men he spoke to on the street said there was a rumour the king's caravan was on its way to Edinburgh and was expected by the next week. She couldn't help but smile at the thought. She would do almost anything to watch him being dragged through the streets for the crimes he committed. But that would only happen if she could deliver the letter to the earl. She had to find him first, and that was going to take some time. And more time would require more sterling.

"Here ye are, Mr. MacKinnon." The innkeeper, an old man with cheeks like withered fruit, dropped a single black key into Edward's palm. "If you or the mistress needs service, I'll be here."

The innkeeper disappeared down a narrow hallway. Edward glanced back once undoubtedly to ensure he was out of earshot. "I hope you don't mind that I told him we were married. If I hadn't, he would not have permitted us to stay as guests in the same room."

"So ye said it out of parsimony, did ye?" she whispered, smiling up at his grinning face.

"We can't afford two rooms, can we?" He kissed her forehead.

"And if he discovers 'tisnae true?" Would the innkeeper send them back into the streets?

"Then make an honest man out of me."

"How will we marry? Ye cannae give yer real name. I willnae marry anyone but Edward Gage." She had never wished more that his surname was MacKinnon.

THE TACKSMAN'S DAUGHTER

He took both of her hands in his. "I know someone who might be willing to perform the ceremony."

"Wake up, laddie. The devil's visiting ye in yer sleep." Cait brushed Taran's damp hair back from his brow. The sparse room glowed with the light of the moon streaming in from the small window near her bed.

Taran sat on his pallet on the floor next to Edward, his little chest rising and falling rapidly.

"Come to me." Cait patted the bed and pulled him close. "What is it that has ye so jittery?"

He buried his head in her chest, his shoulders quaking while he tried to steady his breath. "A big black corbie swooped down from a tall building, spread his wings over Edward, then carried him off."

"'Twas only a dream, laddie. Nothing has taken Edward. Listen."

Taran bowed his head to listen to Edward's steady breathing. She fluffed the meager pillow and urged him to lie down. "You'll sleep up here with me tonight."

He settled next to her, croodling close. "There ye go."

They lay in the dark, and she stroked the back of his head. Her heart ached at the memory she'd done the same thing for Gilli every time she woke with a fright.

"Cait?"

"Aye?"

"'Twasn't a dream. 'Twas a sighting."

The next morning, Cait slipped the earl's letter under a crate that held the washbasin and jug. There it would remain safe until they returned.

"Ready?" Edward asked, his eyes full of anticipation.

She led him away from Taran, who was busy studying his new shoes, his hands running back and forth over the leather. "Are ye certain ye want to do this?"

He brought her hands to his lips and kissed them. "We don't know what tomorrow will bring. I could be discovered—"

"And I will be by yer side."

He stared at her, fear and hope tangled in his gaze. "You should be the one having doubts."

"I have no doubts. I know what's in yer heart. You've shown me time and again." She rested her hand on his cheek. "I cannae deny that I'm no feart of what will come, but that willnae keep me from becoming yer wife."

He kissed her in a way that grounded her to her decision.

The three of them set out on foot to find the minister. Edward had insisted they leave the horses behind so as not to draw attention to themselves. Cait's stomach tumbled being so close to so many people—especially after Taran's sighting of the corbie, even though she didn't understand it.

She'd awakened to find that Edward had shaved his beard clean from his face. It jarred her. He now looked exactly as he did in the warrant Taran had shown them only weeks earlier—youthful and strong with a hint of that carefree playfulness that lived in his crooked smile. It was startling to see him as that same man who'd kissed her on that fateful night back in Glencoe. His face hadn't changed, but everything else about him had. She saw it in the way he walked—guarded and distrustful—and how he protectively ushered her and Taran through the streets, his hands on their backs, keeping them close.

As they passed all the finely dressed women in their shimmering satins and luxurious velvets, Cait was acutely aware of her own plainness, her blue gown threadbare in spots and tattered around the hem. And it was possibly her wedding day.

"Are we close? I dinnae wish to wear out my new shoon," Taran said, drawing her away from her thoughts.

Edward ruffled Taran's hair. "Your shoes should last until you grow out of them, which I suppose won't be long from now, judging by the way you have been eating lately."

Cait smiled to herself. In the more than six months since Taran had arrived in Glencoe, he'd grown almost up to her shoulders. He might even be a head taller than Gilli would have been by now.

It was not a far walk, but it did lead them closer to the castle, and Cait worried that Edward's newly shaven face might be recognized. But as they entered one street after another, no one seemed to pay them any notice. Most kept their heads bowed as they carried on their way, dodging passersby.

Over the tops of great stone buildings, Cait spotted a crown steeple undoubtedly belonging to a kirk. She wondered if that was Mary King's Close, the place where they were headed, but a few steps later, Edward turned down an alleyway and led them through a wynd lined with small homes and shops. They stopped, and he knocked on a plain door painted black. Although gusts of cool wind blew through the dark narrow street, Cait's palms were sweating.

"Are ye sure ye have the right place?" she asked nervously, her fingers fiddling with the new lavender ribbon in her hair.

He smiled. "I spent many days playing cards and sharing a whisky or two with the owner."

"Drinking and gaming? I thought ye said he was a minister."

THE TACKSMAN'S DAUGHTER

"Since when have you ever heard of a clergyman who didn't enjoy a good competitive game of cards along with some spirits?"

She was about to respond when the door creaked open and a straggly brown-haired young man wearing a black cassock answered. Edward took a step back and scanned the doorframe, his brow knitted in confusion. "Is this the home of Ainsley MacLeod?"

The clergyman sighed, his eyes heavy with grief. "My father left us a year past. He is with the Lord now."

Edward seemed deflated by his words. Cait gently ran her hand along his broad back.

"I'm his son, Murray." The clergyman studied his face, his chin jutted out. "I believe we've met."

"Murray. Of course. His second son." Edward smiled sadly. "I apologize, but I don't recall meeting you."

"Och, well. Perhaps I'm wrong. Ye do look familiar, though," he said, brushing back a loose wavy strand of hair with his knuckle. "Yer name is . . .?"

"Edward—"

Cait's breath hitched. "MacKinnon." She gripped Edward's forearm. He couldn't disclose his true identity to this man. It was too great of a risk.

Edward patted her hand with the clear intent to placate her. "Edward MacKinnon Gage."

Cait stared at the clergyman's eyes for a sign that he'd heard his name before, but he remained indifferent. He stepped aside and welcomed them in with the sweep of his arm.

The room was small and dark and smelled of sharp, sweet spices. Smoke from a cluster of candles rose in black swirls up to a low beamed ceiling. A single blotch of sunlight from a window on the far wall pierced the darkness. Reverend Murray presented them with a plate of cheese and some hard black bread.

"Please forgive my meager offering. The kirk does not provide for the clergy the way it used to." He guided them to sit on two stools, but they chose to stand.

"I came here hoping your father would perform a marriage ceremony."

The minister's gaze traveled from Edward to Cait and Taran. "Did you have this child out of wedlock?"

Cait nudged Taran in front of her, her hands affectionately bracing both of his shoulders.

"He is not ours. We are caring for him," Edward answered.

The minister pursed his lips in question. "And when would ye like this ceremony performed?"

"Soon. Today, if possible." Edward wrapped his arm around Cait's waist.

"Urgent, is it? We would need to post the banns. Three weeks." Reverend Murray folded his hands, and they disappeared inside the sleeves of his cassock. He turned to Cait. "Are ye with child?"

She was too shocked to answer. Although she had lain with Edward, she'd had her courses since then.

Edward's answer came quick. "She is not, Reverend."

"Then why so hasty? The punishment for a clergyman who foregoes the banns is time in the pillory or an ear-cropping. And I'll have ye know I am most fond of my ears." He glanced down at the crumb-filled plate of cheese. "Of course, a tithing to the kirk of . . . shall we say . . . two pounds might make the risk of punishment more bearable."

Cait's heart sank. "Much obliged, but we—"

"Ten shillings," Edward said.

Cait gasped.

The edge of the minister's mouth crept upward. "Twenty, and I'll marry ye in a fortnight. I willnae read yer names aloud to the congregation, but they'll be posted outside the kirk. Should anyone ask, it will have simply been an oversight, if ye will."

"Very well. We'll return in a fortnight."

Cait struggled to speak. "Beg pardon, Reverend." She pulled Edward aside and whispered, "Are ye mad? We have no money to give. And he still plans to post the banns."

Edward leaned his head down to hers. "You need to trust me."

She did trust him. It was the minister she wasn't sure of.

Reverend Murray sat at a squat desk near the window and dipped his quill in ink. "Yer names as ye wish them to be posted?"

Edward stepped forward. "Caitriona Cameron and Edward—"

Cait didn't hesitate. "MacKinnon."

Chapter 37

The easy part was finding a card game. The hard part was finding one where none of the players knew him.

Edward had spent ten months in Edinburgh with his regiment two years earlier and had honed his skills as a cardsharp, once raking in seven pounds in a single night. At first, this had created a desire for the most competitive to engage him in fair play, but after his status spread in taverns throughout the city, those not interested in losing their shirts had drifted to other tables with less talented players.

Now, as he sat across from an Irishman in a dingy tavern at the far end of the thoroughfare from the castle, he stared at his third hand of Quinze and intentionally chose to draw a card even though he knew it would break fifteen.

"Lost again!" the Irishman said, sweeping Edward's coin to his side of the table.

"A few more hands, sir. A chance to win back my losses." Edward took a pull of his whisky and shook what was left of his purse. "We can even raise the stakes if you'd like."

The Irishman cocked one eyebrow, staring at the small velvet pouch in Edward's hand. "Very well. I want to be fair, after all."

The greed glistening in the man's eyes told him that fairness was not quite what he was after. Edward smiled and threw down four pence, and the Irishman did the same.

"My turn to deal," Edward said.

The man handed him the remainder of the deck, and Edward dealt the cards—to himself a five and his opponent a ten. All four queens, three kings, two knaves, and two tens were left in the deck, which meant his chances to reach fifteen were just as great as were the Irishman's chances to break. But judging by the way the Irishman paid little attention to the cards played, he didn't seem to be counting them, so in essence, Edward's odds of winning were even greater.

The Irishman rubbed his palms together. "We'll double-up here." He threw down another four pence, then tapped his finger on the table twice. "I'll take another."

Edward dealt him an ace, giving the man a total of eleven. The Irishman scratched at his greying beard, then tapped the table for another card. An eight. He had broken.

Confident, Edward turned over his five, then dealt himself a card. A queen. With a humble shrug, he slid the coins to his side of the table.

The Irishman scowled. "Another game."

A few hours and several players later, Edward had earned back all his losses and almost another three pounds. It was enough to pay the minister, stay at the White Horse Inn for an entire month, and eat daily in a tavern. Edward shoved his now weighty purse into his shirt and stood to leave.

"I'll play ye."

He peered up at the familiar voice, his shoulders rigid. Glenlyon clumsily dropped into the chair across from him and removed his bonnet, his long white hair streaked with red and gold shooting in all directions. His eyes were glassy and bloodshot, his nose red and shiny like a ripe strawberry. He was far from the castle, and it was well after midnight. Edward remembered what he'd overheard John MacDonald say about him to Alexander at Alt Na Munde— Glenlyon would walk a mile in a snowstorm if it brought him a belly full of whisky and a night of gaming.

Edward wasn't sure if Glenlyon recognized him or not. It was difficult to tell in his expression, which was washed over from too much drink. Edward offered a quick nod. "I'm done for the night."

"A couple more friendly games willnae hurt ye." Glenlyon plunked a shilling on the table and reached inside his scarlet coat for his flask. He turned it up, then shook it, clearly unhappy it was empty.

Edward stared at that shilling. He had no idea how Glenlyon had come into possession of that coin, considering the man was notoriously broke and not the savviest card player. Edward wrestled with himself as to whether he should walk away from the table or rob the old hob of his twelve pence. He pressed his hand over the pouch inside his shirt. Cait would want him to return to the inn with his winnings. Or would she? It was Glenlyon, after all.

THE TACKSMAN'S DAUGHTER

"Very well. A few games." He kept his voice low to encourage Glenlyon to do the same. "Do you wish to play that shilling in one hand?"

Glenlyon patted his chest as he searched the room for a barmaid. "I need a wee dram first."

This was going to be remarkably simple. A drunk was always an easy opponent.

Glenlyon snapped his fingers and grumbled loudly for the round barmaid at the other end of the room.

She lazily wobbled over, wiping her mouth on her soiled apron. "Aye. What will ye have?" she asked, scratching her belly with fingers as thick as sausages.

"A dram. Nay. Two, if ye will." He handed her his shilling.

"And you?" She looked at Edward with questioning eyes. He shook his head.

Glenlyon watched her jiggle away. "Looks like that one is eating all the profits." His laugh turned into a fit of coughing.

"Are you quite fine, sir?" Edward asked.

Glenlyon squeezed his eyes closed, coughed a few more times, and dismissed Edward's concern with a sloppy wave of his hand. "Aye, aye."

The barmaid returned with his whisky, dropped Glenlyon's change in his open palm, and waddled off.

Edward shuffled the deck, then handed it to him. "The game is Quinze."

Glenlyon nodded and dealt them each a card—Edward a two and himself a seven. For Edward, any card was safe, but for Glenlyon, anything above an eight would cause him to break. But the truth was, it didn't matter. Edward planned to bet low and lose the first four or five hands regardless.

"Well?"

Edward tapped the table once. A six. Again. A four. That gave him twelve. He couldn't ask for another card or Glenlyon would know he was intentionally trying to lose—that is, if he was sober enough to notice anything above a three would break fifteen—so he rested.

Glenlyon flipped his card over. A nine.

Glenlyon muttered his disappointment and swallowed his whisky in one shot. "Do ye mind if I cut the cards once or twice?"

So you suspect me of cheating. "Please do."

It only took eight hands to claim all of Glenlyon's coin, and Edward hadn't even needed to count the cards. The old fool was too soused to make sound decisions.

After his final loss, Glenlyon rubbed his face briskly with a shaky hand.

"I must go." Edward stood. "Good evening, Captain."

Glenlyon gave a barely perceptible nod. "Sergeant."

Sergeant? Edward's heart leaped. He wasn't wearing the redcoat of a soldier, so he must've recognized him. He took four pence out of his purse and placed the coins on the table. As a bribe to remain silent? Out of pity? Perhaps both. He slipped out of the tavern, but before he mounted his horse, he peeked through the grimy window for one last look at the captain. Inside, Glenlyon brushed the coins into his hand, and within seconds, folded his arms on the table, then dropped his head heavily on top.

On the ride back to the inn, he wondered whether or not he should tell Cait he saw Glenlyon. He was the very reason they had traveled for the last month, the reason they were in Edinburgh. Edward prayed that time had quelled some of Cait's hatred for the man and her need for vengeance had changed from spearing him through to filing a complaint with the king's council. It was a selfish desire, he admitted. He simply didn't want her placing herself in danger.

She hadn't spoken much about Glenlyon in the past couple of weeks, and that gave him hope. But it didn't mean she wasn't still simmering with malice or thirsting for revenge.

He tied his horse to a hitching post in the close and entered the inn, which was dark and silent in the early morning hours. Cait and Taran were asleep on the small bed against the wall, and Edward's pallet on the floor remained untouched with a blue wool blanket stretched neatly over it. On the tiny table beneath the window lay Cait's folded gown with her mother's sapphire placed carefully on top. He smiled to himself, wagering that her black knife was tucked underneath her pillow.

He sat on his pallet to remove his boots, tugging them off with great relief. Then, groping for the clasp, he slid off the strap holding his dagger and pistol. It clanked on the wooden floorboards, and Cait stirred.

"Edward?"

He brushed her hair aside and kissed her on the cheek, then sat on the edge of the bed, the ropes beneath the pallet creaking with his weight.

"Well?" she asked in a whisper.

He removed his purse from inside his shirt and set it in her hand.

She lifted it, measuring its heft. the coins gently clinking together, her eyes open wide. "Did ye rob the king's caravan, then?"

He laughed softly. "I told you to trust me."

She grabbed his hand and kissed his palm. "Aye, ye did."

"We have enough to pay the minister. Are you still willing to be my wife, or have you changed your mind?" His hand drifted to her cheek and down to the neckline of her shift.

THE TACKSMAN'S DAUGHTER

"Do ye think I'd let ye go now that yer purse is full?" She toyed with the hair hanging over his forehead that had escaped his ribbon. A silver wash of moonlight bathed her arm with light.

He ran his fingers along her soft skin now pebbled with gooseflesh. "Is it the coin you want or me?"

She handed him back the coins, smiled with her forefinger placed over her lips, then rolled off the bed with him to the pallet on the floor.

With controlled breath, he drew her close and kissed her. Her mouth was soft against his, her lips and taste familiar now and comforting. They lay tangled and touching, fingers grazing over skin with patience. It was difficult to temper his desire for her, his hand getting lost in her long black hair and grazing the curve of one bare shoulder. Time passed too quickly. Eventually, she turned her back to him, and he rested his hand on the curve of her waist, careful to not make a sound and disturb Taran.

He lay awake in the dark while she slept peacefully. It would only be a couple weeks until they were husband and wife. It was a wonderful feeling, knowing their lives would be intertwined forever. But he was no fool. That soothing feeling of bliss would be short-lived. He had just spent the last part of the evening with the man at least partially responsible for the death of her family. That would not sit well with her once she knew.

He would tell her. In time.

Chapter 38

Davina's ridiculous antics and carrying on about Alexander's little rendezvous with Jenny delayed their departure from Stirling Castle an entire week. She'd refused to permit him even one minute out of her sight, ensuring he remain as far away from Jenny as possible. Needless to say, Alexander missed joining Campden's caravan and all the pleasurable benefits that went with it.

He had to admit he hadn't wanted to get caught with Jenny. It was truly inconvenient and meant, of course, that he would need to be especially kind to Davina—at least until he could figure out what to do with her once they reached Edinburgh. If he had only known he would meet Jenny along the journey, he would've never brought Davina along. He could've left her in the castle with that gaggle of old fussocks, but surely they would've encouraged her to write her uncle and slander him. As angry as she was, the threat of her identifying him as the father of her bastard to Breadalbane loomed as a possibility. How was he to get out of this mess?

He glanced back once at Davina on her palfrey, her expression dour and full of resentment. At least she was quiet.

The steady clop of the horses lulled him into a sedative trance, allowing him to think. If he decided to tell the king about Breadalbane's Jacobite loyalties, it might free him from Davina's clutches. The earl would be hanged, and Alexander's fear of being forced into a marriage with the girl would end. After all, a dead man has no power. Denouncing Breadalbane as a Jacobite might even provide the king with a scapegoat. If William's name should appear on any of the orders for the massacre, he could always blame Breadalbane for intentionally advising him poorly. By turning on Breadalbane, Alexander would be doing the king a favour. That would surely encourage William to forego attainder.

He patted Breadalbane's missives tucked into his coat, the papers crinkling with the pressure from his hand. He considered ripping the one addressed to the king into shreds, then remembered he needed it to gain an audience with him.

A sudden gust of wind brought with it the fresh sweet scent of the river and surrounding trees, but soon enough, the dank smell of the city, musty and rife with the stench of decaying garbage and horseshit would prevail. In the distance, the jagged outline of Edinburgh Castle on the hilltop interrupted the horizon. Heavy grey clouds hung over the landscape, once again promising rain. It all seemed rather dismal, but Alexander delighted in it, knowing the city would deliver his brother.

"Another hour or two and we shall be there," he called over his shoulder, not bothering to turn towards Davina. Her silence told him she was spearing him with some sort of damning look. "I will take you to your friend if that is what you wish. You only need tell me where she is."

Further silence.

"Would you at least acknowledge that you heard me?" If she would only disclose the Scottish whore's whereabouts, he would happily ride there, drop her off so she could pout freely, and arrest his brother.

"I dinnae know where she is. She said she was going after Glenlyon. And *you* said his regiment was here."

He took a deep breath. He need only search for her—them—in a city of thousands.

On the way up to the castle, Alexander left Davina at a rectory that boasted a few spare rooms for a nominal tithe under the watchful eye of the reverend. It was the perfect place to deposit her—quiet, boring, and pious. Most importantly, it didn't allow for male callers, providing him with the perfect excuse to engage in daily matters without the worry of having to visit her.

"We have some things to discuss. Important things." Davina had stood inside the entrance, her bottom lip quivering in sadness. Or was it anger? "When will ye return for me?"

If he were truthful, he would've said, "Probably never." But instead, he'd answered, "When my business is done with the king."

She asked for a more specific date, but he chose to ignore the question and handed her Breadalbane's letter addressed to the Earl of Mar. "Keep this. I will deal with it later."

"But ye told my uncle ye'd deliver it."

"In time." He mounted his horse and feigned a smile for appearance's sake just in case the rector was watching.

The castle was a short ride up the hill, but he decided to take the long route to survey the town and see which new taverns had appeared since his last visit a couple of years earlier. As he rode through a cobbled street, he spotted one of Jameson's sketches of Edward posted by a church near Mary King's Close. He dismounted from his horse to study it. The description was his own except for the mention of blue eyes, the only real thing that set him and his brother apart.

As much as Alexander didn't want to admit it, they were almost identical. It was the very thing Berenice had reminded him of when she'd first announced she no longer favoured him.

In many ways, it seemed like a lifetime ago, but with the memory yet vivid of her fingers gently brushing aside his hair from his brow when they lay in bed, it felt like it had all happened yesterday. In reality, it had only happened a little over two years earlier. Two years that could've been shaped so differently—all changed with the arrival of his bastard brother. What he still couldn't understand was how she could turn so quickly.

He'd been sure the rumours had been all lies. Even now, the servants' gossip about her and Edward's all-too-obvious affection for one another lay like a stone in his gut. But it had been true, and he'd discovered it in the worst way.

With his heart in his throat, Alexander had burst through the door to her bedchamber. He had only meant to confront her about it when he'd climbed those stairs, make certain it was merely misinformed chatter. But when he'd arrived, he heard the low murmur of a man's voice followed by a familiar giggle and swung open her door, his heart pounding as if he'd just run all the way to Lancaster from York.

She'd stared at him wide-eyed, her golden hair splayed over the pillow and Edward lying beside her in the very bed Alexander had slept in the night before. She'd smiled teasingly. "I had no idea there were two of you! How will I choose?"

Every fear Alexander ever had about his future came rushing back to him at that moment. There would be no marriage, no fortune, no land or estates. But even worse, there would be no *them*. He'd been so close to happiness, all to have it ripped from his grasp by his own brother.

He pounded his fist on the sketch. He had to find Edward.

Not far from the castle, Alexander tied his horse to a hitching post and entered the Royal Coffeehouse. More than half of the patrons were soldiers in various

THE TACKSMAN'S DAUGHTER

states of undress. Some leaned back in their chairs with their scarlet coats thrown open. Others wore their waistcoats unbuttoned, cravats untied. A disgraceful lot if he'd ever seen one.

A group in the back laughed boisterously at the expense of some poor sot who was being jostled away from the table. The man shuffled on, his long, tangled hair in desperate need of a good washing. Alexander sidestepped out of his way as he made it to the front of the room.

The soldier tugged on the bottom of his unevenly buttoned waistcoat in a poor attempt to cover his rather robust gut. He turned back to the group, one finger wagging unsteadily in the air. "Ye dinnae believe me, but 'tis true! 'Tis true!"

Alexander stared at the back of his head, the familiar reddish-gold scraggly mess suddenly familiar. Robert Campbell.

"Get ye goin', ye wandought!" someone shouted.

"I'm a captain in the king's army! Show respect or I'll—"

"You'll what? Yer too soused to piss through a window!"

Two soldiers grabbed him under his arms and shoved him out the door. Alexander followed, curious.

"Captain Campbell?" Alexander asked, watching the old man wipe spittle from his chin.

Campbell grumbled something incoherent, then took an unsteady step back, his eyes blinking with effort. "Come to swindle me of my last penny, have ye?"

"Sir?" Alexander asked, confused and disgusted. Campbell reeked as if he'd been dipped in a vat of whisky and sweat.

Campbell moved closer, his eyes narrowed. New lines were etched in his forehead. He flipped his hand dismissively and belched. "Ach. I thought ye were yer brother."

The old fool recognized him. Alexander waved his hand in front of his face to clear away the stench of Glenlyon's breath.

"I willnae play another hand with that one. Robbed me of my sterling, he did." Campbell smiled crookedly, his face lifting with hope. "Ye wouldn't have a bit of coin to spare, would ye?"

"That depends, Captain." Had he seen Edward? Alexander couldn't believe his good fortune. "Tell me where my brother is, and I might spare a coin or two."

His watery eyes lit up. "He's here. In Edinburgh. Played Quinze with him in a tavern."

Alexander smiled. "Which one?"

"Well, I'd like to tell ye, but I dinnae remember. I may've had a wee dram or two that night." He tapped the side of his head with his middle finger. "Makes me forget."

Alexander huffed. "Will tuppence sharpen your memory?"

"Ye misunderstand me, Leftenant. 'Tisnae that I dinnae wish to remember. 'Tis that I cannae."

Alexander grabbed a fistful of his coat and shoved him back. "Worthless mongrel."

Campbell stumbled, then righted himself. "But aren't ye glad to know he's here? Surely, that should be worth something." He held out his hand, palm up.

Alexander reached inside his coat and extracted two pennies. "Indeed it is."

Chapter 39

"Ye must eat, child." Lizbeth, one of the rector's servants, stood above Davina with reproachful eyes. She wore a bright white cap covering most of her grey hair and a green apron over a plain brown gown. "The soul needs a vessel to reside in. If ye continue to starve yerself, you'll surely waste away to naught."

Davina dipped her spoon into her porridge steaming and sweetened with honey. She paused, holding it in front of her mouth, thinking about the moment she'd found Alex in the arms of that horrid woman. How could he be so easily seduced?

"'Tisnae enough to merely spoon it. Ye must eat it too," Lizbeth instructed with her hands firmly set on her hips.

Davina swallowed the spoonful of porridge and smiled weakly at the matronly servant.

"When yer done, ye can visit with the rector in the solar. Be sure not to disturb him in prayer, mind ye." Lizbeth offered her one last look of pity or disappointment or even loathing—any of the three perfectly appropriate—and left the room.

It had been three days since she'd last seen Alex. He hadn't even sent a note to check on her. He probably thought she needed time alone to think.

After the incident at the market, she'd cried and accused him of two years of wrongdoings. She had made a fool of herself in front of all those who ran to see what the fuss was about, then once again in the castle before all the women staying in the king's house.

"How could ye do this to me?" she'd wailed. They'd stood in her small chamber at the castle, the other female guests in the parlour not far from her door.

"You're making more of this than need be," he'd said with annoyance. "There is no need to yell—"

"Ye betrayed me!" she barked. She bristled at the memory of that woman standing so casually and brushing down her skirts after being discovered. She hadn't even seemed bothered by the crowd who'd trickled over to watch. "She must be a harlot!"

He'd closed his eyes and shook his head with what she perceived as regret. At least she was getting to him. She waited while he seemed to work things out, his brow furrowed and lips tight. Her heart continued to beat furiously, impatiently.

Suddenly, the features of his face had softened, and he stared at her with a rueful smile. "I was bewitched."

She blinked, taken aback by his words. *"Bewitched?"*

"She seduced me behind the market square. I was only searching for the trinket you requested when she approached me, and I felt an extraordinary pull . . ." He paced from one end of the room to the other, his hands moving in great theatrics to explain how he'd been entranced by her words. ". . . so I followed her like an ox to slaughter."

Although her heart had continued to beat furiously, her breath began to slow. She had to remain calm for her unborn bairn. She'd walked to the small window near her bed and stared out at the gardens below. Clumps of violet and yellow flowers lining the walls glistened from the light rain that fell. She took a deep breath, then ran her palm over her belly. There were now at least two reasons she should forgive him for his transgression, but the image of him with that woman burned behind her eyes—them together in the tall grass, the rapturous look on the woman's face, her legs pulling him tighter, locking him in a carnal embrace, Alex pinning her arms to the ground. He'd clearly seemed to have the upper hand. She supposed that's what bothered her most—that his account of what happened didn't quite match what she'd seen.

She'd pictured Sawney's little face, his lips and smile resembling his father's. She hadn't dared turn to look at Alex, for she knew she might lose her nerve. She took a deep breath to steady her voice. "Leave."

Several days had passed since the incident, but it seemed as sharp and heavy if it had happened only moments earlier.

Davina shook her head to free her mind of the memory, but the ghost of it remained in everything she saw in the rectory—the horn cup sitting on the wooden table, the iron pots hanging from a beam against the wall, the wavy glass of the tracery windows at the other end of the kitchen.

The father of her son and their unborn child had lain in the arms of another woman.

Seated at the table, Davina listened to the quiet sounds of Lizbeth tending to housekeeping matters on the other side of the door. Although she didn't have much of an appetite, she finished her breakfast.

She wandered into the solar where the rector sat in an armchair, staring out the diamond-paned window at a small cemetery peppered with leaning tombstones, his knobby fingers peeking out of the cuffs of his robe. She turned to leave, but he called her back.

"Is there something I can do for ye, child?" He stood slowly, taking a few careful steps to measure his balance.

"Forgive me, Reverend. I dinnae wish to disturb ye."

He waved her in. "Nonsense. Come sit."

She joined him in the chair beside him, facing the window.

He smiled, his cloudy blue eyes almost disappearing in the deep wrinkles around them. "I find this the best spot to speak with the Lord. 'Tis quiet and looks upon those who are now with Him."

Davina nodded, glancing at the graves in view. "Reverend, I . . ."

What would she tell him? That she'd fornicated with a man outside of wedlock, had his child, and was ripe with his second? He would tell her she was destined for hell. And that was the last thing she cared to hear him say.

He waited patiently for her to continue, his expression calm and compassionate.

"I . . . am in love with a man," she said, finding it hard to control the tremor in her voice.

"Love isnae a sin. 'Tis what the Lord hopes we all aspire to." He folded his hands in his lap. "Does this man have a wife? Is that what has ye troubled?"

"Oh! I would never fancy another woman's husband." Davina's heart raced. "Never."

"Then what is it that bothers ye so?" His brow crinkled in question.

"This man . . ." She took a deep breath before continuing, her throat tight. "He has recently fallen victim to the guiles of another woman."

He nodded thoughtfully. "I see."

"'Twasn't his fault, mind ye. She bewitched him with her flesh," she said, finding it difficult to look him in the eye.

He nodded in what she took as agreement. "Have ye forgiven him?"

She closed her eyes. "I haven't, Reverend. I cannae seem to see past the hurt."

The sun peeked from behind a cloud and cast a beam of light on both of their laps. "Has he repented, then?"

She thought about his question. He hadn't really apologized, but he had explained how it all happened. She supposed the explanation was his effort to show his weakness and get her to understand his plight. Even so, the words, "I believe so," barely made it past her lips.

"In Luke 17: 3-4, Jesus tells us, 'If yer brother sins, rebuke him, and if he repents, forgive him.'"

She wanted to do what was right. It was time. She had made so many mistakes in her life, falling prey to her own carnal desires. She had expected everyone to forgive her for having Sawney, and some had, but now she was acting like those who hadn't. She had to forgive him. It was what the Lord wanted her to do. "How will I know this will never happen again?"

"Marry him." He shifted in his chair, then pointed a bony finger at the ceiling. "But if they cannae exercise self-control, they should marry. For 'tis better to marry than to burn with passion."

It was at that moment she decided they would wed without the consent of her uncle, and she would tell him he was about to become a father once again. It was the only thing that would help both of them heal from his transgression.

That night, she lay in bed wondering if Cait was nearby. She longed to hear her voice, feel her arm around her while she spilled forth all that had transpired over the last month or so. But Davina probably wouldn't tell her about Alex's liaison with the woman in Stirling, knowing what she would say.

She pressed her palm to her belly that seemed to grow thicker by the minute. Soon, she was either going to need to let out the seams in her gown or find a new one. It wouldn't be long before the rector and servants noticed her predicament too. Would they ask her to leave the rectory? She and Alex had to marry soon and legitimize their bairn. She was nervous about telling him the news, but it had to be done.

The next morning, she penned a quick letter to him at the castle, mentioning that she had important news and wanted to reconcile as soon as possible.

"Would you give this to the footpost for me?" She handed the letter to Lizbeth, then sat at the table, pulling the bench in closer to hide the way her stomach seemed to rise when she sat. Lizbeth served her the same porridge she had every morning since she'd been at the rectory, only this time with a hint of cinnamon. Davina leaned into the steam, breathing in the sweet spicy aroma.

"Here ye go." Lizbeth held out a spoon but let go of it before Davina could grasp it. It fell in her porridge, splashing bits all over her sleeve and the front of her bodice. Davina gasped.

THE TACKSMAN'S DAUGHTER

"Forgive me. 'Twas an accident." Lizbeth wiped the wool fussily, bumping Davina's shoulder in the process. "Forgive me, child."

The heat from the porridge burned through Davina's worn gown. She jumped up, toppling over her chair so that it met the floor with a sharp crack. Furiously, she swiped away the glops with shaky hands, anger flooding her chest and settling in her shoulders and neck, turning them to stone.

"Forgive you?" She slapped Lizbeth's hand away, knocking her bowl of porridge to the floor. "How can I forgive you? You've ruined my gown!" She held out her sleeves for Lizbeth to see. "Foolish woman!"

Lizbeth shrank away, a look of horror in her wide eyes.

"Don't ye see?" She tried to control the quiver that found her mouth, her voice, but it was impossible. "I'm ruined." She closed her eyes. She couldn't look at Lizbeth, afraid she'd see the truth that boiled within her. "I'm . . . I'm . . ."

She ran to her room and slammed the door, her heart thundering in her chest. She was ruined. For two years, she'd never understood everyone's judgement after they discovered she was with child. She'd truly believed that no one understood that the love between her and Alex was stronger than any of their disdain for her predicament as an unwed mother. Her mind had been so clouded by false memories and empty promises whispered in alcoves and behind shrubbery, that she couldn't see the truth.

Although she could now see him clearly for the man he was, there was no way to escape the damage that was done. He was the father of her children, and there was no changing that.

She knelt beside her bed and prayed. Her breath grew shallow and measured with each passing moment, her words spilling forth easily and from her heart. "Dear Lord, give me the strength I need to face this trial . . ."

She sat at the small desk to put away the ink, sand, and seal she'd used to pen the note to Alex and accidentally knocked the letter he'd given her days ago onto the floor. She bent to retrieve it, the earl's name—John Erskine, Earl of Mar—written on the front in large fussy letters. When she flipped it over, the wax seal snapped off. It hadn't crumbled or split, so she was sure she could replace it without the earl noticing the contents had been compromised. She opened the flap to examine the seal and noticed Alex's signature inside. It was a private correspondence written in her uncle's hand, so she wondered why Alex's name would be on it. Could it have something to do with her or Sawney? Knowing her uncle, he could be offering her as a servant—anything to send her away and place her in the hands of someone else. Lady Glenorchy certainly wouldn't disapprove. But why was Alex's signature at the bottom?

She looked both ways before unfolding it fully and read her uncle's words in Gaelic that covered the page, her heart racing with each sentence. But it had nothing to do with her or her son as she suspected. It was a letter asking the Earl of Mar to rouse his cronies to provide financial support to members of Clan Cameron who were banding together to gather weapons and ammunition for a future raid. A spy had communicated that two of the king's regiments of foot guards were headed for Fort William with a baggage train loaded with supplies. The Camerons were planning to attack in a matter of weeks. A Jacobite raid.

She was about to fold it back up when she noticed that her uncle had forgotten to sign it. Or perhaps it was intentional. After all, why would he want to identify himself on such a letter? Then she noticed the seal. It was plain, not the large red seal with ribbon he normally used to indicate his status as the Earl of Breadalbane.

Her hands trembled as she refolded it. Carefully, she dripped wax behind the old seal and pressed it closed. She wanted nothing to do with something so dangerous and decided at that moment she would return it to Alex so he could dispose of it. But without knowing when she'd see him again, she slipped it between her mattress and the bedstead as a precaution.

Chapter 40

It was less than a week before Cait would become Edward's wife. She stared at her mother's sapphire, the morning light catching in its facets, its blue reflection dancing on the white wall as she tilted it left and right. She could only imagine what her mother would say about her marrying an Englishman—or marrying at all. It went against everything Cait had ever believed about herself. She had to admit, she was also surprised. But she knew her heart, and she was bound to follow it. She tucked the stone back into her bodice, her mother's smile of approval vivid in her mind.

Edward's voice jolted her out of her musing. "I'd like to find Taran some new breeches today," Edward said. At the sound of his name, Taran's face lit up.

"I told him to stop eating like he had pockets full of gold." She tugged at the waist of his breeks, now too snug. She kissed him on top of his head. "I suppose ye could use a new pair."

"I'm growing, then. Aye?"

Edward smiled at Cait, then tugged on his boots. "Big and strong too."

She stole a quick glance at the crate that hid the letter. She needed the time alone to inquire about the Earl of Mar. She picked up her *sgian dubh*, twirled it a few times between her fingers, then strapped it around her stocking. "You two go without me. I think I'd like to wander about. There's a bit of a clearing below the castle. I need to breathe in the open air."

"We'll go with ye," Taran offered, beaming in her general direction.

"Nay, laddie. Edward cannae go near the castle. 'Tis too dangerous."

"Och, aye." Taran sat next to Edward on the edge of the bed, tapping the leather soles of his new shoes on the wood floor.

Edward peered at her through narrowed eyes. "Near the castle? What sort of trouble are you looking for, Cait?"

"No trouble. I simply need a place without another person within arm's length of me."

Edward shot her a serious look. "I can only hope you listen to me more now that we are betrothed."

"And what does that mean, exactly?" She planted her hands firmly on her hips.

"It means you're a stubborn lass." He stood and held her face, his palms warm on her jaw. "If you should see Glenlyon, you are not to draw your blade. Promise me, Cait."

Although she was glad he didn't suspect her true motive—to find the earl—she would promise no such thing regarding Glenlyon. She turned away.

Edward's hand brushed the back of her neck, his fingers lingering in her hair. "He's a broken man, lass."

"How would ye know such a thing?"

He took his time answering. "I saw him."

She spun to face him, her pulse quickening. "What? When?"

He rubbed his brow. "A week or so ago. At a tavern."

"And why haven't ye told me?"

"Because I was hoping you'd no longer have interest in carrying out this vengeance of yours."

"Which tavern?"

"Cait," he said in a tone that was clearly reprimanding.

"Ye cannae keep me from confronting the man, Edward. 'Tis my right."

"Confronting him is one thing. Killing him is another."

The bogwood handle of her *sgian dubh* pressed against her thigh, reminding her that it was there. She couldn't wait to drive it into Glenlyon's throat. It took great effort to temper her response. "Yer asking me to let the man go?"

"I'm asking you to understand that killing him will not bring back your parents and Gilli."

"Ye think I dinnae understand that? He took them from me. Forever."

"Then committing murder won't change a thing."

Cait knew that, but Edward was missing the point. She hadn't traveled across the country to simply sit down and have a tot of whisky with the man. "And if he should draw his blade first? Am I nae expected to defend myself?"

"He won't. I told you he is a broken man. He can barely hold up his head." Edward drew her into an embrace, and she allowed it—reluctantly. "Promise me you are only going to this *clearing* to free yourself of the demons in your head. Do not go to the castle."

She would agree to that. But if she happened upon him anywhere else, well, she couldn't control that, could she?

Hours later and after meandering through what felt like every street in Edinburgh, Cait plopped on a tree trunk placed as a stool just outside a chandler's shop. No one knew of the earl's whereabouts. She had entered public houses and inns, teahouses and kirks, but no one had ever seen him, and most had never heard of him. How would she find him? She patted the letter tucked inside her petticoat and wondered if she'd taken on a task she couldn't complete.

The smell of rancid animal fat drifted out the door and hung like a heavy cloud right where she sat. She was certain Edward and Taran were probably worried that she'd found herself in trouble and were likely searching that clearing at the base of the castle looking for her.

"Move along now. Ye cannae sell yer wares in front of my shop. Forbye, you'll have better luck up the way." A tall fine-boned man wearing a brown apron smeared with tallow grease appeared next to her, his hands smooth and shiny from his work.

It took her a moment to comprehend what he was saying. But after the initial encounter with the painted lady near the inn and some others she'd seen since then, she knew what he meant.

"I'm no selling my wares. I've simply worked myself into a weary and hungry state." She needed to find the earl, or Glenlyon at the very least, and pierce a hole in his heart. But the chandler didn't need to know her troubles. "I'll be out of yer way. I'm headed to the tavern up the road."

"Ah. The Royal Coffeehouse. But I should warn ye that ye mightn't take a liking to it. 'Tis usually filled with soldiers and ne'er-do-wells."

She perked up. "Soldiers, ye say?"

"Aye. All eejits, if ye ask me. Drinking and gaming until the wee hours of the night." He studied her for a second with concern in his eyes. "Perhaps ye shouldn't go there. They might misunderstand yer purpose."

"I'll be fine, sir."

She bid him a farewell, and with clear intent, headed up the road closer to the castle. If the soldiers weren't there, at least she could inquire about the earl. Her stomach growled as she jingled the coins Edward had given her in a little linen pouch. She wasn't ignoring Edward's caution. He'd only told her not to go to the castle, and this tavern was only *near* the castle.

The Royal Coffeehouse was dim and smoky, the space lit by a half dozen torches burning on opposite walls. Cait held her breath as she entered, the acrid smell of smoke and unwashed bodies a sharp affront to her nose. Other women milled about, but most were either barmaids or whores, she guessed, so even in her faded blue moth-eaten gown, she was the best-dressed lass in the place.

She settled onto a bench near the window and scanned the crowd. At least half of the patrons were soldiers, their scarlet coats and English voices a stark contrast to the Scottish customers. Her heart pounded. The last time she'd been this close to so many soldiers was in Glencoe. She rubbed the back of her neck to free it from the tingling that started there.

"I would do it again!"

Cait froze. It was Glenlyon's voice, loud and sloppy with drink.

He wasn't difficult to spot. He was seated in the far corner, his face bright red and his voice brash and booming. A group of men surrounded him, some standing, some seated on the benches across from him, all with pints or glasses in their hands.

"I would dirk any man in Scotland or England without asking cause if the king gave me orders!" His heavy jaw shook in anger. He held up his drink, the golden whisky quivering precariously in his hand. He drained the last of it, then planted his glass firmly on the table. "So should every good subject of His Majesty!"

As much as she wanted to cross the room and yank him off his pulpit, she didn't. She waited, allowing him to spew his self-righteous prattle to those who would listen, the whisky giving him the false courage to do it. Perhaps it soothed the doubt brewing within him and the guilt poisoning his soul. Or perhaps he truly believed what he had done was right. Either way, she didn't care. He'd led the attack, and that was all she needed to know.

One by one, his audience started to scatter, leaving their empty mugs behind on the long wooden table. With no one to tout his loyalty to, he pushed himself off the bench and wobbled unsteadily as he righted his coat and plaid.

Cait slipped outside, her entire body buzzing with anger. She hid in the alley not far from the tavern, waiting for him to leave. Since she had arrived, the sky had darkened with the presence of clouds, the wind stirring.

Finally, his tall frame filled the door's opening, and he staggered into the street. He adjusted his bonnet, then lumbered over the cobblestones, his coat open and his lace collar untied. Cait's heart pounded as he drew closer, his laboured breath easily heard with each approaching step. He stopped beside a wooden cask to relieve himself, and Cait slid her *sgian dubh* out of her stocking. There couldn't be more than twenty paces between them.

THE TACKSMAN'S DAUGHTER

Her grip tightened around her knife as he grew closer. This was it. Her moment to take the life of the man who'd taken away her family.

She waited until he floundered in front of the alley. The sound of his boots shuffling as they scraped against the cobbles, echoed in her head. He was talking to himself, repeating the words, "I did what I was told." He belched twice, then restarted his chant with his head hung low. "I did what I was told."

Just as he tottered past her, she grabbed him around the neck and pulled him into the alley, her blade held taut at his throat.

He tried to swing around but stumbled in her grip, his bonnet slipping off his head and tumbling into the rubbish at his feet. "What? What is this? Unhand me!"

"'Tis a ghost from yer past," she whispered brusquely in his ear. "One who will force ye to draw yer last breath."

He slumped out of her arms and fell against the wall, crumbling to the ground. "Another ghost?" He swiped his forehead with a soiled hand, dirt wedged under his fingernails. "MacIain's ghost comes to me at all hours. I cannae bear it."

He lifted his heavy head to look at her, his eyes glassy with lines of grief etched around them.

A rush of heat filled Cait's chest. "I hope he haunts ye even after yer in the grave."

He blinked slowly, then belched again. "I remember you. Yer the tacksman's daughter, aye? Malcolm, was he?"

Hearing her father's name stung her heart. She pressed the tip of her blade into the hollow of his neck.

"I didn't want to do it." He peered up at her, his face red and blotchy, his neck tight with fear. "I didn't."

"But ye did." She slid the pointed tip up his neck and under his chin, leaving a thin trace of blood in its wake. He winced at the pain, then leaned back against the wall to escape the pressure of her knife.

"Wait." He fumbled inside his coat, groping blindly and mumbling to himself. He handed her a crumpled piece of paper smudged along the edges with food stains and dirt. "Go on. Open it," he urged with his chin.

She flicked it open with one hand, the blade in her other still at his throat.

For His Majesty's Service, to Captain Robert Campbell of Glenlyon
Sir,
You are hereby ordered to fall upon the rebels, the MacDonalds of Glencoe, and to put all to the sword under seventy. You are to have a special care that the old fox and his sons do upon no account escape your hands. You are to

secure all the avenues that no man escape. This you are to put in execution at five of the clock precisely; and by that time, or very shortly after it, I'll strive to be at you with a stronger party. If I do not come to you at five, you are not to tarry for me, but to fall on. This is by the king's special command, for the good and safety of the country, that these miscreants be cut off root and branch. See that this be put in execution without feud or favour, else you may expect to be dealt with as one not true to King nor Government, nor a man fit to carry commission in the king's service. Expecting you will not fail in the fulfilling hereof, as you love yourself, I subscribe these with my hand at Ballachulish, Feb 12, 1692.

Robert Duncanson

"Who is this *Duncanson?*" she asked, her grip on the missive tightening.

"A Scot. A major under Hamilton."

"Hamilton?"

"Aye. He takes orders from the Earl of Breadalbane, who takes orders from—"

"Enough!" Every word he spoke grated over her skin. She pressed the knife to the tender flesh at the base of his neck.

"Ye must understand, lass." He swallowed hard. "How could I go against orders? The king's orders?"

"'Tisnae signed by the king." She tossed it on the ground beside him.

"Orders like these pass through many hands before they reach me. And the first hand had to be the king's."

So, it was true. Edward was right. And Duncan was right. "If ye think the king's crime absolves ye of yer own, yer wrong. Ye raised yer blade on my kin. Yer own countrymen."

"I dinnae claim to be innocent." Glenlyon shrugged. "Read the missive. I received the orders from someone else, whether His Majesty or no. The attack was nae designed by me."

In the gleam of her blade, she saw her father and mother's faces. Gilli's face. Her breath steadied as she readjusted her grip on her *sgian dubh*. Tucked inside her bodice, her mother's sapphire pressed against her heart.

"Believe what ye wish, but I never came to Glencoe thinking to cause harm on the MacDonalds, lass."

"Maybe no, but ye sure drew yer dirk fast. 'Tis no secret how the Campbells feel about us."

His normally loud voice lost its bravado and lowered to little more than a humble whisper. "'Tis true. But MacIain welcomed us into his home and gave us his food and whisky. I cannae say I would've done the same, but I *can* say

THE TACKSMAN'S DAUGHTER

that 'tisnae the Highland way to turn on a man after he's opened his door to ye. And I'm a Highlander first, mind ye."

"Yer a Campbell first."

He nodded sloppily. "Perhaps. But a Campbell heavy with regret."

Cait stared at him. He was not the same man who'd marched into Glencoe with squared shoulders and his chest puffed out like a gamecock. He was just as Edward had said—a broken man. Perhaps he'd been broken this whole time, his last bit of dignity derived from his role as a soldier. She'd been told he had only one estate left after he'd bankrupted his family, and that was in his wife's name. According to Davina, his improvident ways had left him in debt to many, including his cousin the Earl of Breadalbane. That was what had curdled the earl's opinion of him, she'd said. Glenlyon had only taken the commission as a captain in Argyll's regiment to save his family from complete disgrace. But looking at him now, drunken and sitting in filth with his hair greasy and mussed, he had already disgraced all those who shared his surname.

She didn't want to take pity on him. She didn't care to understand his side of the story. She tried to steady her breath that was now jagged and unsure. She had spent every day since her family was slaughtered, dreaming of avenging their deaths and killing the man who allowed them to be put to sword. But now uncertainty filled her chest as she stared down at the man, a soldier, who claimed he had only followed orders, ones that could not be disobeyed. Edward's words of warning returned to her. His death would not bring her peace. Slowly, she withdrew her knife.

His mouth opened in shock, and he sat a bit taller. "I—"

"Say another word and I'll slice ye ear to ear." She held her blade out in front of her, deflated.

He nodded, then stood to leave, wobbling unsteadily as he stooped to pick up the discarded missive. He tucked it into his coat and held up his hands in submission. "Ye should know that there's a proclamation that all Glencoe survivors must sail to America or Ireland. Ye cannae stay in Scotland."

She tossed him his soiled bonnet, then eyed him warily. "The king decreed that?"

"'Twas from Dalrymple, Master of Stair. But he does as the king says."

The king. The letter at her thigh burned close to her skin. And to think she had traveled all the way to Edinburgh to beg him for his help to evoke justice for the dead.

Chapter 41

Taran sat on the bed, waiting for Cait to return, just as Edward had told him to. He scratched his thighs vigorously to calm the itch of his new wool breeks. The man at the shop had said the more he wore them, the less they'd bother him, but as Taran ran his fingernails over the rough fabric, he figured that it would likely take years before that would happen.

Cait had been missing for hours now. When he and Edward had returned to the inn, the innkeeper had said he hadn't seen her, sending Edward into the streets in a panic and cursing in Gaelic just like he'd been taught. Taran had wanted to laugh but knew that Edward hadn't meant to be funny.

Taran scratched harder, but the itching wouldn't stop, so he lay back on the bed, slipped off his breeks, and flung them on the floor. He breathed a sigh of relief, happy with the cold air that brushed over his skin and gave him gooseflesh.

The door swung open, and he quickly pulled down his sark over his willie.

"'Twasn't that bad." It was Cait's voice, calm and unconcerned.

"I told you not to go there. I specifically said—"

"*He* came to *me*."

Taran slipped off the bed and ran his hands across the floor in search of his breeks.

"You said you pulled him into an alley. That doesn't sound as if he came to you of his own accord." Edward spoke sternly, a lot louder than Taran had ever heard him speak, and it made him want to slide back onto the corner of the bed.

THE TACKSMAN'S DAUGHTER

Cait's voice grew in volume. "Nothing came of it, Edward. I told ye ye needn't fash over me."

"You could've got yourself killed, lass." Edward seemed to soften. His dark shape met with Cait's.

Taran gave up on finding his breeks and slid back onto the bed. "Did ye see the cockard?"

Cait's hand found his head and stroked his hair. The bedstead creaked when she sat next to him. "Aye."

"Did ye run him through, then?" he asked.

"Nay, laddie." She huffed out a deep breath. "Couldn't."

He was shocked. He thought that was what they'd come to Edinburgh for—to find Glenlyon and kill him for what he'd done to her family. And likely his grandda. "Why?"

"'Tis complicated. Edward was right. It wouldn't have made me feel any better if I had." Her voice was sad, defeated. Taran leaned into her, his head resting in the crook of her oxter. "He told me something, though."

"What?" Edward asked.

"He said that all survivors of the attack are ordered to leave Scotland and sail for America or Ireland. Ordered by the king."

Her heart beat fast against Taran's ear. "We have to leave?" he asked.

Edward hmphed but said nothing.

A lump formed in Taran's throat. "Will ye go with us, Edward?"

He tipped up Taran's chin with his finger. "We're not going anywhere, lad."

A commotion started outside, and Taran turned his head to the noise. Shouting and laughing erupted below. "What's happening?"

Edward's heavy footsteps moved across the room to the window. "'Tis the king's caravan."

Taran stared at the blurry light coming in from the window and Edward's dark shadow in front of it. "The king! Can we go?"

"Would ye like that, Taran?" Cait asked with two pats on his arm, a strange challenge in her voice.

"Aye. You can tell me what he looks like and if he travels with piles of gold and how many servants are with him and—"

"Hmm. I dinnae think we can go, laddie," she said.

His heart sank. "Och! And why is that?"

"Because I dinnae believe the king would take too well to a bare-arsed lad cheering him in the street."

Taran pulled on his itchy breeks and followed Cait into the crowds outside. They stood on the opposite side of the street from their inn because she said the walking path in front of the shops was too narrow and packed for her to get a good look at anything. Edward stayed in their room, concerned with being spotted and recognized by one of the soldiers accompanying the procession.

"I want to know everything," Taran said, thrilled with the sounds of horses parading by, the squeaky wheels of the carts, and the foot soldiers all marching to the same beat. It was like nothing he'd ever heard before.

Cait stood behind him with her hands on his shoulders. "There must be a hundred wagons loaded with the king's possessions. Tapestries and pots. Crates and bags."

"What's in the crates?" he asked.

"How would I know, laddie?" She laughed. "Fineries, I imagine."

The wagons rattled as they passed by, laden with items that clinked and jangled. Horses snorted and clip-clopped along the cobblestones. They were so close, Taran could feel the heat emanating off their bodies. "Do ye see the king yet?"

She cursed in Gaelic, and the pressure of her hands on his shoulders increased. She was standing on her tiptoes. "Nay, laddie. But his guards are close. All wearing livery in fine scarlet cloth and gold and silver lace. The banners have gold and silver fringe too."

The names of colours meant nothing to him. He could spot red if he had to, but the other colours were truly all the same. "What would the fringe feel like?"

"Feel like?" The tightness of her grip faded. After a second or two, she hugged him close, her arms resting over his chest. "If ye were to brush yer hand along the ends of sheep's grass, the velvet blades would rain across yer fingers like that fringe."

Taran spread his fingers apart and pretended to run his hand over the grass. It was soft and tickly and made him remember a time last spring when he'd helped his grandda with the shearing of their sheep. Puffs of the tall grasses had brushed against legs as he wandered through the meadow whistling and rounding up the beasties. "I can feel it."

Cait's arms were no longer around his shoulders. "Cait?"

He spun around. "Cait?"

People laughed and cheered all around him. The king must've been within sight. "Cait? Are ye there?"

A shiver ran up his spine. She would never leave him like that—so sudden and without her usual explanation of where she was headed and how he needed to stay put. Taran tapped his cane in front of him, moving away from the crowd.

THE TACKSMAN'S DAUGHTER

"Cait?" he called.
She didn't answer.

Chapter 42

"We dinnae allow our female guests to have gentlemen callers, Leftenant."

Alexander rolled his eyes and flipped Davina's note out of his coat. "I was sent for. I am the mistress's . . . patron."

The old trug took the letter and scanned it briefly before she handed it back. "Wait here while I fetch her."

Alexander stood in the doorway as the servant toddled away. The rectory smelled musty, like aged books and damp boots. He fluttered his fingers back and forth beneath his nostrils to clear his nose of the odor.

Davina appeared at the old woman's side, pale and desperate as always. Her blonde hair had been pinned up close to her scalp, a rather severe look for a woman with her disposition.

"Ye came," she said, stating the obvious.

"You said you wished to discuss something of great importance?"

"I do. But nae here." Davina turned to the servant. "Would ye mind if I stepped out with the leftenant, Lizbeth?"

The woman glanced back and forth at the two of them. Alexander made sure not to give her the courtesy of making eye contact.

"Make haste, though. There's no time left in the day for long conversations, mind ye." She waddled to the rear of the house, turned back once for a last look, then disappeared behind a closed door.

He scanned the shops for his brother as they walked towards the castle to a clearing just below the great hill. Edward was nowhere to be seen. But Edward would never chance being close to the castle, undoubtedly aware there was a price on his head. Not that Alexander wanted to go anywhere near it either. It

THE TACKSMAN'S DAUGHTER

only reminded him of his insufficient accommodations there. He had to share a room with three other officers, one of whom smelled like the decaying flesh and leather found in a tannery. He settled on a spot near a clump of trees that would provide shade from the sun or protection from the rain—whichever decided to make its appearance in the unpredictable moody weather of this godforsaken country.

"What is so important that you needed to call me from my duties?" he asked, bored already with the whole ordeal. He had no duties to perform, but she didn't need to know that.

Davina urged him to sit next to her. He reluctantly obliged.

"I've been speaking with the rector," she started, her hands fumbling with one another nervously.

"And?"

"He believes we should marry." Before he could protest, she added, "And I do too. I have forgiven ye for yer dalliance with that woman. I know ye couldn't help it."

He'd never met another woman so easily played. But how could she possibly talk of marriage after she'd caught him in the act of tupping another woman? "You want to—"

"The rector said marriage will cure ye of yer ways. 'But because of the temptation to sexual immorality, each man should have his own wife and each woman her own husband.' That's Corinthians, mind ye."

He wasn't much one for the Bible. "That's lovely, but we do not have your uncle's blessing. 'Tis impossible."

"We dinnae need his blessing. He willnae even care."

"Then what of your parents?" He knew that was a foolish question, but he asked it anyway, hoping things might have changed and they'd suddenly found interest in their wreck of a daughter.

"They would care even less." She suddenly straightened. "Or perhaps they would welcome it. Ye are, after all, Sawney's father. I could tell them that ye never meant to leave me. That ye always meant to return and give me and yer son yer name. 'Tis our chance to be a family."

He started to panic, heat creeping into his neck. "Wait, wait, wait. We need to think clearly here."

"I *am* thinking clearly. We should marry. And soon." An unsteady smile stretched across her face. "There is something ye should know, Alex."

He flinched. Memories of Berenice's golden curls tickling his chest as she lay in his arms, settled in his mind. The lilac perfume on her wrist as he kissed the palm of her hand, invading his senses. He swallowed hard.

"I have asked you not to call me that," he said, his voice made weaker by his struggling heart.

"'Tis my pet name for ye." She kissed her finger, then dabbed his chin with it. "Alex."

"Stop or I shall leave." No one would ever take Berenice's place. No one. Davina's ridiculous smile dripped from her face.

He was losing patience. "Now what is it that you feel the need to tell me?"

She bit her bottom lip and looked down at her lap, finding invisible bits of lint to pick from her gown. She took two deep breaths as she brushed her hands across the front of her skirts, smoothing out the wrinkles.

He rubbed his temple in circular motions to stop the pounding in his skull. "If you have nothing to say, I shall escort you back."

He started to stand, but she grabbed his hand and coaxed him to sit. Her eyes began to water. "I'm to have another bairn."

A bolt of heat shot up through his spine. "What?"

"I said—"

"I know what you said!" He stood abruptly. "And if that is indeed true, 'tis not my child."

She appeared perplexed, her brow crumbling inward. "Of course he's yers. I havenae lain with another man."

"How would I know? I do not follow you about like a mongrel as you do me!"

She sucked in her breath with a squeaky sound.

"I will have none of this!" He began to leave, but she leaped up and remained at his heels. Finally, he stopped. "I will not allow you to try and trap me with another child. They are *your* bastards. Not mine."

"Why are ye saying this? I thought—"

"That is the problem with you, Davina. You do *not* think."

"What?"

A searing rumble of anger raged inside of him. His chest filled with vitriol as he grabbed her just below her shoulders and shook her roughly. "Must you be so daft? I have been fucking my way through Scotland for years, and I do not intend to stop. Do you hear me?"

She froze, her mouth and eyes wide in shock.

He shook her again. "I do not love you! You are nothing but another whore to me."

Her lips quivered and her nostrils flared. She swung out of his grip and slapped him hard across the face. She pointed a shaky finger at him, her shoulders shuddering heatedly. "You *willnae* make a fool of me! I will tell my uncle and the king, if I must, that yer a coward and a liar. That ye stole my maidenhead from me!"

"Do you honestly think they will believe you?" He couldn't help but laugh. "I will denounce you as an opportunist, another desperate whore looking for a man to hand over his purse and raise her bastards. Be my guest," he said with the flourish of his hand. "Tell whomever you please. It will only prove you as the simpleton you truly are."

She lunged at him, flailing her arms at his face and chest, pushing and pounding with little effect. Her face was the colour of a beetroot and her eyes bloodshot. It was almost arousing. He stepped aside and she fell to the ground, landing hard on her knees.

"I have had quite enough," he announced.

As he walked away, she laughed. Not a measured, amused laugh, but a cackle, shrill and manic. He vowed not to turn around.

"Go on," she yelled. "Ye forget that I have the power to take away everything ye have. Yer titles, yer land, yer fortune! All I need to do is deliver that letter to the king and you'll be ruined!"

He stopped and turned. "*I* have the letter to the king."

She laughed again, this time more sinister. "But *I* have the letter to the Earl of Mar."

"So?"

"Have ye forgotten ye signed yer name on it?"

He thought back to Breadalbane's request for him to sign it. It was peculiar at the time, but the earl had explained it by stating that the recipient would only receive it if it had both signatures on it. "What of it?"

"I read it," she said, a menacing grin on her red splotchy face. "Do ye know what a *Seumasach* is?"

A Seumasach? The whole damned thing had been written in Gaelic.

She waited. "Of course ye don't. It means Jacobite."

He was sure his face was as blank as his mind. What was she talking about?

"Yer a fool. Do ye know that?" She scrambled to her feet and shoved him hard. "Ye signed yer name to a document asking the earl to help the Jacobite cause."

"I did no such thing." The pulse in his neck thrummed.

"But ye did. And I have the proof."

He sneered. "You understand that if you show that letter to the king, you are looping a noose around your uncle's neck."

She threw her head back and laughed. "Oh, *A-lex-an-der*, ye fool. *He* never signed it. Only *you* did. So *yer* neck is the only one in jeopardy."

He remembered signing it but couldn't recall if Breadalbane had done the same. He had thought penning his name on another man's correspondence odd at the time—but he'd done it, too famished to argue and in exchange for a good horse and a fine coat. *Damn him!* Breadalbane had purposefully left off his signature just in case the letter was intercepted. Alexander's chest grew tight as if a vice were cinching it smaller.

He couldn't let this happen. Not after everything he'd endured—serving as a soldier, sleeping in tents, billeting in homes not good enough for livestock—to save himself from attainder. He grabbed her throat and squeezed. Her hands fought to pull him off. "Where is it?"

Her face changed from pink to red, her mouth struggling for air.

"I said, *where is it?*"

She opened her mouth and gagged, a bubbling noise barely escaping. He let go of her, and she plummeted to the ground, gasping and coughing unattractively.

His life would be ruined if she showed it to the king. Being attainted didn't even matter anymore. He could be hanged for treason. He had to destroy that letter.

He reached down and grabbed her by the hair, inadvertently knocking out a few of her hairpins. She scratched at the skin on his hands, clawing and pulling to free herself from his grip. "Tell me where you put that letter."

Her mouth curled down into a moue of disgust. "Yer life is over!"

His grip tightened. "Tell me! Is it at the rectory?"

He threw her down, and she curled into a ball, her green tattered gown now covered in leaves and dirt. He loomed over her. "I swear I will kill you if you do not tell me where it is. Answer me!" Fueled with fury, he yanked her by the hair once again, and her head wobbled awkwardly.

He held his breath, unsure of what he had just done. With the jerk of his hand, he let her go.

She lay with her mouth open and eyes closed, unmoving. He began pacing, his boots striking the earth angrily. How could this have happened? How could he have been so careless?

He lifted her hand and let it drop. Nothing. Had she fainted or . . .?

He dragged her to a tree, then shoved her body beneath some bracken. *Damn her.* He had to find that letter.

He raced through the thoroughfare to the rectory just as the last sliver of sun set behind the horizon. Pacing in front of the door, he wiped his hands down his face and ran his fingers through his hair. How would he explain Davina's absence to the rector? It would certainly create an alarm of suspicion.

THE TACKSMAN'S DAUGHTER

He knocked on the door and waited, brushing debris from his coat and straightening his cuffs and cravat. After what seemed like a minute, he knocked again.

The servant answered, her hands set on her hips. "Just in time. I thought ye mightn't return before—"

"I am here to retrieve Mistress Davina's belongings." He tried to step past her, but she blocked his way with her arm.

"Where is she?" She stretched her neck to look beyond him and into the street. "We have rules here."

Alexander took a deep breath. The stench of the fusty parlour affronted him. "I am moving her to another rectory. She is complaining of the dust and smell."

The servant eyed him suspiciously. "She never complained of that to me."

"If you would just step aside so I can collect her things . . ."

Again, he tried to shove through, but this time she grabbed the edge of the doorpost and wouldn't budge. "You'll stay right here, ye will. And *I'll* fetch her things."

She shut the door behind her. Alexander stood on the front step, his heart pounding furiously and beads of sweat forming on his upper lip. Could she have sent the letter by messenger? If she had, he would need to disappear. Find some place to hide in England under a new name. He would lose all his money and titles, but he would be spared his life.

Or he could capture Edward and turn him in to the king to prove his loyalty before word of the letter reached his ears. He had to find his brother.

The woman returned with a small bundle wrapped in linen. He unraveled it quickly, but all he found was a single hairpin, a comb, and a black ribbon. "There should be a letter."

She shook her head. "That's all she had."

He squeezed his hands into fists, desperate to keep them from shaking, a sharp pain forming in the back of his throat. "Let me look. I am certain I will find—"

"Good evening, Leftenant." With one hand on his chest, she nudged him back and shut the door.

Chapter 43

Cait grappled with the hand covering her mouth as she was dragged away from the king's procession into a narrow wynd. The dirt and sweat caking the palm and fingers of her assailant found their way into her mouth and eyes during the struggle. She wrenched her head left and right, gagging on the salty, gritty taste. She tried to blink the dirt away, but it was impossible, rendering her incapable of seeing where she was being taken. Her own desperate muffled screams were drowned out by the crowd's cheers and laughter flooding her ears.

Her attacker grunted as he heaved her up against some wooden crates, then flung her to the ground. Her eyes watered from the scratchy dirt, blurring the two figures before her. She scrabbled for the knife in her stocking.

"If it isnae the tacksman's daughter. Ye enjoying yerself watching the king?"

Her heart plummeted. Sionn. She swiped at her eyes to see him clearly. Finnean stood two paces behind him.

She thrust her knife at him. "Touch me again, and you'll no live to see another day."

Sionn stood with his arms folded and legs braced apart, an amused smirk spreading across his face. Edward's dirk lay at his hip. "Did ye hear that, brother? She's going to kill me with that wee blade. Again."

Finnean snickered, his cheeks twitching nervously.

"Ye tried that once. Didn't ye, bitch?" Sionn held his arms out in presentation. "But here I am."

THE TACKSMAN'S DAUGHTER

Even after three months, the scar on his neck was angry and red. It was a clean line that curved around his throat just below his jaw. She couldn't believe he'd survived the injury. She stumbled to her feet and raised her *sgian dubh*, aiming it at his neck. "Consider that a gift, aye. This time I willnae spare ye."

He glanced back at Finnean, pointing and waving his thumb between them. "But there are two of us now. You'll have to kill us both."

"Aye." Finnean rested his hand on the hilt of his dirk, his shaggy pale hair hanging in his eyes.

Cait shrugged. "I will if I must." She took a step and jerked her *sgian dubh* at him. "Back away and I'll leave ye free to go about yer business."

Neither budged.

"Leave *us* free?" asked Sionn. He pulled Edward's dirk from its sheath and pointed it at her, his voice lowered. "Yer no going anywhere. I'm here to finish what I started in Kinlochbeg."

She considered throwing her knife into his chest, but that would leave her without a weapon if Finnean came after her. She'd have to fight him straight on.

"I'll go first." Finnean moved closer, his hand cupping the front of his breeks.

Sionn pushed him back with one fist curled around the fabric of his sark. "We're no doing that. Get her weapon."

Finnean's shoulders sank. "So *you* get to decide when we take a lass? 'Tis my turn for a go, Sionn."

"You'll get yer turn! Now get her weapon!"

He shoved Finnean from behind, and he stumbled into her. In the seconds it took him to regain his balance, she slid his dirk from its strap and held him at bay. "So now I have two weapons. One for each of ye."

Sionn glared at his brother. "Ye *amadain!* Look what ye did!"

A look of humiliation and panic swept over Finnean's face. In a sudden move, he reached for Cait's wrist to wrangle away the dirk, but she swung it at his arm, sending him howling in pain. A dark red line appeared in the open tear of his sleeve. His eyes widened in shock as blood streaked down his arm. He dropped on top of a crate and sat, squealing like a stuck pig and squeezing together the gash she'd created.

Sionn glanced back at the entrance to the alley, then yelled at his brother. "*Sguir a ghabhail dragh!*" *Stop yer fussin'!*

But even with Finnean carrying on like that, Cait knew no one would hear him. The crowd was too busy shouting and applauding for the king.

"Let me pass or you'll be next," she said, holding both weapons in front of her. Auntie Meg's weak smile appeared in her memory, and her stomach sank.

She wasn't sure she could do it. Edward was right. Murder *was* a heavy burden to carry, especially since Sionn was kin.

She'd given Glenlyon a second chance. But this was self-defense. She readjusted her grip on the knives.

Sionn's eyes darted towards his brother and back. He had to know that Finnean would be of no use. He slid Edward's dirk into its sheath and held up both hands in concession. "Then go."

He took a half-step back and stared at her, waiting.

She edged closer, pressed to the wall of the building. Her heart knocked riotously against her chest. He had done this once before, and she had fallen for it, but this time she held two weapons in her hands. "If yer foolish enough to move, yer foolish enough to die," she reminded him.

He smiled insincerely.

She circled around him, close enough to smell the sourness of his breath, gripping the blades tightly. Just as she cleared him, he tripped her, sending her staggering to the ground, her black knife escaping her grasp and tumbling onto the dirt by his feet.

She reached for it, but he kicked it aside and fell on top of her, squeezing her wrist to force her to let go of Finnean's dirk. She wriggled under his weight, trying to buck him off, but he was twice her size and angry. With his other hand, he pried open her fingers and wrestled away the knife, locking her wrists together. She screamed for help, but like Finnean's cries, hers were also unheard.

He slid his tongue over her lips, and she pressed them tighter, gritting her teeth. She swung her head back and forth, her eyes squeezed shut. Suddenly, he hit her, the back of his hand smashing into her cheek and forcing her to still. A dull pain spread to her temple and into her skull.

"Did ye think I was going to do it, *siùrsach?*"

Although she didn't care for being called a whore, she found the spittle that landed in her ear more offensive.

He rubbed his groin against her, the fetor of his sweat seeping out of his rank clothing. He laughed. "Nay. I'll no give ye the pleasure."

Her legs kicked furiously as she twisted to get away. "Get off me!"

"Ye ruined everything for me back home, ye did." With one hand, he slid the dirk out of its sheath and pressed it to her chest. As he shifted his weight, he raised his chin, once again flashing his scar. It made her think of her own scar that ran across her palm, bringing her right back to the brewhouse where the soldiers had attacked her. And her brief encounter with Sionn in Kinlochbeg when she left him for dead. She had thought quickly both times and managed to escape. Now she would have to do the same.

THE TACKSMAN'S DAUGHTER

Out of the corner of her eye, she saw a flash of red, but with Sionn blocking her view of the alley entrance, she couldn't make out what it was. Could it be someone coming to help? A soldier?

Finnean whined not ten feet away. "Ye promised I could have the next lass. Ye promised, Sionn."

Sionn ignored him, his eyes intently focused on hers.

The thought that they had forced themselves on other women sickened her. Auntie Meg had raised a couple of beasts. Finnean mumbled to himself, his words caught in between groans and sharp intakes of breath.

Sionn gritted his teeth, lips taut. He pressed the tip of Edward's blade into the hollow between her breasts. Her pulse raced and throbbed in her throat. She had to do something.

He lowered his head, his face only inches from her own. "Ma blaming me for everything. Ye filled her head with tales. Do ye think I care about yer fancy meals and MacIain's whisky and wine? Och, I heard enough of that. Ye think yer so special because yer da was one of MacIain's tacksmen."

She couldn't believe that was what had made him so angry. A few stories—memories—about her life in Glencoe. She tried to steady her breath to keep the point of the dirk from piercing her skin.

"Now she's talking back. Havering on about nonsense." Spit sprayed her face as he spoke. "'Tis all yer doing."

"If the two of ye weren't such useless doltons, perhaps ye'd have enough to eat every night too," she said between gritted teeth.

His face tightened, and the pressure of Edward's knife left her chest momentarily. Quickly, and with a force that surprised her, she slammed her head into his nose, a sharp crack marking the impact. Sionn reared back, releasing her wrists and clutching his face. Pain stretched across her forehead and white dots bloomed before her eyes, blinding her momentarily. But knowing this was her only chance to escape, she threw her weight forward, causing him to lose his balance and fall back against the wall.

She scrabbled for Edward's dirk.

Chapter 44

"Cait's missing."

Edward spun from the window and stared at Taran as he entered the room, a lump of heat settling in his chest. "What?"

"She was standing with me, watching the parade of horses go by, and then she was gone. I came as fast as I could, but it was hard to break through the crowd. Even they didn't want to let a blind lad by."

She would've never left Taran on his own. Something had happened. He strapped on the dagger belonging to the Earl of Breadalbane and tucked the pistol inside his coat. "Where were you two last?"

"Just on the other side of the street. I cannae tell ye how many paces because I had to jump and dodge a wee bit to get here. But 'twasn't far from a vennel. I could smell it." He wrinkled his nose in disgust.

Edward grabbed Taran's shoulder, his mouth suddenly dry. "Stay here. Do not leave this room. Do you understand?"

Taran nodded, and Edward flew out the door. The crowd was thick and almost impossible to jostle his way through. Nevertheless, he forced his way between bodies tightly abutted against one another, bumping and shoving with little mercy.

"Mind yerself! We all wish to see!" someone shouted behind him.

He waited for a break in the procession, guessing from the cheering crowd closer to the palace that the king had already passed by. He cut between two of the king's guards seated on white stallions. The horses skittered sideways and jerked their heads upwards, frightened by his sudden presence, but regained their composure as he made it to the other side.

THE TACKSMAN'S DAUGHTER

What could have happened? He could not help thinking it had something to do with Glenlyon. Could he have taken her for ransom? Revenge? He didn't seem capable of such an act, but perhaps he had someone else do it for him.

The stench of the alleyway hit him almost immediately. He pushed through the hordes of people to get there. It was very narrow, barely wide enough for a horse and rider to fit through. He turned in and instantly heard the sounds of scuffling and a man's groan. He hoped he was only stumbling upon a drunk suffering from being too deep in his cups, but when he heard a female gasp, he knew it was more.

He slipped his dagger from its sheath and edged along the side of the wall, listening, his head pounding. Hard as he tried, he couldn't help thinking he'd found her and she was in a bad predicament.

He slid around the corner into an open space and discovered Cait reaching for a dagger that lay in the dirt only feet away from her. Her cheeks were smeared with tears, her face blotchy and red. Her hair was tousled and filthy, and the back of her gown was covered with dirt.

"Cait?" He started to run towards her.

"Edward!" she shouted, her eyes round with fear.

Before he took another step, he was shoved to the ground from behind, the force sending his dagger flying. He jabbed his elbow into his attacker and flipped on his side. The man straddling him was bloodied from brow to neck, his face a deep raspberry colour and his nose swollen and purplish. Edward tried to wriggle free, to grasp the pistol in his coat, but the man jammed his palm into his throat, causing him to gasp for breath. Edward choked, twisting furiously to escape from underneath him, a handful of his shirt clutched in one hand. The man broke free and dragged him up against the brick wall, his forearm pressed against Edward's neck. Just as Edward managed to pry his arm away, his attacker's eyes sprung open in shock. A trickle of blood spilled out of his mouth and down his chin. He grew rigid, and Edward shoved him to the side before he collapsed to the dirt face-first. A knife that Edward recognized as his own stuck out from the dead center of the man's back. Cait stood not ten paces away, her arm still extended from the release, her eyes wide and lips trembling.

Edward reached for her hand, her face red and flustered with purple marks starting to form on her cheek and brow. He drew her close, checking every part of her he could easily see.

"I killed him," she mumbled, her chin quivering.

He couldn't imagine what she'd been through. "If it is ever brought to light, we'll say I did it, *mo gràdh*. I already have a price on my head."

She fell into him, her cheek resting heavily on his chest.

He kissed her brow, then bent to reclaim his dagger. Gently, he nudged her towards the entrance of the alleyway. "We need to leave quickly before we're seen."

Behind him, he heard shuffling. He spun around and faced a man with hair the colour of dirty cream, a shaking black knife in his hand. Cait's.

"Ye killed my brother," he said, advancing, one sleeve drenched in blood. "Ye killed him."

Edward pushed Cait behind him. "Did you touch her?"

He stared at him, dazed. "'Twas my turn." He edged forward, blood dripping in a steady stream from his fingertips into the dirt. His head tipped back briefly then shook, his eyes dazed. "She's a whore, and 'twas my turn. I—"

He stumbled, and Edward lunged out of his way. He wasn't going to have to kill him. He was already halfway there. "It looks as if the devil will take you."

The man's head circled and flopped lazily onto his chest, then jerked backward. He fell to his knees and dropped the black knife into the dirt. Air escaped his mouth in a long burst, breathy and loud, then he slumped forward, his head and shoulders landing on top of his brother's stomach.

Across the way, behind a heap of crates and casks, Glenlyon stood in his scarlet coat, his mouth agape in alarm. He tipped his bonnet, took a long draw from a flask, then walked away.

Edward had given Cait the time she needed to tell him what happened. It had only taken a day for her to spill forth all the horrid details about the soldier in Glencoe after the attack and her cousins' behaviour during her stay in Kinlochbeg. Before that, he had assumed her time there with Davina and Sawney had been pleasant. Cait had only spoken of her aunt with affection, but now he knew the truth, and it hurt as if he had done all of this to her himself. He had, hadn't he? He and the other soldiers had entered the glen—her peaceful village—and taken her life away from her, placing her in danger from that cold day in February until now. If he could take it all back, he would.

The incident in Glencoe as she fled Alt Na Munde and Sionn's assault were more than justifiable. He brushed the tears from her cheeks. "One doesn't hold a pistol—or a knife—to a person's chest without the intent to use it. You acted in self-defense."

"Aye, but yer right. It does weigh heavily on my conscience. Especially since Sionn was kin. I dinnae regret it, but I'm nae proud of it." He could see she was trying to sound brave, but her voice erupted in jagged bursts, her hands still trembling steadily. "I never want to do that again. To be in that place where I must decide . . ."

He stroked her hair as they sat on the small bed in their room. "I fear Glenlyon saw what you did. If he should go to the constables as a witness, there will be no way of escaping the inevitable."

"What are ye saying?"

"I think we should leave Edinburgh as quickly as possible. You've done what you came for. There's no reason to stay."

"We must stay, at least until we're married." She pulled out of his arms. "Or are ye saying ye no longer wish to marry me?"

He wiped a tear from her eye. "I want you as my wife. But so much has happened and none of it good."

"So ye wish only to be with me when times are fair?"

"That's not it, *mo gràdh.*"

"I suppose the right thing to do would be to let ye go. I've killed a man, after all," she stated frankly, her lips quivering and concern drawn in the lines stretching across her forehead.

He tucked a wayward strand of hair behind her ear. "And I've committed treason against my king and country."

She leaned into him, speaking softly. "Then we are meant for each other."

The three of them remained in their little room for days to avoid being seen by any of the king's soldiers or anyone searching for the lass who killed a man in plain daylight. On the fourth day, they left for Mary King's Close, Edward guarding the twenty shillings tucked in his shirt for Reverend Murray. Cait wore the violet ribbon in her hair that he'd purchased in Falkirk. She'd done her best to wash the stains out of her gown, but the ghost of them remained on the back of her bodice and skirt. They bothered her but not him. Those stains reminded him that he had chosen a strong, courageous woman to spend the rest of his life with. She looked perfectly lovely.

Just as they turned the corner into the narrow street where the minister lived, Taran tugged his sleeve and waved him to bend down to his level. "When are ye going to give her the surprise?"

Edward patted the pouch in his shirt. "When we get there, lad."

They hurried into the close, Edward feeling better than he'd felt in weeks. They planned to leave immediately for England after they were wed. They couldn't go to his home in Boroughbridge because that would be the first place the army would look, so they decided to settle on somewhere near the Borders where neither he nor Cait had family. If only he could figure out a way to free himself of his past and his brother's wrath, but he sensed that was not in his immediate future.

They arrived at Reverend Murray's door, Taran looking up at him expectantly with unfocused eyes. Edward reached into his shirt and extracted the pouch. With two fingers, he fumbled inside for the very thing that might settle Cait's nerves. He fished it out and held it securely in his hand. "Before we go through that door, Cait, I want you to know that I will do whatever is in my power to make you happy."

"Ye already do," she whispered.

Taran bounced up and down, unable to contain his excitement. "Give it to her, Edward."

Edward laughed. "Very well."

He reached for her hand and turned it palm up, the scar reminding him of all the terrible things she'd already endured. In it, he lay the chain he and Taran had purchased the same day they bought his new breeches.

"'Tis for yer sapphire," Taran said. "Do ye like it?"

Cait stared at her hand, her mouth open, her other hand pressed to her chest. Tears welled in her eyes, and she shook her head.

"Shall we put it on so you look like a proper bride?" he asked.

She reached into her bodice and retrieved the sapphire she always kept close to her heart, then handed it to him. "My mother had meant to give me her necklace on my wedding day."

He slipped the new chain into the little ring at the top, then fastened it around her neck. It fell just below the hollow of her throat. "*Mo chaileag uain'-shùileach chalma.*" *My brave green-eyed lass.*

Her fingers closed over it protectively. She opened her mouth to speak, then closed it and fell against his chest.

Edward knocked on the door, unable to shed the grin from his face. Cait stood at his side with Taran in front of her. Inside, a chair scraped across the floor with a sharp squeak. Cait squeezed Edward's hand.

He smiled. "We shall head for England as soon as we're wed."

Reverend Murray came to the door in his black cassock, his expression eager but distracted. He nervously glanced down the street in both directions.

"Is there a problem?" Edward asked, reflexively scanning the street as well.

"Nay, nay. Come in." He stepped aside, pressing himself against the doorpost, then shut the door behind them. "Do ye have the money, then?"

Nothing like getting right to the point. Edward pulled out his pouch and handed it to him. With quick fingers, the minister untied the knot at the top and peered inside, clinking the coins together by bouncing the pouch in his hand. "One pound?"

"It is." Edward found his demeanor unflattering for a man of the cloth. Although his father enjoyed gaming and a dram of whisky or two, he was never greedy. Murray was definitely nothing like his father. "You said you would marry us after a fortnight so . . ."

"Aye, aye." He held up a finger. "Wait one moment while I put this somewhere safe."

With a lack of celerity, he bumped into the doorframe before disappearing into the back. The sound of furniture moving and knocking across the floor echoed from behind the wall. Edward glanced at Cait and shrugged. After a few minutes, Reverend Murray returned wiping his brow with a begrimed cloth.

"Are you quite fine, Reverend?" Edward asked. He noted the minister's shaking hands and darting eyes.

Murray offered a perfunctory smile, a glistening droplet of sweat trailing over his temple.

Taran's squeezed Edward's elbow, tugging at the fabric of his shirt.

"What is it?" Edward asked.

"What is he wearing?" he whispered.

"Who?"

"Reverend Murray," Taran said, his face turned up.

"He's a minister, lad. He's wearing a cassock."

"Black?"

"Of course. Black."

Taran gasped. "He's the corbie!"

"What?" Edward had no idea what nonsense Taran was referring to, only that it was delaying the ceremony. He turned to Cait, whose face melted before his eyes. "Cait?"

The door burst open, and a flock of soldiers poured into the room, their bodies blocking the light in the doorway. Scarlet coats filled the tight space, forcing Edward back against the far wall. Edward stilled, his chest and shoulders tingling.

Reverend Murray scuttled to the side, pointing in Edward's direction. "That's him!"

"Sergeant Edward Gage?" A stout man holding an official document bearing the king's seal squeezed his way through the soldiers, almost losing his grey periwig when it snagged on a drawn rifle. He righted it, then proceeded forward.

Edward stood straight, knowing this day was bound to come.

Cait clung to his arm, Taran at her side.

He stretched open the document and read. "Sergeant Edward Gage, officer of the regiment under the command of Colonel John Hill, you are hereby arrested for treason against His Majesty, King William of England, Ireland, and Scotland."

The bewigged man gave a cursory nod to no one in particular, and two soldiers grasped Edward's arms, while another removed his weapons.

Cait jumped in front of them, eyes sharp with worry. "Ye have the wrong man. He is Edward MacKinnon. Ye cannae—"

"Shh, *mo gràdh*. We will find a way."

As they led Edward out, Reverend Murray shouted after them. "Remember my reward! One hundred pounds! Remember!"

Part Five

Chapter 45

July, 1692
Edinburgh, Scotland

Alexander waited in an outer chamber at Holyrood Palace for the guard to call his name. He'd been there for three hours with Breadalbane's missive in his coat, hoping for a moment with the king. The guards had inspected the seal, holding it close to their noses to examine the crest before letting him pass through to the inner royal apartments.

He was in a fairly good mood since hearing that his brother had been taken into custody and sent as a prisoner to Edinburgh Castle. It was the very thing he could use to state his case in front of the king. After all, what could prove more painful, more traumatic than accusing one's own brother of high treason? The only thing that might be more effective would be turning in his own mother. He would do that, too, if it would prevent his bloodline from being attainted.

The doors opened to the king's audience chamber, and a jowly guard emerged. "His Majesty will now see Baron Mansfield," he called absently into the room.

Alexander's heart pounded in his throat. "I am Baron Mansfield."

With a cursory wave of his hand, the guard motioned for him to enter. The audience chamber was littered with gold accents on finials and frames and in the crests engraved in the ceiling. Enormous tapestries depicting pastoral scenes hung on the walls and covered the wood-planked floor. King William sat in an ornately carved throne with his back to the wall and two stern-faced guards flanking him. He wore a dark brown periwig parted in the middle and curled beautifully, the perfect ringlets hanging well past his shoulders. His blue velvet cloak trimmed in ermine draped partly over his red and white satin clothing and puddled to the floor in elegant folds. Alexander was suddenly struck by his imposing nature.

The guard cleared his throat, reminding him to bow. Alexander hurried into the subservient position.

"We understand you have come to deliver a missive from the Earl of Breadalbane." The king's voice was subdued, almost apathetic, his Dutch heritage present in every word.

Alexander straightened. "I have, Your Majesty. But there is something you should know before reading it."

William nodded almost imperceptibly.

"As your most humble servant, I should tell you that the earl's loyalties are suspect."

The king leaned to the side and rested his chin on his hand, his index finger scratching at the corner of his eye once before settling on his cheek. His gold collar, beset with plum-sized ruby cabochons surrounded by sapphires, shifted with him, catching the light streaming in from a nearby window. "This is a most serious accusation. Have you proof?"

Alexander had to be extremely careful with what he said. He couldn't mention Breadalbane's letter to the Earl of Mar because—with his signature on it—it would only implicate him as well. And the truth was, he didn't know if that letter would ever surface anyway. Then there was the matter of what lay on the page of the missive he held at his breast. He had no idea what Breadalbane wrote in that letter, and considering he had set up Alexander as his scapegoat in Mar's, he had to assume that the old cockard had done the same in this one.

He cleared his throat. "I can only tell Your Majesty that he has had dealings with persons of questionable repute who have strong ties to the Jacobite cause."

"And you know this how?" He breathed rather easily for a man who was just told one of his closest allies was plotting with James Stuart to overthrow his throne.

"I was told by someone residing in his castle at Kilchurn. Apparently, that is where their clandestine meetings take place."

William seemed to consider what he said, his extended finger now tapping his cheek rhythmically. "Why should We believe you, Mansfield?" He sat upright. "You could be telling Us this to save your own neck."

"Your Majesty?"

"Your father is in the Tower, is he not?"

THE TACKSMAN'S DAUGHTER

"'Tis true, but—"

"A Jacobite in his own right."

Alexander swallowed hard. He hadn't realized the king knew who he was.

William played with the bejeweled ring on his finger. "And word that We are considering *corruptio in sanguine attainder* has certainly reached your ears."

His heart hammered in his chest. "If I may, Your Majesty."

William offered a desultory flip of his hand, indicating he could continue.

"I have served most honourably as an officer in Your Majesty's service under Colonel Hill for almost three years now. I have spent the last five months searching for my own brother to turn him in as a traitor for disobeying orders in the attack at Glencoe. 'Tis only now that he has been—"

"Glencoe." He smiled sourly, the corners of his mouth turned down. "It seems that is all We have heard about these last few months. Like a bell constantly ringing in Our ears."

Alexander tugged at the lace at his throat. Although he had worn his blue velvet coat, which was of a lighter weight than his wool coat, it seemed as if someone had just stoked a fire nearby.

The king continued, "Why would you wish to see your own brother executed? You understand that is what will happen if he is proven guilty of high treason?"

"I am loyal to King and Country before all else," he said, the corner of his mouth twitching erratically. "Surely, I have proven myself loyal—"

"And you are hoping this will convince Us not to pursue attainder. Is that it?" William leaned back, elbows resting on his armchair, fingers intertwined at his waist.

"I am, Your Majesty. It would be foolish of me not to beseech your forgiveness for my father's alleged transgressions against you."

"Foolish of you, indeed." With the wiggle of his finger, William signaled to the guard waiting at the door. "Please escort Baron Mansfield out."

"Forgive me, Your Majesty, but I was hoping I could get some sort of promise from you—"

"*You* want a promise from *Us*? Choose your words carefully, Mansfield."

"What I mean to say is . . ." Alexander wiped his brow, searching for the words. "An agreement. I—I . . ."

Alexander felt the pressure of the guard's hand on his forearm, urging him out of the king's audience chamber.

As he was forced to step back in retreat, the king spoke. "Wait."

Alexander pulled out of the guard's grip. Could it be that he was reconsidering hearing his plea? His pulse thrummed in his ears.

"You never presented Us with the earl's missive." One of the guards at William's side strode to him, then waited while Alexander pulled Breadalbane's letter from inside his coat. His hand shook perceptibly as he handed it over.

"Again, Your Majesty, I should warn you that the earl may have written something—"

He held up his hand, quieting him at once. "You may leave now."

Alexander bowed, praying that Breadalbane had not duped him again.

He rode back to the castle in a fury. They could all go straight to the devil for all he cared—the king, Breadalbane, and his brother.

There was nothing else he could do to prove his loyalty to William. If he was going to attaint him, so be it. He would have to sell some of his smaller holdings as quickly as possible, though. Perhaps his mother's jewels, some of their furnishings, artwork, livestock. Anything that might slip past the eyes of the king and place sterling in Alexander's coffers. His mother would likely be upset, but he couldn't worry about her. He'd write a letter assuring her that selling what they could was best for the both of them—if only to get her to agree. Then after it was all done, he'd send her off to fend for herself.

As he approached the portcullis, Sergeant Robertson stopped him. Alexander was thankful that they stood outside in the open air where his offensive roommate's stench would dissipate in the breeze.

Robertson smiled, displaying his missing lower front teeth. "Yer brother was sent to a cell. Just brought him in not two hours past."

Although he'd known of Edward's arrest, he was not certain of his whereabouts within the castle. Alexander's chest warmed with the idea he was right under his nose. The letter to his mother was going to have to wait. "Where?"

"Vaults under the Great Hall. But he's no with all the shabbaroons." He handed Alexander a paper listing the crimes Edward was accused of. "They have him in a separate cell below. Pit prison. Must be dangerous."

Alexander rolled his eyes. There was nothing dangerous about his self-righteous pillicock of a brother.

He stabled his horse and hurried past the barracks to the castle vaults. The halls were dark and dank, pungent with the odor of unwashed bodies and urine. It was eerily quiet, considering there must have been a hundred men locked behind the iron bars in the larger cells. Only the occasional belch or fart followed by an angry curse broke the silence.

Edward's cell was empty—unlike the others, which had wooden platforms with pallets and hammocks for sleeping—and lit only by a single torch mounted outside of the bars at the entrance. Edward sat in the back, his head resting on his folded forearms and one ankle fettered by a heavy iron band and chain attached to the wall. A pathetic sight.

It was more than Alexander could have ever hoped for. "Nice to see you again, brother."

Edward lifted his head.

Alexander unrolled the paper Robertson gave him and read. "It says here that you are accused of treason, murder, theft, sodomy, assault, and rape." He laughed, amused that Sterling Struana's formal complaint had reached all the way to Edinburgh. "It sounds as if you have been quite busy since last I saw you. Father would be so proud."

Edward's fists clenched.

Alexander held up the paper and pressed it against the bars. "You are much more interesting than I ever thought you were. Sodomy, Edward? I had no idea you had it in you."

"You know those charges are false."

He searched through the paper once again. "Theft too. It says here that you were found in possession of weapons belonging to . . . the Earl of Breadalbane. A serious charge, I am afraid."

Edward studied the back of his hand, a sure sign he was guilty. Alexander could hardly contain his joy.

"And murder." Alexander shook his head with disapproval. "Really, brother. Killing innocent drovers? You must be horribly ashamed."

Edward stood, his jaw tight with ire.

At the bottom of the sheet, a note indicated that a clergyman had turned him in, claiming he was asked to perform a marriage ceremony, but instead thought it was his moral duty to report him for treason. Alexander clicked his tongue. "And on your wedding day. 'Tis all so sad. Tell me, is your bride that Scottish whore from Glencoe? How does she feel about this charge of sodomy?"

Edward lunged, clearly forgetting he was chained to the wall, and was jerked back violently a few feet short of reaching the cell door. His chest heaved with each breath, but his voice was steady. "Why don't you join me in here, brother, where we can continue this conversation on the same side of the bars?"

"Understand this." Alexander's chest filled with light. He had dreamed of this scenario since the first time Father had spoken of his favour for Edward. He pressed himself up against the bars and glowered. "You are a bastard born. We will never be on the same side of anything."

Chapter 46

A slow stream of water trickled into Edward's cell from a crack in the wall. It had rained hard the night before, leaving behind a thickness in the air that somehow found its way into the prison. Every now and again he shifted to avoid sitting in the cold puddles that traveled between the ridges and gullies of the stones.

He knew Alexander had to have something to do with those erroneous charges of sodomy, assault, and rape. He wasn't sure what, but they reeked of his brother. Edward couldn't imagine what Cait would think once she discovered the charges. He hoped she could see right through them. He closed his eyes, feeling shame for something he hadn't done. The stigma of the accusations would likely leave its indelible mark on his name for years to come. And even if he didn't live much longer, people would always whisper behind their hands that he was the man who'd committed such unspeakable crimes.

The murder charge wasn't true either. He assumed Glenlyon reported him for killing Sionn and his brother. He supposed it may have appeared that he was the assailant. After all, just as Glenlyon emerged, both of Cait's cousins fell dead at his feet. The accusation was a relief, however. Cait needn't pay for defending herself, so he would take the blame happily if it set her free.

The charge of theft was a little more complicated, but no one had to know that. He'd worn those weapons knowing they rightfully belonged to someone else, and when he was stripped of them during his arrest, he knew it would amount to something. He only prayed that Cait wouldn't confess to taking them herself.

As for the charge of treason, they could call it what they liked, but he wasn't sorry for that either.

THE TACKSMAN'S DAUGHTER

The sound of his name startled him out of his thoughts. "Gage?"

A guard unlocked his cell door and stepped inside, a wooden bowl in one hand and the keys in the other. "Yer meal."

He set it on the floor in front of Edward. The grey porridge inside sat like a stone, thick enough to be shaped into a round clump.

The guard stood with his hands on his hips, his gut protruding below the open buttons on his coat. "Ye can eat it with yer fingers. I'll be back for the bowl in an hour."

Edward set it aside. Although he hadn't eaten since he was arrested early the day before, he had no appetite.

The guard shut the gate behind him, his keys jangling in the lock.

"Has anyone come to the castle asking about me?" Edward asked.

"A visitor?"

"A woman."

"None that I know of." The guard hooked his keys on a ring at his waist. "But yer hearing is in a few days. I imagine quite a few people will show for that."

After the guard left, Farquhar and Kennedy's voices came to him through a crack in the wall. Although Edward was sad they hadn't been able to escape, he breathed in their voices like fresh air. It was the only thing that provided Edward with a little comfort in his dingy surroundings. They told him the story of how they'd managed to elude capture for two months and were ultimately caught north of Fort William, trying to hire a boat to the Isle of Skye. They'd said the reward money was what did them in.

Edward pressed his ear to the wall to listen to Farquhar, the stone cold and damp against his cheek. "There's going to be an inquiry. Too many folks griping about the attack on Glencoe."

Edward doubted that Parliament would hold an honest inquiry, especially if it implicated the king. "William must not be too pleased with that."

"He ordered it," Kennedy said. "Pamphlets are being distributed from here to London, trying to incite a rebellion. The king is hoping this inquiry will prevent it."

Edward was surprised. How would the king hide his participation in the massacre? Surely, Parliament would discover his signature on a document or two somewhere. "How do you know this?"

Farquhar's voice lowered. "The guards talk. You'll learn soon enough to shut yer gob when they parade through. 'Tis the only way to discover what is happening outside these miserable walls."

"Do you know who is going to be implicated?" Edward was thinking about Glenlyon. If he didn't drink himself into the grave before he was arrested, it would be a miracle. But the idea of the blame falling on Glenlyon didn't sit well with him. It was true that he was a drunkard and a lout. And perhaps he also harboured spiteful feelings about the MacDonalds over the years that made drawing his sword that early morning in February easier than walking away. But he was a man with nothing. His only possessions were debt, malice, and kinsfolk who loathed him for his clumsy drunken ways. And seeing him a week earlier spending his last penny on cards and whisky, he'd never felt so sorry for a man in all his life. Glenlyon was merely a servant of those happy to take advantage of his desperation.

The true criminals behind the attack were those whose signatures lay at the foot of the orders. Alexander had told him Major Duncanson had sent the orders, but he had to have received them from higher up. Hamilton?

"Dalrymple and Breadalbane's names have been tossed about a bit." Kennedy spoke with spite.

That made sense. Hamilton answered to Breadalbane, who answered to Dalrymple.

Kennedy continued, "'Tis no secret that Dalrymple dances a jig every time a clan chief falls. I doubt he was hoping the chiefs would swear their oaths to William in time. It would give him the perfect excuse to exact his revenge."

"And Breadalbane?" Edward asked, confident the serpent knew neither honour nor religion. Greed was his companion.

"That sly fox?" Farquhar asked. "He'll likely slip through the fingers of justice. Ye dinnae see him here, do ye?"

Kennedy added, "Glengarry told us that Breadalbane made a secret pact with the Highland chiefs that if James were to get support from France, he would withdraw his oath to William."

"Who else knows this?"

"All of the chiefs who were at the gathering in Auchallader last summer. MacIain included. That's when he said it."

That was sloppy of Breadalbane. A dozen or so Highland chiefs now knew of his Jacobite intentions.

Kennedy coughed a wet hacking eruption that lasted the good part of a minute. When it was quiet once again, Farquhar continued. "Glengarry said Breadalbane blamed MacIain for interfering with his bargain to keep the peace with the other Highland chiefs. Glengarry thinks that is what started the burn in Breadalbane's wame for vengeance against MacIain."

"But would the king have listened to him?" Edward asked, doubtful.

THE TACKSMAN'S DAUGHTER

Kennedy spoke with a strained voice. "Some say he leads the king around by his nose. But I think 'twas Dalrymple."

Footsteps approached, the scraping of boots across the cobbles echoing down the hall. The three of them sat silent. Edward listened carefully as the hushed voices grew louder. The guards stopped at Farquhar and Kennedy's cell, their shadows cast on the wall behind them. Through the bars, Edward gathered there were two of them.

"Either of ye MacDonalds?" one asked, his voice low and raspy as if water were lodged in his throat.

Farquhar answered, "Nay."

"Too bad, then."

"Why is that?"

"The king says all MacDonald survivors can return to the Valley of the Dogs."

He meant Glencoe. Edward's pulse quickened. Cait had just told him that Glenlyon had said there were orders for them never to return, that they had to board ships bound for America or Ireland. She was a Cameron, but Glencoe was her home. Would she want to go back? Who would be left?

The guards shuffled away, their voices growing faint with each step.

When the sound of their footsteps vanished, Farquhar said, "It seems as though William is seeing the error of his ways."

"Or is he simply afraid of what the inquiry will reveal?" Edward guessed that the king was preparing for a backlash of accusations and insults, and this was his way of softening the blow of the revelations to come.

"Either way, 'tis a good thing for the MacDonalds. They've been hiding in the braes all these months."

Edward couldn't imagine that. He had holed up in a cave for only a month before he could take it no longer. He had to tell Cait. But as he sat on the floor in one of the few spots that remained dry from the night before, he had no idea if he'd ever see her again. He hoped the next time wouldn't be looking down at her from a scaffold.

"Edward?" Drips from somewhere behind the walls punctuated the silence. "They're calling it 'slaughter under trust.'"

He sighed. "That's what it was."

No one spoke. A grey mangy rat skittered across the cobbles just outside Edward's cell.

"Are ye nervous, man?" Farquhar asked.

"Nervous?" Edward wanted to laugh but was incapable. "I can only hope Parliament convenes to cast blame on the parties responsible long before I dangle at the end of a rope."

Chapter 47

"Who do I speak to?" Cait asked the guard posted at the outer gate of the castle. It had taken her a day to discover where Edward had been imprisoned. She'd gone to the Tolbooth first, where she'd waited for hours to speak to someone, only for the clerk to tell her that traitors were taken to the castle.

He crinkled up his nose and scratched his beard. "That would be the Provost Marshal, but he's no here presently."

"Is there no one I can speak to, then?" she asked.

"Ye could try the Captain of the Guard," he offered with no sense of certainty. "He'll be in the barracks. You'll need someone to escort ye there."

He called over a soldier standing by the entrance to the guardhouse, too busy picking at his nails to hear him yell the first time. "Nesbitt!"

He hurried over, brows lifted in question.

"Take this woman to see the Captain of the Guard."

She stared straight ahead while Nesbitt searched her, his hands running briskly over her gown as if he couldn't be bothered, then followed the soldier up the cobbles to the barracks on the opposite side of the courtyard. They passed through two more sets of guards before entering a small room decorated with portraits of stern-faced, red-breasted officers and a boar's head mounted on a wooden plaque. A large desk set with a crystal decanter and four glasses sat in the center.

Nesbitt directed her to sit in the chair in front of the desk while he searched for the Captain of the Guard.

Cait stared at the prickly brown boar with tusks turned upward at the corners of its mouth as if extending its smile. The trophy was probably meant to

THE TACKSMAN'S DAUGHTER

demonstrate the captain's prowess with a rifle, but it didn't impress her. She had killed boars much larger than that one with her blade and the flick of her wrist.

"Captain Sutherland at yer service." The captain appeared, wearing the gold lace and sash of an officer. He edged around his desk and rested comfortably in the chair. "How may I be of assistance?"

She was about to speak when a soldier knocked on the doorjamb. "Forgive me, Captain, but yer horse is ready."

Sutherland ran his fingers over his brow. "I am afraid we must make this short. I am meeting with the Earl of Mar, and I mustn't keep him waiting."

Had she heard him correctly? "Ye have business with the earl?"

"We have a dining engagement. The ride to Prestonfield isnae far, but I'm expected within the hour, ye see."

She couldn't believe her luck. "Perhaps I may escort ye there. I need to meet with the earl myself."

Sutherland's face crinkled. "The earl and I have some private matters to discuss. You understand."

Her heart sank, but at least she knew where he was now. She had to get to Prestonfield.

"But since yer here, I can give ye a few minutes of my time. 'Tisnae often I have such a comely lass waiting for me in my office. What brings ye to the castle?"

She cleared her throat. "There's been a mistake. A soldier I *know* to be loyal to King William has been arrested and imprisoned here."

"For treason, I assume?"

"Aye, but he isnae guilty." She probably sounded like every other woman who came seeking a pardon.

"And how do ye know this?"

"I was there. 'Twas in Glencoe last February. Ye see, a regiment—"

"I know exactly to what ye are referring. Ye must understand this is a highly complicated matter, mistress."

"Complicated?" Her voice rose uncontrollably. "He should be heralded as a hero for not taking up arms against us! We were defenseless! And we billeted and fed those devils for more than a week!"

"What is this I hear?" said a voice all too familiar. Cait's chest turned to stone.

Alexander stepped into the room, a smug expression on his face. His speculative gaze flowed over her. "How lovely to see you, Mistress Cameron."

She wanted to pull her knife right then and there. How could he possibly be in Edinburgh?

297

Sutherland wagged his finger between the two of them. "You two are acquainted, Leftenant?"

"We are," he answered quickly.

Sutherland searched Cait's face for agreement, but she only managed a tight smile.

"I suppose you are here to discuss Edward's imprisonment." Alexander tilted his head to the side, his lips pouted in a conciliatory manner.

"Ye know that I am." She wasn't going to fall for his false sentiment.

He turned to the captain. "I would be happy to handle this matter. I am familiar with the details surrounding the prisoner's case and have his paperwork at my disposal." He patted his chest, and it crackled.

Sutherland's fingers drummed the desktop as he considered the offer. Cait swallowed, feeling suddenly ill.

The captain stood. "Would ye mind terribly if I handed this matter over to the leftenant, mistress?"

Cait froze. "It might be better if I were to speak with someone else."

Alexander tilted his head, a consoling look on his face. He turned to Sutherland and spoke in an appeasing tone. "I am certain I can address her concerns, Captain."

Sutherland stood, brushed down his coat, and retrieved his hat from a small wooden stand behind him. "You may use my office if it suits ye."

Alexander offered a curt nod and stepped aside to let the man pass. "Much obliged, Captain."

Cait stared straight ahead, nervous and angry all at once. The door shut behind her. Her only solace lay in the fact that should Alexander try something foolish, the hallway just outside was busy with soldiers, their voices muffled on the other side of the door.

"So, Cait—"

"Dinnae call me that."

He sat in the captain's chair, his hands folded neatly over his waist. "Very well, Mistress Cameron."

"I am not here to be toyed with, Leftenant."

"Of course. You are here to free your beloved from prison." He reached for the decanter, held his nose to the open top and inhaled. A smile emerged on his face, a genuine one—something she had never before seen on him. He poured himself a drink. "Would you care for some Claret?"

She took a deep breath to steady herself. "Where is Edward?"

The corner of his mouth lifted. "I heard your nuptials were interrupted. I had no idea you two were so . . . entwined."

She clenched the folds of her skirt in her fist. "Where is he?"

THE TACKSMAN'S DAUGHTER

He closed his eyes as he drank, then held his glass in front of him to study his wine. "What do you see in him anyway?"

She controlled her breath to refrain from smacking the glass out of his hand. "He's everything yer not."

"Oh. That hurt." He frowned sarcastically, then finished his glass and poured himself another. "I would like to help you, but I do not see how I can. Edward is wanted for high treason. He will stand trial, and a jury will determine his fate."

"But *you* are the one accusing him of it. Ye must have the power to withdraw yer accusation," she prodded, insistent.

"I wish it were that simple."

"What he did was insubordination at best," she argued.

"Not when the orders come from the king."

A heavy weight filled her chest. She'd heard those familiar words too many times. As much as she found it hard to believe, it had to be true.

He interrupted her thoughts. "Besides, those are not his only crimes. He has been accused of theft, murder, assault, and . . ." He leaned forward in his chair, an amused smile on his face. "Sodomy and rape."

She tried to mask her shock behind an unflinching smile, but she couldn't deny that those two words pierced her heart. She had no idea where the claims had come from, but as sure as the sun would rise in the morning, she knew Edward was not capable of such things. The charges were clearly false.

Unfortunately, the theft charge was another story. The soldiers had removed Breadalbane's dirk and pistol from his hip when they arrested him. That was completely her fault, and she would report herself immediately to clear him of that charge.

But murder? That charge had to be made by Glenlyon. No one else had seen them in that alleyway. Could he have misunderstood what he saw? She supposed it was possible. She suddenly wished she had used a little more pressure with her knife when she'd found him and penetrated his flesh, sending him to his grave at that instant.

"His indictment is at the end of the week." Alexander appeared expressionless, but there was a smile hidden behind his closed mouth, his cold brown eyes unnerving.

"Indictment?"

"That is when his charges will be read and his trial set," he explained in a condescending tone. He swirled his glass, the burgundy liquid spinning evenly. "A bit different from your Highlander ways, though. No clan chief to play favourites."

Parliament Hall was close to Mary King's Close, where Edward was arrested. Cait shuddered, knowing she was only a shout away from the home of the man who'd changed her single moment of pure happiness to utter devastation. She would never forget the look of excitement on Reverend Murray's face when the soldiers stormed into the room. It would be forever branded into her memory.

She stood outside the building and took a deep breath. Parliament Hall was imposing, standing in the square with thick round columns set above lower arches. The stone figures of Justice and Mercy stood over the main entrance. She understood little about the law outside of Clan Donald, but from what she witnessed so far, justice and mercy were no part of it.

In a large hall with men seated on either side in rows of benches, she stood amongst the crowd behind a rail, hoping for a glimpse of Edward. It was more than three hours before they called his name, and he was led closer by two guards with a tight grip on his arms. Edward's hands were shackled together and connected to a heavy chain around his waist. His shirt and breeks were black with grime, and a light peppering of stubble covered his jaw.

The Lord Advocate sat in a chair at the head of the room, his voice booming over the sea of mumbling in the hall. Cait steadied her breath as he read the dittay from a paper held before him by the solicitor-general. "Edward Gage of Boroughbridge, England, aged four and twenty years or thereby, charged as an officer in His Majesty's army of extraordinary and heinous crimes against the people of Scotland and His Majesty, King William of England, Scotland, and Ireland. The most abominable crime of high treason perpetrated against King and Country. The crime of murder being another against two persons of unknown name and birth, but witnessed by one Captain Robert Campbell, also known as Campbell of Glenlyon, of His Majesty's army, committed with a blade in the public area near Holyrood Palace in the presence of King William's court and caravan. The crimes of rape, sodomy, and assault with intent to ravish against Wynda Bruce of Stirling but residing in Fort William under the employ of Struana Wallace, proprietor of a gentlemen's establishment of ill repute. The crime of theft against John Campbell, 1st Earl of Breadalbane, 11th Laird of Glenorchy, and member of the Scottish Privy Council, in that the prisoner had in his possession one pistol and one dirk highly engraved and with the earl's crest upon them. All these crimes wickedly and most egregiously carried out with malice and ill intent upon all those parties injured. How do ye plead, Sergeant Gage?"

Gasps and angry outbursts filled the room. Cait wiped away the tears that fell down her cheeks. "He isnae guilty of theft or murder," she shouted.

THE TACKSMAN'S DAUGHTER

Edward spun in her direction. His eyes were wide with shock. She leaned against the rail, her heart pounding in her throat. "I did it!"

His eyes met hers, his gaze fixed. In the space of a few heartbeats, he relayed all his thoughts to her with just that look. *Nay, mo gràdh. Stay quiet. Trust me.* She could almost hear him saying those words aloud. Edward faced the Lord Advocate. "She knows not what she's saying. Drunk again, I suppose."

He faked a laugh, and the crowd tittered with him. Cait tried to scream out again, but someone pulled her from behind and led her through the crowd to the back of the room.

"What do ye have to say to this indictment?" asked the Lord Advocate.

Cait struggled to break free of the guards who held her.

"I would like to say —"

"Milord, may I approach the prisoner?" It was a woman's voice, smooth and slippery like an eel.

"This is highly inappropriate at this time, mistress."

"I am here on behalf of one of the injured parties. I'm Struana Wallace."

Cait stood on tiptoe to see what was happening, but all she saw was the back of a dark-haired woman as she sauntered through the crowd, wearing a red silk gown and a black hat, her shoulders straight and squared. She stopped in front of Edward and stared silently at him.

Cait trembled, wondering what further harm this woman could do. After a long silence, she spoke. "'Tisnae the man. I would've remembered those blue eyes."

Cait inhaled sharply.

"Are ye certain, mistress?"

She studied him again, circling around him this time. "Aye. I'm certain. But I'll be damned if he doesn't look like him."

The crowd didn't seem to know what to make of her statement, but Cait had her suspicions.

"Do ye wish to drop the charges of rape, assault, and sodomy, then?"

"Against *this* man? I do."

Noise erupted from the crowd, some complaints and some sighs of relief. The Lord Advocate quieted everyone. "The charges will be removed, but the prisoner still remains charged with that of high treason, murder, and theft."

The guards holding Cait let her go and resumed their places at the edge of the crowd.

"Wait, milord." Another person spoke up, but this time, Cait knew that voice. If he was close enough, she'd pull her knife and end his life like she should have days earlier. The mob exploded with exasperation.

"Robert Campbell here, and I have something to say." Glenlyon shoved his way through the crowd, his blue bonnet clutched in one hand.

The Lord Advocate rubbed his forehead. "Aye, aye. Ye may approach."

He stood nervously, wringing his bonnet in both hands now, his head shaking as if with a tremor. "Ye have the wrong man, milord. 'Twas a different man I saw bearing his blade."

Cait stilled.

He looked up. "I was mistaken."

The Lord Advocate pointed a finger at Glenlyon. "Did ye no make a complaint accusing . . ." He glanced down at the paper, then continued, "one Sergeant Edward Gage?"

Glenlyon shifted his weight from one foot to the other. "Aye, but 'twasn't him."

"Have ye been partaking in any spirits, Captain?" he asked, one brow lifted in question.

Cait snickered. Glenlyon's reputation had reached as far as the courts.

"Not today, milord. My mind is clear at the moment, and I can say with certainty 'tisnae the man." He ran his fingers through his wild hair. "Perhaps whisky is what had clouded my vision when I saw what happened."

People shook their heads and muttered their disappointment. But Cait stayed quiet, wondering what the old messan was up to.

"Do ye wish to say we should drop the charge of murder against this man?"

He nodded solemnly. "I do."

Clearly annoyed, the Lord Advocate took a deep, labourious breath. "Very well."

Glenlyon turned, then stopped to pat Edward on the shoulder. They exchanged a quick look before Glenlyon skirted his way around the crowd to where Cait stood. He was going to pass by her without a word, but she grabbed his arm. "Why did ye accuse him? Ye know 'twasn't *him* who killed those devils."

He closed his eyes for a moment. "I suppose I was angry at him for making the rest of us look poorly, throwing down his blade while we bore ours."

She also imagined he wasn't too happy about losing the last of his coin in a card game to Edward either. She leaned into him and lowered her voice. "Ye could've told the truth. Ye know I—"

"Nay." He held up his hand to stop her from saying any more, then pressed his lips together and smiled ruefully, his eyes watery. "Ye could have killed me, but ye didn't. Truly, it would've been the right thing to do too."

She wanted to hate him, but she couldn't. Not after what he just did. "Ye were feart to die then. I saw it in yer eyes."

THE TACKSMAN'S DAUGHTER

"A man's guilt can cause him to be disquieted about his own death. I have no fears now." He tugged on his bonnet and offered her a perfunctory yet humble nod. "I've already taken enough from ye. I hope what I've done brings ye peace, lass. He's a good man."

She watched him leave the hall, then shut her eyes to hold back the tears, but it was pointless. They came of their own will, raining down her cheeks and bringing the pain of the last five months with them. She struggled to make sense of her feelings. Could she forgive Glenlyon for what he did, especially now that he'd refused to accuse her of a crime she committed?

The Lord Advocate's voice echoed off the beams in the ceiling. "Trial is set for three days from now."

With his announcement, Cait opened her eyes just as Edward was escorted out the door.

Chapter 48

Alexander raced back to the castle, stewing over the dropped charges. What the devil was Struana doing in Edinburgh anyway? And why on earth did Glenlyon retract his accusation?

He was glad he'd escaped from the hall before Struana caught sight of him. That would have been a fortuitous disaster. He would have to stay out of the taverns and brothels for a while on the chance she might be frequenting them herself, looking for a potential customer or stray mopsy to recruit. He could do it if pressed—and he was pressed.

At least the other two charges remained, and without his help, Edward would never be cleared of high treason. Like father, like son, he supposed. But that reminded him that Breadalbane's letter to the Earl of Mar was yet missing and could implicate him as a traitor as well. He could probably explain his way out of it by saying that he'd signed it without knowing what it said. It sounded more like a child's excuse than the explanation of a man who should know better. But it was written in Gaelic, so there was a chance that he might be believed.

And as far as Breadalbane's missive to the king, it had been three days since he'd handed it to William, and no one had come to arrest him or accuse him of misdeeds of any sort. Alexander could only assume there was nothing incriminating in that letter after all.

Not a word had been heard about Davina either. He had to imagine her corpse was rotting away under the heavy brush in the clearing below the hill. With no witnesses, there likely wouldn't be any accusations. Her death had been an accident of sorts. He hadn't truly wanted to kill her—only scare her into giving him Breadalbane's letter.

He passed through the guardhouse and portcullis and wound around the esplanade to the barracks, then stopped. He needed something to calm him, to release him of his anxious thoughts. He turned to the vaults and headed for Edward's cell.

Edward sat inside much like before, his back against the wall and his head resting on his forearms. Alexander's heart lifted.

Alexander leaned against the bars, his arms folded across the horizontal brace as he spoke. "Your Scottish whore paid me a visit."

Edward's head lifted slowly at the sound of his voice, his hair hanging in messy waves across his brow and on either side of his face.

Alexander gave a little wave of his hand and smiled. "Pathetic, that. She wanted to see if I would consider releasing you from the charge of treason."

Edward stared at him, unspeaking.

"There was a price to pay, of course," he added.

Edward straightened, his shoulders rising noticeably with each breath. He was such an easy target.

"A good fuck, that one. Now I understand the attraction."

Edward's nostrils flared. "She'd sooner cut out her own heart than let you touch her."

Alexander laughed. "Oh, she put up a good fight, but, well, you know. Her. Me. An uneven match. She had no chance."

"You're lying."

"Am I?"

"You better pray you are. Because if you aren't, you're a dead man."

Alexander laughed. "Why, dear brother? I am certain 'twas all the same to her. We look alike, after all. I am simply the better lover."

"I don't believe it. I won't. 'Tis a lie," he said, shaking his head.

"Once we got started, she seemed to like it. Understandably, of course." Alexander tugged at the lace at his wrist, barely able to contain the euphoria bubbling in his chest. "She's quite petite beneath all those layers of skirts."

Edward clenched his fists and slowly stood. "I swear I'll kill you, Alexander."

"And how will you do that, brother?" He took a step back and opened his arms in presentation. "You are in there. Chained like a beast. And I am out here. Free to do as I please."

He bowed with a flourish before leaving and headed back to his quarters.

It felt good to do that. All those years watching Edward best him with the women he'd wanted, and now the bastard would likely go to his grave believing

Alexander had taken the one woman he truly loved. It would serve him right. A tit for tat, if you will.

The truth was those women didn't matter. They were simply a way to pass the time. He'd enjoyed some of the gifts that came with a good tumble—the lace handkerchiefs, the fine leather gloves, or the occasional piece of remembrance jewelry. For many of them, that was the best part of the deal, but not Berenice. She was different. He loved her. And until Edward had arrived in Lancaster to ruin everything, Alexander had believed she loved him too.

He paced back and forth in his quarters, luxuriating in the memory of Edward's torn visage moments earlier. There was no doubt he believed him about Cait. And in time, it *could* be true. Cait could offer him nothing. But ruining her then leaving just to spite his brother would make it worth the trouble.

Sergeant Robertson entered the room, bringing his fetor with him. His coat was unbuttoned, and his cravat hung sloppily from his neck. Alexander shook his head in disgust. What happened to a soldier's dignity?

Robertson extracted a flask from inside his coat and drank, a trickle of whisky dripping out of the corner of his mouth. He wiped it away with the back of his hand. "You were there. At Glencoe. Were ye not?"

Alexander cringed at the name of the village. "I was."

"Well, then, ye may need some of this." Robertson stuck out his flask in an offer.

Alexander pushed it away. "And why is that?"

"There's going to be an inquiry into the massacre. An investigation of officers from each regiment."

The *massacre*? Is that what they were calling it? Alexander's chest burned. "The officers? We were only following orders."

"Aye, aye. But that's nae the way folks are seeing it." He took a strong pull from his flask, this time managing to keep all the whisky in his mouth. "They're screaming that you and all officers, should be tried for murder."

Robertson's words buzzed in his ears. He took a deep breath to steady his thoughts and his heart. Would they come after him? He grabbed him by the arm and shoved him out the door. "Go bathe yourself, Robertson. You smell like a barn."

Now he had to add to the pot the prospect that he'd be tried for murder. But it was only a possibility, not a certainty. Incidentally, so was the charge of treason. Either way, he had to be prepared.

There was only one thing to do. Sell everything.

He needed to write that letter to his mother. His wealth—or what was left of it—must be protected immediately. The properties would undoubtedly be

THE TACKSMAN'S DAUGHTER

sequestered the moment the king announced his decision whether or not to attaint. Losing everything was almost a foregone conclusion now. His mother was going to have to accept that. He could only imagine her reaction when she heard she had to start selling off her jewelry and fur-trimmed cloaks.

He darted downstairs in search of a quill and ink.

Chapter 49

A beam of white light traveled through the tiny window and across Captain Sutherland's desk, illuminating the deep red Claret in the decanter. Cait hadn't expected to find herself in his office again, but he was the only person she thought she could persuade about Edward's innocence regarding the theft charge. Yet he barely paid attention to her as she spoke, one hand clutching his throat, explaining he was suffering from a bout of quinsy.

"So ye understand, he isnae a thief," she insisted.

He squeezed out his words in a grumbly whisper. "Then how did the weapons come to be in his possession?"

She wanted to tell him a variation of the truth—that she took the weapons before she left Kilchurn to use as a safety measure when traveling and then gave them to him for safekeeping until they could be returned. But that sounded too much like a confession, and Edward would not be happy that she implicated herself.

She decided to use the art of prevarication to explain. "What ye need to know is that Edward Gage didn't steal Breadalbane's weapons."

"But that doesn't explain—" Sutherland leaned to look past her at the door and croaked out a call. "Ah, Leftenant Gage."

Cait's stomach clenched.

"Perhaps ye can finish with the mistress here. I need to find the chirurgeon." He pointed to his throat, eyes clenched.

She didn't turn around. She couldn't.

"It would be my pleasure, Captain." He stepped inside the office.

"When?"
"Just before dark."

THE TACKSMAN'S DAUGHTER

Sutherland stood, a pained expression on his face. "I'm afraid I must bid ye a good day, mistress."

Cait considered leaving. There was no chance Alexander would listen to her plea to release Edward of the charge of theft.

Sutherland scooted past her and tipped his hat before exiting the room. She smiled weakly in return.

"Do ye hide around the corner waiting for my arrival?" she asked acerbically. "Placing you in charge is like putting the cat amongst the pigeons."

Alexander ignored her, too busy searching the captain's desk for something. He opened a drawer and pulled out a couple of sheets of parchment, then gathered together a bottle of ink, two quills, and a vial of sand, setting them aside in a neat little pile.

"So, we find ourselves together once again." He leaned back, his hands linked behind his head. "Let me guess. You are here to argue Edward's innocence."

She used to think he and Edward looked almost identical, but now their dissimilarities accosted her, striking her like a cold splash of water. There was an angle to Alexander's face that wasn't present in Edward's. It could be seen only in the profile of his brow, but it was there, angry and brooding. His eyes lacked the brightness of Edward's too. Although a clear light brown—almost golden—Alexander's contained a heaviness that carried years of bitterness and jealousy. His mouth was the same shape as Edward's, but when expressionless, his lips turned slightly downward at the corners, casting his face in a smug darkness. She closed her eyes for a second, erasing Alexander's features and replacing them with Edward's. How could she possibly help him?

The charges remained. Treason and theft.

And then it occurred to her that perhaps she could help Alexander instead.

Chapter 50

Alexander almost felt pity for her. After all, she'd returned to the castle to argue a foregone case.

"Yer forgetting something, Leftenant." Cait seemed too smug for a woman whose lover was presently rotting away in prison. Nevertheless, he'd hear her out.

A slice of red sunlight piercing through Sutherland's wine decanter slashed across the sleeve of her faded blue gown. "If Edward is tried for treason, it will only strengthen the king's desire for attainder."

He looked at her sideways. Clearly, Edward had told her about their family's predicament. He wasn't sure how he felt about that, another person aware of his potential doom.

"One more member of yer family with the heart of a traitor?" She shrugged halfheartedly. "That *is* what most concerns ye, is it not?"

He leaned in, hoping to appear as if he was sincerely interested in what she was saying.

"Edward told me that besides the forfeiture of yer family property, yer father will be accused of having a corruption of blood. Edward being found guilty of treason would only prove that further. As Edward's brother and yer father's son, yer blood would be corrupted too."

She spoke of this as if it were the first time he'd ever bothered to consider it. As if it hadn't been weighing on him heavily for the last two years.

She apparently didn't know there was now an inquiry into the attack as well that could likely place him in chains, or she wouldn't have thought he could help her. The only thing he had any power over, at this point, was selling as much personal property as he could before the king claimed it as his own. He needed to get busy writing that letter to tell his mother to begin the purge.

"You and yer children to follow. Ye stand to lose everything, it seems," she continued, her mouth grim. "I suppose ye must decide what ye wish for more. To take revenge on yer brother or to keep yer titles and fortune as yer father's rightful heir."

She evidently had no idea what Edward had done to ruin his future. How convenient of him not to tell her the truth. If Berenice would've gone through with their marriage, her properties would have become his as her new husband. Although he might have lost his titles with attainder, he would've acquired exorbitant wealth with her as his wife.

Alexander snickered inwardly. He'd play along with this game. "You believe if I rescind my accusation, the king will be less likely to pursue attainder."

She didn't seem to realize that the soldiers who followed orders witnessed Edward's treachery with their own eyes. Too many of them saw him unarmed and trying to prevent others from carrying out their orders. They could've just as easily named him as a traitor. The fact he was the accuser might save his own neck in the eyes of the king, but it wouldn't save Edward.

"Two loyal sons—officers nonetheless—doing the king's bidding?" she said with confidence. "Remove the charges and you, too, will remain free. Free to go about yer life in the manner ye please as Baron Mansfield."

Poor thing seemed hopeful.

He sat motionless, then helped himself to a glass of Sutherland's Claret, the dark berry flavour with a hint of smoke coating his tongue. He drained it, then poured another.

"'Tis what you've always wanted," she added.

He rested his chin on his fist, hoping his pensive stance was conveying sincerity. He could almost see her thoughts meandering in all directions. Would he swallow the bait and agree to free the whoreson? He could tell she was holding her breath, waiting for his response.

"Perhaps you're right," he said, taking another sip of his wine.

She exhaled, perceptibly surprised by his acquiescence.

He stared into his glass as he spoke. "Meet me here tomorrow evening. I will take you to Edward."

"Will ye retract yer accusation of treason?" she asked hopefully.

He shrugged. "Come tomorrow and then we shall discuss our options

Chapter 51

The next day, Cait rode to Prestonfield with the earl's letter hidden in her petticoats. It was only a mile or two from the inn, but the ride gave her plenty of time to think about tonight when she would finally see Edward. Had he suffered at the hands of his gaolers? She had to imagine that those suspected as traitors were treated roughly. Had he been tortured? A chill ran through her spine and she closed her eyes, desperately trying to replace the image of a bruised and tattered Edward with the way he'd looked on their last night together before they'd gone to Mary King's Close. He'd seemed so at peace, his eyes half closed as he spoke of a future with her, one hand stroking her back. He'd talked about one day taking her to England to meet his mother and, in time, filling their home with children. It had all sounded so lovely. Her new life. A future.

But she had to do this first. Make the king pay for taking away her past.

When she reached the estate, she was taken aback by the verdant lawns decorated with statues and flowing fountains. It was undoubtedly the estate of a grand family. A liveried groom approached almost instantly, and she handed him her horse.

"Are ye the new kitchen maid?" he asked, scanning her worn blue gown disapprovingly.

He was right for thinking she was a servant. She hadn't considered how she might be perceived. She lifted her chin. "Nay. I've come to see the Earl of Mar."

The groom twisted his mouth to the side. "Is . . . he expecting ye?"

"I have a letter for him. If ye tell him it's from Duncan, I'm certain he will accept me." She wasn't certain of anything but thought it sounded convincing enough to pique the earl's interest.

He held out his hand. "Give it to me, and I'll see to it that he receives it."

She took a step back. She couldn't give him the letter and risk it landing in the wrong hands. She'd be discovered as a traitor if anyone reported her to the king. "I was told to deliver it only to him."

The groom exhaled loudly in irritation. "Very well. Come with me to the back. Ye will need to go in through the servants' entrance."

She followed him to the stables, where he passed *Ciobair* to another stable hand, then entered a plain door in the rear of the house. Two women stood at a long table kneading dough, their skin powdered white with flour. The older one reminded her of Lilas, her sleeves rolled up to her elbows and her powerful hands moving in a sure, steady rhythm.

The groom removed his hat. "This woman has a letter for the earl. Would ye tell Mrs. Nimberton for me?"

The younger woman nodded, then disappeared up a small set of stairs. The older woman cleaned her hands on her apron and smiled at Cait. She thought her heart would break right then. "Stay right here, mistress. I'll get ye a bannock while ye wait."

Cait ate the warm bannock with a tot of jam. It was almost as good as the ones Lilas baked back at Alt Na Munde. Her throat tightened with the memory of Lilas's sweet smile and the white bits of hair that always seemed to wrestle their way out of her cap.

The kitchen maid returned with a woman wearing a navy silk gown with bows up the bodice and delicate lace at her cuffs. It was the finest gown Cait had ever seen.

"You have a letter for the earl?"

Cait's heart pounded. She couldn't hand over this letter. "I was instructed to give it to him directly, mistress."

"That would be impossible. I cannot allow you to see him."

A young man in a gold silk coat and fawn-coloured breeks sauntered down the stairs. He seemed Cait's age, perhaps younger. "I hear there is a letter for me."

Mrs. Nimberton swung to face him, clearly shocked that the earl, even as young as he was, wouldn't know better than to venture down to the kitchens. "Please do not trouble yourself, milord. I will bring it to you upstairs in the parlour."

THE TACKSMAN'S DAUGHTER

He was taller than she was, but only by a few inches. His hair was brown and curled on the sides, tied back loosely with a black ribbon. He stared at her with the confidence of a much older man.

Cait curtsied. "I have a letter for ye, sir. From Duncan."

His lips pressed together in concentration. Heat crept into her chest. Had she made a mistake? Did he not know Duncan?

Suddenly, he smiled. "Ah. Duncan. Of course. The Highlander."

Cait let out a breath of relief. She nodded, then turned away to remove the letter from under her skirts. It felt good to get rid of it. With a shaky hand, she offered it to him.

He shoved it inside his coat without looking at it. "Why did Duncan not deliver it himself?"

She lowered her voice. "He was killed. He never had the chance."

The earl quickly glanced beyond her at the women, who all stood unmoving in deference to his presence. The news was clearly something he didn't want them to hear. "Will I see you again?" he whispered.

"I'm afraid I am simply passing through Edinburgh." She needed to get out of there. She leaned closer. "'Twas the only message I have."

"Then I bid you safe travels." He nodded once, then hurried up the stairs and out of sight.

Cait rode as fast as she could back to the inn. She couldn't believe what she had just done. Had delivering that letter sealed the king's fate? Had she moved James closer to taking the throne? Or had she just secured her demise upon a scaffold? Only time would tell.

She climbed the stairs to her room, her hand slipping from the rail as she collapsed to the floor. She was now a Jacobite.

⸻ ❈ ⸻

"Why can't I go? I want to see Edward too," Taran pleaded, his head resting against her as they sat on her bed at the inn.

It broke Cait's heart to see him so sad, his little mouth pouting over his crinkled chin. "With any luck, you'll see him soon enough when he is released."

"Do ye think they'll let him go right then?"

She didn't know. How did these things work? Would Alexander do what she hoped? Would it take a long time for him to have Edward released? Could he be beside her by tomorrow night at the White Horse Inn? "I hope so, laddie."

"I dinnae think I can take the wait. We should all be together, don't ye think?" he said, his leg bouncing up and down.

It was the only thing she thought of—the three of them connected by unexpected tragedy but somehow always meant to be together. "Aye, Taran." She brushed her fingers through his blond curls. "There is no other way for us to be."

Cait waited at the gatehouse—having left hours before—watching the sun creep across the sky at a frustratingly slow pace. Dusk could not come soon enough.

She didn't trust Alexander, but as much as she knew she was getting into bed with the devil, she had to take this chance.

She peeked inside the yellow cloth that held the small bit of meat and bread she'd brought for Edward just in case he hadn't been fed properly since his imprisonment. She folded it back up and laughed sadly at herself. *That* was what she was worried about?

"Is someone available to escort me to the office of the Captain of the Guard?" she asked the nearby soldiers sharing a block of cheese between them. Her heart pounded in her throat.

One guard backhanded another in the chest, volunteering him for the task. He brushed his hands on the front of his scarlet coat and jogged up to her, strands of his brown hair flying freely about his face.

"Captain of the Guard? Visiting a prisoner, are ye?" he asked, ogling her breasts. "I'll have to search ye."

She crossed her arms in front of her. "Whatever ye have in mind, I dinnae recommend it—unless ye think ye willnae have need of yer hands anymore."

He snickered, flashing one side of his teeth in a crooked grin. "Someone's going to search ye. It might as well be me."

She hesitated, then dropped her arms to her sides. Better him than Alexander.

"What have ye got there?" He gestured towards the sack in her hands.

"Food." She unfolded it just enough for him to peek inside.

"Very well."

He stood behind her and ran his hands over her gown, spending an unnecessarily long time over her breasts. She stilled when his hands ran over her legs, afraid he might feel the blade on her thigh through her clothing, but he merely skimmed them, too excited about touching her breasts once more. His fingertips inched inside her bodice, and she slapped his hands away. "Are ye done, then?"

He took a step back and licked his bottom lip. "Lucky prisoner, this man."

THE TACKSMAN'S DAUGHTER

"He'd crush yer bollocks under his heel if he knew ye touched me like that."

He paled instantly, and she spun towards the portcullis with him at her heels. Unlike her first visit, only a smattering of guards stood in the courtyard. The castle grounds seemed eerily quiet, sending a sudden chill up her spine. *Where is everyone?*

The sun tipped below the horizon, washing the sky in a bright orange. Over the Firth of Forth, a flock of starlings circled wildly in undulating waves of black, forming moving pictures, then breaking apart. Cait was instantly reminded of the day the soldiers had arrived in Glencoe. The day her whole life had changed. She drew in a deep breath and prayed it was a sign that this time, that change would be for the good and Edward would be released.

Alexander stood outside the barracks waiting for her. "Somehow I knew you would be punctual."

She was thankful he'd kept his word. Had she realized that she need only appeal to his greedy nature, she would've reasoned with him much sooner. She'd never thought it possible before this moment, but it seemed her life with Edward would be returned to her. "Ye said you'd take me to Edward."

"I did." He held out his arm for her, and although it made her bristle inside, she took it.

They entered an arched hallway lit with torches on either side, their winking light casting an amorphous glow on the uneven stones. They passed two cells filled with filthy shoeless prisoners lying on thin pallets and hammocks strewn about in disordered rows on either side. Some jeered as she hurried by, and others lay motionless and silent.

Down some stairs and around the corner, she spotted three more cells. The air was heavier in the back of the vaults. Damp and cold. Her heart ached for Edward.

When Alexander stopped to retrieve a torch from its cradle, she peered into one of the cells. Two men stared back at her through the darkness. Farquhar and Kennedy. She was about to blurt out their names when Farquhar placed his index finger over his mouth to silence her, alarm in his eyes. She realized it was to protect her more than anything else. They were traitors, after all, and knowing them would further cast all sorts of suspicions on her—and Edward. Alexander surely knew this, but if there were guards posted in the shadows, she certainly didn't want them to know. She bit her bottom lip and nodded weakly, thankful for the warning.

With his hand on the small of her back, Alexander urged her to the end of the hall. She wished he wouldn't touch her and thought of chiding him for it, but she realized she had to swallow her revulsion if she wanted his help.

Her heart leaped when she saw Edward lying on the floor, his back to the wall. He had removed his shirt and used it as a pillow under his head. His breeks were torn on one knee, and his shoes were missing.

"Edward?" she whispered, her throat burning with despair.

His eyes blinked open slowly, dreamily. "Cait?"

Alexander's fingers grazed the back of her neck and toyed with her hair. She clutched the cloth filled with food to her chest and leaned away, trying not to unveil her disgust.

Edward stood, one ankle fettered by a chain anchored to the wall. His gaze danced between her and Alexander, a pain in his expression she had never seen before.

She turned to Alexander. "Can I go to him?"

He seemed to weigh her request, leaning against the bars casually, legs crossed at the ankles. They hadn't discussed her entering the cell, but the keys dangled from his waist in invitation. "That would likely go against regulations . . ."

"But who would know? There's no one here," she said, beseeching him with her eyes to show some mercy.

He smiled, this time at Edward. "Who would know?"

The sadness in Edward's gaze made her heart melt. She had to go to him and let him know that she'd never believed those charges of sodomy and rape, and she would do what she could to free him of the charge of theft. That there was hope for them. "Alexander said he would consider retracting his accusation of treason."

Edward shook his head. "*Tha e breugach, mo gràdh. Na cuir earbs' ann.*" *He's lying, my love. Don't believe him.*

Alexander wagged his finger at Edward. "No Gaelic, brother. Everything should be shared freely between us." He leaned over her, and his breath was hot on the crown of her head. His hand landed gently on her shoulder.

She stiffened, disgusted by his touch. Edward speared his brother with a look meant to kill. It took everything to steady her heart and hold her tongue, but she had to diffuse the situation. It was the only way Alexander would let go of the animosity he carried for Edward.

"Ye dinnae understand, Edward. We've come to an agreement," she said softly. "He's going to help us."

THE TACKSMAN'S DAUGHTER

Edward ran his hands through his hair and huffed out a breath. "I don't wish to hear it. I've heard enough."

She didn't know why he was being so stubborn. Couldn't he see what she was trying to do? Alexander stood on the precipice of change, and one small mistake on her or Edward's part could ruin their chance of a future together. If this was going to work, Edward needed to make an effort.

Alexander draped his arm around her shoulder, and she flinched. "You should listen to her, Edward. I tried to tell you."

"Will ye open the gate, then?" she asked, her skin tingling with the thought this could all be over soon. Edward only had to play along, at least until he was freed and Alexander held no power over him. Then he could do as he wished, even if that meant severing all ties to his brother.

Alexander tilted his head. "Of course, dear sister."

With that, he unlocked the gate and let her in.

Chapter 52

Edward drew Cait into his arms, holding her tight to his chest and smelling the sweet scent of her hair. His hands covered her, gliding over her back and neck, his palms remembering her curves. He kissed her, grateful he could touch her once again. For a second, he forgot where he was and that the last week had stripped him of his happiness. She stared up at him sadly, her hand caressing his cheek.

"Have ye eaten?" She pulled away from him and handed him a yellow sack. "I brought ye some—"

Suddenly, Alexander jerked her away and dragged her back, one arm around her neck and the other low on her waist, pinning her arm to her side. Cait's eyes sprang open in shock.

Edward lunged but was yanked back by the chain. "Let go of her!"

Cait struggled to free herself from his grip, but she couldn't pry his arm from her neck. Edward tugged at the chain, the iron band cutting the skin around his ankle.

"What . . . why?" Cait wriggled in Alexander's grip.

Alexander grinned, clearly amused. "Did you honestly think I would help you? Help *him?*"

"Yer only hurting yerself!" she cried.

"Don't do this, Alexander!" Edward tried to steady his voice, but inside he was boiling over. "You have me exactly where you want me. Let her go."

He shook his head smugly. "You are going to watch me do to her what you have done with my women in the past."

"If that is what this is about, then 'tis a problem between you and me."

THE TACKSMAN'S DAUGHTER

"That is most certainly true, brother. And now you are going to pay for your misdeeds." Alexander hugged Cait tighter, the crook of his arm forcing her chin up, likely hindering her ability to speak. "Do you know about your *beloved's* sordid past?"

Edward steeled himself. "I'm warning you, Alexander."

He laughed. "Edward is a philanderer. Maids, married women. *My* women."

"Stop, Alexander."

"We are more similar than you dare to admit."

Edward hated hearing that because he knew it to be true, at least it had been at one point in his life. But that was years ago.

He ran his lips and tongue along Cait's ear, a smirk directed at Edward. "He has had more than his fair share. Stealing women from my bed. You remember that, Edward. Do you not? Lady Berenice?"

"Alexander."

Alexander's fingers crawled down Cait's skirts, inching them up as he spoke. "She was a widow with no heirs. I could have married her and never joined this godforsaken army."

"You're upset about her fortune! 'Twas not as if you loved her."

"I *did* love her!" Alexander blurted, red-faced. He closed his eyes and shook his head, his voice escaping in a whisper. "I did love her."

He'd never heard his brother suggest that over the years. Edward knew the only person Alexander ever loved was himself.

"You came to Lancaster to steal her from me." Alexander's fingers continued to climb over Cait's skirts, the muscles in his jaw pinched.

Edward's glare fixed on Alexander's. "I did no such thing. I came to tell you that Father had arranged for us to be commissioned as officers in the king's army."

"Yet it took you less than a fortnight to do *so* much more." Alexander wrenched Cait's face towards him and kissed her lips. She fought to turn away but couldn't.

Edward struggled against his ankle cuff. "I had no idea you and Berenice were lovers. She never let on there was anything between the two of you. Not until . . . after. And then I never laid another hand on her."

Alexander's head lifted, the vein at his temple pulsing wildly. "We were more than lovers!"

Edward softened his voice, hoping it would calm his brother. He had to get Cait away from him. "I understand that, and I regret what transpired . . . but neither of you had disclosed the true nature of your relationship to anyone at the time, so no one knew."

"*She* knew! *We* knew!" Alexander jerked Cait's head back, his fingers pressing into her neck with far too much force.

"You're right. And now I understand too." Edward leveled his breath in an effort to sound composed and reasonable. To get him to release his grip. "Unhand Cait, and we will settle this once and for all. You have the advantage here. I am chained—"

"You are damned right I have the advantage," Alexander scowled with gritted teeth. "And now you are going to watch me take the one who means so much to *you.*"

Edward's blood raced through his veins with searing heat. He pitched forward once more, reaching to wrap his hands around his brother's neck, but Alexander stepped back, pulling Cait with him. She screamed.

Alexander rubbed his cheek against her temple, his lips brushing against her ears and his eyes fixed on Edward. "No one is going to hear you. The guards are whoring in town. Why do you think I had you come at dusk?"

He tugged up her skirts, his hand disappearing behind the layers of fabric and between her thighs. A single tear trailed down her cheek.

"There we are," Alexander cooed, a slow smile forming on his lips. "Feels good, does it?"

Convinced he could snap the chain holding him back, Edward lurched, and a sharp crack sounded behind him. He fell to his knees, ignoring the sting from his torn skin on his ankle and the bloody bone sticking out of his foot.

"Beyond your grasp, are we?" Alexander kissed the top of Cait's head. "Pity."

A dizziness engulfed him. It started behind his eyes and spread to his chest. A painful tingling sensation traveled down his limbs and into his fists. His mind spun—thoughts of the first time he'd kissed Cait in Glencoe, finding her at Eilean Munde, her skin glistening with river water, the way she pressed against him for warmth when they lay under the stars.

Fight, Cait. Fight, he pleaded. Had he said it aloud? Could she hear him?

Edward caught a glimpse of the bottom of the sheath of Cait's black knife on her thigh, but he couldn't tell if the castle guards had confiscated it. "*A bheil do sgian dubh agad, mo gràdh?*" *Do you have your blade, my love?*

Cait stared at him, panic in her eyes, both cheeks now wet with tears. She nodded cautiously. "*Chan urrainn dhomh ruighinn air.*" *I can't reach it.*

Alexander growled. "I said no Gaelic!"

Edward swallowed back the pain, the smell of his own blood making him nauseous. "*Dèan nas urrainn dhut a dhol an comhair do chinn agus beiridh mise air. An urrainn dhut sin a dhèanamh?*" *Do what you can to throw yourself forward, and I'll grab it. Can you do that?*

THE TACKSMAN'S DAUGHTER

Cait arched her back, trying to make it difficult for Alexander to reach low enough to touch her underneath her skirts. In response, he wrapped his arm around her and swung her to the right, causing both of them to lose their balance. She lunged, and they toppled over just in front of Edward, her arms now free from Alexander's grip. She scrabbled to get away, one hand fumbling for the blade at her thigh.

Edward panicked. She couldn't be the one to kill Alexander. She might not get away with it this time, and he couldn't let her have another man's death on her conscience.

He tried to grasp her stocking to get to the knife first, but she yanked it out of its sheath and spun it in her hand so the blade was in her palm. She was going to throw it.

Alexander stood and backed away towards the gate, fear in his eyes.

Edward swallowed hard. "*Leig leamsa a' dheanamh. Chan eil cail agam ri chall.*" *Let me do it. I have nothing to lose.*

Before she could draw back, Edward knocked it out of her hand. It slid across the uneven stones not far from him. Alexander lunged for it, but Edward grabbed it, and slashed at Alexander's arm, catching his flesh and shirtsleeve.

Alexander jerked back and grunted, flinging Cait to the side. She crashed into the wall, banging her head and shoulder into the unforgiving stone.

Edward tried to scramble to his feet, but he slipped on the pool of blood gathering under his injured foot. He stumbled to his knees. Alexander punched him hard in the jaw and his head swung to the side in sharp agony. The next thing he knew, Alexander was on top of him, grasping furiously for the knife. Edward sliced at his arm and missed, his vision blurring from the pain in his ankle.

Suddenly, Alexander stopped his attack.

From beneath heavy lids, Edward watched him. For a moment, indecision played across Alexander's features, but then he grinned, spotting the source of Edward's pain. Edward held his breath, knowing his brother all too well. He tried to slide his leg away from Alexander's reach, but he was too slow, and Alexander kicked at his injured ankle with the toe of his boot. White light flashed in front of Edward's eyes, and bile rose in his throat. Unwittingly, he loosened his grip on the knife, and Alexander snatched it from his hand.

His brother stood clumsily and jerked Edward's head up by his hair, holding the blade at his throat. "Shall we end this here, brother?"

Edward swallowed back the bile, his vision fading. "Let her go first, Alexander. Leave her be. And you can take my life as you please."

"Wait!" Cait lumbered closer, blood trickling out of a gash on the side of her head and holding her arm below her shoulder. "I'll give ye anything if ye let him live."

The strain in Alexander's face melted away, and he turned to her, releasing Edward. "I already plan on taking what I want, but don't flatter yourself. It won't spare his life."

"But I have more to offer."

"What could you possibly have that I would want?"

Edward's throat tightened, afraid of what she would say.

She fell at his feet and kissed him, her tears hot on his skin. Her lips were soft and salty, fragile beneath his own. "Ye damned fool," she whispered. "I could've—"

He shook his head, pressing his finger to her lips.

His thoughts started to jumble, and it became increasingly difficult to focus. He sucked in his breath, trying to fight the pain.

"How pretty, the two of you." Alexander pointed at them with the knife. "It makes me want to retch." He pressed his lips together in a thin line and shoved Cait away, sending her reeling onto her back.

Edward snatched his brother's forearm just above the open wound. Alexander grimaced and held the blade at the base of Edward's neck.

Cait scrabbled to sit up, her hands out in supplication, begging him to stop. "I—I have something!"

She reached into her bodice and slipped out her mother's sapphire on the chain he gave her on what should have been their wedding day. "You can have it. 'Tis believed to be the largest sapphire in all of Scotland."

Edward froze, the muscles in his chest and stomach tightened. "Don't do it, Cait."

She shoved it at Alexander. "I'll give ye this if ye let Edward go."

Edward couldn't believe she would offer the only thing she had left of her mother, her family. "Please, Cait."

Her hands shook as she spoke. "Ye said ye were angry about the women, the money. Take it. 'Tis worth a fortune."

She dropped the necklace into his hand. Alexander stared into his palm, a sickening grin slipping onto his face. He dangled the gem from its chain, a spark of blue light flashing through its center.

"A sapphire?" he mused.

"Give it back to her, Alexander," Edward said, the words spilling from his mouth sloppily, slowly.

She stuck out her hand in protest. "'Tis fine, Edward. Let him have it."

His brother had won.

THE TACKSMAN'S DAUGHTER

"You will not take Cait. Understand?" The room began to spin, the stone walls swirling above his head like leaves caught in an autumn gust.

Alexander ran his knuckles over her cheek and across her jaw. "Perhaps later."

He slipped the necklace into his coat and withdrew the blade. "As much as I would love to see you die at my hands, I will let the noose have the pleasure. A public execution would be much more entertaining. The humiliation. The jeering. Watching you shit yourself. I suppose I could forego this moment of having you at my mercy for all of that."

He snatched Cait under her arm and threw her out of the cell. She grabbed the gate as he locked it, her face peering back through bars at Edward. "Ye cannae leave him here. He'll die. He's bleeding!"

"Death is a fate he will not escape." Alexander shoved her away, and she disappeared from Edward's view just before he collapsed into darkness.

The bonesetter did a fair enough job with Edward's ankle. He couldn't see it beneath the linen wraps, but only a small amount of blood seemed to have escaped his wound to stain the white cloth red.

He learned from one of the guards that Farquhar and Kennedy had shouted loud enough to wake the dead that same night he was left to bleed to death, alerting a soldier who was returning from a night of cavorting at a local tavern. It was what had saved his life, and he would forever be indebted to them.

Now he lay on a straw pallet in a different cell with three other prisoners, all with some injury or ailment. Except for the company, the conditions were almost the same as before.

His trial had been postponed until he could walk into the hall before the High Court of Justiciary with no more than the help of a cane. It had taken him well over a fortnight to be able to hobble around, but it didn't offer him any hope since it would only render him competent to stand trial, thus bringing him closer to his death.

He hadn't seen Cait since the night Alexander had attacked her, and he wondered if he'd ever see her again. He'd been told that she came daily but was turned away at the entrance, undoubtedly due to orders from his brother. Perhaps it was for the better. He was likely going to be hanged for treason. She could go on with her life and find a more suitable husband. It pained him to admit that, but he couldn't be selfish. She was young, beautiful, and full of life, and she deserved to find happiness, even if it wasn't with him.

"Are ye ready, Sergeant?" A young guard named Nesbitt jingled the keys to his cell, his shoulders hunched as he pushed open the gate.

Edward leaned on his cane and hopped out. He'd been given one shoe and a shirt to wear—he was told they had been taken off the body of a prisoner who died from a bee sting. He and four other prisoners were hoisted onto a wagon and carted to Parliament Hall. Of the five of them, he was the only one with an obvious injury but somehow seemed to be the one in the best shape, the others covered in open sores and bruises.

After they were unloaded, they were escorted into the hall by a half dozen guards and told to wait until their names were called. Edward sat outside the courtroom listening to the cheers of the crowd every time a sentence was announced.

After a couple of hours, the heavy wooden door opened, and the courtroom guard appeared. "Edward Gage."

Edward grabbed his cane, and two guards followed him through the entrance. He scanned the curious faces for Cait's, but there were so many, he couldn't possibly spot her in the short walk to the rail. He plodded ahead, feeling more alone than he had in his cell. Despair settled in his chest like a heavy stone.

He had been provided with a solicitor, a diminutive man with a head as round as an onion and a red-tipped nose. He spoke with his eyes closed, one hand resting between the buttons of his coat, the other periodically twirling a curl on his periwig. "The care which the law has taken for the personal safety of the king is not confined to actions or attempts of the more flagitious kind, at assassination or poison, or other attempts, directly or immediately aiming at his life; there would be little difficulty, provided a man was to attempt a thing of that sort, in saying that he was intending the death of the king. 'Tis extended to everything willfully and deliberately done or attempted, whereby his life may be endangered . . ."

Edward searched the faces of the crowd, many of which seemed to have no idea what the little man was saying, their eyes glazed over in a watery haze. The men distractedly scratched at their beards, and the women sighed with boredom.

"And with that, 'tis understood within this branch of the statute, that the accused's behaviour cannot be deemed an act of treason which defies the orders of the king, but rather is lawfully defined as . . ."

Edward rolled his shoulders to relieve his stiffness. The Lord Advocate shifted in his seat, then exhaled loudly.

"The chancery has also sent forth a proclamation stating that there will be an inquisition into the massacre at Glencoe, which occurred on the morn of February 13th, the year of our Lord sixteen and ninety-two. Therefore, I request a postponement of the trial for high treason until the process has been employed under the eyes of Parliament."

The Lord Advocate whispered something to the solicitor-general standing next to him, and he nodded. "Very well. The accused shall await trial until further notice. With regard to the charge of theft, I—"

Out of the corner of his eye, Edward glimpsed a raised hand. Cait's. She opened her mouth to speak but was cut short when a woman's voice, meek but clear, interrupted the solicitor, turning every head to the back of the room.

Davina.

Chapter 53

"Milord? May I be heard?" Davina asked, determined to hold her head high. Her throat yet hurt from the damage Alex had done to it a month earlier, the dark purple bruises now faded to various shades of green and yellow.

"We are in the middle of the proceedings, mistress. Ye shall not—"

"I know that, but I have information regarding the matter of theft."

Although she spoke softly, she felt as if her voice roared in the cavernous room.

"Step forward, then."

The crowd parted and Davina strode ahead, one hand resting on her swollen belly. She forced a smile but knew her face appeared gaunt and sad, touched with the heaviness of truth. Someone whispered her name, and she turned to her right to find Cait edged between two tall men. Their glances met if for only a second, and Cait tentatively reached out for her, her other hand covering her mouth.

Davina stood at the rail while the guard opened the little gate and allowed her into the pannal where Edward stood. She glanced at him once with a pained smile, then turned to face the Lord Advocate.

"State yer name, please," he commanded.

She cleared her throat. "Davina MacNab of Glenorchy. Niece of John Campbell, 1st Earl of Breadalbane, and 11th Laird of Glenorchy."

The crowd murmured an acknowledgement of her relationship with the earl.

"Do ye have information about the stolen weapons?"

"I do." She swallowed, then continued. "I gave those weapons to Sergeant Gage myself. He had somehow lost his own in Glencoe during the attack. I know him to be a man of honour, milord, and I awarded them to him as a gift for saving me and my son in an unrelated matter."

She understood she was lying in court, but she knew Edward to be a righteous man—so unlike his brother—and she would not see him charged with this crime. She glanced at him briefly, hoping he would not betray her false words.

"Is yer uncle, the earl, aware of this?"

Davina locked eyes with Cait, who wiped at tears on her cheeks. "He is. So ye see, a theft was never committed."

The crowd rumbled. The Lord Advocate sat silent and stared at Edward. Davina held her breath until he spoke. "Return the prisoner to his cell."

People stood to leave, clearly disappointed that Edward wasn't going to be sentenced to hang at that moment.

"Milord?" Davina spoke again, interrupting the crowd's departure.

"Aye."

The masses returned to their seats or places behind the rail.

She took a deep breath, filled with the courage she hadn't felt before the day Alex had struck her. "I have in my possession a letter containing the treasonous words of one of the king's soldiers." She reached into her sleeve, her hands steady and sure, and removed the letter she knew would cinch Alex's fate, then turned to the guard at her side. "Would ye please give this to milord?"

The guard handed it to the Lord Advocate, who glanced at it briefly, then passed it to the solicitor-general. "'Tis in Gaelic."

While he read it, Davina stood straight, staring ahead but looking at nothing in particular. A sudden movement amongst the rapt crowd caught her attention. It happened quickly, but there was no mistaking what she'd witnessed. Slipping behind a row of onlookers, Alex had scuttled out the door.

The Lord Advocate and solicitor-general whispered with their heads close, the crowd intently waiting for an explanation.

When they were done, the Lord Advocate spoke. "This will be delivered to the king immediately."

Davina exhaled. She was finally free—free of her past, her fear, her pain. She no longer would make excuses for a man who deserved none. She would no longer see what was never there. She would no longer wait for something that would never come. A lightness filled her breast, and she breathed easily.

A hushed murmur passed through the crowd, then stopped abruptly when she spoke again.

"The same man who signed that letter tried to murder me and my unborn child, then left me for dead. I was discovered under some brush in the clearing below the castle by a few good souls who showed me kindness and helped me heal from my wounds. 'Tis by the grace of God that I stand before ye today."

Edward turned to her, his brow furrowed and lips tightened in recognition of who she was speaking of.

"Guards, escort Mistress MacNab to my chambers for further discussion." The Lord Advocate stood. "Ye can file yer complaint then."

Later, Davina sat opposite the Lord Advocate, and although her hands shook the entire time, she relayed her story with confidence. "As ye can see, the last of the bruising remains."

His gaze settled on her mottled neck. "And ye said the man knew ye were with child."

"Aye. 'Twas his own."

He and his assistant exchanged looks of pity. "And yer sure ye wish to bring charges against the father of yer bairn?"

"I've never been so sure of anything in my life."

It was a sad truth, but the truth nonetheless. Her thoughts of vengeance had morphed into the need for justice long before her black and blue marks faded to yellow. It was an uncomplicated desire, no longer convoluted with emotion, for her heart had truly left the matter the moment she'd regained consciousness on a pallet in a stranger's home. This new feeling of lightness was welcome as a release from all that had enslaved her over the years. A release from seeing what was never there and wanting what could never be had.

It had been a shock to the rector and Lizbeth when she returned for her belongings. She told them the truth of what happened and naturally, they were horrified. Lizbeth had felt wretched about giving her few possessions to Alex the day he attacked her. But all that mattered was that he hadn't taken the letter to the Earl of Mar, so if no one believed Davina's story about a well-respected leftenant in the king's army trying to kill her, the letter would prove his abominable nature. Did it bother her that she knew the truth behind his signature inside? Not at all. Not anymore.

The bairn kicked twice, and she smiled, her hand instinctively gliding over the spot low on her belly. At least Alex hadn't killed the one hope she had left that something good could come out of this.

The assistant scratched a few more words on the parchment and set down his quill, the fingers on his right hand smeared with ink. "Unless ye have anything further to add, we are done here."

She shook her head, pleased with her courage. "My conscience is clear. 'Tis up to *you* now to see he's brought to justice."

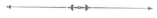

THE TACKSMAN'S DAUGHTER

Cait stood with her head bowed outside the massive building, pacing when Davina spotted her. "Cait!"

Cait looked up and ran to her, pulling her into an embrace that spoke of uncertainty, desperation, and love. "I had no idea—when did ye arrive? What happened to ye?"

It soothed Davina to hear her voice and be touched so affectionately. But her questions made Davina's stomach drop. If it were anyone else but Cait, she probably would've changed the subject or skirted around the truth. But it *was* Cait. "Come sit."

They sat on a bench, and between sobs, Davina relayed the terrible events of the recent past. Her shame. Her naiveté. Her foolishness. Cait remained quiet the whole time, listening and wiping away her tears. Never judging.

"I must apologize to ye, Cait," she said. "I remained true in my heart to Alex even after the attack. He told me he played nae part in it, but I know now that was unlikely. 'Tis his nature to lie. To hurt."

Cait pressed her lips together, obviously struggling to hold back her words.

"I suppose I thought I could change him. Make him a better man. I thought he'd do it for me. For Sawney." She ran her hand over her growing stomach. "But I was wrong. I spent years remembering the few fine moments we shared and forgetting the darkness that surrounded each one of them. 'Twas easier to live a beautiful lie than dwell in the ugly truth, ye see."

Cait nodded. "Aye. I do."

Davina took a deep breath. "I'm nae the same lass. God has a plan for me."

Cait's head tilted to the side, her eyes sad yet encouraging. She patted her hand gently. "I can see yer expecting another wee one."

"I'm almost five months along now." Davina assumed she would do the mathematics in her head. She'd gotten with child the night she'd lain with Alex in Glencoe.

Cait smiled and ran her hands over Davina's protruding belly, her worn green gown patched with side panels. "'Tis still a blessing."

"Aye. 'Tis."

They walked arm in arm to the White Horse Inn, where Cait was lodging. Taran sat in the parlour, his cane leaning against his chair and an elderly woman pressing his hand between her palms. He nodded as she spoke, asking questions of him that Davina couldn't quite hear but knew from her tone were of a surreptitious nature.

It warmed Davina's heart to see him there with his blond curls hanging loosely over his brow and his dimples framing his mouth. He was a reminder of the beauty of the past and the possibility of things to come. He made her pine for Sawney and his silly little smile. She would do anything to feel his arms around her neck and his noisy, sloppy kisses on her cheek. But until she could return to Glenorchy, the memory of him would have to suffice.

The woman who'd been sitting with Taran scooted by her and Cait and out the parlour door.

Cait crossed the room and planted her fists on her hips. "Are ye doing what I think yer doing?"

"Depends on what ye think I'm doing," he answered, hiding his hand behind his back.

"Oh, no ye don't. Show me what ye have there, laddie."

Taran's shoulders dropped as he brought forth his hand, palm open. *"Three pence!* These Edinburgh folks are flush in the fob."

"If ye dinnae wish for me to give yer ear a good tug, you'll stop yer—"

"Och! Yer always fussin' at me."

Cait softened, her expression sorrowful, tired. She knelt at his feet. "Am I, laddie?"

He reached for her, and she pressed his hand to her cheek. "Aye. But I know 'tis because yer worried over Edward."

She kissed his palm. "I am. But I have good news to share with ye."

"Ye do?"

"He willnae be tried today. The court will wait for Parliament's inquiry. He could be freed!" she explained with quivering lips and a forced smile. "And the charge of theft has been dropped."

"Did ye tell them, then?"

Davina knelt beside Cait. "Nay, laddie. *I* did."

Taran's mouth dropped open. "Davina? Is that you?"

Davina cupped his chin. "Aye. 'Tis a great blessing to see ye, Taran."

He hugged her, his head resting on the crook of her neck and shoulder. She held him tight, thankful he had escaped the horror of what happened that day in Glencoe. "Oh, I missed ye so."

"How did ye come to Edinburgh?" he asked.

"'Tis a long story, laddie." She stood and handed him his cane.

"Will ye be staying with us, then?" he asked, excitement in his voice.

Cait placed her hand over her heart. "'Twould do us a great deal of good, Davina."

Davina smiled at the two of them. Though she was far away from Glenorchy, she finally felt at home. "Then 'tis settled."

Chapter 54

August, 1692
Dunbar, Scotland

Soldiers burst through the door and dragged Alexander off the surprised whore, who scrambled to cover her nakedness with a badly stained sheet. He fought to escape their grip but was no match against the three of them.

"Did you tell them? Was it you?" he yelled at the skinny whore with skin like a lizard.

"Shut yer gob, Leftenant!" barked the fat soldier, his heavy beard dusted with bits of his morning's breakfast. "She had naught to do with it, ye clot. Ye left a trail of debt and a long list of angry innkeepers and alehouse skinkers from here to Edinburgh."

"And in bawdy houses too. Plucking a few withering roses along the way, were ye?" an older soldier quipped, his eyes fixed on the deflated breasts of the naked whore on the bed.

The bearded soldier tied a coarse rope around Alexander's wrists, binding them together. "That reminds me—ye were identified as the cockard who *mistreated,* shall we say, that whore in Fort William. Apparently, the owner of the establishment saw yer likeness in a proscription posted near Mary King's Close, and a woman from the rectory below the castle named ye."

That was Edward's likeness! Not his!

"Yer an interesting man, Leftenant," he added, chuckling to himself and snatching the small pouch where he kept his valuables.

It had taken Alexander two weeks to ride to Dunbar, the distance of which he could have accomplished in a matter of days if the weather hadn't been so miserable. He could've been in Newcastle by now, lodging with Englishmen who'd likely be ignorant of his true identity and safely in search of someone wealthy enough to purchase the sapphire. *Damn this country!*

"At least throw me my breeches!" he barked, yanking his arm from the older soldier's grip.

The fat one tossed him his clothes and crossed his arms. "Ye might as well put them on. Ye willnae be needing yer cock for a long time."

Alexander rode on his horse behind the others, his hands tied at the wrists and the reins controlled by the commanding soldier. It rained mercilessly on him for three days straight, the men not bothering to stop to find shelter from the weather. He'd slept on the boggy ground, both feet tethered to a tree while the others slumbered under tents to shield them from the downpour. In the morning, he was so numb and cold, he wasn't sure if he'd pissed himself in his soaked breeches or not.

They reached Edinburgh Castle in the midafternoon, and he was ushered to the vaults as a prisoner. Immediately, he was stripped of his boots and shackled at the ankles with heavy iron bands connected by a foot-long chain. He was free to walk about his cell only because the wall chains were currently being used on other prisoners. He leaned heavily with both hands on the cold stone, planning what he would say at his indictment the next morning.

"A bit of a surprise to see ye here, Leftenant." Robertson stood outside his cell, eating an apple, the rank air molested by the man's pungent odor.

Alexander peered at him out of the corner of his eye. Juice dripped on Robertson's chest, and he swiped at the spot ineffectually. "Didn't know I'd been sharing a room with a skellum. Not to mention a traitor."

"I am not a traitor, fool," Alexander snarled.

"Of course not." Robertson laughed. He held up what remained of his apple in salute.

He disappeared, chortling loud enough for Alexander to hear the echo long after he'd turned the corner.

"So, they finally have the correct Gage in custody." Edward's voice came from the other side of the wall, even-toned and punctuated by a slow drip from somewhere nearby.

Alexander chose to ignore him.

"I wonder, though—how is it that your signature lies at the foot of a treasonous letter? Could you be a Jacobite?" Edward hesitated, allowing the

THE TACKSMAN'S DAUGHTER

silence to fill the void. "I suppose you could. There isn't a single revelatory accusation against you I wouldn't believe."

Alexander gritted his teeth, fighting the urge to respond.

"But I won't begrudge you that, brother. I can't."

He knew what Edward was saying. He had never resented their father for his Jacobite sentiments either, but Edward was a fool—just like Father.

"And I don't begrudge you proclaiming me a traitor. I know what the indictment stems from, after all. It has been years in the making. Father. The money. Berenice."

Smug bastard. Edward was always part of the problem. Why no one else could see that remained a mystery.

"But what you did to Davina is reprehensible. That . . . cannot be forgiven." Someone coughed down the hall, breaking the momentary silence. "Tell me, brother. While you were brutally beating her, were you hoping to kill her child—your child—too?"

Alexander had enough. "I suggest you shut your mouth, Edward."

"You like hurting women, don't you? Easy targets, I suppose. Davina and who knows how many countless others?" The dripping echoed in the silence. "And then there's what you did to Cait. I would kill you with my bare hands if I could."

"You may climb down from your pulpit. I am no longer listening." Alexander shuffled to the opposite side of his cell, the chain between his feet dragging across the cobbles.

"Then I leave you with this: Pray, Alexander. Pray for a quick death—and not the one you deserve."

Alexander stood like a common criminal, his hands bound and feet bare, in front of the Lord Advocate and a couple hundred of the local townspeople in the great hall. He hadn't eaten the slop they'd served him, and now his stomach growled madly.

"Alexander Gage, leftenant in the king's army and Baron Mansfield, ye are hereby charged with the crime of treason against His Majesty, King William of England, Scotland, and Ireland, the crime of attempted murder against one Davina MacNab—and her unborn bairn—of Glenorchy, the charges of sodomy, rape, and assault with intent to ravish against one Wynda Bruce of Stirling yet residing in Fort William. How do ye plead, Mansfield?"

Alexander rolled his eyes. "Not guilty, milord."

"Return him to his cell," the Lord Advocate said airily, waving his hand towards the door.

He sat with his back to the corner of his cell, ruminating over his circumstances. How was it that his questionable—*at best*—liaisons could be considered criminal? He understood that sodomy was thought to be an unnatural act considered an abomination by the Church, but it was *expected* in a brothel. That was what whores were for, for God's sake! And the assault with the intent to ravish? Of course he planned to ravish her, but one could hardly consider tying her hands with a hair ribbon an act of assault.

And treason. He could maintain that he understood not a single word of Gaelic and therefore could not possibly have known to what he signed his name. The letter to the earl was written in Breadalbane's hand, so it shouldn't be too difficult to argue his innocence. Of course, if Breadalbane were arrested for supporting the Jacobite cause, he would retaliate by arguing that Alexander had conspired against the king with him.

Then there was the matter with Davina and her misbegotten child. He might be able to argue that although not married in the Church, he'd treated her as his wife since they already shared a child together, and he had a right to beat her as her husband. He hadn't used a weapon or drawn blood, so it was perfectly acceptable in the eyes of the law. He could even add that they'd discussed marriage while in Glenorchy but were only awaiting the approval of her uncle, the earl. He smiled at himself, pleased and impressed by his ingenuity.

Footsteps approached from down the corridor. "All the way at the end, miss. Watch yer step there."

Alexander listened as they grew nearer. Two people stopped in front of his cell, the torchlight behind them blanketing their faces in shadow.

"May I have a bit of privacy, please?" It had been over two months, but he'd know that voice anywhere. It was Jenny. Had she come to help? To speak on his behalf?

"I'll wait at the end of the hall. Holler if ye need me," the prison guard offered.

Alexander stood, his heart pounding. "Do not believe anything they are saying about me. None of it is true."

She laughed softly and gripped the bars of the gate with both hands. "Of course what they are saying is true, my pet. Most of it, anyway."

Alexander shambled closer, eager to see her, to smell her again. She wore her hair down over her shoulders, her auburn waves cast in light from behind. He reached through the bars to touch it.

"'Tis a pity, though. We would have been good together," she said. Her hand slipped down his chest, grazing his nipple and stomach, then over his cock.

THE TACKSMAN'S DAUGHTER

"We *are* good together," he moaned, silently cursing the bars that separated them. He pressed himself against her hand, his breeches growing tighter. She licked her bottom lip.

"Such a good lover," she cooed, her hand gripping and moving over him. "Confident, demanding, desirous. But not all women appreciate that type of ardour the way I do."

He loved the way her mouth moved as she spoke, her lips full and wanting.

"Why did you have to be so foolish?" she whispered, drawing his mouth to hers.

Their lips met, gently at first and then more frantic. She tasted of wine and sugar.

He wanted, needed to embrace her, but the bars were unforgiving. He closed his eyes as she stroked him. "You cannot possibly believe the charges."

"You forget I know your true nature, Mansfield."

Could she be jealous? "You yourself share a bed with the viscount. You cannot judge me—"

"Judge you? Is that what you think? That I am judging you?" she asked, her face pinched in question, her hand leaving his breeches and landing on his cheek. He brought it to his lips, and she sighed.

She smiled. "Bedsport is a perfectly useful weapon. You use it, as do I."

He took great comfort in knowing that she understood him. "We are one in the same."

She tilted her head and held up her index finger. "Except I use it for good."

"For good?"

Her playful tone became serious. "Why do you think I latched onto a sour-smelling old gundigut like Campden? For the money?"

"Is that not the reason all women become mistresses?"

"Well . . . some of his money did prove useful." She leaned closer and whispered, "But nay. I did it for my country. For the rightful King of England."

What was she saying? "The rightful king?"

"Campden—as meek and dull as he is—is an enthusiastic supporter of King William. The perfect cover." She dabbed a finger on the tip of his nose. "And you, my pet, were the perfect source of information."

He shook his head, confused.

Her voice once again turned kittenish. "Granted, you are desirable in your own right. Tall, alluring, imposing. And the tupping . . . well, *that* was indescribable. But our acquaintance had nothing to do with that." She ran her finger across his lips. "It was because you are a soldier. An officer who could answer questions."

He thought back to the conversations they'd had during their rendezvous, all related to his regiment or the king. And then there was the evening at the Duke of Argyll's lodgings when the viscount had said Jenny insisted on stopping in Stirling—perhaps not so coincidentally—at the same time there was a Jacobite rally. It suddenly struck him. "Are you a Jacobite?"

She shrugged one shoulder in confession, a smile playing on her features.

"You used me as a spy," he said, astonished that he could have been so oblivious to her true intentions.

"The truth is never simple, is it?" she said. "Why do you suppose I took you as a lover that first night in less time than it took me to finish my meal?"

He took a step back. He wasn't sure what to make of this information. Perhaps he could use it against her to free himself of suspicion. "I could report you."

"Do you think the court will believe the desperate tales of a man with his head on the block or the mistress of one of the most renowned staunch supporters of King William?"

"Who knows about this?"

"That you were my scout?" she asked, brows raised in question. "I told no one."

He took a deep breath, his chest pounding through his shirt.

"*You* did," she said.

"I did no such thing."

"Ah. But you did, my pet." She reached for him through the bars, but he pulled back. "You delivered a letter directly into the king's hands, telling him you were a spy."

The only letter he'd given the king was Breadalbane's.

"You should have married the girl and set her aside like most husbands do. We could have still been lovers."

How did Breadalbane know? His mind raced back to the time the earl had seen the three of them together, Davina pressing her bastard into his chest, Breadalbane piercing him with his eyes at the spectacle, then handing him the letter to the king just afterward. This was all about revenge.

"You were working for Breadalbane," he said.

"As were you."

He ran his hands over his face and paced. "Why did you come here? To gloat?"

She shook her head sadly. "To say goodbye. Had you only kept your cock to yourself, things would've ended differently. We could've banded together for the cause."

"I am not a Jacobite."

THE TACKSMAN'S DAUGHTER

"I know that, my pet. But in time, you could have been."

Chapter 55

Cait could hardly contain her excitement. She, Davina, and Taran stood open-mouthed as the town crier read the news. Parliament had ordered the removal of John Dalrymple as Master of Stair and the imprisonment of Breadalbane in Edinburgh Castle, all as a result of their dealings in the Glencoe attack. Nothing was said of the king's involvement. Even if it were proven that he'd ordered the massacre, Cait imagined the public would never be told.

She hugged Taran to her side for support and tugged on the crier's sleeve. "What are they saying of the prisoners being held for refusing to follow orders during the attack?"

"They are to be released immediately," he replied, posting a list of names outside Parliament Hall.

Cait held her breath as she scanned the list. Francis Farquhar and Gilbert Kennedy were both on there. She slid her finger lower, and there it was. Edward Gage. Tears flooded her eyes. She couldn't believe it was all finally over.

"We should hurry to the castle," she said, tugging Taran and Davina behind her. "Make haste! Make haste!"

Davina pulled away, her eyes sad. "I think I'll stay behind."

"Are ye certain?" Cait asked, suspecting Davina wanted to avoid possibly seeing Alexander.

"Aye. I need to make arrangements to return to Glenorchy before Kilchurn is sequestered. Sawney is still there." She kissed Cait's cheek, shooing them away. "Go on with Taran and bring back yer man."

THE TACKSMAN'S DAUGHTER

They hurried up the hill hand in hand, Cait imagining their life together from this point forward. She'd been thinking about it a lot lately. She didn't want to return to Glencoe just yet and thought traveling down to Boroughbridge to meet Edward's mother might be what Edward would want to do. They had the horses, so the journey shouldn't take long, and Taran would probably enjoy the adventure of entering a new country. She smiled at the thought they could get married in a church with his mother present.

She and Taran were searched for weapons by a guard. The familiar weight of her *sgian dubh* on her thigh was no longer there, Alexander last having possession of it. It felt odd not to have it with her, the security of knowing she could defend herself in a second now gone. She'd had that knife since she was fourteen, when her father had given it to her before her first lesson. He'd told her never to pull it on a man without good reason—never to attack and only to defend. She'd listened to his advice, except when it came to her encounter with Glenlyon, and wondered what he'd think of her for it.

A guard ushered them to the vaults, her heart beating vigorously with each step. Edward stood in front of his cell, leaning on a cane and talking to Farquhar and Kennedy. He wore one shoe and was covered in the filth of more than a month. His hair and beard were long and shaggy, and he'd lost a stone or so in weight, but he was finally free and all hers.

She bit her lip, watching the three of them bid their farewells with slaps on the back and few words. After the two men left, she approached, her skin tingling with the exhilaration of seeing him.

"Edward?"

He looked at her, his blue eyes glistening. "You came for me."

"I . . . I tried many times, but the guards—"

"I know, *mo gràdh*. They told me." He spoke softly, woefully. "I truly had no idea how much my brother hated me. I only regret that he chose to hurt you to get to me."

"'Tis but a memory." She swallowed back tears, her hand brushing back his unkempt hair. She leaned up to kiss him, her body pressed against his, their fingers intertwined. It felt like they had been separated forever, and she couldn't wait to have him permanently in her arms. "Only a memory."

"I want to explain a few things. What my brother said about Lady Berenice." She felt his heart pounding through his sark. "I am not proud of my behaviour in the past. I hope you don't think my intentions with you bear any resemblance—"

"You've asked me for my hand in marriage." She shook her head, surprised that he'd worried about that all this time. She'd never doubted him. She recognized his love in the way he tilted his head ever so slightly to listen to her speak. The way he pressed his lips to her palm when she needed his reassurance. The way he smiled crookedly every time she twirled her blade between her fingers. And the way he'd taken her under his wing, when she'd lost everything and everyone she'd ever held close to her heart. "Ye needn't say more."

He closed his eyes and leaned his forehead against hers, his shoulders lowering with each breath. The heat of his body warmed her.

"Let's go," he whispered onto her lips. She felt the words as much as she heard them.

She walked back to the inn with Edward on one side and Taran on the other, their hands in hers. Although Edward seemed to be used to his cane, occasionally he faltered on the uneven cobbles, increasing the pressure on Cait's hand. She loved it, though, that sudden tightening a reminder that he needed her. There was no awkwardness between them. No hesitation or bashful glances. Their time away from each other had not changed anything nor diminished her need for him. His mere presence reassured her, soothed her as it had in the past. Taran seemed comforted as well, easily falling into his rogue routine the moment they exited the castle gates and peppering him with a thousand bizarre questions.

"How could ye stand that smell in there? It could kill a horse." Taran shuddered, crinkling his nose.

"After a while, I didn't even notice it." Edward sniffed his sleeves and grimaced. "Perhaps a good bath is in order."

Cait smiled up at him. "And a good shave too."

Edward scratched at his beard and raised one eyebrow. "I suppose I look like a beast."

Taran tapped his cane ahead of him. "I dinnae know. But ye smell like cow farts."

"Taran!" she cried.

"Och. Fine, then." He turned to Edward. "Since you've been gone, all she's done is snip at me."

Edward ruffled his hair. "Someone has to keep you in line. You won't find a lass if you talk about cow farts."

"Gilli didn't mind it. And she was my lass."

Cait's throat stung at the mention of her sister's name. But Taran was right. Gilli had probably giggled when he talked like that. He stayed quiet until the inn was in sight, allowing Cait to relish the moment of having the two of them by her side.

"Where did ye piss, then?" Taran suddenly asked.

THE TACKSMAN'S DAUGHTER

"Ye ask such strange questions, laddie," Cait said, rebuking him with her tone. "Ye should—"

She stopped midsentence, spotting Taran's grandda talking to the innkeeper outside the inn, his blue bonnet in his hand. Her heart sank. The innkeeper pointed a finger in their direction, and the old bard's face brightened.

"I should what? What were ye going to say?" Taran asked, oblivious to the fact he was going to be stripped away from her.

Edward squeezed her hand, his palm warm and large, his grip firm and assuring. He gazed at her sympathetically. "'Tis for the best."

How could his grandda have found them? They walked closer, Cait's heart splitting in two. The bard called to him and Taran stilled, his grey eyes searching the empty space before him.

"Taran," he called again.

Taran sucked in his breath. "Grandda?"

The bard rushed towards them, hope and relief in his features. Cait reluctantly released her proprietary grip on Taran's hand. She blinked away the tears forming, stunned that her new little family had just been returned to her only to be ripped apart minutes later.

"Thig an seo, mo laochan bàn." Come here, my fair-haired laddie. The bard bent low and pulled Taran into his embrace. "Thank God."

Cait's heart leaped in her chest as Taran's arms folded around his neck. She leaned into Edward, her lips pressed into a wavering smile. She wanted to be happy for Taran but somehow couldn't help but feel the loss as if she were losing Gilli all over again. She knew she was being foolish. That losing her sister to heaven was so much more. But nonetheless, her heart was cleaved in two.

His grandda scrugged on his bonnet, pulling it low over his brow. "'Tis a blessed day."

Cait's throat constricted, the first tear falling. "Aye. 'Tis a blessed day."

Taran stood in front of the horse his grandda had laden with bulking saddlebags, his hand resting on top of his cane.

"Must ye leave so soon?" Cait asked, hoping for just a little more time with Taran and Edward together.

"Has been long enough, mistress. Forbye, we've been away from Harris since late last autumn. 'Tis time." His grandda waited while Edward whispered something funny in Taran's ear, then hugged him hard. He patted Edward on the back and led him around the horse, giving Cait a moment alone with Taran.

She tried to speak but swallowed instead, her hand absentmindedly playing with his curls.

"Och. Ye know I'm going to miss ye something terrible," Taran said, his head bowed shyly.

"Ye will?" she asked, his words stabbing her heart.

"Aye. But nae yer fussing and all the bathing ye make me do."

She laughed. "Well, the next time I see ye, ye better smell like river water and nae like a stable."

He swatted his hand at her, then rubbed his nose. "Do ye think we'll meet again, then?"

"Aye, Taran. I do." But she knew it was improbable. He lived far north on an island she'd only heard about in tales and one she'd likely never see. "Until then, I'll carry ye in my heart."

"The way ye do Gilli?"

She kissed the crown of his head. "Aye. The way I do Gilli."

"Are we ready, then?" his grandda asked, hoisting Taran onto the saddle with Edward's help. "Och, you've grown!"

As they rode away, Edward hugged her, tucking her close to his chest.

When they stepped inside the inn, the proprietor was waiting for them. "Mistress, I have a note for ye. From the woman staying with ye."

He handed Cait a small piece of paper, her name written on the front in a neat feminine hand.

"Could you send up a basin and ewer?" Edward asked the innkeeper before he slipped away.

They climbed up to their room, Edward's cane tapping on the wooden stairs, reminding her that Taran wasn't with them. Right behind, the proprietor arrived with the fresh water and a porcelain jug.

Cait sat on the bed while Edward washed, thinking about how quickly her life had once again changed in a matter of minutes. How decisions were constantly being made that reshaped her little world instantly. It was a frightening thought that others could have so much power over her life.

"Are you going to read it?" He jerked his chin in her direction.

"What? Oh." She'd forgotten about Davina's note. She unfolded it and read.

My Dear Cait,

I have been offered permanent lodging at the rectory as an assistant to Lizbeth, the woman I told you about, who helped me when I first arrived in Edinburgh. With the rector advancing in years, her burden of keeping the household has grown to a point where she can no longer handle it herself. I

THE TACKSMAN'S DAUGHTER

have written Lady Glenorchy to send Sawney with the caravan that is bringing my uncle to Edinburgh for his imprisonment. Every day I regret leaving him there, but I was blinded by my own gullibility, blinded by what I thought was love, and I made all the wrong decisions. But now I am a different person, not the foolish lass you remember me to be.

The rector is happily anticipating Sawney's arrival, delighted to have children brighten these old rooms. He and Lizbeth are fully aware of my circumstances and have offered to pay for a midwife when my time comes. I feel so fortunate to have people around me who truly care as you always have. It has been a difficult lesson, but I have learned that family has little to do with blood and everything to do with the heart. As we will make our family here at the rectory, I will burden you no longer, for it is time for you to be with your Edward and Taran as the family you have grown to be. I will always cherish your friendship and love.

Humbly,

Davina

Cait set the letter on the bed, thrilled that Davina finally sounded settled. It was all Davina had ever wanted—a family. Not the one she'd hoped she'd have, but one that was better.

Cait stared at Taran's name in the letter. "How do ye suppose Taran's grandda found us?"

Edward vigorously scrubbed his face and behind his neck. "I sent a letter from Falkirk to the parish church in Glenorchy, telling the minister you were taking Taran to Edinburgh. I signed your name at the bottom."

She thought back to the time the minister from the Glenorchy parish kirk had told her to visit St. Conan's Well in order to soothe her heart and find what she was looking for. That's when she'd found Taran. And it had soothed her heart. "Why did ye sign *my* name?"

"I couldn't sign my own. I was a wanted man." He threw off his shirt and ran the wet cloth over his chest and arms. "I told them to let his grandfather know."

"Did ye know he was alive, then?"

He shook his head, his flesh turning pink from all the rubbing. "But if he was, he should know. Do you not agree?"

She stared at his hand as it moved across his body, stripping the grime from his skin. If only it were that easy to scrub away heartache. She answered him half-heartedly. "Aye."

"Come now, Cait," he said, shooting her a suspecting side-glance. "If we had a child who was missing, wouldn't you want someone to return him to us?"

She wasn't sure what touched her more—the idea of having a lost child or having a child at all. She reached out for him and pulled him down on the bed beside her. "We were a family, though."

"We were a *borrowed* family." He brushed his knuckles across her cheek. "But once we are married, we can start our own."

"Can we?"

He swept a tendril from her brow, and their lips met. His kisses often surprised her. They were soft, tender. Strange coming from such a large, powerful man. He leaned down and kissed her more purposefully, easing her back on the bed, then leaned away. He started to speak, then fell silent, his hand playing with the hair that framed her forehead. Although his lips barely grazed hers, she felt softly pinned in place by his touch. "I want nothing more."

Five days later, word arrived from Holyrood Palace that King William had attainted Edward's father, proclaiming the family name as corrupted. Edward stood at the window, looking out at the drizzly rain that washed the sky grey. Cait lay in bed, staring at his profile, the lines of his naked body limned with dull light. He was a study in perfection, sinewy and smooth—a slightly thinner version of the man he was before he went to prison. His face, now shaded with only a day's growth of a beard along his jaw, turned to her. He closed his eyes and exhaled audibly, his chin falling to his chest.

"That means he'll be hanged," he said glumly.

"But he's a noble. I thought . . ." She couldn't finish the sentence. It would be too cruel.

He sighed. "He's been attainted. He's no longer considered a noble."

Edward's father wouldn't be beheaded, the quicker, more honourable death. Instead, he would endure a humiliating demise at the end of a rope. Alexander's guilt had undoubtedly encouraged the king to make that decision. She rose to join him at the window, her skin instantly covered in gooseflesh after leaving the warmth of the bedclothes. "Does that mean your brother will suffer the same fate?"

Edward's finger tapped the windowsill methodically before he answered. "It does."

The day before, they were told that Alexander had been convicted of the charges set against him. Edward had chosen not to attend the trial at Parliament Hall, and Cait hadn't questioned why. She assumed that although his brother had treated him poorly—had wished for his death—he was still his brother, his flesh and blood, and that thought left Edward brooding. It was a hard thing to understand, losing family in such a violent manner. She would know. But at least, he still had his mother.

THE TACKSMAN'S DAUGHTER

"Edward?"

He remained staring out the window, answering with only a soft grunt.

Cait took a deep breath to steady her nerves. "I have a confession."

He bristled visibly, his shoulders stiffening in anticipation.

She rested her hand on his back. "I'm guilty of the charges Alexander is being hanged for."

He turned to face her, his brow crinkled. "What?"

"I delivered a Jacobite letter that would help pluck the king from his throne," she whispered, her voice catching on the word *Jacobite*. When he didn't say anything in response, she told him the whole story—the letter Duncan showed her the morning the drovers left, how she slipped it from his corpse, the search for the Earl of Mar, and the delivery of it the day Alexander attacked them in the cell. "I know I have disappointed ye. But I want ye to know I would've hanged with a clear conscience if I were caught."

"You played a dangerous game, *mo gràdh*."

She nodded. "And now yer brother hangs for my crimes."

His blue eyes darkened. "His crimes were far worse. 'Tis divine justice."

"Will we go? To see him?" she asked, unsure of how she hoped he would answer. He was scheduled to die the following day.

He folded his arms around her, the heat of his body entering her everywhere they touched. She rested her cheek against the hard planes of his chest.

He inhaled deeply before answering. "Only to make sure the rope doesn't snap and he draws his last breath."

The sun broke from the clouds the next morning, casting light and heat over the city. The Firth of Forth glistened in the sunlight, tiny sparkles flickering on its bouncing current. Muffled drums beating a solemn cadence announced the arrival of the prisoners as they entered the Grassmarket square and slowly made their way to the scaffold. Cait and Edward stood amongst the crowd as the men marched past with their heads bowed. Once they settled, armed guards directed them to form a line and wait their turn to be called to their deaths.

Alexander was easy to spot, standing taller than all of them, his patrician nose and dark glare prominent next to the pale-faced defeated stares of the other prisoners. He stood barefoot and covered in grime, his jaw working back and forth beneath his scowl. A soldier read the garrison orders one by one, revealing the crimes of the prisoners, all soldiers accused of mutiny, sedition, or some other form of treason.

It was late August, only seven months after Cait's entire family had been sent to their graves. So much had happened since then. She'd suffered great loss yet gained more than she'd ever imagined in that short time. Her mother had always told her that loving, or failing to love, always came at a tremendous cost. And it was true. But the cost of heartache could not outweigh the benefits of love—the love for her parents, Gilli, Lilas, Davina, Sawney, Auntie Meg, MacIain, Taran, and all the others who had crossed her path. But above all, Edward, the most unlikely of the group—the Englishman, the soldier, the stranger. For him, she would risk anything.

Cait stiffened at the sound of Alexander's name being called. It could've been her name instead. Edward stood behind her, one hand on her waist and the other on his cane.

"Alexander Gage, of Wetherby, England, aged four and twenty years or thereby, guilty as an officer in His Majesty's army of extraordinary and heinous crimes against the people of Scotland and His Majesty, King William of England, Scotland, and Ireland. The most abominable crime of high treason . . ."

The words were almost the same as they were when Edward's crimes were read aloud in Parliament Hall. A chill ran up Cait's spine at the thought.

". . . the crimes of rape, sodomy, and assault with intent to ravish . . ."

Cait searched the crowd for the woman who'd proclaimed Edward innocent of the charges against the whore in Fort William. She was easy to spot, standing in the same bright red gown and black hat she'd worn in court, her head held high, neither a smile nor frown upon her blank face.

". . . a charge of attempted murder against one Davina MacNab of Glenorchy . . ."

Alexander stood on the scaffold, his head bowed. Cait scanned the crowd for Davina but doubted she'd be there. Even after everything he'd done to her, Cait imagined it would still be too painful for Davina to watch the man she shared two bairns with die in such an undignified manner.

When the guard finished reading his crimes, a noose was placed around Alexander's neck. His lips were taut, and Cait realized he neither begged for mercy nor prayed for it, perhaps believing death could not possibly come to him.

Alexander lifted his head and locked eyes with Edward. Cait flinched, her stomach flipping uncomfortably. Edward's grip tightened around her waist, and his strong heartbeat banged against her back. Alexander narrowed his eyes at Edward, proving he wasn't searching for forgiveness. He was cursing Edward, blaming him for every bitter moment he'd ever had. She was sure of it.

Without warning, the guard shoved Alexander, and he fell from the platform. The weight of his body yanked the rope once, his legs kicking furiously, jerking him back and forth. He wriggled spastically for an interminable length of time, then stilled, his eyes bulging and the front of his breeks wet.

Out of the corner of her eye, Cait spotted the worn green dress she knew so well with its patches sewn into the sides, make an exit through the crowd and down the square. Davina was stronger than she'd thought.

Edward pulled her back through the entranced mob and away from the spectacle that was his brother, showing little emotion.

"How are ye, my love?" she asked in a whisper, her hand cupping his cheek.

He kissed her palm and drew her close. "Glad 'tis over."

They skirted around the horde to the back, the castle looming overhead in the distance. She shivered at the bad memory of his imprisonment that still lived between her shoulders like a tightly pulled string. Edward hobbled on his cane, his features stern.

"Sergeant Gage!" They both spun in the direction of the voice. "Sergeant Gage!"

Captain Sutherland raced up to them, waving a small pouch in his clutches. He reached them slightly out of breath, his free hand pressed against his chest. "I'm so pleased I caught ye."

Edward narrowed his eyes in question. "What can I do for you, Captain?"

He tipped his hat at Cait. "Mistress."

She nodded.

"I thought ye might want the prisoner's . . . ah, yer brother's belongings." Sutherland handed him the pouch, then straightened his coat. "'Tisnae much, but they're yers now."

Edward nodded. "Much obliged, sir."

He left without another word and disappeared into the crowd. Edward loosened the string at the top and peered inside.

Cait asked, "What could Alexander possibly have that—"

Edward reached in and pulled out her *sgian dubh.* She took it in her hand and twirled it once between her fingers. One side of Edward's mouth curled up in amusement. He was about to tuck the pouch into his shirt, then he stopped, a new smile spreading across his lips. *"Mo gràdh."*

Cait held her breath as he reached inside and slipped out her mother's sapphire. The sunlight caught it just right, suffusing it with bright blue light. He placed it in her palm. It was missing the chain he'd given her on their wedding day, but other than that, it remained unharmed. She pressed it to her lips, knowing her mother and all those she loved were watching over her that very moment.

"Are you ready to go home?" Edward asked as soft as a whisper.

"Home?" She wasn't sure what that meant anymore, but she'd go anywhere with him.

He nodded once.

She tucked the stone into her bodice over her heart and peered up at the tall buildings surrounding her. Overhead, one solitary starling flew to join a spiraling flock, hundreds of black dots in the bright blue sky. They dipped and rose, then dipped again in a broad swirl before soaring off over the river. The sun beat down on her face, filling her with warmth. This time, they came to tell her everything had changed. All for the better.

Edward squeezed her hand, and she smiled up at him.

"Aye. Take me home."

THE TACKSMAN'S DAUGHTER

If you enjoyed *The Tacksman's Daughter*, please consider writing a review on Goodreads or Amazon. This helps other readers discover the story. Thank you!

Goodreads:
https://www.goodreads.com/book/show/59923078-the-tacksman-s-daughter

Amazon:
https://www.amazon.com/Tacksmans-Daughter-Donna-Scott/dp/1734924845

If you would like to be informed about new releases and special offers, please sign up for my Newsletter at http://eepurl.com/g06zzz

Historical Note

The Glencoe Massacre may have occurred more than three hundred years ago on February 13th, 1692, but it remains a very sensitive subject for MacDonalds and Campbells even today. For twelve days, soldiers—both English and Scottish—billeted in Glencoe and were given food, drink, and entertainment until the weather improved. Instead of leaving peacefully and thanking the clan chief MacIain, the troops committed one of the most heinous crimes in Scottish history.

Both Highland clans carry a deep respect for Highland law and customs but disagree as to who is truly to blame for the horrible early morning slaughter on that fateful February day. Both sides do agree, however, that certain individuals should have been prosecuted for their involvement, but because of the politics at the time and King William's probable hand in the matter, those people were not sufficiently punished.

In a desperate measure—just after it became known that dissent was beginning to rise regarding the attack—the Earl of Breadalbane sent a messenger to the survivors, promising he would secure full pardons and restitution if they would swear under oath that he played no part in the slaughter. It mattered little, for in 1695, the inquiry committee found that although he could not directly be blamed for the massacre, he was accused of having Jacobite loyalties as demonstrated in his dealings to negotiate with the Highland clans. He was imprisoned in Edinburgh Castle for only a few months, professing his innocence and loyalty to William and claiming he only pretended to be a Jacobite in order to infiltrate the Jacobite clan movement. In 1715, he cleverly avoided implication in the next Jacobite Rising by claiming his mind was unclear due to his advanced age of seventy-nine.

The Master of Stair, Sir John Dalrymple, was removed from his office as the Secretary of Stair but punished no further, even after much civic protesting. Because of his notorious disdain for Highlanders, many believe that he was the true orchestrator of the Glencoe Massacre. He returned to government five years later and was instrumental in securing the Treaty of Union that created Great Britain.

Colonel John Hill, an advocate for the Highlanders, was absolved of any crimes during the inquiry. Although he was later knighted, he was discharged from the army and awarded half-pay.

THE TACKSMAN'S DAUGHTER

Glenlyon never stood trial and died penniless in West Flanders only a year after the inquiries, destroyed by his own guilt. He was buried in an unmarked grave.

In the end, almost 80 deaths could be attributed to the massacre—some by slaughter and others from freezing temperatures (including MacIain's wife) as victims attempted to escape and hide in the braes.

An iron and stone monument commemorating the event stands near the River Coe in the village, and to this day you'll see a placard stating "No Campbells" at the entrance of the Clachaig Inn on Old Village Road.

DONNA SCOTT

Author's Note

I fell in love with Scotland many years ago from reading books about its history and viewing images of the castles and beautiful geographical landmarks the country boasted. It wasn't until early 2015, however, that I was able to travel to all the places I had dreamed of visiting.

I went with my friend, and on our drive into Glencoe, we stopped to listen to the piper play against the backdrop of lush green peaks dusted in fog. Sprigs of fuchsia foxglove and thistle, deep purple Scottish primrose and bluebells, and yellow bog asphodel grew in wild bunches along the roadside. It was magical. Serene. When we reached Glencoe, we were greeted by the quaint little village at the foot of the braes nestled between Loch Leven and the River Coe. After checking in to Glencoe House, we realized we had arrived at a very special place. As I wrote this book, I tried to capture the essence of the village and people, honouring their history with my retelling of Glencoe's tragic past.

In this novel, all the events regarding the massacre were taken directly from historical documents and references. In some cases, even the dialogue was taken verbatim from eyewitness accounts and journals. The orders that were given to Glenlyon were also verbatim. I tried to stay true to the facts with regards to the timing of events, the nature of the deaths, and those who perpetrated the attack. There was a complicated web of players involved, and historians disagree as to who may have been the *most* responsible for the heinous attack on the MacDonalds. Although it would be easy to blame Robert Campbell (Glenlyon) for the attack, considering the long history of feuding between the two clans, he was not the one who ordered it. Because absolute culpability remains in debate, I intentionally left it unclear in the book.

A fantastic source on this subject is John Prebble's book entitled *Glencoe*. It proved an invaluable resource for information regarding the attack and the aftermath as well as the politics before, during, after the inquiry—clan politics included.

The fictional characters—Edward, Alexander, Cait, Davina, Taran, and some secondaries—helped me tell the story of others who survived. For example, Edward's seclusion in the cave in the high braes and his visits to Eilean Munde, the burial island, were similar to those by several MacDonald men who came down from the caves and corries to bury the dead on the sacred island after the attack. His refusal to comply with the orders was representative of the few (like Farquhar and Kennedy) who did the same that early morning. Cait and Taran's survival gave me the opportunity to show the devastating

THE TACKSMAN'S DAUGHTER

impact on those who lost all or some family members. There happened to be a visiting bard from the Isle of Harris there at the time, who I conveniently made Taran's grandfather. Davina's character allowed me to create a connection to Breadalbane, giving the reader an intimate glimpse into who the man really was. And Alexander? He epitomized the soldier who merely put aside his humanity to follow orders, no matter how heinous they were. And there were many just like him.

The other characters, Alasdair Ruadh MacIain MacDonald or clan chief of the MacDonalds of Glencoe (MacIain), his wife and sons (Lady Glencoe, John, and Alasdair Og), Angus MacDonald (tacksman), Captain Robert Campbell (Glenlyon), Colonel Hill, Major Duncanson, Captain Drummond, Leftenant Lindsay, the Earl of Mar, Earl of Breadalbane, Sir John Dalrymple, King William, Big Henderson, Dunkin Rankin, Captain Sutherland, Gilbert Kennedy, and Francis Farquhar were all historical figures.

Although MacIain was the chief and had a larger home than the local crofters, it no longer stands where it once was, so I placed it in the most likely location in the novel. My expert Iain McDonagh was responsible for naming it Alt Na Munde—stream of the mouth or valley of the river—where it would've sat perched between the loch and the River Coe. I also mentioned that Edward—a fictional character—engraved MacIain's name on his tombstone on Eilean Munde. Although MacIain is buried in a tomb there, I have no knowledge as to who erected the structure or marked his grave.

There's a sporran at the West Highland Museum in Fort William that is said to have belonged to Glenlyon, its dark brown leather worn and brass tarnished. A few other "found" items are also there as reminders of the dark history of this special place in the Highlands.

So how many survived the attack? More than the soldiers had intended. Although it is believed that most of the soldiers had no idea what was to come, some did. According to sources, a few of Argyll's (Glenlyon's) soldiers hinted warnings to their hosts the night before, causing them to flee from their homes and search for safety, sparing their lives. Unfortunately, no one warned the clan chief and his wife.

I hope you take the time to learn more about the massacre. If you are able to visit the beautiful village of Glencoe, I highly recommend it.

To learn more about the Glencoe Massacre, the links below provide a good starting point:

https://www.highlandtitles.com/blog/the-glencoe-massacre/

http://www.bbc.co.uk/history/scottishhistory/union/trails_union_glencoe.shtml

https://www.historyextra.com/period/stuart/glencoe-massacre-scottish-highlands-what-happened-why/

https://www.livescience.com/62056-glencoe-massacre-archaeology.html

https://www.scotsman.com/whats-on/arts-and-entertainment/looking-back-massacre-glencoe-1483135

https://www.nts.org.uk/visit/places/glencoe/the-glencoe-massacre

https://www.scotclans.com/scotland/scottish-history/scottish-unification/1692-glencoe/

https://discoverglencoe.scot/key-information/history/about-glencoe/glencoe-massacre/

Acknowledgements

When I set out to write this book in 2015, I had no idea how many wonderful people I'd meet along the way, many of whom lived in or around Glencoe, Scotland. The first of my experts, Iain McDonagh, walked right into my suite at Glencoe House while I was eating breakfast in my bathrobe. He was all decked out in traditional Highland garb, wearing a kilt, vest, tie, sporran, kilt hose and garters, and Ghillie Brogues—a real sight to see. With a warm smile and Scottish charm, he introduced himself and we quickly became friends. As the resident historian of Glencoe, he and his wife, Jackie, run the Beechwood Cottage Bed and Breakfast in the village below. Iain led me to many sources on the massacre to help with my research, and his knowledge and expertise proved priceless. What he *didn't* do was advise me not to wear flip flops to hike up to Signal Rock. That was a mistake.

But there were also many others who contributed in one way or another to make this book possible—some of whom I was able to meet personally—and I extend my humble gratitude to every one of them: Fiona Marwick of the West Highland Museum; Kirsty Ferguson of the Glencoe Folk Museum; Dr. Stuart Allan (Principal Curator in the Department of Scottish History and Archaeology) at the National Museum of Scotland; Dr. Kirsty Owen (Cultural Resources Advisor) of Historic Environment Scotland; Emma Bowie, Duncan MacCallum (Senior Guide), Rachel Pickering (Cultural Resources Advisor), and Rachael Dickson (Regional Collections Manager) of Edinburgh Castle; Innes MacNeil (Gàidhlig/Language Influencer) of LearnGàidhlig, and Professor Boyd Robertson (Principal) of the National Center for Gaelic Language and Culture. Stateside, I consulted with Yasmin Morais of the David A Clarke School of Law at the University of the District of Columbia; and Erin Kidwell (Curator of Legal History Collections) at the Georgetown University Law Library.

However, even with all these wonderful experts, mistakes can be made, for all of which I take full responsibility. That also holds true with regards to my wonderfully talented editor, Jessica Cale, who took on this project with excitement. When I mentioned this novel was my most research-intensive, she said 'bring it on'. Got to love an editor like that!

To my beta readers, Julie Edelstein, Emma Lombard, Karen Moser, and Lisa del Valle, I am forever grateful for your suggestions, all of which help make my books better.

And to my book club of eighteen years—your encouragement and faith in me as a writer mean the world to me.

Thank you to Jenny Quinlan for another striking cover design and again to Emma Lombard for listening to my late-night rants about marketing and social media.

Most of all, thank you to my husband, Scott, and my two sons, Caleb and Coby. They have always cheered me on and supported my new ideas and travel adventures for every project. They are the reason I smile.

To discover the historical inspirations behind the novel, please visit my website www.donnascott.net and please follow me on . . .

Facebook: Donna Scott--Author
Twitter: D_ScottWriter
Instagram: DonnaScottWriter

Also by Donna Scott, *Shame the Devil* and *The London Monster*:

THE TACKSMAN'S DAUGHTER

Questions for Readers

1. Cait's fear of Englishmen, especially soldiers, is prominent throughout the story. Is her fear warranted? Why or why not?

2. Edward's relationship with his brother is complicated. When they first met at 17, it was combative, but once their father was placed in the Tower, they were forced to reconnect. Although they serve the king as officers in his army, their relationship soon falls apart. Who is to blame?

3. Many of us have a person in our lives like Davina, who makes excuses for others' bad behaviour. Throughout the novel, she rationalizes all her past interactions with Alexander. How does she grow as a character, and what causes her to change?

4. Alexander's poor relationship with his parents affects who he is as a man and how he feels about his brother. Does this make him a sympathetic character? Why or why not?

5. Edward tells Cait that murder is a heavy burden to bear, even in self-defense. How does this affect Cait's decision to use her knife with Glenlyon. Sionn, and Alexander?

6. Knowing the contentious history between the MacDonald and Campbell clans, do you think Glenlyon's claim that personal malice played no part in the attack was true? Why or why not?

7. What did you know about the Glencoe Massacre prior to reading the novel?

8. Although the Glencoe Massacre happened over three centuries ago, we still see evidence throughout history of people taking orders blindly from their superiors even when they know it is not the ethical thing to do. Unfortunately, in 1692, it resulted in the death of dozens of innocent people. Have you ever been in the position of doing something you were uncomfortable with or opposed to? How did you handle it?

Donna Scott is an award-winning author of 17th and 18th century historical fiction. Before embarking on a writing career, she spent her time in the world of academia. She earned her BA in English from the University of Miami and her MS and EdD (ABD) from Florida International University. She has two sons and lives in sunny South Florida with her husband.

Made in the USA
Columbia, SC
17 February 2022

56396171R00219